Pat,

Thankyou for all your
support, love and friendship.

For all your character help
and your love of our
'little' character – Emily.

Br...

x

Redway Acres

By
Trish Butler

Book 1 ~ Helena

ISBN-13: 978-1539712398
ISBN-10: 1539712397

Cover design by Adriana Tonello

For Emily
And
Richard

Helena (he-LAY-nah)
Shining light. The bright one

~

Coverture

By marriage, the husband and wife are one person in law: that is, the very being or legal existence of the woman is suspended during the marriage, or at least is incorporated and consolidated into that of the husband: under whose wing, protection, and cover, she performs every thing; and is therefore called in our law-French a feme-covert; is said to be covert-baron, or under the protection and influence of her husband, her baron, or lord; and her condition during her marriage is called her coverture. - **From William Blackstone's Commentaries on the Laws of England in the late 18th century.**

~

"It is a truth universally acknowledged, that a widow in possession of property, must be in want of a husband."
Variation on the opening line of
Pride and Prejudice by Jane Austen.

~

www.redwayacres.com

Table of Contents

Map

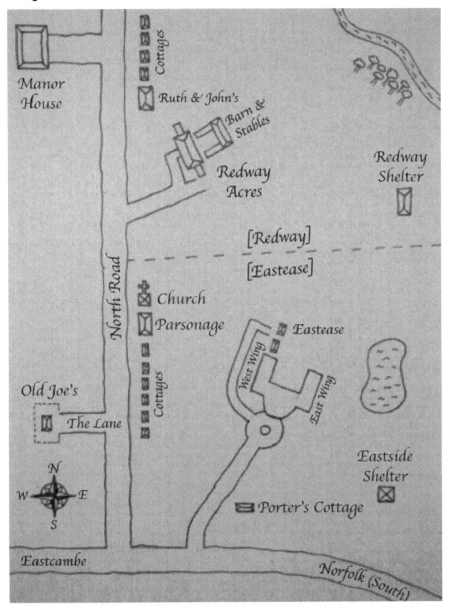

Manor House

Cottages

Ruth & John's

Barn & Stables

Redway Acres

Redway Shelter

[Redway]

[Eastease]

North Road

Church

Parsonage

Eastease

West Wing

East Wing

Cottages

Old Joe's

The Lane

N
W · E
S

Eastside Shelter

Porter's Cottage

Eastcambe

Norfolk (South)

Prologue

Mrs. Helena Andrews, née Billings, travelled north in the carriage her grandfather had sent for her. The journey was approximately sixty miles from Fairfield Market, the village closest to her family's home in Norfolk, to Redway Acres, her grandfather's stable in Lincolnshire. She was almost one-and-twenty and had been married and widowed in a short amount of time. The child within her should be born sometime in October.

It was June 1808 and they had been favoured with three days of good weather for their journey. Her companions in the carriage were her family's cook, Ruth Robertson, and Ruth's two children, Jacky and Molly. Ruth's husband, John, was driving their cart of belongings behind them. He had been a Billings' stableman and easily managed Colossus, her grandfather's steady, black Shire horse. Both he and Ruth were close with the young Helena, who followed her grandfather's love of horses and had spent much of her time in her family's stable with John.

The parting from her family the day before had not been very emotional. Mrs. Billings had barely spoken to Helena for months, as she blamed her daughter for becoming a widow. Her brother had muttered a goodbye and followed her father out to wave her off, but barely looked up from the ground. Her father felt it most she thought, but not enough to shed a tear. So, she kept her own tears and fears within her as she held her head high and climbed into the carriage with the aid of the driver, Dom.

They had crossed the border of Lincolnshire late the first day and stopped for the night at a nearby inn. After two more days, they passed the entrance to the grand estate of Eastease, and the children clambered over their mother for a glimpse of the large house, but barely a chimney could be spotted. Before they reached the village of Eastcambe, they turned down the North Road. It was only a few miles more to Redway.

Eastease was owned by a young gentleman called Alexander Harker. Although he was midway through his twenties, he was unmarried, but did care for, as his wards, the twin stepdaughters of his childhood friend, Lieutenant Wyndham. Their mother had died in childbirth when they were six years old, and their stepfather in battle three years later.

Helena's grandmother had told her of four young men who had been friends since childhood. The oldest of them had been Mark

Wyndham; then his second cousin and son of Lord Aysthill, Nathaniel Ackley; thirdly Alexander Harker and the youngest, Robert Davenport, the son of a local gentleman.

The grounds of Eastease joined Redway Acres on Redway's southeast side. In fact, all the land east of the North Road belonged to either property, with the larger amount attributed to Eastease. As they passed the pretty cottages that were dotted along the roadside, they saw a quaint church with a well-kept parsonage adjoining it. Finally, they turned gratefully into the welcoming gates of Redway.

It had been many years since Helena had last seen her grandfather, George Stockton, but there he stood awaiting them, a large ox of a man with a head of thick, red hair, and green eyes. The latter two were traits that had skipped his daughter and were inherited by his granddaughter. She had not been allowed to visit him in almost six years, but to her he had not changed one bit, except that she could see a slight sadness around his eyes due to the loss of his wife. Two years ago, Isabella Stockton had been taken ill and never recovered. Helena had begged to be allowed to visit her grandmother, but her mother had refused and Helena had never forgiven her for it.

Heedless of her condition, she flew from the carriage when it had barely stopped and into her grandfather's strong arms. Although she was tall, her head only just reached his broad chest. She started to sob, her ordeal prior to arriving this day, finally over.

Chapter One

The smoke was billowing on the battlefield, around noon on a late June day in 1813, that had started sunny and bright. Colonel Nathaniel Ackley was in northern Spain near the French border. He sat astride his horse, Thor, wiping the blood off his sword onto his coat sleeve, then sheathing it while taking stock of the situation. There was a lull in the fighting and the French who had not fled were lying dead or dying on the ground. He could see English uniforms, too, and swallowed down bile. It was not the first time he had seen this sight, and as much as he hoped it would be, he knew it would not be the last. They had not defeated Napoleon Bonaparte, and until they did the battles would continue. He had managed to be in England last year for his friend's wedding, and returned briefly for Christmas, but had seen little of his beloved England and friends in the six months since.

He scanned the carnage as the smoke from the cannon fire started to clear and saw a figure rise from the bodies. The colonel tensed, then relaxed again as he realised the uniform was English. The soldier stood awkwardly and hobbled, as he tried to walk. Colonel Ackley started Thor at a slow trot over to the injured man. He focused on the face and recognised Tommy Smithson, an army stableman. One of the few who loved working with Thor, who could be troublesome.

"Colonel!" Tommy called out in acknowledgment.

Lifting his eyes from Tommy's face, he noticed another horse moving toward the man at full speed. The rider's sword was drawn in his right hand and aimed at Tommy's heart.

"Tommy, beware!" the colonel called, pointing at the Frenchman as he legged Thor to a canter. At full gallop, he should get to Tommy first, but would not be able to get him onto such a fast horse. The French soldier, seeing another bearing down on his quarry, shifted to pass Tommy on the opposite side. He moved his sword to a downward pointing position, crossing his sword arm over his reins.

The rest happened fast, but to Colonel Ackley it seemed so slow. Tommy leaned down to his boot and removed a dagger that he threw, with accuracy, at the enemy bearing down on him. It caught the soldier in the chest but the horse did not slow. Turning, Tommy reached up for the colonel's outstretched left arm to swing himself up and behind him onto Thor. In that moment, when the colonel was leaning to his side, the Frenchman's sword swooped down in front of them where the colonel's body was protecting Tommy. The movement of both horses carried the sword upwards as it sliced across him. Even through his heavy coat he felt the blade cut into his flesh, as it swiped upwards from ribs to shoulder. With all of his strength, he hoisted Tommy behind him and righted himself in the saddle. Warmth spread across his chest as blood poured from his wound, everywhere else he felt suddenly cold.

Tommy, seated behind the colonel, wrapped his strong arms around him and took the reins. Thor continued to canter toward the relative safety of the encampment under Tommy's guidance; had it been anyone else he probably would have bolted. Colonel Ackley tried, for as long as he could, to stay conscious, and make the journey easier on both passenger and horse. Finally, as light narrowed to a pinpoint in his vision, he succumbed. His last thought, a hope that his body would make it back to England for burial. Tommy was the only one to witness, with some satisfaction, the Frenchman fall from his horse, dead.

In England, at Eastease in Lincolnshire, Alexander and Genevieve Harker, were getting used to married life. Genevieve had started to grow larger with their first child and life was, in stark comparison to that of their friend, Colonel Ackley, peaceful and good. Only one problem was troubling Alexander as he sat behind his desk, in his study, and that was Harriet Wyndham, to whom he was guardian with the colonel.

Harriet was the shy one of the twin stepdaughters of Alexander's late friend, Mark Wyndham, but she was becoming more outspoken and opinionated. True, it was something Alexander had hoped for her, because she had been so timid, particularly since her sister's marriage. She used to be painfully shy and it could make life difficult, more so he felt for a woman than a man. A woman needed to be outgoing and somewhat flirtatious to secure a husband, whereas a man need only be wealthy. Certainly, he had hoped that Genevieve's wit and charm would rub off on his ward and happily that had been the case. Harriet had started to become more willing to enter into conversations with him, Genevieve and some of the Hopwood family who had visited.

However, a recent connexion that had struck up between Harriet and their widowed neighbour, Mrs. Andrews, had Alexander concerned. Mrs. Andrews was the young widow of a captain who died fighting in France, and the granddaughter of George Stockton, the man who had previously owned Redway Acres stable. Mrs. Andrews had come to live with her grandfather when she was widowed around five years prior and at the time she was with child. Her grandfather had died just six months ago, the victim of influenza, and had left the stable in its entirety to his granddaughter. Mr. Stockton had asked Alexander's opinion on the matter of his will, about a year before he passed, not realising his time would be due so soon. He had expressed a hope that the stable might provide an inducement for a potential suitor and that his granddaughter might make a suitable marriage, despite being a widow with a child. Alexander had promised the elder man that he would provide his expertise in business management to Mrs. Andrews should the need arise, but so far it had not. Mrs. Andrews seemed more than capable of running the stable. Her grandfather had taught her well.

No family was ever seen visiting Redway Acres, though it was known that Mrs. Andrews' mother was still alive and living in Norfolk. Her mother was remembered by some as a mean girl, who did not share her parents' love of horses. She married a much older man because he was wealthy and she was keen to leave her home. Mr. Billings had mines and mills in the north, which their son would inherit.

Some speculated that Captain and Mrs. Andrews had not actually been married and that was why family did not visit. Others said that was tommyrot, because it was easy to tell that Mrs. Andrews was a woman of breeding, who loved her husband so much that she still kept mostly to herself and showed no interest in marrying again. Most did not care either way, as Redway horses were the healthiest, best-bred and well-trained horses in the county.

In the past, Alexander would have erred on the side of caution and forbad Harriet to see the woman, but Gennie had softened his views on the strictest guidelines of society he had been brought up with. She mentioned that forbidding anything to his ward might make it more attractive. However, since making the acquaintance of Mrs. Andrews, Harriet had been more outspoken about a woman's role in a marriage and decision making. Now she had said she wanted to wear breeches beneath her skirts and ride astride a horse, rather than side-saddle. A knock was heard at his door.

"Come," he ordered and then rose from his chair when Genevieve entered, "how is she? Is she still angry with me?" His eyes were so bleak that Genevieve put out her hands to comfort him. When Harriet had made her request, he was so shocked that he was afraid he had not reacted very well. She had been upset, saying she only wished to ride astride at Eastease, '*I am not planning on riding through the village of Eastcambe naked, like Lady Godiva through Coventry!*' she had exclaimed, before storming out.

"Yes, she is, but it will pass. She is still not yet eighteen and this is the price we pay for allowing her to spread her wings. I thought I might write to Mrs. Andrews and introduce myself. I never heard from her when I first arrived, because her grandfather was ill and then he passed. I should have made some time to make this visit then." He smiled, recalling how little time he actually allowed Genevieve for social meetings when they were first married. He had barely let her out of his sight, or his bed.

Having got a smile, which was her aim, Genevieve sat down on a small loveseat. Rubbing her round stomach, she continued, "I could go in the new carriage to visit her. I am sure I would be most comfortable in there. What do you think?"

"If you are sure you should be comfortable, my dear, I think that might be the best course of action. How on earth did I manage to do anything without you?" he sat down next to her.

"I am sure I have no idea," she giggled and then exclaimed, "Mr. Harker!" as he pulled her up out of the seat and back down again onto his lap.

Over the next week, due to the large amount of blood he had lost, Colonel Ackley barely gained consciousness for more than a few minutes at a time and he was probably better for it. Once Tommy got him to the tent for the wounded at their encampment, he had been stitched up and the bleeding was stemmed. Later he remembered only the pain.

The camp doctor told Tommy that the colonel should not be moved, but word had spread of supplies and reinforcements due to land at port about forty miles away. Tommy knew he had to get himself and the colonel on that ship, if either of them were to have a chance of survival. He suspected his own leg was broken and if they stayed, they would both succumb to infection.

They travelled mile by slow, painful mile in a basic covered cart, to meet the ship and return to England. Tommy sat in the back with the colonel, trying his best to keep him still and cool, while Thor, tethered to the cart, walked behind them. The colonel had a fever, which had started the day after his injury. He was too weak and not sufficiently conscious to eat, but Tommy did what he could to get him to drink. He hoped to get him to England and get the stitches removed, before he developed an infection. Tommy's leg, which he had bound tightly, was causing him a lot of pain.

Near to where they landed on the south coast of England, a week to the day of the battle, was a convent hospital. Tommy got himself and the colonel onto Thor's back and walked him up the hillside to their door. He and the colonel had to be carried into the hospital to be tended, while Thor was taken to the stable.

Genevieve Harker made her visit to Mrs. Andrews at Redway Acres in the splendour of the shining carriage pulled by two handsome chestnuts. Mrs. Andrews had heard enough village news to know that, although the daughter of a gentleman, Mrs. Harker came to Eastease with very little. She wondered, while she waited for her guest in the parlour that overlooked the pretty little garden her housekeeper tended, what Mrs. Harker was like. She hoped she should like her as it would be good to have a friend. As nice as Harriet was, the young woman looked up to her more as an older sister and horsewoman, than a friend.

Although Mrs. Andrews had been living at Redway for five years, she did not do much visiting. She was a person who liked working with horses and was happy to pitch in to get the work done. She could not turn her hand easily to sewing or an instrument. She was an avid reader, but her subject in that area was horses. Her daughter's talent was in making up stories. She tried to join in, but most often Isabella told her to stop because she was *'doing it wrong'*. She liked to make the princess outwit her opponent, rather than wait for rescue by a prince or knight.

"Mrs. Harker, ma'am," Ruth had opened the door and taken her away from her reverie.

"Thank you, Ruth," she said to her housekeeper. She turned to her guest, "I am pleased to meet you, Mrs. Harker. Refreshments?"

"That would be most welcome," was the reply. Mrs. Andrews gave Ruth a nod and she departed.

Ruth thought of Mrs. Andrews like a daughter, *"how wonderful that my girl has a female visitor of her own age. If she had her way, her only company would be Isabella, horses, John and I."*

Mrs. Andrews took stock of her visitor. Mrs. Harker was a handsome, young woman in her early twenties with light-brown hair and pale blue eyes. By her estimation, she was perhaps seven months into her child bearing. No wonder she had arrived in the comfortable carriage, "are you feeling quite well after your carriage ride?"

"Quite well I assure you, Mrs. Andrews, and it is nice to meet you, too." The housekeeper arrived with the refreshments, which allowed Genevieve time to take her own review of the neighbour who was causing a stir at Eastease. She saw a woman with a flame of red hair, tamed into a simple bun, and escaping in red tendrils around her freckled face. Mrs. Andrews obviously spent much of her time outside, a shared interest, although her own interests did not extend as far as horses. She had noticed, before they sat, that her hostess was taller than herself by several inches. Her back was ramrod straight and she was slender, but soft and curved.

While tea was served and refreshments were eaten, they talked of the weather, village news, Mrs. Andrews asked after Mrs. Harker's family and she, in turn, complimented Redway Acres and the view of the small garden from the window.

"I hear it is nothing compared with the gardens of Eastease."

"Well, I am biased, but must confess that I have not yet seen all of it. In my current condition, I can hardly walk very far from the house."

"As you know, I have been in that condition myself. With your family so far away, please feel free to talk to me, if you need any advice or someone to share concerns with. I am more than willing to serve if I can, Mrs. Harker."

"If we are to talk of such personal things, I think you should call me Gennie, as my sisters do," she blushed.

"Then you must call me Helena. I am afraid my brother never gave me a nickname."

"Do you see much of your family?" Gennie asked, not letting the opportunity to find out more pass. Helena however, said that she did not, with little by the way of explanation and then steered the conversation back to the previous subject. They passed several happy minutes talking of babies, before a small, red-headed whirlwind entered the room and ran to her mother.

"Mama! Mama! I have finished my studies." Mrs. Andrews dismissed the young girl who had been looking after her daughter, with a nod and a smile. Then she looked up at Genevieve with her arms full of a beautiful, four-year-old girl.

"Mrs. Harker, may I present my daughter, Miss Isabella Andrews. Issie, this is Mrs. Harker, the wife of Miss Harriet Wyndham's guardian," at the mention of the much-admired Harriet, Isabella sat up and paid attention to this new adult.

"You know Harry?"

"I am married to her guardian, Mr. Harker."

"I am going to marry Jacky. He works in our stable and knows all about horses," the little girl declared.

"Jacky is my stable manager's son," explained Helena, "he loves you like a sister, my sweet girl, but I am afraid he has his eye on Mrs. Harker's scullery maid, Rebecca."

"Is that so?" Genevieve looked amused, "well she is a pretty thing, as I recall," she made a mental note to look into the prospects of the girl. If she was to marry, she would need to improve beyond scullery maid.

"The girl with Miss Andrews seemed young for a governess."

"Rachel has a measure of learning for a good start for Issie. She would love to be a governess, so I plan to keep her when we get one." Genevieve approved, it seemed Helena was of the same mind as herself when it came to serving the people who worked for them. She found herself warming to her neighbour, and dare she say friend?

The rest of the visit passed quickly as Isabella regaled them with stories of dragons and princesses, whilst brave princes saved the day. When Genevieve departed, it was with the promise of a return visit, which should include an excited Isabella. Her opinion was to be sought on the new nursery for the heir of Eastease.

Over the next few weeks, Tommy, whose broken leg had become gangrenous and was removed below the knee, convalesced at the convent hospital with Colonel Ackley. After a week, the colonel had regained full consciousness and was surprised to find he was still alive.

Tommy talked of his home, with his parents, in Sheffield. They did not have much and relied on his money. The colonel pondered on this and decided that he should be sure to send that family money whenever he could spare it. There was no doubt in the colonel's mind, had he remained longer at the encampment, he would have died of an infection. The man who he was sharing his convalescence with, had not only revenged his assailant, but saved his life.

Colonel Ackley was surprised to see an Aysthill carriage arrive and his mother descend from it. She was horrified when her son informed her Tommy would be travelling back with them. She insisted that propriety be upheld and, despite his injury, Tommy should ride with the driver.

The journey took many days to complete. Thor made the journey, too, and the colonel often wished that he was strong enough to ride him. The carriage in July was stifling, the conversations with his mother bored him easily, and he felt restless. He often feigned sleep as each mile rolled slowly on.

Harriet mounted her horse and rode over to Redway. She was so welcome at the stable, that she could approach from the fields of Eastease and dismount in the stable courtyard. As usual at this time, she found Mrs. Andrews making her rounds of the stalls. John was with her and they were discussing each horse. They looked up and waved as she walked her horse toward them.

"We must move Perceval and Grenville on to the next stage of their training. Their buyer is hoping to take possession in September," Mrs. Andrews finished saying, as Harriet approached.

"Bloody daft names if you ask me," John turned to Harriet adding, with a pull on his forelock, "good morning, Miss Wyndham."

"Prime Minister buff, is he?" Harriet asked, adding, "good morning, John, Mrs. Andrews."

"Unfortunately, yes," declared Mrs. Andrews, "good morning, Harriet. How are you today? Has Hudson had a good enough run or shall I join you? I wanted to take Perseus out today. Alternatively, we could have refreshments in the drawing room, like proper *ladies*," the last part was said with a tease, knowing full well that it was the last thing Harriet would want.

"It is a delightful morning. Let us ride!"

While Mrs. Andrews saddled Perseus, Harriet took her own turn around the stalls, peering into each. Fresh straw lay on clean floors, the stablemen had been at work early. Each horse should have had time in the paddocks while this was done. Harriet had known Mrs. Andrews to get involved in this process herself. She admired the woman, but was sure her admiration would not go as far as doing *that* job.

Mrs. Andrews rode Perseus side-saddle. She knew Harriet was not allowed to ride astride and thought to keep the girl company. They rode over green fields, allowing their horses free rein to race across the grass. She led them to a favoured spot by a small stream. A willow hung low over the water and several trees grew in a little copse. It was perfect for hide and seek or chase with Isabella. They dismounted and walked the horses over to the stream to drink.

"I suppose you are interested in what Mrs. Harker had to say the other day?" surmised Mrs. Andrews, her face flushed with the exertion of riding. Harriet looked sheepishly at her, a mild blush to her cheeks, *"does anything make this young woman look unpolished?"* wondered Helena. She knew her own hair was escaping its confines; her bonnet had fallen and was held only by the ribbons tight at her neck. Harriet, in stark contrast, still looked perfectly groomed from head to toe. Helena recalled having to submit to her mother's ministrations every five minutes, due to some hair out of place or ribbon untied.

Mrs. Andrews described Genevieve's visit, leaving out anything she felt was intended only for her. The fact was, they had never discussed Harriet, "I think she was happy to get to know me. We will return the visit and I have a feeling Mr. Harker will talk to me then."

"Do you think they will forbid me to come?" Harriet looked forlorn, which raised an affectionate smile from Helena. Sometimes the girl still showed herself through the woman.

"I hope not. Issie and I love your visits, and so do the horses! I will do all I can to show that I hope only to open your mind. Not force my views upon you, but to encourage you to think for yourself. You are intelligent enough to listen to a friend, and your guardian, then make your own decisions. Neither of us should be upset with you, if you agree with the other," she saw immediate relief in Harriet's demeanour.

"You would not be angry with me, if I did not agree with you?"

"Of course not."

"Alexander is not my only guardian," Harriet revealed, satisfied enough to change the subject, "my stepfather's second cousin, Colonel Ackley, is also my guardian. He is to come home soon."

As the women continued to walk and enjoyed the day, they talked of the two mares due to foal in a month. Harriet was as excited for that as she was for the birth of the Harkers' child, due shortly thereafter.

At the end of July, in the middle of the day, their coach finally arrived at Aysthill House. Colonel Ackley, who was still not fully recovered, was unable to do more than watch Tommy being ushered to the kitchens for a meal. The colonel's mother with several servants, took him to his rooms, where he was to lie in his bed. The room was stiflingly hot and he was frustrated, but he was not left alone for a moment.

Finally, when everyone had gone to bed, he was able to slip down to the kitchens. As expected, Mrs. Rollins, the old cook who had worked for his family for over forty years, was overseeing the cleaning of the last pots and pans from dinner and was thrilled to see the colonel.

"Colonel Ackley," she bobbed, "what are you doing down here when you should be resting?"

"My dear Mrs. Rollins, I am sick of resting. I am fine, I tire easily, that is all. Tell me how things are with you and your family?" he desperately wanted to ask her of Tommy, but politeness made him ask after her first.

"We are all doing well, sir, I thank you for asking. My first great-grandbaby is on its way, should be here in a couple more months," she smiled indulgently. "Can I get you anything, sir?"

"No, I thank you, but you did feed Tommy Smithson well I hope?"

"Oh yes, sir, of course, sat right in there he did," she pointed to the staff dining room, "fed him up, while he told us of how you saved him. Not sorry for himself at all with his poor leg. God bless you, sir, for what you did for that young man. I am so happy we did not lose you instead though. I was not sure we would see you again. Used to love it when you would run in here, begging for biscuits or whatever I had baking," she covered her mouth with her hand, to hold in the tears welling in her eyes.

"Would you happen to have one of those biscuits available now?" he asked with a grin, hoping to help her gain control of herself, yet touched that she had worried about him.

"Awe, Colonel, I made a fresh batch today, knowing you were coming home and hoping you should ask me," as she made for the larder to collect the biscuit tin, she continued to talk, "I got the impression from that young Tommy, though he did not directly say, that he saved you as much as you saved him."

"More, in my opinion. I was hoping to see him before he left. I wanted to make sure he was sent off with plenty of food and money, but they would not let me out of bed."

"Do not worry about that, Colonel," she assured him, "I packed a good food parcel up for him and we had a little collection by way of thanks for bringing you back to us. He would not take the money though. A credit to him that was, but I snuck it into the food parcel. He will not see it until he un-wraps the pork pie!" at this she let out a laugh that sent her ample bosom rising and falling.

"Then I am in your debt, Mrs. Rollins. I will repay you of course."

"You keep your money, sir. We were all happy to do it, as thanks."

"Thank you, Mrs. Rollins, for the aid to Tommy, and the biscuits," he took the plate from her. "Please have the driver who took him to Sheffield provide me, and only me, with the address. I want to be sure that Tommy and his family have enough to manage." He turned and left, so did not see the older woman hold her hand to her heart to say a quick prayer that such a good man was not taken from the world too soon.

July turned into August, the roses in the gardens wilting in the hot summer sun. Mrs. Andrews and Miss Isabella visited Eastease as promised. Rachel spent considerable time trying to train Isabella's unruly hair into a suitable style for visiting Eastease. Mrs. Andrews submitted herself to the ministrations of her own maid just as unwillingly as her daughter, but Eastease was a good ally to have in the world and she wanted to make the right impression.

They took their curricle on the North Road and then turned into the luscious grounds. After passing the Porter's cottage, they took the main route that led to the front of the magnificent house.

"Mrs. Andrews and Miss Andrews, ma'am."

"Thank you, Mrs. Hopkins. Refreshments as soon as you are able, please." Mrs. Harker turned from the housekeeper to her guests, "so good to see you both again. Harriet, I believe you know Mrs. Andrews and Miss Andrews already."

"Indeed, I do. Helena and Isabella, I am so glad to see you at Eastease."

"Harry!" exclaimed the younger girl and flew to Harriet to wrap her arms around her skirts, "how is Hudson?" she was eager to ask after Harriet's favoured mount.

"Isabella, is that any way to greet a friend in such a house as Eastease? How will we show Mrs. Harker how refined you are, if you behave in such a manner?" Harriet's voice was tinged with humour and she proceeded to give Isabella the correct words to use. They all played their part as Isabella repeated the words to Genevieve, and then praised her for her efforts.

Mrs. Hopkins re-entered the room and oversaw the serving of the refreshments. Once she was satisfied all was in order, she nodded her approval and exited the room, leaving the women with their charge to enjoy the finery before them. When refreshments had been eaten, and talk of horses and babies had lapsed, Isabella sat kicking her heels together. She looked around for something to catch her interest. In a far corner stood a pianoforte and she walked over to inspect it. She had not seen one before and wondered about its odd shape. With the other ladies engaged in conversation, Harriet watched the progress of the child, then followed her and lifted the lid to reveal the keys.

"Would you mind if I played a small piece, Gennie?" Harriet asked. Receiving assent, she proceeded to play a light melody for the girl. Delighted, Isabella turned in circles and shifted her feet in time to the music, much as she did to her mother's singing. Once the piece was over, she sat down with Harriet, in the hope that she might be invited to try the instrument for herself. Harriet played the first measure of melody from the first bar and invited her to copy it. She did it perfectly. Harriet added a second measure, again the child copied it flawlessly.

"Mama, it is so wonderful!" Isabella played the two measures she had learned, twice more.

"If neither of you have an objection, I should love to teach Isabella. She seems to be a very willing and capable student," to prove the point, Harriet added the chords with her left hand to the two measures of melody. Isabella copied her.

At that moment, Alexander came striding into the room. Catching the mood and situation immediately, he insisted on meeting the accomplished musician he had heard playing so well.

"It was me, Mr. Harker, it was me!" exclaimed Isabella.

"Alexander, my dear," interjected Genevieve, delighted at her husband's humour with the child, "please allow me to introduce the maestro, Miss Isabella Andrews and of course her mother, Mrs. Helena Andrews. Ladies, as Miss Isabella correctly surmised, this is Mr. Harker."

"Mrs. Andrews and Miss Andrews, so delighted to make your acquaintance, at last," he bowed to each. "I should love to hear some more of your playing, Miss Andrews," he indicated to Isabella to show off her newfound skills.

"I should love to teach her," Harriet repeated, after the two measures had ended and a suitable applause delivered. Alexander considered it an excellent idea. Mrs. Andrews expressed a concern about imposing, but it was waved away with the suggestion that it be an exchange for Isabella's advice on the new nursery. At that, the party exited the room to the stairs, heading to the nursery to view it.

Mr. Harker, however, stayed Mrs. Andrews asking for a quick word in his study, while the rest of the group went ahead. With a glance first at Genevieve, Mrs. Andrews, receiving an encouraging nod, followed Mr. Harker toward a dark oak door across the hallway.

Mrs. Andrews entered the study of Mr. Harker, and took in the rich sights and smells approvingly. She imagined he worked hard at the old desk that he moved behind effortlessly. The room was very functional, but with views out to the luscious gardens of Eastease, it was restful, too.

As comfortable as the room looked, it did not afford any to her. She had an idea that Mr. Harker wanted to speak to her of her relationship with his ward. As was her habit, she sat straight-backed in the chair that Mr. Harker had indicated.

"Mrs. Andrews, I would like to apologise for being remiss in expressing my condolences for the loss of your grandfather, in person. He was an admirable man, who discussed business with me often and I find that I miss him."

"Thank you, Mr. Harker," she did not move from the chair as she felt he had more to say.

"During one of our many consultations, he did discuss his decision of leaving Redway Acres to you. He appealed to me to assist you if ever the need arose. I would like to encourage you to make use of my knowledge of business. I should be happy to be of service to you and fulfil his wishes."

"Thank you again, it is very generous of you to offer your time," she waited.

"Mrs. Andrews, I should like to make a request of you," Mr. Harker leaned forward onto his desk. Resting his elbows there, he joined his fingertips to form an arch. His intense, brown eyes looked over them at her, "I am very happy, for both Harriet and my wife, that they have found a friend in you. However, I should like to request that you refrain from imposing your, let us call them independent, opinions on Harriet, who is at an impressionable age." Interesting that he only mentioned his ward in that request she thought. Before he could assume her silence as acquiescence, in the way that men do, she responded.

"Mr. Harker, let me ask you this. If I were to require your business opinion, as you have so generously offered, would you be informing me of a course of action I must take, or would we have a discussion over the merits of possible courses of action for me to be free to choose from?"

"The latter of course," he exclaimed with surprise.

"Then please be assured, that when Harriet has sought *my* opinion on any matter, we have always discussed the merits of varying viewpoints. I have given her my views, with my own reasoned arguments. She has been free to make her own decision. You have no need to make this request, as your ward is an elegant, intelligent, caring and very charming young woman, Mr. Harker. She is also a first-rate horsewoman. You have done very well raising her and I value her friendship."

"On Harriet's finer points we most certainly agree, Mrs. Andrews!" Harker nodded with a wry smile. Genevieve had warned him that this woman was quick witted. She had outsmarted him, quite calmly. He looked forward to talking business with her in the future. "Let us join the others in the nursery and see what your daughter has to say."

In the weeks since Colonel Ackley returned to Aysthill, he felt he had returned to his childhood. Once again, he was fighting to find his own way in the world. His mother's instructions to staff, to report his movements to her, were as stifling as the heat in his room from the fire constantly built up. For the first week, his only escape was at night, when he finally was able to sneak outside to the stable to look in on Thor.

After a while, his mother had allowed him out, although she insisted the fire be built up in every room he went in, much to his father's annoyance. To his own annoyance, she talked of him giving up the life of a soldier and bachelor. She had her own idea as to who he should marry.

During this past week, he found his stamina improved greatly and decided that a visit to his longtime friend Harker was needed, before he behaved very badly toward his well-meaning mother. With this in mind he put pen to paper.

Harker,

I hope this finds you, Mrs. Harker and my dear Harriet in good health. After my previous letter sent from the convent, I am very happy to confirm that I am much recovered.

I think the final step in my recuperation should be a trip to Eastease, some lively conversations and superb music. All of which I am sure your wife and my cousin could provide.

What say you Harker? Can you endure me for a few weeks, before mother drives both father and I completely mad? I think that she may wish to see me in situ before she rests at ease at home. Perhaps an invitation to dinner would not be too much of an imposition? I promise to remove myself once the heir to Eastease is born, if not before.

Write as soon as you can. I am already packing. Your's

Ackers

Upon reading his friend's letter, Harker smiled. He had been worried about him, but so much of the colonel's humour shone through in the short note, that he was relieved of most of it. After dashing off his reply, he went to find his wife and Harriet.

Fortuitously, he found them in a meeting with Mrs. Hopkins. Genevieve's aunt and uncle, Mr. and Mrs. Ridgefield, were to visit Eastease before Genevieve's confinement. They were to continue north to visit Mrs. Ridgefield's family in Newcastle, after the weekend. He informed the ladies of their latest impending visitor and request for a dinner. Then he left them with their happy preparations.

The women agreed that this was a wonderful opportunity to include Mrs. Andrews in a dinner party at Eastease. Leaving them a gentleman short for the best dining arrangement, they decided the most appropriate man to fill the spot should be Mr. Brooks. He had recently taken up the post of the local clergyman.

Harriet was keen to go out on Hudson. She agreed delivering the invitation in person to Redway, should be the best way to get an acceptance. It was well known at Eastease, that Mrs. Andrews was not one for social outings that did not involve horses.

The young woman had an idea about the entertainment for the evening. She had known for some time that Mrs. Andrews was an excellent singer. If she spent time with Genevieve or Alexander during

Isabella's pianoforte lesson, Harriet persuaded her to sing an aria from Beethoven's opera, while the child enjoyed a treat from the kitchens.

Helena's voice was so beautiful and the character, Leonore, was strong. She dressed herself as a man, to pretend to be a guard, at the prison where her husband was being held unjustly. Harriet's romantic heart just burst at the thought of it. She hoped to persuade Helena to sing it after the dinner.

Chapter Two

At the beginning of the last weekend in August, Colonel Ackley rode the ten miles west from Aysthill to Eastease under a blue sky and a high sun. He was a bit too warm, with his cravat snug at his neck, his waistcoat buttoned up and his top coat on. However, as he was visiting his friend's impressive estate of Eastease, he had to arrive appropriately attired. On a summer day, his preference would be to ride with the neck of his shirt open and his sleeves rolled up.

The rest of his family followed in a carriage. They were joining him for dinner at Eastease, with a brief overnight stop. He should be staying as long as he could without wearing out his welcome.

He was glad to be taking Thor with him. He understood the animal, as neither of them liked to be confined for long. It was why the excitement and danger of battle suited them. Thinking of the battlefield he rubbed at his chest. The scar cut across him diagonally from ribs to shoulder. It was still raised and occasionally sore. He had seen, and inflicted, enough death and debilitating injuries to know he was lucky.

Colonel Ackley was not a violent man. Killing was part of war and when victorious the losses could be considered worthwhile by those who remained. However, when a battle was lost and retreat was sounded, the deaths seemed senseless.

Occasionally, he speculated on how God might judge him when his time finally came, but being young and optimistic, he did not dwell on it for long. For now, he was on his way to see a friend who he considered more like a brother. Genevieve and Harker had been married for a year and an heir for Eastease was due shortly. Harker had asked him to be the child's Godfather. He smiled, if children were not in his own future, then Godfather to a Harker was a pretty good second best. He should like to have his own children, but that would mean a wife.

His Father's cousin, Lady Agnes Bainbridge, had been writing to his mother. Her daughter, his second cousin, Lady Grace, was of marriageable age. All three women wanted to keep the Bainbridge estate, in Norfolk, within the family. However, he had never wanted either Grace or Bainbridge, no matter how many times she had made him groom in her pretend weddings, when they were children. He had only consented then because, as a ten-year old, he enjoyed rescuing the fair maiden from the dragon first, even if she was five years his junior.

Once, he had resolved that, if he were to marry, it would be to a woman of fortune. Witnessing the Harkers' marriage, his priority had shifted. To find a woman that he could love, who could love him in return, was where the true fortune lay. Until then he would remain a bachelor.

He had spent the previous Christmas at Eastease, with Mr. and Mrs. Ridgefield. His cousin and ward, Harriet, was also present and he felt it his duty as her guardian, with Harker, to see her as often as he could. Now that she had a woman in the house for guidance, he looked forward to seeing her again and seeing the young woman, he had no doubt, she was blossoming into.

With these pleasant ideas, he turned his horse into Eastease Park and with the welcoming destination so close, Thor gladly cantered the remaining distance to the house.

"Colonel Ackley, welcome to Eastease!" Genevieve Harker greeted him with a curtsey, as gracious as always. Marriage and impending motherhood served her well, as she looked radiant.

"Thank you, Mrs. Harker. And I thank you for the invitation to stay awhile," he bowed, adding "I rode ahead of the rest of my family," in response to her raised eyebrows and slight glance behind him. "We have but a few minutes' respite before they descend."

"How are you, Nathaniel?" she asked. Last Christmas, he had asked Harker for the privilege of a brother and allowed her to use his given name, "are you fully recovered?"

"I am well I assure you," the noise of Harker striding into the room, prevented him from having to provide any further detail. He turned to greet Harker and was quickly in his friend's firm embrace.

"It is good to be at Eastease again, Harker. Thank you for inviting me or should I say accepting my invitation to myself. My word! I have to say that marriage suits you." Harker's frown did not directly disappear. He looked at his friend intently, searching his face for signs that he had not yet recovered. He had obviously been worried for him. Remembering their long-time friend, Mark Wyndham, who had died in battle many years' prior, the colonel smiled, getting the smile to reach his piercing, blue eyes. "I am well, my friend, I am well. A good dose of Eastease, and escape from mother, is just what I need."

"Then you are welcome, Ackers!" Harker found his voice at last, as his concern receded.

"Cousin!" this exclamation came from Harriet, who forgot all her training and wrapped her arms around his neck. The strength of his embrace and the familiar smell of him was such a comfort to her. He was the closest thing she had to a father, since her stepfather's death.

"Harriet," he said softly, as he returned the embrace, "I see you have not lost any of your youthful exuberance. You are quite the handsome woman I always knew you would grow up to be."

"Thank you," she stepped back, dropping her gaze to the floor.

"Worry not, my dear. It was the best welcome I have received since setting foot back in England."

The noise of the rest of the Ackley family arriving, filtered through the open door of the sitting room. Shortly thereafter, Lord and Lady Aysthill entered announced by the Eastease butler, followed by the Viscount and his wife the Viscountess. All were welcomed, refreshments were requested and seats were taken.

"So, you see for yourself, Alexander, Nathaniel is recovering quite well," said Lady Aysthill.

"Indeed, I do, My Lady. Your ministrations have worked wonders."

Seeing the colonel's discomfort, Genevieve directed the discussion to another path, "my aunt and uncle arrive this afternoon. I know they will be glad to reacquaint themselves with you, Colonel."

"And I, them," he replied, continuing to ask after all her family. The awkward moment forgotten, she addressed the whole group, advising them that the final members of their party for dinner would be the local clergyman, Mr. Eliot Brooks, and Mrs. Helena Andrews of Redway Acres stable.

"Mrs. Andrews is a recent particular friend of mine and Harriet's," explained Genevieve, "of course they have horses in common, which I understand is a failing of mine."

"Quite so," added Harker, "her stable is where the two Yorkshire Coach Horses, that you hanker after, come from, Ackers."

"And does she also share your love of music, Harriet?" the colonel asked, attempting to draw her into the conversation, "or do you only talk of horses?" clearly her reticence in a group of more than three or four still stuck with her.

"She does not play an instrument," she replied, "says she has not the time or the patience for it. Claims that she would rather spend her time with a living, breathing thing, preferably a horse!" at that they all laughed. "She does, however, have a wonderful singing voice and we have been practising a surprise for you tonight. Providing neither of us loses our nerve."

"Then I cannot wait to meet her, Harriet."

While the Harkers greeted their guests early that afternoon, Mrs. Andrews strode anxiously around her horses' stalls. Horses had always calmed her, but this afternoon nothing was going to achieve that. *"Oh, why did I agree to this dinner party?"* she asked herself for the hundredth time. *"Why did I agree to sing that ridiculous aria?"* She had agreed, because she had not been able to resist the charming sight of Harriet, so enthralled by the romance of the music, that none of the usual qualms about performing marred the young woman's face. She had talked of Leonore's love for her husband, and how she had posed as a guard to free him from unjust imprisonment. Singing as a strong woman, willing to serve her husband in such a daring way, certainly appealed to Helena.

She had thought the audience would be the Harkers and their friend. Now there would be an audience of ten, including Lord Aysthill and his eldest son, with whom she had a heated disagreement about the sale of her horses. She could not back down now. Harriet seemed to think her singing worthy of her own playing and that was praise indeed, given that young woman's talent. She should pick out one person and sing it to them. She should focus on Genevieve. Her face would be friendly and encouraging. That was the solution. With renewed determination, she paced another circuit around the stable, before heading off to discuss with Ruth the arrangements for Isabella's care. Then she would spend some time with Isabella, prior to heading over to Eastease in time to dress for dinner.

She had decided to ride Perseus. She wanted to wake early in the morning and get back to Redway without much in the way of assistance. She should be home in time to help with the morning routine and training schedule. She hated to leave Isabella for too long, not to mention the two mares foaling within the month. At least, those were the reasons she gave her hosts for her plans. Her overnight necessities and evening gown, which was dusted off and adjusted accordingly, had been sent with Isabella, when she had her last music lesson.

In order not to be noticed arriving on horseback, she rode Perseus across the fields. Leaving the horse in the capable hands of the stable manager and giving instructions for her early departure the following day, she entered the house through the back. As arranged, she found Harriet in her music room practising for the evening performance. Together they ascended the stairs to their adjoining rooms, to prepare for the evening with the service of Harriet's maid and Rebecca, the scullery maid. Helena was pleased that Genevieve was giving the girl the opportunity to learn the ropes of being a lady's maid.

Colonel Ackley had enjoyed the rest of his day at Eastease. The Ridgefields had arrived and the acquaintance renewed. To have a discussion and allow the matter *not* to be resolved upon, but each person to keep their own opinion was enjoyable, and was something his father and Cousin Grace, would never usually allow. For the Ridgefields, the joy of a discussion was more about the discussion itself, rather than the necessity of reaching a conclusion.

His mother was seen instructing Mrs. Hopkins, the Eastease housekeeper. He suspected she was giving orders about his care. He politely asked the woman to disregard Lady Aysthill's requests.

"Do not worry about it, Colonel. Mr. Harker has informed the staff to agree with Lady Aysthill on all matters regarding you, and then to proceed to treat you the same way we always have. I hope that meets with your approval?" relieved, he had confirmed it did, and smiled at Harker's forethought.

He had time to visit Thor and discuss his care with Adam, a stableman who was good at managing the beast. Thor was happy with the treats the colonel brought with him from the kitchens, but less so that he chose to share them with two young, Yorkshire Coach horses. They were indeed handsome, strong, yet temperate and he envied Harker's possession of them.

Curiously, he found a large, grey stallion there. He glanced toward it twice, before he realised that he knew it. He must be wrong. How could *that* horse be here at Eastease? He had a carrot left in his pocket, which, if he recalled correctly, was this horse's favourite treat. With the carrot in his open palm he had approached the stall.

"Watch out for that horse, sir. He is particular as to who he lets near him," the warning voice of the stable manager had come from behind him.

"If he remembers me I will be fine, thank you," he responded, then in a gentle voice, "do you remember me, old fellow? Remember your friend? Have a good sniff," the horse had sniffed at the colonel's hand and took the carrot. While its mouth was occupied, he had quickly moved that hand to stroke the horse's neck and pat a muscular shoulder. All the while, murmuring reassuring words. The horse put its head over the colonel's left shoulder and rubbed none too gently in greeting. Looking over his other shoulder he saw the stable manager standing frozen in astonishment. Smiling he opened the stall door and entered.

"You do remember me then, boy," he crooned, and ran his expert hands over the horse's back and haunches. There, as he had expected, he had felt the ridges of old scars.

"I have got a few scars myself, including a really good, new one. It is not quite as well healed as these." The stallion looked healthy and there were no recent scars on him. In fact, all of the ones he had felt, were many years old. Where the devil did Harker get him? This wonderful specimen was supposed to be dead. The horse nuzzled into the colonel again, which he flattered himself was because it was pleased to see him, but it was probably looking for more carrots. With his forehead resting on the horse's neck, he was overcome with a sense of peace that he had not felt in some time.

"Sorry boy, I have no more treats on me," he patted him once more and exited the stall. Had the stable manager still been around, he would have asked him how this particular horse came to be in Harker's stable, but blast it, the man had disappeared.

Colonel Ackley dressed for the evening with the service of the Eastease footman, James, who doubled as his valet when needed. When in the army, he was assigned a soldier to serve him, but in truth he was more than capable and quite happy, to dress himself. Still, *"when in Rome..."* he thought as he submitted himself to the ministrations of the man tying his cravat.

It should be interesting to meet this old widow that Harker had said owned the stable which produced those Yorkshire Coach horses. He wondered if she had much information of horses or just left that to her stable manager. If the former, he hoped they might talk of his favourite subject. He also planned to get to the bottom of why a grey stallion, that was supposed to be dead, was ensconced in Harker's stable.

He found Harker, his father and brother in Harker's study. The topic of discussion was the very one that had been occupying his own mind while he was getting dressed, the old widow, Mrs. Andrews.

"She is certainly opinionated, Sir, but not overbearing. However, we do not see it as a problem for Harriet to be exposed to others' opinions, and Mrs. Andrews encourages discourse, not acquiescence. Harriet is coming out of her shell more and expressing herself well," Harker reasoned.

"How is she supposed to get a husband if she is far too opinionated? No man worth his salt will endure her," countered Lord Aysthill.

"I agree, Father. Phoebe would never disagree with me!" said William.

"Are you sure that is the only reason you object to her?" Lord Aysthill's face turned puce.

"What was Harker alluding to?" the colonel raised an eyebrow in Harker's direction.

"You would think," a similar colour rising in William's face as he spoke, "that people selling horses, should not be so particular about to whom they were sold! What does it matter to her what becomes of a horse, once she has sold it and reaped her profits?" So, the widow had refused to sell horses to both his father and brother. He had seen their treatment of the more temperamental animals in their possession. His respect for this woman doubled in an instant. Nay tripled!

"With respect, Father," the colonel joined the conversation and really meaning no respect whatsoever, "neither you, nor William, is Harriet's guardian. That honour falls to Harker and me. I have not met the lady as yet, but I trust Harker's judgment. We know old widows well enough to know them to be opinionated. I am sure Genevieve can help Harriet determine what is useful and what is not, from the information she learns from Mrs. Andrews."

Harker smirked and covered it with a scratch to his nose, but the colonel saw it. He glanced at his father who surprisingly was covering a small smile of his own. Mr. Ridgefield entered the room and the subject was changed.

The men joined the ladies in the sitting room, next to the dining room. The colonel scanned the faces for the one unknown to him. His mother; sister-in-law; Genevieve; Harriet and Mrs. Ridgefield; all were looking resplendent in their finery. In amongst them, was the face he did not recognise, but he realised, with a jolt, that it was not a face he was expecting. Did the old widow have a daughter? He had never asked if she had children. If so, then where was the widow? He looked at Harker and saw the sparkle in his friend's eyes, as he noted the colonel's reaction to the woman. He realised he had been tricked. It was his fault for making the assumption that a widow should be an old woman. As a soldier, he had seen enough young men die to know there must be a lot of young widows. This was a particularly attractive one.

She was not coiffed and powdered, like the ladies of the ton he had met with his brother or Harker, prior to their marriages. Her thick, red hair was loosely tied up, with only slight curling. Her skin was pale, as befitted her overall colouring, but freckles fought with the minimal powder on her face. She obviously spent a lot of time outside.

Her green eyes turned to him as the introductions began and took their own assessment. He was almost as tall as Mr. Harker, lean, too, but in the same way that she judged the muscles of a horse beneath its coat, she could see the muscles of the man. His were stronger than those of his friend, both in his arms and across his chest. As she looked up from his body, she saw his eyes were upon her. Genevieve was making the introduction, "Colonel, please allow me to introduce Mrs. Helena Andrews of Redway Acres; Mrs. Andrews, my husband's dear friend, and Lord and Lady Aysthill's son, Colonel Nathaniel Ackley."

Colonel Ackley stepped forward and bowed, "Mrs. Andrews, I am pleased to make your acquaintance. I have long admired my friend's Yorkshire Coach horses and understand he obtained them from your stable," rising from his bow, he was surprised to see that she had taken a step backward. Judging from her blush it was unconsciously done.

"I am pleased to meet you, Colonel," she replied recovering quickly and making a quick curtsey, "yes, those were my grandfather's horses. Cleveland Bays bred to Thoroughbreds. It gives them a longer-legged stride, with unmatched ability for a combination of speed, style, and power. They do make a striking scene on the roads here and, I am sure, on the streets of London." So, the conversation was to be horses, his spirits lifted. Nodding an 'excuse me', he turned to attend his mother, who was calling him over to introduce Mr. Brooks.

She realised that she had fallen back onto horse details to cover her embarrassment. He had caught her looking at his body and noticed her step backward. She said, *"stupid, stupid!"* under her breath. Not being in society much, she had learned some general, conversational and hopefully witty things to say. None had come to mind under the stare of those blue eyes. That horses did not interest him was evident, he was so eager to get away. She knew, however, that he rode in the Army and had seen his magnificent horse in the stable. Perhaps the horse was a means to an end for him, like his father. She was, surprisingly, disappointed.

Once introduced to Mr. Brooks, the colonel had but a moment to enjoy the view of Mrs. Andrews before dinner was announced. It was evident she was not relaxed in company. She sat ramrod-straight, replying with short answers when Genevieve attempted to draw her into conversation. However, he noted that she smiled animatedly at Harriet, when she leaned over and whispered something to her. Dinner was announced and everyone stood. The men then chose the appropriate partner with whom to walk into the dining room. Harker with Lady Aysthill and Lord Aysthill with Genevieve; William moved toward Harriet, so it fell to the colonel to walk in with his sister-in-law; Mr. Brooks politely offered his arm to Mrs. Ridgefield, and her jovial husband was left with the honour of walking in with the attractive Mrs. Andrews. It was not often the colonel envied a portly, older man, but at the moment that slim, pale hand rested in the crook of Mr. Ridgefield's arm, he would have happily changed places with him.

Chapter Three

Colonel Ackley thoroughly enjoyed dinner, though the same cannot be said for all those present. Conscious of Mrs. Andrews' refusal to sell horses to Lord Aysthill and his son, Genevieve did not sit her next to either one. A fact for which she was profoundly grateful. The colonel found himself sitting opposite her, with Harriet and Phoebe either side of him.

The first course was served, and as etiquette demanded, he spoke to Harriet on his right. Truthfully, she spoke mostly to him and he listened. What music she had recently learned, how excited she was for the arrival of the Harkers' baby and her endeavours at making simple clothing items for it, which were *'disastrous'*. How much she loved having Genevieve to turn to and was she not *'the most excellent person there ever was?'* He noticed that Mrs. Andrews and Mr. Brooks did not have a whole lot to say to each other, though the man seemed eager to draw her into conversation. By lending half an ear to it, the colonel heard only trivial subjects such as the weather, Eastease and the meal.

Too soon the course was cleared, he had hoped to question his cousin about the mysterious Mrs. Andrews. The conversation became more general, including the whole group. Genevieve looked over to Harker expectantly and he dutifully complimented his wife and Harriet on their successful preparations for the evening. With sounds of agreement, and added praise of Mrs. Hopkins and her staff, all present raised their glasses.

During the second course, the colonel rightly turned his attention to Phoebe, while Harriet was engaged in conversation with William. After a couple of inane exchanges about the weather and the ton, boredom prompted him to poke at a hornet's nest and quietly ask of Mrs. Andrews' refusal to sell his brother horses.

"Dreadful woman!" she exclaimed under her breath, "what is it to her who she sells her horses to? Said she knew he was only buying them on behalf of father, whom she had refused. Then she has the insolence to suggest she buy Moses from him!"

"What were her reasons?" the colonel smiled, Moses was his father's prize horse.

"For not selling, she said she had not loved and trained these beautiful animals to be beaten because they had lost father a bet. For buying Moses, she said she wished to save him more of the same!" he

31

nodded in agreement. Phoebe took this to mean agreement with her, when, in truth, he was agreeing with the opinions it seemed Mrs. Andrews held.

"William insisted that, being beaten, the horse was unlikely to lose him a bet again. She responded that being animals that naturally loved to race, there was no need to beat them into running faster. Encouragement was more effective. Did you ever hear such a thing, Colonel?" he surprised her by saying that he had and used such techniques himself. Phoebe's conditioned response of agreeing with a male opinion put her in a difficult position. How could she agree with both her husband and brother-in-law when they were at odds with each other? Her dilemma amused him.

He looked at Genevieve, a woman he knew would weigh up both opinions and draw her own conclusion. He followed that with a glance at Mrs. Andrews. She was engaged in a meaningful and spirited conversation with Mr. Ridgefield about... fishing? Did he just hear them mention fishing? She seemed to be miming a technique using her hands. Mrs. Andrews may well be cut from a similar cloth to that of Genevieve, and should that not make life interesting? He smiled as she laughed pleasantly at the older man's story.

At the same time, Mr. Brooks was considering the interesting Mrs. Andrews. He was a youthful, serious man, who had the good fortune to benefit from Harker bestowing the living at the local village of Eastcambe upon him. With his path truly settled, he hoped to find a wife and start a family. Mrs. Andrews was handsome, if headstrong, a little intimidating in fact. Once she was his wife he would be her master and that should give him confidence. He wished he was a little taller, as she was much taller than the admirable Mrs. Harker. He had a subject matter ready for his second opportunity to talk with her, assured that Mrs. Andrews would submit to his better opinion.

"Mrs. Andrews, I have not yet had the pleasure of seeing you at Sunday service," he was sure the tone of his voice was pleasantly inquisitive, not judgmental.

"The sauce served with this pudding tastes almost as if the fruit were picked only this morning," she adeptly changed the subject matter.

"Quite," he conceded, but undeterred, continued, "do you not think it prudent, for an owner of a residence, such as Redway, to set a good example in godliness by being a churchgoer?" Her eyes narrowed, Colonel Ackley noted, as he had picked up on the conversation, whether in annoyance at Brooks ignoring her avoiding the subject or at the insult implying her imprudence, he was not sure, but she looked dangerous.

"Is being a churchgoer the only requirement to prove godliness, Mr. Brooks?" she enquired.

"Well yes, quite," he stammered, "attending church is not the only proof of godliness, or its close neighbour, goodliness."

"Exactly!" she exclaimed, catching the attention of Mr. Ridgefield to her right and Harriet beside the colonel, who was a little annoyed with him for not distinguishing her, as he should have. "Pray tell me, how has the church behaved goodly recently? Perhaps in the aid of a local family to buy shoes for its children?" Here Mr. Brooks thought himself on solid ground, though the colonel shook his head thinking she was leading him by the nose. He could imagine a bridle around Brooks' head.

"Mrs. Andrews, you have found me, I mean the church, out. A mother did ask for some assistance the other week. After consulting the church coffers, I was able to give the money to her husband when I saw him in the village on Saturday. He attended church on Sunday and thanked me, nay the church."

"Mrs. Robinson had gathered all her courage to ask you for that money. She felt such shame, but did so anyway for the good of her children. Did so, despite knowing she would face the wrath of Mr. Robinson. And this money you gave to her *husband*?"

"Of course I did, as man of the house it is his responsibility to manage money matters."

"If Mr. Robinson could manage money matters, *Mr. Brooks*, his family should all have suitable shoes," she retorted, "so, how well shod are the Robinson children?" Colonel Ackley could see anger in her demeanour, even though she showed control, keeping her voice even. Her green eyes sparked with it. He wondered the clergyman had not combusted in his chair.

"I do not know the answer to that," he blustered, realising he had made a mistake, but unsure as to what it might be.

"Unhappily, I can tell you they still wear the same shoes with holes in them. After meeting you last Saturday, Mr. Robinson proceeded to the local tavern. There, he got well into his cups. Upon returning home, he felt it within his rights to beat Mrs. Robinson for daring to ask for the money he had happily spent on ale. Then he showed *his* 'godliness' by attending church the following day and thanking you."

Chastised, Mr. Brooks only had two courses of action to the colonel's mind. Retreat or push on. He could see that Mrs. Andrews held an ace up her sleeve. He did not do well at the card table because he was only lucky. Unfortunately, Mr. Brooks took the latter course.

"As unfortunate a situation as that may be, I do not see what that has to do with me, or why it means you should not attend church yourself," poor man, it was a lamb to the slaughter!

"Firstly, you should have given the money to the person who asked for it."

"How was I to know he would spend it on ale?" his defence was poor and his face was red.

"You should know your parishioners, Mr. Brooks," a voice came from the far end of the table, where Mrs. Harker sat, listening carefully to the exchange. "It is well known, that Mr. Robinson has a habit of drinking in excess and getting violent when he does so." Mr. Brooks nodded politely in the direction of his hostess. The matter seemed to be closed and everyone turned back to their own conversations. Always the mischievous one, however, the colonel asked Mrs. Andrews a question.

"...And secondly?" his amused eyes were on Mrs. Andrews. She turned her green ones directly to his gaze as she answered, without reciprocating his amusement. Hard jade were words that came to his mind, her earlier timidity forgotten.

"Secondly, I spent my churchgoing time last Sunday attending Mrs. Robinson's cuts and bruises, and measuring her children's feet. They will have new shoes within a week." Delighted with her response, the colonel picked up his wine glass, raised it toward her and drank well from it whilst looking at her over its rim. She was splendid! Beautiful and eloquent. His time at Eastease had taken an upward turn and his spirits rose. He felt happier than he had in all of this abysmal year.

After the women withdrew, Harker, William and Lord Aysthill had a good chuckle at the colonel's mistaken conclusion that the widow was an old woman. As they partook of port and cigars, he took the opportunity to find out what Harker had learned of Mrs. Andrews.

Her husband was Captain Andrews, whose information of horses put him in the cavalry and in touch with Mr. Stockton at Redway Acres stable. His granddaughter, Miss Billings as she was then, had stayed with her grandparents often and fell in love with Captain Andrews. He had pursued her to Norfolk, on her return to her parents' house, and when she was old enough they were married. The captain was killed in battle, prior to the birth of their daughter, Isabella, over four years ago. At that time her parents wanted no more to do with her, so she came to live with her then widowed grandfather. George Stockton died last winter. The tall, strong man was taken down by influenza. The stable was willed to Mrs. Andrews in its entirety. Her stable manager, is a man named John Robertson, a lifelong horse man who knows his trade well. Apparently, she was lucky to have him. He and his wife, who is the Redway housekeeper, travelled with her from Norfolk. Harker mentioned he had business discussions with her often. That wording had the colonel's head snapping up from his port to look at him, *"discussions?"*

Colonel Ackley did not know a Captain Andrews in the cavalry. That did not mean much, there were many Captains and this was more than four years ago. He would have to see if he could find out more of him. He wondered where in Norfolk her family lived and why they did not have any contact with their daughter and granddaughter.

Once back in the drawing room with the ladies, various conversations struck up around the room. Genevieve had been sitting on a comfortable couch with Mrs. Andrews and Mrs. Ridgefield flanking her, they had been laughing at something when the colonel crossed the threshold.

Harker marched straight over to his wife and took the place of Mrs. Ridgefield as she was rising. She took Mrs. Andrews over to Mr. Ridgefield and encouraged her to repeat the obviously funny story. His round belly lifted up and down as he laughed with the women. Mr. Brooks had moved to stand on the periphery of this group, close to Mrs. Andrews, and tried to join in the laughter. Harriet rose and joined them, too, while the colonel's father and brother joined his mother and sister-in-law, to whom Harriet had been talking.

He observed them all, before sitting down with much satisfaction, on a chair close to the couch where Genevieve sat. Harker was doting on her and asking if she had enough to eat, did she need to rest, was she comfortable? She smiled at him and patted his cheek, before turning to the colonel.

"Genevieve, I would like to thank you for allowing me to escape to Eastease for a few weeks and for this welcoming dinner party. I have enjoyed myself immensely this evening."

"Do not think I missed your mischievousness at the dinner table, Ackers!" she exclaimed, "if you misbehave we shall send you back to your mother."

"Now Gennie, you cannot spoil *all* my fun. It is, after all, part of my recovery," he jibed. His eyes caught a swish of green skirt, as Mrs. Andrews moved around Mr. Ridgefield, only to rejoin the same group. Mr. Brooks, who had been moving ever closer to her, seemed about to make the same manoeuvre, when, the apparently all-seeing Mrs. Ridgefield, stayed him with a hand on his forearm and a firm,

"Mr. Brooks, please give me your opinion on…"

He wondered if Mr. Brooks had intentions toward Mrs. Andrews. Well too bad for him, she obviously had no interest. Brooks would have to challenge him, too, and he never bet against himself. Having surprised himself with that last thought, he had missed what Genevieve was saying. He thought he caught her say something of Harriet and it was about the usual time for a performance.

"Yes, I am sure that would be wonderful," he replied, hoping it was vague enough. Then, at Genevieve's expectant look, spoke loudly to the group, "is it about time for some entertainment? Harriet, I believe you and Mrs. Andrews have prepared something for us?"

The two women moved toward the pianoforte to a light smattering of applause. Harriet settled herself at the instrument and Mrs. Andrews stood at her side ready to sing. They looked at one another, each waiting for the other to speak. In a series of nods and squeaks they seemed to be communicating. The colonel found it all most amusing and smothered his snorting laugh with his hand, pretending to rub his chin. He felt a pinch in his arm. Genevieve had reached over and nipped him! His surprised 'ouch' had all eyes turning to him. The reprieve from being stared at, allowed Mrs. Andrews to find her voice and she explained the aria. It would be sung in German and was from Beethoven's opera, Leonore. Leonore's husband was wrongfully imprisoned and she dressed as a man, to pose as a guard, to set him free.

The music began and the colonel was just beginning to appreciate the improved talent of his cousin when Mrs. Andrews started singing. He stared at her and in doing so, realised she was looking directly at him. My God, the woman's voice was haunting. Her range was incredible and she seemed lost in the part of Leonore, who was rescuing her husband. Being fluent in German, the colonel appreciated how she showed nervousness over what Leonore was doing, the love she had for the man she hoped to save and the duty she felt in rescuing him. He translated as she sang...

"Abominable one! Where are you going?
What will you do? What will you do in wild anger?
The call of sympathy,
The voice of humanity,
Does nothing move your tiger sense?
Like turbulent seas,
Anger and hatred rage in your soul,
So appears to me a rainbow,
That bright on dark clouds rests.
A quiet gaze,
So peaceful,
That mirrors old times,
And new appeased my blood flows.
Please, hope, let the last star, the last star,
From fatigue not fade!
Please, illuminate, illuminate my destiny, even if it's far,
Love will reach it. Love will reach it. Love will reach it.
O please, hope, let the last star,
From fatigue not fade!
Illuminate, illuminate my destiny, even if it's far, even if it's far,
Love, love will reach it. Love, love will reach it.
I follow an inner drive,
I will not waver,
My duty strengthens me,
My duty of true marital love.
I will not waver,
My duty strengthens me,
My duty of true marital love.
O you, for whom I bore everything,
If only I could be at your side,
Where evil has you bound,
And bring you sweet comfort!
O you, for whom I bore everything,
If only I could be at your side,
Where evil has you bound,
And bring you sweet comfort!
I follow an inner drive
I will not waver
My duty strengthens me

My duty of true marital love.
I follow an inner drive,
I will not waver,
I follow an inner drive,
I will not waver,
My duty strengthens me,
My duty of true marital love."

He was swept away in it, and in her eyes, that stayed on him for the whole piece. All too soon it was over. She looked away, as the room erupted in applause, and he felt bereft. Harker, of course, was standing and loudly applauding Harriet. Mr. Brooks was overdoing it, trying to catch Mrs. Andrews' attention and Mr. Ridgefield was, as always, enthusiastic. The colonel could only sit there staring. Genevieve looked at him amused, and thought him lucky everyone was focused on the performers and did not see how dazed he was. She fondly recalled her first dinner at Eastease, when she had played and sung for Alexander in this very room. His expression had been remarkably similar to the one she now saw on the colonel's face.

"Would you like me to pinch you again, Ackers?" she enquired quietly. That seemed to bring him out of his stupor. He started to clap as everyone else was stopping. Discussions were breaking out about Harriet playing some more and with renewed confidence she found another piece to play.

Mrs. Andrews stepped, hesitantly, away from the instrument. She was wondering what had made her lock eyes with the colonel as she sang. She had intended to look at Genevieve to calm her nerves, but at the last moment his eyes were on her, the brightest blue she had ever seen. She had felt entranced and it seemed the most natural thing to sing to him, *"oh no, now his father is heading this way."*

"What a surprise, my dear, what a surprise!"

"You had better get over there, Ackers. He has had several glasses of wine," said Harker, noticing his friend was observing Lord Aysthill's approach toward Mrs. Andrews.

He sprang to his feet, walking toward her, as she was trying to extricate her hand from his father's, "thank you, My Lord. I think your wife is in need of you," she almost had to drag him over to Lady Aysthill.

As the colonel reached them, she was accepting, more graciously than it had been given, that lady's praise. He grimaced as he heard his mother, "my cousin's daughter, Lady Grace Bainbridge, sings terribly well, too. If she had been here, she would have been considered by far the best singer in the room."

Mrs. Andrews smiled at her, with what he thought might have been a pitying look, then turned away from him in the direction of Mr. and Mrs. Ridgefield. As she received their praise, she generously gave all the honour to Harriet. The colonel moved away to the back of the room to observe her more.

She seemed to be tricky for a man to engage in a conversation. Earlier, with Mr. Brooks and now with his father. He wondered if that were by coincidence or design? The only exceptions seemed to be Mr. Ridgefield and Harker, probably because they were both happily married.

As he watched, Mr. Brooks joined her group and complimented her, too. To the colonel's mind he was standing a little too close again. It seemed Mrs. Andrews agreed with him, because she took a step away. *"Oh, that was a mistake,"* he thought. Mr. and Mrs. Ridgefield chose that moment to approach the pianoforte and Harriet, as her second piece came to a close. This left Mrs. Andrews alone with the clergyman, but she was quick and turned to walk side by side with him. As he talked, she walked him closer and closer to Harker and Genevieve, depositing him into the chair the colonel himself had vacated. With a well-aimed question to Genevieve, the two became engaged in conversation, leaving her free to walk away.

In the meantime, Harriet had graciously allowed Phoebe to take over at the pianoforte. William saw this escape from his wife as his opportunity to approach Mrs. Andrews and compliment her singing. She had only managed a step or two away from Genevieve and Mr. Brooks, and stood in close proximity to Harker. She turned to ask him a question that set him into a heated discussion with William, leaving her, once again, able to walk away.

Colonel Ackley watched all of this from his vantage point with much amusement. It was like watching a dance. The principal was Mrs. Andrews and each time she was alone for a moment, she picked up a new partner. Moving across the room she deposited him elsewhere. If he were to approach her, he would, undoubtedly, receive the same treatment. He wondered what her motives were. She was not allowing a man to talk to her alone or stand too close.

The colonel considered his strategy. He would need another

woman with him, keep his distance and a subject to hold her interest. Horses were good and it was close to foaling season. She must have mares ready to foal, excellent. Harriet was approaching her, which was good timing. He must remember to do her a good turn sometime soon.

He arrived as Harriet was trying to persuade Mrs. Andrews to sing again, but she was refusing, "no need to bully her, Harriet," he said as he approached, but kept a step further back than he usually would, "although you did sing beautifully, if I may say so. You played well, too, Harriet, as always."

"Thank you," they said in unison.

"Tell me, Mrs. Andrews, do you have any mares ready to foal? I am right in thinking it is almost foaling season, am I not?"

"This season we have two," she felt comfort in the subject and the fact that Harriet stood there. He was not standing too close to her either, which made a nice change from many of the other gentlemen there.

"They are wonderful. I cannot wait to see the babies," said Harriet.

Mrs. Andrews continued to talk with some enthusiasm of the mares and her hopes for the foals. These would be the first foals to be born to Redway since her grandfather had passed, so were truly her responsibility. She obviously loved what she did. After some discussion, Harriet had left them to go to the pianoforte to play again. The colonel had achieved his goal of getting her to talk alone with him. It was incredible how happy it made him.

For Mrs. Andrews' part, she was astonished to discover his interest in horses. She had wondered why her earlier, nervous talk, had been met with indifference. Now that she recalled the moment, she remembered that his mother had called to him, so she must have been mistaken. She had been watching his interactions with his family at dinner and realised how stiff and formal he was with them. It was in total contrast with how warm and relaxed he was with the Harkers, Ridgefields and of course, dear Harriet. She had thought that she had fallen into the first category, but now it seemed, by his relaxed demeanour, that he had placed her firmly in the second. A pleasant feeling spread inside her at that realisation.

She had relaxed so much, in fact, that she had not noticed Harriet had returned to her playing and she was standing by herself in discussion with him. The moment of that realisation was evident to the colonel as she stiffened and her eyes widened, almost imperceptibly.

To avoid being rejected, he spoke before she could, "I wonder if you are rested sufficiently to sing? Harriet is looking annoyed with me for monopolising you. She is probably worried that someone will insist that she sing," he gestured toward the instrument and she nodded. He made a slight move toward her to offer his arm, but again she stiffened. He reminded himself to be cautious or lose all good favour. Instead, he clasped his hands behind his back and walked side by side with her the short distance to the instrument. Harriet was delighted she would sing again and picked a well-known, lively song, of summer days.

"Cousin, would you sit by me and turn the pages, please?" unable to deny her anything, he dutifully pulled a chair beside her stool and set to his task. Harriet was surprised she had to nudge him once or twice, as she was coming to the end of a page. Then she realised he was distracted by watching her friend sing, and imagined how wonderful it would be if they fell in love. She got an idea into her young, romantic head.

Once the song was finished and the applause began to die, Harriet quickly launched into another of love and loss. Mrs. Andrews continued to sing. One page into the song, Harriet glanced at her cousin and indicated that he should take over the playing. He gave a wry look at her meddling, but obliged her indulgently. Moving stealthily, they switched places, fingers replacing fingers seamlessly on the keys. As Harriet stood to move behind him and take the seat he had vacated, Mrs. Andrews turned slightly. Singing of her love that had left her, she looked straight into the colonel's eyes as he played. It provided a contact with the bewitching red-head, that he had not yet been able to attain. To her credit, she did not falter in her singing, but finding her inner courage, that had never failed her yet, she rose to the challenge.

"Thank you, Colonel, you play well," she said as the song ended.

"Not as well as my dear Harriet, but your splendid singing allowed me to get away with it."

"You are rusty, that is all," exclaimed Harriet, "he is being modest. He is an exceptional player." The applause was dying down and Genevieve was getting to her feet.

"I am afraid I am a poor hostess these days, but I must get to bed or I will be asleep on this couch within minutes." Harker had been helping her to stand and she leaned upon him heavily, wishing he could come with her to bed. However, both of them knew he could not leave his guests without a host. Mrs. Andrews and Harriet were soon by her side, exclaiming about their own tiredness and Mrs. Andrews' early start in the morning. Goodnights were exchanged and they escorted Genevieve off to bed.

Harker, and Colonel Ackley who had walked over with the performers, stood side by side. Both were feeling the loss of the retreating forms. Lord Aysthill's loud voice stirred them, suggesting cards. They adjourned to the games room across the hall, where they formed two tables of card players. Harker joined the colonel, his father and brother, to play Brag with high stakes. He was sure that Ackers was looking to fleece his father, who was well into his cups. Lady Aysthill, looking disapprovingly at her husband, joined Phoebe, Mr. Brooks and Mr. and Mrs. Ridgefield, to play a game of Bridge, with Mr. Brooks keeping a points tally. After a while, the more respectable game broke up and the participants declared themselves off to their respective beds.

Harker, who had stood to see his guests to the door, was looking longingly out of the room at the stairway to his own bed and wife. The colonel took pity on him, "go, Xander. You really should see that *your* family members make it to their rooms safely. I can play host to *mine* and gain a little extra spending money. We will of course be raiding your brandy and cigars."

Thinking that was a small price to pay, and with a grateful smile to the colonel, Harker turned to the other men, "my house is your house, gentlemen. I am leaving you in the colonel's capable hands and will see you in the morning."

Chapter Four

An hour earlier, when the card players were first taking their seats, Mrs. Andrews had wandered to her own room. They had put her in Maria Wyndham's old room, which adjoined Harriet's via a connecting sitting room.

She allowed Rebecca to serve, only with her unbuttoning and the unpinning of her hair. She could manage everything else herself and dismissed the maid, telling her to get some rest. It would be no good for her to have dark patches under her eyes, when next she saw Jacky!

Dressed in her nightgown and brushing her hair, she wandered to the window. Setting the last lit candle in the room on a nearby side table, she opened the curtains. She sat on the narrow window seat and looked out into the darkness. By her calculations, her room faced southeast, which was perfect because the early rising sun should slant through the window and wake her. Redway, of course, sat northwest, in the opposite direction, and there was a new moon, not much moonlight to see by. She could make out the dark shape of the east wing of Eastease, with the bedrooms above, including the room where she and Harriet had left Genevieve. Those windows were all dark or with curtains drawn closed. There was light to be seen in the rooms below, however. The east wing was where the dining and drawing rooms were that she had just been in, but their windows faced out to the gardens on the other side. So what room was she looking into now?

Through the farthest window lighted she could make out a billiards table, so it must be the games room. Four windows across from that was a more brightly lit window, through which she could make out two tables of card players. Nearest the window were four men. The stout figure, with his back to the window, was Lord Aysthill. She closed one eye and made a pinching movement with her thumb and forefinger, pretending to squash him, then giggled. It was a game she and Isabella played sometimes. Either side of him, sat two tall, dark-haired men, the Viscount and Mr. Harker, which meant the lean figure, lounging back in his chair and facing the window, was that of Colonel Ackley. She watched his languid movements. Mostly he stayed lounging, except to take an occasional sip of port or to collect his winnings, which was something he did more often than any other man at the table.

She was not tired and the cushions on the window seat were comfortable, so she pulled the cream, woollen coverlet that lay there over her legs to keep away the draught, and thought of this man that attracted her. She had seized the opportunity to leave his company, when Genevieve announced she was tired, because she was worried about the way she was feeling. It was all so new to her. Never before had she reacted so to a man. She recalled the way he had looked at her as she sang the aria to him, and how singing while he played the pianoforte felt so intimate, in a way it did not with Harriet. She had noticed him watching her after the aria, as she spoke with various dinner guests. When he had finally approached her, he had kept his distance, unlike Mr. Brooks or Lord Aysthill. It was confusing, yet comforting, and she had felt relaxed talking to him of her mares.

In the games room below, she noticed the people at the other table starting to rise. It looked like they were making their goodnights. Standing, the colonel slapped Mr. Harker on the back, smiling broadly enough that she could make it out. Mr. Harker turned, bowed to Lord Aysthill and left. The colonel swiftly went to the sideboard and procured a decanter, three large cigars and three brandy snifters from it, before returning to the table with them. He poured the drinks, and Lord Aysthill and his older son, who had already removed their topcoats, lit their cigars.

Before sitting down and lighting his, the colonel took off his topcoat, unbuttoned his waistcoat and loosened his cravat, so it hung loosely either side of his collar. He undid the top button of his shirt and then proceeded to roll up his sleeves. Rubbing his hands together, he sat down, and as he did so, he happened to look out the window. A light in a top window caught his attention and he stopped for only a second or two, at the sight of the beauty in a white nightgown, before glancing quickly back at his father and brother paying attention, once again to dealing the cards.

In her shock at being caught observing him, Helena sat up at once and blew out the candle. She did not move from the window seat, reasoning that she did not want to bring more attention to herself. Truthfully, she wanted to continue watching him. Confident she was no longer silhouetted by the candle, she remained still. At first, she could see that he lost a few hands, but then the familiar lounging and winning took over. Amused, she watched and her eyes drifted down as she fell asleep on the cushions.

After another hour of card playing, Lord Aysthill declared that he had drunk enough of Harker's brandy to make a dent in it, lost enough money to Nathaniel to keep him funded for the rest of the year and was off to bed. William agreed, and they all picked up their coats, stubbing out their cigars as they stood. The colonel had surreptitiously glanced at the darkened window often during that hour, but only when he felt his father would not notice him. He could make out a pale shape, that may have been cushions or could have been Mrs. Andrews, but she could not have watched them for over an hour. If she was still at the window, she must have fallen asleep.

He followed his relatives up the east wing staircase and said goodnight. Each had his own wife waiting in bed. A warm woman in his bed, he thought, and the image of Mrs. Andrews in a white nightgown drifted into his mind. Shaking his head to clear it, he pulled off his cravat, dropping it and his coat onto a nearby chair, and frowned at his bed. It seemed less welcoming than it had when he had left the games room. His valet came in from the dressing room.

"Can I serve you, Colonel?"

"Good lord, James, are you still up? Of course you are. My apologies, I really am used to taking care of these things myself. There was no need for you to wait for me, I should have said so earlier. Get yourself off to bed, man, and do not get up early for my sake, either," the valet hurried, gratefully, from the room, closing the door behind him. Less than two minutes passed before a hurried knock was heard at the door again. It would seem that the man was back.

"Begging your pardon, sir. Your father, that is, Lord Aysthill, has just headed down the west wing, but his rooms are in this wing. He seems a little unsteady on his legs and I thought I had better let you know."

"What was father thinking of?" he wondered, *"surely he was not going to 'teach her a lesson'?"* he had heard him say that of many an impertinent woman.

"Helena."

"I beg your pardon, sir? Is there any assistance I can give you?"

"No, I thank you. I expect he is a little too merry and forgot where he is. I will lead him back to his rooms." The valet left and the colonel marched down the west wing. He saw his father deciding which door to try and reaching for a handle, he gave it a turn. The door did not open, it must have been locked. Thank the heavens, the woman had some sense.

"What are you doing here, Father?" Lord Aysthill was startled at the sound of his son's voice, sounding deep and menacing behind him, he had not heard him approach. The colonel was angry with his father for his intentions toward this young woman, and in Eastease, Harker's home no less.

"What are *you* doing here?"

"Following you." When his father had turned to him, he had been surprised to see fear in his eyes and saw him change in that moment. No longer was he the formidable Lord Aysthill, but an old, scared man. He decided his usual amiability should diffuse the situation much better, "you seem to have misplaced your bedroom, Father. Have you really had that much to drink?"

Laughing, Lord Aysthill muttered, "must have, me boy, must have," then wound his way back to the east wing and his rooms with his wife. The colonel sorely hoped that he would not take out his frustration on her.

Looking around the wide corridor, he decided he had better sleep on the ornate couch, lining the opposite wall. He could not be sure his father would not return. It did not look too comfortable, but he doubted he would sleep much back in his own rooms. Sighing, he walked over to it. He sat down gingerly, rubbing his face in his hands, as the shame of his father's actions overcame him.

As his eyes lifted, he saw a pillow had appeared in front of him, with a pale hand holding it. He looked up into her green eyes and stood, as taught to do in front of a lady. She was a vision in white, with red hair cascading around her face. She had wrapped a white, silk dressing gown around herself, over the nightgown he had seen from the window. It was a minimal barrier and it took all his self-control not to scoop her up, march with her in his arms back into the bedroom, deposit her on the bed and ravish her himself. He was not like his father, though, and did not feel the same entitlement to take whatever he liked, whenever he liked.

"Thank you," his voice was gruff, and he took just the pillow, "I am sorry, you must have been frightened. He should not come back, but I will sleep out here tonight."

She *had* been frightened. In fact, she had woken only a few minutes before and nearly fallen off the window seat. Seeing the darkened games room and feeling the need for the pot, she had scrambled around in the dark, searching for it under the bed. She had just finished squatting over it, when the door handle had rattled. Thank goodness, she had thought to lock it!

Moving quickly to listen at the door, she had heard the anger in the colonel's voice when he spoke to his father and a glow came over her, that there was a man in this society prepared to protect her. She had not felt so since her grandfather's death. Hearing receding footsteps, she had peeped out of the door and was surprised to see Colonel Ackley walk to the couch and sit down. Realising his intention, she picked up the pillow and coverlet and went to him. She should not tell him all of that though, and thinking to lighten the moment she simply said, "I nearly fell off the window seat."

He laughed at her acknowledgement and reached down to push some of her hair behind an ear. Her eyes fell to glance at his exposed neck and she bit on her lower lip. He smelled of brandy and cigars. Then her other hand came up between them, bringing the cream coverlet from behind her back, and diffusing the tension, as she had hoped, "I found this was quite warm enough on a summer night, perhaps you would find it so," as he took it from her, he felt that it was still warm from being wrapped around her.

"How did you know he was coming here?"

"The Eastease manservant they give me here, James, saw him staggering this way. He returned to inform me."

"And you came after him, because you knew his intentions?"

"Yes."

"Because it is something he has done before?"

"Yes," he confirmed again, "but he has gone too far this time. A guest at Eastease, no less."

"Well, I am afraid we do not agree, Colonel. I would say that *'too far'* was the very first time he forced himself on a woman. Evil will succeed, if a good man does nothing," her eyes bore into his and the realisation of what she was saying shocked him. She was right. The fact that each time his father's actions had been covered up, had led to this moment. An uncomfortable night on this couch now seemed more like a penance for his inaction, than the admirable office of protection, as he had hoped she would view it.

"A servant could be brought up here to take your place on the couch or I could share Harriet's bed. It would save you a night out here.

But, I suppose that would take explanations you would rather not give, if this matter is to be forgotten."

"Quite, but thank you for these," he gestured with the pillow, and the coverlet that he had been holding to his chest.

"Thank you," she said with emphasis, "for doing something." She walked to the bedroom door, then turned to look at him again, "goodnight, Colonel Ackley."

"Goodnight, Mrs. Andrews."

Safely back in the room she closed the door and leaned her forehead on it. Out of habit she went to turn the key, but realised she really did not feel the need to do so. He was outside guarding her. How thrilled Isabella would be, by a soldier guarding the lady. What might have happened had he not stopped his father? She did not want to think of it, those nightmares were not conducive to a good night's sleep.

Before waking on the windowsill, she had been having a much more pleasant dream. It was one she had experienced several times before. The first time was after she had seen John and Ruth sharing an intimate kiss in her kitchen. They did not see her, but the gentleness of the moment had surprised her. In her dream, there was a faceless man in shirtsleeves. The man had taken her face in his hands and kissed her gently. Dreaming on the windowsill this night, that man had the face of Colonel Ackley.

On the other side of her bedroom door, the colonel lay down on the couch and placed the pillow at his head. He noted that he had not heard the turn of the lock, so she trusted him, that was good. Still clutching the throw to his chest, he bent his head to it and sniffed. He fancied that he could smell her perfume of roses on it, and started to doze.

Through the open curtains in Mrs. Andrews' room, the sunbeams slanted across the bed to wake her the next morning. She had woken off and on during her few, short hours of sleep. Again, she had the dream of the colonel kissing her, and had woken with a throbbing and frustration through her body like she had never known before.

Tiredness and this frustration, brought her anger to the fore and many ideas went through her mind as she dressed herself. What right did Colonel Ackley have to make her feel this way? She did not need a man in her life. She managed quite well without one, and certainly would not want to give over her independence and marry one. Why was she even thinking of marrying? She sat in front of the mirror, loosely pinning up her hair. She did not know the first thing about him, except he was handsome and charming; gallant and honourable; thoughtful and handsome.

"Oh, you already thought handsome!" she silently admonished her reflection, pointing a hairpin toward it.

She shook her head. It would not do. She would have to get out of this house and away from the Ackley family. No returning to Eastease until he had left. He would probably die in France fighting Bonaparte and she would never have to see him again. The horror of that thought hit her so hard, that she clamped her hand across her mouth, as if she had said it out loud. She felt ashamed that it should even cross her mind. Having already lost her stepfather to war, Harriet would be distraught if the same were to happen to her cousin.

Leaving her things for the maid to pack and send back with Isabella, she picked up her bonnet. She felt guilt about the poor night of sleep the colonel must have received on that uncomfortable couch. Then in equal measure, anger with the thought that it was not her fault and she should not feel guilt.

Armed with that anger, she opened her bedroom door. The colonel's eyes were closed and he hugged the bunched coverlet tight to his chest, which she thought was odd, as more warmth would have been gained from it had he draped it over himself. She contemplated not waking him and letting him know that he need not sleep there any longer, but it would not do for a servant to find him.

"Colonel," she said softly and then a bit louder, "COLONEL!"

"What the blazes!" he almost shouted it, and her hand came down over his mouth in reflex, to stop him waking Harriet in the next room. Mortified that she should do such a thing, she quickly took her hand away.

"Sorry," she whispered, "but you were loud. I wanted to let you know you could go back to your rooms before the servants come, and to say thank you," with that she strode down the hall and did not look back at him. He shook the sleep, late night and the feel of her fingers on his lips, from his head, as he gathered his bearings and strode after her.

"Mrs. Andrews," he called as loudly as he dared, but she seemed to walk faster. What was she wearing? It had looked like a riding habit, but as she walked away, he could see that each of her legs was surrounded with separate material; like voluminous, skirt-like trousers. Not willing to wake the whole household, he did not catch up to her until she had exited the house and reached the stable. Damn the woman, why was she leaving so early?

He stopped her from closing the stable door behind her and stepped into the short corridor that led to the stable proper.

"Wait!" was all he managed as her retreating back disappeared around the corner. She stepped back into view to look at him.

"Why are you following me?"

"I wondered why you are leaving so early and without a hint of grace, after I had a very uncomfortable night. Also, if I might add... what on earth are you wearing?" she looked, affronted, down at her attire.

"It is a riding habit, not that it is any concern of yours. I said thank you quite gracefully I believe, more than once and your uncomfortable night was not my fault. I am, however, annoyed that I seem to feel guilt over it. Leaving early was always in my plans, as you see my horse is ready for me," she gestured for him to look around the corner. He saw the mysterious grey stallion fully tacked, but not with a side-saddle. Surely, she was not going to ride the horse astride? It was most inappropriate.

"Astride? Like a man? On this beast?" he blurted out.

"Yes, yes, and absolutely yes," she took the reins from Adam, who was patiently holding Perseus. She was surprised how calm the animal was, given the colonel's presence and outbursts. She led him out of the larger barn doors at the back of the stable, which led to the green fields of Eastease. Adam made to follow, presumably to assist her in mounting the horse. Colonel Ackley stayed him with a hand to his chest and followed her himself.

"Where did you get this animal from?" he asked her.

"I fail to see what business that is of yours," she was haughtier than she had intended.

"I knew his previous owner," her eyes flashed to his.

"I think you must be mistaken," but he had seen the fear cross her face, "are you going to help me mount, as you have sent the stableman away?"

"No," he stated simply and folded his arms across his chest, "you should not be riding this horse," he would not help her break her neck. To his astonishment, she simply led the horse to a water trough and stood on its edge. Putting her hands on the horse's withers, in front of the saddle, she hoisted herself upward and swung a leg expertly over it. She was obviously much stronger than her womanly form led one to believe.

"I think you and your father, need to stop trying to tell me what to do and stay away from me," with that she turned the horse toward the fields and legged him into a canter. She had not meant to be so cruel comparing him to his father, but she should not lead him to believe that there might be any future with her. Even though the glorious sight of him so dishevelled from sleep and in such a state of undress, made her breath come out of her in a sigh.

"Would you like me to saddle Thor, so you can go after her, sir?" offered Adam, who was leaning casually on the barn doorframe and was obviously amused.

"Yes, saddle him please, but no hurry, I will not stand a chance of catching up to her." Mrs. Andrews and her magnificent horse, were speeding across the green fields. It was obvious to him that she was a better rider than any man he had met, and had the full respect of that stallion, "as I am here, I will take him out for a ride."

Chapter Five

The colonel rode Thor out across the fields, to the farthest Northwest corner of Eastease where it joined Redway Acres land. As instructed by Adam, he had kept the various cottages and the church that lined the North Road, to his left. A mile after the church, he looked for the boundary marker that showed the transition from Eastease to Redway Acres. From there, Eastease's magnificent house was no longer in view, but the stable buildings and Redway Acres' house could be seen another mile away.

He had ridden Thor out in quite a temper. The horse, happy to have been given free rein, ran steadily for him. It was the first time in his convalescence that he had pushed his body to such rigorous exercise. He found that he felt well for it, despite the short hours of sleep and excesses of the previous evening.

On the return to Eastease, he kept Thor to a manageable canter and then trot, to allow both of them to cool down. He decided that while he was at Eastease, he would ride along Redway Acres' boundary and see how far her property extended. For today, he planned to return Thor to the stable, clean himself up and, after eating breakfast, he would have to talk to Harker of last night.

His father had overstepped his bounds, though it was doubtful he would see it that way. It would require the two of them to take him to task over it. If Mrs. Andrews was vulnerable here at Eastease, she might be vulnerable at Redway Acres, and that scared him the most.

The colonel planned to write a few letters to see if he could find out more of Captain Andrews. Despite Mrs. Andrews' request, he was not planning to stay away.

After getting cleaned up in his rooms, he headed downstairs for breakfast. His bed had looked inviting, but he did not want to miss his opportunity to talk to Harker before his father left. As he stepped from the staircase toward the breakfast room, he ran into Mrs. Hopkins.

"Oh, Colonel Ackley, how are you this morning, sir?"

"Well, I thank you. Can I assist you, Mrs. Hopkins? You look a little perturbed."

"Oh, sir, I do not know what to think. I was going to find Mr. Harker. One of the maids found a pillow and a coverlet from Mrs. Andrews' rooms, on the couch in her corridor this morning. It seems someone slept there, but what an odd thing to do. I cannot ask her of it as she has left." Oh lord, in the hurry to catch up to the woman he had just left the pillow and coverlet there and forgotten about them.

"Allow me to explain, Mrs. Hopkins," he gestured to a small, sitting room, "I am planning to talk to Alexander, as soon as he has finished his breakfast. He will speak to you of the matter later. However, please let me put your mind at ease. *I* slept there."

"You, Colonel? Surely not," she had known this young man just about all his life. What on earth was he thinking of, sleeping outside the two young ladies' rooms?

"I am ashamed to say that my father drank a bit too much brandy last night and was roaming the corridors. I believe he was confused, thinking he was at Aysthill House instead of Eastease. James quite rightly informed me of the matter, and having directed him back to the east wing, I thought it might be wise to stay, in case he returned. Mrs. Andrews heard our voices, and seeing my intention kindly gave me the pillow and coverlet from her rooms. I left them there, after seeing her safely to the stable this morning. So, you see, all quite innocent, but given the conclusions people can draw from this kind of thing, I would appreciate you ensuring the usual Eastease staff discretion."

Mrs. Hopkins narrowed her eyes. She was not fooled, at all, and what was more he knew it. She had seen that steely light in his eyes before, and she knew folk who worked for Lord Aysthill. She knew what that blaggard had been about. Seeing the colonel's knuckles turning white, as he gripped the back of the chair he stood behind, was all the confirmation she needed of his anger with his father. She would see to it that James' vigilance be rewarded in some way.

"Of course," she put a hand on his arm, looking up at him warmly, "may I say thank you for taking the trouble, sir? Mrs. Andrews is a favourite of ours here, ever since that business with Adam's poor sister a couple of years ago," he stared at her mouth agape, while the words she had just said sunk into his sleep-deprived consciousness. She turned to leave the room.

"What business, Mrs. Hopkins?" she hid her small smile before turning back to him. Adam had told her of the colonel's interaction with the lively Mrs. Andrews early this morning, and him riding Thor out in a temper. She was glad to see that he was on the way to full recovery, and thought Mrs. Andrews a very suitable woman to lock horns with.

"Well, two years back, Adam's sister, Rachel, was walking to Eastease to see him on her day off. They only have each other left. She worked for one of those families who come up from town and have a country house hereabout. Ah bless her, she was only fourteen at the time, but these two scoundrels set upon her. After they left her at the side of the road, John Robertson's boy, Jacky, happened by. He brought her straight over to Redway, where she was taken care of by Mrs. Andrews herself, who sent Jacky over here to fetch Adam. Rachel knows her words and numbers and has an aptitude for learning, so once she was recovered, and they were sure there were no consequences, Mrs. Andrews employed her as Miss Isabella's first governess. Intends to keep her, too, when Miss Isabella needs a bit more learning than Rachel has. She says Rachel can learn it at the same time and then get a good position elsewhere, with references from Redway," she looked up at the colonel again and could see he had a thoughtful expression, "from what I understand from Adam, Mrs. Andrews has given the girl a small dowry. Just enough to overcome the stigma, should she want to marry."

"Tell me, Mrs. Hopkins. Are there other people she has served?"

"Well now, let me think," she tapped her finger against the side of her mouth, amused that his interest had been peaked, "she is not one to make a big song and dance of it. Mr. Watkins told me, she was goaded into talking of Mrs. Robinson at dinner last night, so you know about her. There's Old Joe, who lives in that ramshackle place down the lane a way. He is a widower and does not take care of himself as he should. She goes down there with Miss Isabella of a Sunday, with a basket of vegetables that her housekeeper grows. Gives him a bit of money, too, but he just spends that on beer. Ruth says she knows he does, but she laughs and says at his time of life, maybe that is all he has to look forward to. There was young Lilly Stubbins, whose husband was put in prison. She had nothing to pay her rent and was evicted. Now she works in Redway kitchens. Part of her pay is one of the Redway cottages to house her brood of three. Mrs. Andrews helped a couple of widows around here. Got them on their feet at Redway, before they moved on, with references. That is all I can think of, I should not be surprised if there were more."

"Thank you, Mrs. Hopkins. You have given me an idea, or I suppose, Mrs. Andrews has."

Entering the breakfast room, the colonel saw Harker and the ladies, enjoying their breakfast with Mr. Ridgefield and Mr. Brooks. He walked over to his mother first, bending to kiss her cheek, he embraced her and she winced slightly. So, his father had not been gentle when he had returned to his rooms, and the son hated him all the more for it. After greeting everyone else, he turned to Harker.

"Might I have a word with you after your breakfast, Xander?" Harker consented and continued with his breakfast. He did not notice his friend's severe demeanour, as he was distracted by Genevieve. She was eating such small amounts these days and it concerned him. Mrs. Hopkins had assured him it was all quite natural. With the baby so large, and taking up so much room, there was little left for food.

The colonel ate quickly, so that he would be ready as soon as Harker had finished. They left the breakfast room together and crossed the hall to Harker's study.

"What is troubling you, Ackers?" Harker, who moved to sit behind his desk, now noticed his friend's unhappy countenance and indicated a chair opposite for him to sit in.

"Mrs. Hopkins wanted to ask you about a pillow and coverlet that was left on the couch outside Mrs. Andrews' room this morning. She said it seemed as if someone had slept there," Harker looked at him incredulously.

"Good God! Who on earth would do such a thing?"

"I would, Xander. I slept there," he proceeded to relay the events of the evening, from when Harker had left them playing cards, until Mrs. Andrews had kindly given him a pillow and coverlet to make the night on the couch more comfortable. He did, however, leave out seeing her at the window and their exchange this morning. Harker looked furious, "I am sorry, Harker. For this to have happened in your house, for what *could* have happened. He has gone too far. We have to take action. We cannot cover it up again. What if he were to go to Redway Acres?" panic crept into his voice at that thought.

Harker had heard enough. He got up and strode toward the door, but the colonel stopped him.

"No. Do not speak to him in anger. We must work out a plan. I have something in mind, but it will take the two of us to convince him," with a pained expression he looked at Harker, "Mrs. Andrews said something to me, something that shamed me to my core. That I had known what he was planning to do, because he had done it before. That the first time he had done it, should have been unacceptable. She was right. Had I done something before now, it would not have come to this."

"If *we* had done something my friend, your family is my family. None of us is innocent in this," he put his hand supportively on his friend's shoulder.

"Lord Aysthill," Watkins stepped aside to allow the older gentleman passage into Harker's study, after confirming that his master was ready to receive the Earl.

"Little formal there, Harker," he walked into the room and begrudgingly took a seat. He had slept late and did not appreciate being summoned to Harker's study before his breakfast. Harker bowed his head toward his friend's father, trying to control his temper.

"I wish to address the matter of your behaviour toward Mrs. Andrews last night, Sir," his temper blazed in his dark eyes, though his voice was controlled. Lord Aysthill shifted a little in his chair, uncomfortable under the gaze of this man for the first time in his experience. What did he know? He decided to bluff.

"I have no idea what you mean, Harker. I do not appreciate the tone you are taking with me. You are forgetting yourself, boy!"

"It is you who have been forgetting yourself, Father," ice shivered its way down Lord Aysthill's spine. There was that voice again. He turned to see his youngest son leaning casually on the side of a large bookcase, with his arms folded. He was wearing his full regimentals, with the sword sheathed at his side. His casual stance belied the fury in his face. Hidden back there in the shadows, he had not noticed him. He had stood so still, had the man even breathed?

He *was* a man. He had never thought of his sons in that way, despite their age. And this man was a soldier. It occurred to Lord Aysthill, though again he had never thought of it before, that this man had killed men. Shot them and used that sword on them. True, it was all for King and Country, a noble reason, but it must give a man a dark side. That was what he was seeing in his son's face and stance at this moment. That was what he had heard in his voice, in that dark corridor last night.

"My boy," he started with a conciliatory tone to his voice, "must we talk of this? I was hoping to keep it between ourselves. I admit to being a little too drunk, but as you are aware nothing happened. Let bygones be bygones. You know I will make it worth your while."

At that, the colonel pushed himself off the bookcase with a flex of his shoulder, keeping his arms folded, "keep your money," he snarled, as he took a few steps toward his father, pleased to see the man recoil.

"It is for Harker to decide what must be done, as this has taken place in his home," he managed to gain some control of his temper, "I have told him all of the particulars and we have discussed it. Now you will listen to him have his say. Then I will have mine," a few more steps and he stood directly behind his father, regimental straight this time. He nodded curtly for Harker to begin. Harker covered his surprise at the drastic change in his friend's demeanour, and addressed the older man.

"Lord Aysthill," he began, "in order to secure my secrecy over what took place here last night, I require the following from you. You must find all the women that you have violated in the past and make restitution. If they are no longer living, you must make restitution to their families. By restitution, you must ensure their health and that of their families; that they and their family members are gainfully employed and have suitable living arrangements. If there was issue from your *assignation* with any of these women, you must set up a financial arrangement that will see to their needs for the rest of their lives. You will do all of this anonymously, but I expect to see evidence in the form of a ledger, on a regular basis. I am employing, at my own expense, the services of a discreet man. He will find the relevant women for you and make any arrangements you need. As your memory may not serve you as well as it should, in remembering the names and circumstances, your son will ask Lady Aysthill to assist you. Genevieve assures me, that these are particulars your wife will not have forgotten." Harker had discussed it all with his shocked wife earlier. He wanted her to make sure that her friend was not upset over what had occurred, and to ensure that she knew Lord Aysthill would not be allowed to harm her at Eastease, or at Redway Acres.

"I will do no such thing!" Lord Aysthill blustered. He was astonished at the task Harker had set him. He had not even got into the woman's room. She probably did not even know that he had been there. The men had anticipated this reaction and had discussed their best leverage. Harker spared a glance at his friend and swiftly brought his eyes back to Lord Aysthill.

"You *will* do it, Sir. You have no choice. If you do not, the colonel and I will see to it that all your acquaintances here, and in London, know that you attempted to..." he paused, searching for the right word, "...fornicate with an unwilling, young widow, a guest in my household, whose husband died honourably in battle, and who is much beloved in this community. No one will ever invite you to their houses again, for fear of what might happen to their own guests or families. You will not be able to show your face in society. You will be forced to live out the rest of your life rarely leaving Aysthill. Only seeing your wife and eldest son. Do I have your agreement, Sir?"

"Well, it seems you leave me little choice in the matter. I will do it. Send me your man and I will get him started. Although I must say, that I am not happy," he made to stand, but the colonel's hands shot to his shoulders and prevented it. My goodness, he had no idea the man was so strong. Why had his mother been fussing over him these past weeks? He was no invalid.

"Wait a moment, Father," he was still using that voice, "you have not heard me out. This is what I require of you to ensure *my* secrecy. You will no longer force yourself on any unwilling woman. You will not take your frustrations out on my mother, by treating her so roughly that it causes her to wince if I embrace her. Being drunk is no longer an excuse for this behaviour. Finally, you will not set foot on Redway Acres property. You have no business there. If I hear that you have touched one hair on that woman's head, I will take my sword and run you through. Do you hear me, old man?"

At this, Lord Aysthill did stand up and face his son. He was all bluster and bully, pushing his chair roughly away. In stark contrast, Colonel Ackley stood still and steely. He did not flinch. At almost the same height, they stood nose to nose. Harker stood, but stayed behind the desk when, without taking his eyes off the bloodshot ones of his father, the colonel put out a hand to stop him.

"Kill me? In cold blood? You think you could?" roared the older man.

"Yes, yes and absolutely yes." How ironic, he thought, that he should end up using the same phrase she had used with him earlier that morning.

"You would not get away with it. I would see you hang!"

"You would not see me hang, you would be dead. You would see me in hell."

The older man slumped back into the discarded chair, rubbing his face with his hand, and the younger strode to the door.

"Those are my terms, Father. Take them or leave them," he had the satisfaction of seeing the man's curt nod, before marching out of the door and slamming it behind him, leaving Harker to deal with the remaining particulars. He took a deep breath, straightened his red coat and strode purposefully into the library, where he expected to find his mother.

Harker, after finishing the details with Lord Aysthill, had a quick word with his housekeeper to confirm the colonel's story and make his own request of his loyal staff, to keep it out of the village news. He need say nothing further, for her to know that more had taken place than what was disclosed. Mrs. Hopkins' mind was at ease, as she knew that, whatever it was, her master and Colonel Ackley had taken care of it.

Then Harker found his wife, so he could feel her in his arms and have her words of love cleanse him of the dirt.

Chapter Six

In church, on Sunday, the colonel scanned the congregation for the familiar red hair, without luck. Although disappointed, he smiled, wondering what her excuse would be to Mr. Brooks, should he dare to ask her. When the singing of the first hymn was coming to an end, the clergyman climbed up to the pulpit, the colonel fancied that the man scanned his flock looking for her, too.

"*'The LORD is good to all; he has compassion on all he has made'.* Psalm one hundred and forty-five; verse nine," the clergyman brought his flock to attention with an unusually commanding voice. "God said, *'Let Us make man in Our image, according to Our likeness; and let them rule over the fish of the sea and over the birds of the sky and over the cattle and over all the earth, and over every creeping thing that creeps on the earth'.* Genesis chapter one; verse twenty-seven." Colonel Ackley's ears pricked up. He had not heard the man speak before, but in his experience preachers tended to do just that. He listened a little more attentively.

"The Psalm," Mr. Brooks continued, "is simple enough. God is good and He has compassion for everything, because He created everything. He has compassion for man and *woman*; for animals; for trees and flowers; and the earth and the sky," he paused, "God is good. God is compassionate." Some people in the congregation repeated those two statements.

"The Verse: God made man in His image. As God is good and compassionate so must we be, must we not? We know though, that some of us are not good or compassionate, so it is a choice. God wants us to choose Him and to choose goodness and compassion, as He does. You may say to me *'Mr. Brooks, we are good and compassionate. Here we are attending church.'* Yes, you are and I thank you, and God is pleased, but is attending church being Godly or goodly?" at this point, the clergyman caught the colonel's eye and gave a small smile. The colonel smiled broadly, remembering Mrs. Andrews' comments at dinner and nodded. The man seemed to want him to answer.

"Godly, I believe, Mr. Brooks," his loud voice carried to the back reaches of the church.

"Colonel Ackley, who is attending with his friends from Eastease, is correct. We are being Godly today, respecting and praising God together on His day, as we should. But when were you last good? When were you, a good neighbour, a good friend or a good master? When and to whom have you shown compassion?" Mr. Brooks was in fine form, thought the colonel, he really must have taken, what Mrs. Andrews had said to him, to heart. She would love this sermon, what a shame she was not there.

"God is compassionate over all He has made, and He has made man in his image. The verse also says, 'let them rule over the fish of the sea and over the birds of the sky and over the cattle and over all the earth, and over every creeping thing that creeps on the earth'. God wants us to be compassionate like Him, and has given us rule over everything He has made. He wants us to be compassionate in our rule over everything He has made. Good and compassionate to the animals and over all the earth. Should man beat the horse? We would only be teaching the horse to kick the dog and the dog, in turn, learns only to chase the cat," there was some laughter at this image, as Mr. Brooks had hoped there would be.

"We should be good and compassionate, and treat our animals well. God is good and compassionate, in all He has made, and God made man and woman. We should be good and compassionate to each other. To that end, I implore you, on this day of the Lord, to spend no more time here, listening to me, but let us say a final prayer, sing the final hymn, and go from here, and do something good, something compassionate. Perhaps you need to make amends and ask for forgiveness, of someone to whom you have not been so. Rest assured, that I have someone I need to apologise to. Let me add, that the person who has inspired my sermon this week, unfortunately is not here today. Undoubtedly, she is somewhere doing some good, as she was last Sunday." The colonel thought of Old Joe, who lived in the ramshackle cottage, down the lane and had an idea of his own.

There was a smattering of mumblings, as people looked around to see who was absent. He heard a voice whispering behind him, "he must mean Mrs. Andrews!"

Someone else said, "she is always serving somebody."

The final hymn ended and they trooped outside. Many people were talking of what good they could do that day.

"Mrs. Smith is not at all well. I think I will take her one of my pies."

"I think I will go help Mr. Taylor dig up his old tree stump. Who is with me?" several men assented to that task.

The conversations faded away, as the congregation left the

church. Colonel Ackley looked back toward the pulpit, to see the clergyman step down and head toward Mr. and Mrs. Robinson, no doubt to make his apology.

They exited into bright sunshine and the colonel noticed a small, open carriage waiting outside, next to the Eastease coach, with two superbly muscled, but lean horses ready to pull it. A working man, dressed in his Sunday best, was standing at the heads of the horses.

"Mr. Robertson, it is so good to see you. How are you and your family?" a confident Harriet stepped forward to greet the man and stroke the noses of the two horses. She declared they were named Perceval and Grenville, because their new owner was a Prime Minister buff. Mr. Robertson was telling her how she had just missed his son, Jacky, who was driving the cart, with the whole family in it, back to Redway. She took care of the introductions.

Mr. and Mrs. Harker first, followed by Colonel Ackley, because he was closest and then Mr. and Mrs. Ridgefield. John pulled at his forelock at each introduction, saying, "pleasure," each time. After he had been introduced to the Ridgefields he said, "then I must tell you both, that I am to collect you and take you to Redway, as per the instructions of Mrs. Andrews." Exchanges were made of how thoughtful that was, however, the Ridgefield's had planned to stop at the rectory for tea on their way back to Eastease. John assured them this would not be a problem and Mr. Ridgefield handed his wife into the carriage, before following her.

While this was happening, the colonel was having a few words with John about the horses and running his expert hands down their necks and legs, as much in admiration, as to check for soundness. Even this short contact with horses, particularly Mrs. Andrews' horses, soothed his troubled mind.

For his part, John was taking the measure of the colonel. His girl, as he considered Helena, in the same way his wife did, had been out of sorts since the dinner at Eastease on Friday night. He suspected that this gentleman had much to do with it.

John and Helena did not talk much of people, unless it pertained to their horses. So, he was surprised yesterday, while they were working in adjoining stalls, that she asked him why men were so sure their opinions were always the right ones and that they, therefore, were entitled to tell women what to do? He was not sure she was actually asking his opinion, so he kept stumm. She had continued though,

"Just because he is a colonel and used to telling people what to do, does not mean I *have* to do it. Thinks he is so charming and handsome, with those blue eyes and that boyish smile. He said, he knew Perseus." John, who had been smiling while he worked, and thinking that his girl finally sounded like she was interested in a man, popped his head up over the stall wall, to look at her. She was rubbing down another horse and turned to look at his shocked face, "I told him he was mistaken. I do not know if he believed me. He is so damn sure of himself. Thinks he is so damn handsome."

"You said handsome twice," he pointed at her with the curry comb he was using, shrugged and they both returned to their work.

"Yes, I keep doing that," she had sighed wistfully, and John had smiled again.

Now the man was in front of him, and he could see what she meant by him being commanding, but also of the charm and good looks. It remained to be seen, whether he was good enough for his girl though.

"So, you are doing your *'something good'* for today?" the colonel gestured to the Ridgefields.

"This? Nah, s'pposed I would stop over at Old Joe's later and see what I can fix up for him, sir."

"This would be the widower, in the ramshackle cottage down the lane? I had the same thought. What time are you planning? I will meet you there." They arranged it and took their leave of each other.

With the Ridgefields safely in the carriage, John climbed up to the driver's seat and promised to return their guests to Eastease in time for dinner. Goodbyes were said and off they went.

Thoughtfully, Colonel Ackley watched the Ridgefields depart. He desperately wanted to run after them, but was not sure to what end. Not feeling like being cooped up in the closed carriage, he told Harker he would walk back to Eastease. Immediately, Harriet insisted on walking with him. She had told him before, how Harker and Genevieve could be embarrassingly affectionate in front of her sometimes, so he took pity on her, providing she was prepared to ramble over the fields with him. She said, it was lucky she had worn her boots.

It turned out to be the tonic he needed. They walked back through the graveyard and over a stile, into the field that would take them back to Eastease. Over the first hill and the house should be in view.

Harriet talked of how pleasant it was to have him there and would he stay for the baby's arrival? She talked of books she had read and how her music was progressing. She intuitively asked him of Spain's weather and land, and how much he had learned of the language, without asking him about the battles and his injury. He had always had an ear for languages and spoke French and German, fluently. He had been learning Spanish and Portuguese, and delighted her with some phrases.

Then they had talked of Mr. Brooks' sermon. He agreed with her conclusion, that Mrs. Andrews had influenced the clergyman.

"Do you think he likes her, Cousin?" she asked him.

"Yes, I think he does. Though any man worth his salt, would be foolish to do what he did today, just because he liked her. I assume he must believe in his interpretation of the text," then he added, "not that he stands a chance."

"Because you want her for yourself! I saw you looking at her while she sang. You missed turning several pages." God be damned, she was teasing him.

"I will give you a ten-count head start, Harriet," she screamed and ran as fast as she could, picking up her skirts over the long grass. It was so good, he thought, to see her run and laugh. "That is ten!" he shouted, and laughing caught up with her easily. He grasped her around the waist and swung her around.

When he put her down, finally, he hugged her to his chest and kissed the top of her head, as he had often done when she was younger. He loved both his wards and had missed them. They were the only remaining part of his friend, Mark, left in the world. He was glad he was able to be with her at Eastease, again.

As they walked on, she talked of her friendship with Mrs. Andrews. How she had met her when out riding and was not Perseus a wonderful horse? How handsome her stable was, and that she hoped he would get to see it before he left.

"I am not sure that Mrs. Andrews wants to see me, right now."

"I know something happened on Friday night, that no one will tell me of, but I am not going to worry about that. Helena says, that it is pointless to waste time on things you cannot control. Accept or do not accept a situation, and then move on. I am not accepting that I am not included in the secret of what happened, but as I cannot control it, I am moving on. But tell me this Cousin, you have been a gentleman toward her, have you not?"

"I have, Harriet, I assure you. We had a disagreement. If I get the opportunity, I will apologise."

He had heard *'Helena says'* from Harriet, many times in his few days at Eastease, so he asked her of a conflict Harker had told him of, "what does *'Helena say'* of riding astride a rather, than side-saddle?"

She laughed out loud again, "now it is my turn to keep a secret. Something that she said about it that was only between us. She did say, however, that she felt it was safer to ride astride. She has heard of women who have been killed, because their skirts were caught up in a side-saddle when they fell off. Is that not awful? Apparently, though, it is less comfortable riding astride and takes longer to learn. What do you think?"

"Well, she is in the unique position to tell us, because she has done both. However, I doubt women would have been allowed to ride side-saddle, if it was not safe. Does she ride everywhere astride?" the vision of Helena hoisting herself up and astride Perseus, as she called that stallion, came into his head and he shook it away.

"Of course not! She only rides that way for training a horse who will be ridden by a man or when she is alone, riding around Redway. She says she prefers it. I love the split-skirt riding habit that she wears. When she is standing, you can hardly notice that it is not a regular riding habit, but she wears men's trousers underneath her skirts sometimes."

"Which do you have hidden in your dressing room, ready for when you get permission to ride astride?" she looked at him aghast, "well done with the innocent look, my dear, but you are no cousin of mine, if you are not prepared to take advantage, the moment Harker changes his mind."

"I have some trousers that Helena has given me, they are a little loose, but as she is as tall as me they are long enough."

"It would seem that Mrs. Andrews is trying to get you to follow her lead," he shook his head. It would not do for this headstrong woman to unduly influence Harriet.

"Not at all, I assure you, Cousin. I had to ask, every time I saw her for over a fortnight, before she would give them to me. When she did, I had to solemnly swear that I should only use them if I had permission from my guardian. You are as much my guardian as Alexander, you could allow me to ride astride and when I do you could try riding side-saddle. Then your opinion could be decided, having first-hand information on the subject."

Here was Mrs. Andrews' influence coming to the surface. The girl made a sound and reasonable argument, and had cornered him nicely. He was proud of her despite it. They were almost at the house. As he looked at her, considering, he remembered that he had promised, in his mind, to do her a good turn, when she had unknowingly helped him talk with Mrs. Andrews Friday evening. He had time before his meeting at Old Joe's.

"Challenge accepted, Cousin. Go and change, while I arrange the horses to be saddled."

"You should ride Hudson, Nathaniel. He is used to side-saddle commands," she said, and then added hopefully, "I could ride Thor."

"*That* is not going to happen."

When they arrived at the stable, Mr. and Mrs. Ridgefield praised the look of the place to each other. John loved Redway. Although he worked for Helena, having known her for so long he took pride in their praise. As he handed Mrs. Ridgefield down from the carriage, his wife Ruth arrived at the doorway to greet them.

"Mr. and Mrs. Ridgefield, ma'am," Ruth smiled as she showed the visitors into the parlour. She liked the couple immediately. So gracious, and Mrs. Ridgefield, so very beautiful.

"It is so good to see you again," Helena greeted them with a curtsey, "I am so glad you were able to come."

"Thank you for the invitation, Mrs. Andrews," Mr. Ridgefield bowed, "and for the transportation. It is a perfect day for an open carriage jaunt and such magnificent animals."

"Not mine, I am sorry to say, Mr. Ridgefield. Those two are a commission, but your transportation was a training exercise for them, so we both benefitted," as she had found at the Eastease dinner, she felt immediately at ease with this couple. Genevieve was lucky to call them family.

Ruth arrived with a maid and refreshment trays. She oversaw the arrangement of the meats and breads, pies and sweets, and poured the tea before leaving. There was plenty of food for their luncheon. Mr. Ridgefield praised the food as enthusiastically as, Helena had learned, he did most things that pleased him. As they ate, the couple talked of Mr. Brooks' sermon and how they believed, as most of the congregation seemed to, that she was the source of his inspiration.

"I am all astonishment and am sure I deserve no such praise. In fact, I do not look back on my behaviour at the dining table that evening with satisfaction. I feel that I may have embarrassed the poor man in front of your niece and nephew, in my anger over how things had turned out for Mrs. Robinson. Maybe my good deed for the day should be to apologise to him."

"Well, we are stopping for tea with him, when we leave here. You would be welcome to join us, I am sure. It is your carriage that will be taking us, after all," Mr. Ridgefield generously offered.

"I would suggest, if you have the opportunity, to impart that you have only neighbourly interests with him, and not encourage him in any way," said Mrs. Ridgefield, "I hope you do not mind me saying so, but I do think he has an interest in you, and I think I am right in ascertaining, that your ideas lie in a different direction?" Helena gave a quick nod of understanding, before a noise was heard outside the door.

"I understand from Genevieve, that you have several children of your own."

"Yes, we do, and we said today, for the hundredth time at least, how much we miss them." A cherubic face appeared at the door, looking in to see if it was time for her to be allowed to join them. Seeing her mother nod, she smiled and walked in the room, eyeing the new adults.

"Mr. and Mrs. Ridgefield, may I introduce to you my daughter, Miss Isabella Andrews? Isabella this is Mr. and Mrs. Ridgefield, Mrs. Harker's aunt and uncle, from London." Mr. Ridgefield had stood and bowed. Isabella performed her best curtsey and they all laughed.

"Adorable," said Mr. Ridgefield, "I am pleased to make your acquaintance, young lady."

"It is lovely to meet you, Miss Andrews. We have four children, but have left them all in the care of Mrs. Harker's two sisters and mother at Thornbane Lodge, in Cambridgeshire," Mrs. Ridgefield sounded forlorn.

"Were they naughty?" asked Isabella, who thought that being away from her mother for such a long time, would be a punishment.

"Not at all, dear," Mrs. Ridgefield replied with a laugh, "we miss them all terribly, but it is a long journey, and they have so much fun with their cousins." Isabella decided she liked the Ridgefields.

"Would you like to come and see my horses?"

"Splendid idea, child, splendid," Mr. Ridgefield allowed himself to be pulled toward the door, knowing it would give his wife the chance she needed to talk to Mrs. Andrews, as Genevieve had requested. Helena rose to protest, but Mrs. Ridgefield stayed her.

"He is fine. She is adorable and he will love her showing him around. I would like a quick word with you if possible?" surprised, Mrs. Andrews sat down again.

"Of course, is there something wrong?"

"Colonel Ackley apprised Mr. Harker of what happened with his father on Friday night."

"Oh, I see," was all that she could think to say.

"Mr. Harker and Gennie wanted to assure you that all was being done to ensure that situation will never arise again. That you will be safe at Eastease, and here at Redway."

"Here? Of course I will be safe here," it had never crossed her mind that she should not.

"And what if Lord Aysthill were to visit you here? Who is here to protect your good name?" she knew she sounded stern, but Mrs. Ridgefield felt it important, to let this independent girl know the reality of her situation.

"John is here and Ruth, and all the stablemen."

"Wonderful people all, I am sure, but consider who you would be asking them to protect you from." Helena started biting her lip, a nervous habit.

"I had not, I did not think," she stared around rather frantically, and would not have been surprised if Lord Aysthill appeared in the room at that moment.

"Do not fret, my dear," Mrs. Ridgefield patted her hand, "Mr. Harker's message was that Lord Aysthill will not dare to come here. In fact, considering Colonel Ackley's mood yesterday, I rather think that he had more to do with it than Mr. Harker. Mr. Ridgefield was rather surprised to see the colonel leave Mr. Harker's study in his full regimentals, including his sword, after they met with Lord Aysthill. I believe my husband's description of him was *'formidable'*."

"Oh!" Mrs. Andrews almost breathed the word, as she took in the implication of what Mr. Ridgefield had witnessed.

"I do have two other questions to ask of you, and they are my questions, not those of Mr. Harker or Gennie. Was Colonel Ackley right in saying Lord Aysthill found your door locked and nothing happened?"

"Yes, that is right. Thank goodness, I had thought to lock it. I had a disagreement with him before you see, about horses."

"So I understand," Mrs. Ridgefield paused. She had to ask the next question, even though Gennie would not be happy with her for doing so, "and nothing happened with you and the colonel?"

"I gave him a pillow and coverlet, to aid him in sleeping on the couch outside my rooms. That was all." A slight blush rose to her cheeks remembering their exchange, but she gave nothing away to Mrs. Ridgefield who seemed satisfied. "Why do you ask? Did he say something had?"

"No, not at all. But I am a mother and I feel it would be remiss of me not to ask you the question. Colonel Ackley is not my direct friend and I have no assumptions as to what might have happened one way or another. Whereas, Mr. Harker and Gennie have of course assumed the colonel's story is the true one."

"Do you not believe him honourable then?"

"Of course I do! Mr. Harker and Gennie's trust goes a long way with me. However, he is a second son with no fortune of his own, and I wanted to be sure that nothing happened."

"I thank you for your concern, but it did happen as Colonel Ackley has told," she hesitated, then decided that this woman might be able to answer a question that had been bothering her since Friday night. "I thought on Friday, that Colonel Ackley might like me, but I am inexperienced."

"You are?" Mrs. Ridgefield was rather surprised and gestured toward the door that the woman's daughter had exited just a few moments ago.

"Isabella's father and I only had one night together, before he went to war and never came back. It really was more of an arranged establishment, than a courtship."

"Oh, I see. Well, in my experience, men who are not interested in a woman, do not stare at the woman the way the colonel stared at you, while you were singing that evening. They do not sleep outside the woman's bedroom, and they most certainly do not threaten their very powerful fathers with a sword, to ensure her safety."

"Do you think that he is more interested in Redway, than of me?"

"That question is harder to answer. However, let me ask you this. Have Gennie or Miss Wyndham ever spoken to you of Colonel Ackley's second cousin, Lady Grace Bainbridge?"

"No, I do not think so, but Lady Aysthill did mention she had a superior singing voice to mine."

"I doubt that, my dear. My understanding, is that since the colonel's injury, his parents have been looking to him to stop being a soldier and marry her. They want to keep the Bainbridge estate in the family. Yet, here he is at Eastease, watching you sing and sleeping outside your room."

"Oh, I did not know that," Mrs. Andrews looked at the woman and then shook herself as if to clear her head, "well, it is to no avail. I am not the marrying kind and I cannot give over Redway to anyone. Let us go and see if Isabella has Mr. Ridgefield up on a horse!"

Laughing, Mrs. Ridgefield followed this extraordinary woman outside, to see her stable, and wondered why, she should consider marriage to Colonel Ackley, as giving up Redway Acres. It was obvious that she had not, yet, truly known the love of a good man.

After his enlightening dinner with the Harkers, Mr. Brooks had considered the points that Mrs. Andrews had made to him. At first, he thought that she should see things his way, until he realised that his pride had been bruised. She was a beautiful woman, and he had hoped she would fit his ideal of what a wife should be, because he found her attractive. However, she was far too headstrong for him to consider a good alliance. He had seen the way that Colonel Ackley had looked at her. He, Eliot Brooks, would step aside.

Mrs. Andrews had challenged him, however, and having set his pride aside, he realised that she had been right. He had not known the full situation with the Robinsons and it had humbled him to take some of the responsibility of that man's actions. It was not only with them that he had made this mistake. He had not really got to know his parishioners well, at all. He had prided himself in not asking questions of a too personal nature, of the people he visited, and maybe he should have.

Following his sermon, he had gone to the Robinsons and apologised sincerely to Mrs. Robinson. Mr. Robinson stood at her side looking rather embarrassed. Mr. Brooks had explained to them, that he felt that he should visit them once a week, to talk of God's and the church's views of marriage. Mrs. Robinson had looked at her husband pleadingly, and he had agreed.

Mr. Brooks then accepted lunch with a local, well-to-do family who had a handsome, if rather dull, daughter that was of marrying age. The lunch was delicious, but not good enough to tempt him to consider her a possible wife. He had walked several miles home, to arrive in time for tea with the delightful Ridgefields.

He was surprised to see Mrs. Andrews riding her horse behind her carriage and asking his permission to join them. He acquiesced, but was concerned that she had heard of his sermon and might now be thinking of him in a more favourable light. Maybe she was flattered at the thought that she could influence him. He started to think again how very beautiful she was, but stopped himself.

She did, however, apologise to him for her behaviour at dinner. He insisted there was no need. She had made her point, though eloquently, quite forcefully. He realised that it had been needed for him to see his mistakes. He endeavoured to tell her of his plans regarding the Robinsons and she approved whole-heartedly.

He had asked her if she would consider meeting with him occasionally. He found her quite challenging and would like to discuss the bible with her. He suspected that she was a non-believer, and he hoped that he might persuade her toward his view point. After all, it was the vocation of a clergyman to see that the souls of all his flock passed through to heaven, when the time was upon them. He would hate to see Mrs. Andrews in the hands of the devil.

Helena agreed to meet with him. She had questioned her parents about passages in the bible and the rules of the church, but they had been unwilling to explain, insisting that she accept. Now that she was in charge of her own actions, she had avoided going to church. Instead, she preferred to attend to her community duties at that time. Here was her chance to get some questions answered, or at least discussed.

She had teased him about the Cuthbertson's daughter and the

lunch he had shared with them. Asking if they were soon to be calling Miss Cuthbertson, Mrs. Brooks, but he assured her that would not be the case. He had been thinking in another direction, but had cause to rethink his plans. To this, Mrs. Ridgefield had said, that Mrs. Harker had two unmarried sisters and maybe he would find one he liked, when they came to visit the baby. To which they laughed, that Mrs. Harker might like to marry both her sisters locally, so she could keep them near to her.

While the Ridgefields had tea at the parsonage, Colonel Ackley met with John Robertson at Old Joe's cottage. Old Joe was quite a character, who spoke highly of Mrs. Andrews and her daughter. The colonel had taken a look around the cottage and hated the idea of Mrs. Andrews being anywhere near it. It was dirty and indeed a *'ramshackle'*, as Mrs. Hopkins had described it. So was the man who occupied it.

"It will need some money thrown at it," John had said, resignedly, "the thatcher will be needed to fix the roof, before owt else is done, and we will need some new wood for these areas here," he pointed at the posts, that barely held up the front door porch, and some rotten floor boards.

"Well, I have some money I won playing cards, with my father," the colonel told him. He had intended to give it back, when he dealt with his father the day before, but he decided to give it to Tommy, instead. Now, he would split it between Tommy and this cottage.

"Then we had better head to the tavern, as the thatcher will be there, for sure, on a Sunday."

So, it was agreed, that the colonel should take Old Joe with him to Eastcambe, on Thor, while John took the Ridgefields back to Eastease, before he followed them. Thor had not been too happy about having two men on his back, once again, but it was worse for the colonel, who had not been in this situation since the battlefield. Memory flooded back of the blood seeping out of him and losing consciousness, thinking he was dead, then John started laughing at the sight of them and the situation had been diffused. Warmth had flooded back into the colonel's body, as he had laughed heartily, too. Then he urged Thor on to the Eastcambe tavern. He could do with a pint, or two.

When John called to collect the Ridgefields, he told Mrs. Andrews that he had just been at Old Joe's with Colonel Ackley, looking at the help they would be giving the old man. He explained they would be discussing the particulars, with some tradesmen they would find at the tavern. The colonel and Old Joe had gone on ahead, and providing Mrs. Andrews did not mind, he would be following on after going to Eastease. She did not mind, on the understanding that the horses were taken care of while John was enjoying a drink, and agreed that she would inform Ruth of his whereabouts.

Mr. Brooks then surprised everyone, including himself, by jumping up on the driver's seat with John, saying, that as he wanted to get to know his parishioners, going to the tavern should be a good start. Mrs. Andrews agreed that any willing hands from Redway could help out on the following Saturday, once the horses had been attended, and that she, Ruth, Rachel and Isabella, would personally bring refreshments to the workers. John and Mr. Brooks left the Ridgefields at Eastease, with a message that the colonel might be late for dinner, and drove to Eastcambe.

Eliot Brooks had never been inside a tavern. It was loud, raucous even in one part of the room, where several dirt covered men were telling the story of finally pulling up Mr. Taylor's tree stump. They were drinking the beer the grateful man had bought. Mr. Brooks saw Old Joe and Colonel Ackley in one corner of the room, finishing off their first pint of ale. Seeing the two arrive, and giving a surprised look at the clergyman, Colonel Ackley had proceeded to catch the barman's attention and held up four fingers.

As John and Mr. Brooks sat down, a thick hand, clasping four tankard handles, placed the drinks in the middle of the table, spilling some over the rims. The colonel, he was sure, suspected his discomfiture and smiled widely, "it is a different side of life, is it not, Mr. Brooks? Old Joe, here, has not seen the thatcher, yet."

"Tha's 'im," Old Joe, pointed at a tall, thin man, who had just walked into the tavern.

"Over here, Reg!" shouted John, pulling up another chair to their table, as the man strode toward them. "Another pint, please, Big Jim. How's the missus, Reg? Ruth will have at me, when I tell her I saw you, if I do not ask after her." Reg Smith's wife had been under the weather, and a recipient of a great many foodstuffs this afternoon, for which he dutifully thanked Mr. Brooks.

So, they had bartered and drank. Agreed a plan of action and drank some more. The colonel would meet the tradesmen, most of whom arrived in the tavern at one point or another, at Old Joe's house during the week and agree what materials were needed. He would foot the bill for the materials as well as the pints they were drinking that evening. They would all donate their labour as their goodly deed, as the clergyman had encouraged them to do, providing he chipped in, too. John confirmed that he would bring as many Redway men with him as he could, and the colonel promised to ask Harker if some of the Eastease men could join them.

John drove Mr. Brooks back home a little worse for wear, leaving the colonel and Old Joe still drinking. The old man had not had such a match for a long time and was enjoying himself. Eventually, when the colonel felt if he drank any more, he would not be able to ride home, he and Joe had mounted Thor, with some difficulty, and sang songs of obliging women all the way back to the cottage.

Chapter Seven

The Ridgefields left Monday morning, after breakfast. Colonel Ackley had seen them off, with Genevieve and Harker, and then deposited himself at the desk in the library. He wrote letters to his connexions in the army, who could find out more of Captain Andrews. He hoped he might have at least two replies before the end of the week. He organised sending half his winnings, from his father, to Tommy in Sheffield. The other half he would use on materials for Old Joe's place.

At the breakfast table, he had asked Watkins to let Adam know he wished to ride Thor when he had finished his letters. The dry Watkins had said, "would that be your usual saddle, sir, or should I ask Adam to fit him with the side-saddle?" much to the amusement of all present.

Having given his letters to Watkins to get to the post coach, he made his way to the stable and mounted Thor. He set out on the north road, toward the church, before turning down the lane to Old Joe's.

As her workers would not be there for most of Saturday, Mrs. Andrews spent much of Monday morning with John, going over the needs of Redway for the week. There were various fences that needed mending, and some feed and hay was coming in. Their winter planning had to be started. They would begin with restocking the various shelters on the outskirts of the property. These were used if stranded in bad weather. All of this, was in addition to the routine of cleaning out stalls, exercising and training horses and, at some point, foaling the two mares.

They agreed she would supervise much of the routine work, and John, the winter preparations. The weather was still good, even though it was September, and she hoped it would stay so. It would be best for them, but also for the repairs to be done for Old Joe, this coming weekend. Ruth had told her how proud she was of her inspiring Mr. Brooks' sermon, which in turn seemed to have inspired the village. Everyone was being kind and helping others. There was a feeling of goodness in the air.

Harriet visited, glowing with pride over how she had managed to get permission to ride astride around Eastease and Redway. She had arrived riding Hudson astride, but was most annoyed with Helena for being too busy to notice. Helena had been thrilled for her and laughed heartily at the thought of Colonel Ackley riding side-saddle. He certainly was an unusual man.

Thursday morning, after a slow turn around one of the smaller gardens with Genevieve, during which he had regaled her with stories of his week dealing with tradesmen at Old Joe's, Colonel Ackley received two letters with the army seal on them. He had forgotten all about the inquiries he had made of Captain Andrews.

When he was not out, either at Old Joe's or riding Thor, he had been in the library pretending to read, but in reality, thinking of the redhead, in a white nightgown, at a window. He had gone back into the games room several times and looked up to the window she had sat in. Once he had gone into that room and looked out from her perspective, then turned and strode away shaking his head in disgust, at how he was acting like a lovesick boy.

He hoped that he might see her at Old Joe's house on Saturday. John had mentioned, that she had suggested, the ladies should bring some sustenance to the workers, during the day. Her last words, before she had ridden off on the grey stallion, still rang in his ears. She had compared him with his father and said he should leave her alone. Well, he had left her alone for nigh on a week and he would be damned if he would do so any longer. She was interesting to him, and he wanted to see her again. He wanted to find out just how interesting she was.

Alone in the library, after lunch, he read the letters. Given the sensitivity of the information contained therein, he burned them in the fireplace. Genevieve had said she felt a storm coming that afternoon and he would need to ride Thor before then. He wanted to ride along more of the Redway boundary. Who was he trying to fool? He wanted to see her today. Armed with the information he had from the army, he wanted to confront her, though all sense told him it was not the best course of action. He would ride out and decide what to do when his head was clearer in the brisk wind.

The mare had bolted. John's team of stablemen was mending the fence to the paddock while Mrs. Andrews and John looked on.

"Truly closing the door after the horse has bolted," she stated as a matter of fact rather than criticism.

"I am sorry. It was on Dom's list of things to do. I thought it done before I let Missy out into the paddock. It was entirely my fault and I will make it up to you anyway I can, if we have lost her."

"Let us see what state she is in when we find her. I need you here to see to Lady," she was referring to the other mare, that was showing the first signs of foaling, too. "I will take Perseus and some supplies with me. Just hope I find her close to shelter," it looked and felt, like a late summer storm was rolling in. The air practically rippled with it.

"I do not like the idea of you riding that horse, let alone in the kind of storm that is brewing."

"John, I will be fine. It is you he does not like. Remember he is a battle tried horse and has experienced cannon fire. He will be steady under me."

"It seems he does not like anyone, except for you. Be sure to take the gun with you," he added.

She went to her room and considered what to wear. Although it was warm, the storm would cool the day, and of course there would be rain. Supplies would be needed for her and the horses and anything she may need for the foaling. At least they had freshly stocked and made repairs to the outer shelters on the property, earlier this week.

She was concerned that Missy's foaling might not be an easy one. It was just an instinct, no specific reason, but she trusted her instincts and prepared. She remembered another difficult foaling, when her grandfather had been alive. He had shown her what to do, but unfortunately it had been too late for the foal, that had been stillborn, and the mare that had lost too much blood. She shook herself, declaring herself foolish, and turned to concentrate on what she could control.

"Layers," she concluded. Propriety insisted that she wear a gown, but her riding breeches should do underneath. With luck if caught in the rain she could remove the gown and the breeches may still be dry. It did not matter what she wore once she got the horse to a safe haven. Assuming she should have to bunk overnight, her gown should be dry to put on again, before departing for home in the morning.

Dressed, she went to her daughter and explained where she was going. Isabella understood how important horses were to her mother. She felt the same way.

"Good luck, Mama, I will take care of everything here."

"Thank you, my sweet girl," she replied, with a smile. Then she left the room, turned toward the kitchen to pick up her supplies, and from there onto the stable to mount Perseus. All the while she was considering her route. She knew her land well and mapped in her head a path the mare may have taken. She would not have jumped anything and would have kept to low ground as much as possible. Helena was sure Missy would have followed the route she had mapped in her head, in the direction of Eastease. She planned to keep that route in her view while she rode, keeping as much land as possible in her vision in other directions. Thank goodness Missy was a grey and should stand out in the darkening light.

She rode out with determination, within minutes her hair was flying free. Her bonnet was holding on by its ribbons around her neck and flying behind her.

That was how Colonel Ackley saw her, as he rode Thor over the fields of Eastease. A streak of blue gown that was covered by a man's long-coat. Her hair, loose and flying in the wind, looked like red fire. A stormy sky silhouetted them. Studying her, he realised she was not riding side-saddle. She was up in a half-seat and giving that beast of a horse of hers, if indeed he was hers, free rein to gallop across the terrain.

As she rode, she scanned the horizon, moving her head from side to side. He recognised a sense of urgency and he wondered what caused it. Could the child be lost? That was his first thought, as she slowed slightly and looked in his direction. He had taken off his greatcoat and his redcoat was easily spotted across the terrain. She rode on. Curious, and keen to offer help, were the only reasons he allowed himself to think, he urged Thor toward the racing duo.

Mrs. Andrews saw the rider in the redcoat, as she scanned the land toward Eastease. It gave her a jolt and memories tried to flood in, but she pushed them back. She had to find Missy. Her mare, and the foal she was due, were her priority. Just over the next rise she saw her. She was stopped and marching around, obviously in distress. She slowed Perseus to a trot and then a walk, getting within fifty yards of Missy, as the redcoat streaked past her. She shouted at him.

"Slow down you fool, she will run!" to his credit he did rein in his horse, but it was a big beast and he could not hope to stop suddenly. He turned the horse back toward the east, and the startled mare did not move far, mainly because she was in such difficulty. Helena could see afterbirth hanging from her, but clearly the foal was still within. She walked Perseus a little closer and dismounted smoothly. Leaving him there, she approached the mare from the front, with soothing noises and a treat in her hand. She deftly swept the halter over the horse's head and fixed a rope to it, before she noticed Colonel Ackley had turned back toward them. He dismounted and approached Perseus.

"Do not approach him," she warned, keeping her voice even, "he does not like men, especially redcoats." Perseus however was looking pleased to see the colonel, which confused her no end. If John approached him without her close by, he would try to escape or cause bodily harm.

"We became reacquainted last Friday, did we not boy?" he put on his greatcoat and grasped the reins she had left dangling.

"Reacquainted?" she wondered. She did not say anything, but felt fear creeping up into her throat. She looked at Colonel Ackley standing straight and confident between the heads of the two beasts he controlled. As she did, lightning flashed, splitting the sky and the rain started to pour, as the thunder rolled loudly. She roughly fixed her bonnet back in place and tucked her long hair into her coat.

"I understand from Adam that there is a barn not far from here, with some stalls?"

"Yes, over the next slope and to the left, you will see it. Go ahead, as you will be able to get there faster than me. I fear we will be at a snail's pace. Get the boys settled with a stall between them, please, and light some lamps. There are packs on Perseus' back that I will need, too. Thank you." Not wishing to risk being thrown and crack his head, Colonel Ackley marched the two horses over the next slope. He caught sight of the barn with the next flash of lightning.

When she approached, he was at the door, holding it open for them. He had not put his hat back on, and his hair was soon wet and plastered to his head. He closed and secured the door, then he removed his drenched coat and hung it on a nail in the wall nearby to dry. The exhausted mare collapsed on the floor, on the hay he had thrown around for that purpose.

Helena removed the large overcoat and handed it to the colonel. He hung it alongside his, then turned back and was startled to see her undoing the fastenings at the front of her gown.

"What on earth are you doing?" he turned away again.

"No need to worry, Colonel. I have the same amount of clothing on, under this gown, that you are wearing. These skirts are soaking wet, but served their purpose. I can move more freely now, to attend the mare," she removed the gown to reveal a man's shirt and trousers, and then she sat down on the floor, to remove her boots.

"Why take off your boots?" he asked, hanging up the gown to dry, and removing his redcoat, so he could also move more freely.

"I will need to put my feet on the mare, to gain some leverage and pull out the foal. I am not going to do that with boots on. Where are my packs? I need a knife from one of them." Quickly, he retrieved a knife from the packs that he had deposited on the bunk, at the back of the barn, and handed it to her. He picked up the gun John had slipped in there and started to prime it.

"No need to do that," was all that she said to him. Then she was all about the business of helping her mare. Without any qualms, and with the confidence of someone who had dealt with this before, she set up what she needed. She looked him over and requested he remove his cravat.

"She is too exhausted, I will need something to use to pull out the foal and the rope is too thick," as he started to remove it, she asked him to do what he could to calm the mare and keep her still. Missy seemed to know that they were there to help her and was really too exhausted to do much more than lie there. He stroked and soothed her, with his strong, competent hands and deep voice.

Helena took up the knife and carefully cut into the afterbirth. She had rolled up her sleeves, and blood covered her hands and forearms, but she did not flinch from the job at hand. With her way now free, she was able to see two hooves side by side, this was no good; the shoulders of the foal would be too wide for the mare straight on. Putting her hand as high up on one foal leg as she could reach, she pushed back and managed to get them staggered to ensure the shoulders would not be aligned coming through.

She wrapped the cravat around the foal's legs and looked at him again. Her glance took in his open collar, where she glimpsed a red scar crossing diagonally over his chest. She could not see where it started or where it ended. His sandy hair was curling around his face where it was drying and gave him that boyish look.

"Ready?" he nodded, as she put each foot on the hind quarters of the mare and pulled at the hooves, the cravat preventing her hands slipping. Now it was positioned correctly and the afterbirth was out of its way, the foal slid out reasonably easily. A colt. Getting out of the way, she untied the cravat and cast it aside. The foal was already moving and he helped her guide it toward its mother. Their eyes met over the sight and she smiled, a huge smile of relief, as he had never seen on her face before. My God, she was so beautiful, he had to take a deep breath before he smiled back.

There was still a lot of work to be done. Being a practical man, the colonel had put as many pails as he could find outside before she had arrived with the mare. He now brought in one for them to clean off the blood. That done, they each took to the stall their ride was stationed in, and took off the saddles and bridles, and brushed the horses down. A fresh supply of hay, stored in the barn, was given to each horse, and each got a pail of the rain water. After providing the same to the mare and ensuring the foal was well, they turned to their own needs.

In Helena's pack, she had enough food and water for a good meal and drink for one. Her plan had been to eat, drink and sleep. Still, a good meal for one, could be a reasonable meal for two, and she shared out the provisions between them.

The bunk in the far corner of the room, that was half-partitioned off from the mare, was the only place to sit. She spread the food in the middle, like a picnic, and sat near the end of the bunk with her back against the wall. Colonel Ackley noticed that she had not taken the corner of the bunk to sit in, but chose the end nearest the exit. After the practicalities of dealing with the mare and taking care of their horses, she had become wary of him and the situation they found themselves in.

The rain still hammered, relentlessly, on the roof of the barn and the late afternoon light had dimmed. Journeying back to the main house in the dark and the rain would be ridiculous to contemplate. He stood in front of the bunk, but she gestured to the corner.

"Colonel, would you care to join me at the dining table?"

"I accept, and thank you for your generosity!" he picked up on her playful tone. Sitting with his back to the far corner, he took a look at their meal. Bread, cheese, pie and some cake, with a flask of water, was spread on a linen cloth. It had been kept dry in her pack. To it he added his hip flask of whisky.

"I must look a dreadful sight. I was not expecting company on this mission," she was not looking for a compliment, but simply stating that she would not purposely look this way in front of anyone else. He studied her. Her red hair was progressively coming loose from the tie that she had used to hold it back when delivering the foal. Her bonnet lay discarded on the floor. The man's shirt was tucked into the trousers, but without a cravat was open at the neck. Despite the fact that it revealed less of her neckline, than the gown she had worn at dinner last Friday, it seemed more decadent. She had replaced her boots to care for Perseus, as she called him.

"You may not be dressed for society, but to me you are more beautiful, by showing greater concern for your horses, than for your appearance," she made no response to that, not even a blush rose to her cheeks, but she stared at him, still wary. Frustrated over her lack of trust in him, the letters he had received earlier sprang back to his mind.

"I tried to find a Captain Andrews, who died in battle and worked with the cavalry horses. I received replies to my inquiries today. Nothing known of a Captain Andrews. Who was your husband?" the question was met with a stony silence and a glare. She looked toward Perseus' stall and then back at Colonel Ackley. Fear crossed her eyes.

"As soon as I start to think better of you, Colonel, you do something that confirms your belief that you are better than me. You are a man, you have a powerful family, and you can do as you please. You are so much like your father."

"I am nothing like my father!" she had meant to hurt him because he had scared her, but his anger brought hers to the fore.

"Then why did you 'make inquiries' about my husband? If you had suspicions that no such man existed, why not ask me of him?"

"Would you have told me the truth?"

"*That* we will never know, will we?" they continued to glare at each other until the colonel picked up his whisky flask. Rather than offer it to the lady first, he took a long defiant swig from it and spun it across the bunk to land beside her.

"You should try some, it will calm you," he suggested, feeling the warmth from the alcohol sooth his own temper, "unless whisky is too strong a taste for you," she knew he was goading her and he knew she would not turn away from the challenge. She picked up the flask and knocked back a considerable mouthful of the liquid it contained. Valiantly, she managed to avoid spluttering all over the bunk and swallowed, but he could see her eyes watering with the effort.

With a small smile at her defiance he tried again, "please allow me to apologise and start this conversation again. Mrs. Andrews, I know that the horse over there is not called Perseus but Pegasus. I knew his previous owner, General Alcott, was killed by him, and that horse was supposedly destroyed because of it. It happened when the general was visiting friends in Norfolk and I know you hail from that county. I have no doubt he was beating the animal, as I had seen him do many times before. The Eastease housekeeper, Mrs. Hopkins, would give me some wonderful healing ointment that I would use on Pegasus, and I would bring him carrots whenever I could. I was sorry to hear he had been killed"

"The general?" she half croaked the word, the whisky still burning her throat.

"No, Pega... Perseus. I was very surprised, and pleased, to see him in Harker's stable."

"Reacquainted."

"Quite so."

"Carrots are his favourite."

"The general's?" he quipped and raised a small laugh from her. Having broken the mood, he tried again, "would you do me the honour of trusting me. Would you tell me how a horse, that is supposed to be dead, came into your possession, and who your husband really was?"

He had asked her directly and she could stall no longer. Taking another long swig of the whisky, she swallowed it with more relish now that she was ready for its strength. She considered what she should do. It seemed unfair not to trust him with the truth and insulting to try to lie to him further. Could she trust him? She thought she could, but how sound was her judgment given her attraction to him? She had heard how he had spent the past few days organising, and paying for, the repairs they planned for Old Joe's house, that had to count for something. Perseus trusted him and that counted for a whole lot more in her book. Had he not helped her with the dam foaling and caring for the horses, rather than just helping himself to her? They had been together hours and he had not even tried to touch her. As he had not touched her the night he slept outside her room at Eastease. It was a moment to stop being afraid.

"I, too, must apologise, Colonel. In temper, I have compared you to your father, twice. I want to assure you that I do not think of you that way." He wanted to ask her in what way she did think of him, but did not, as she seemed about to open up to him. "To tell you the truth, I have to go back to my childhood and tell you my whole story. It would seem that we have plenty of time for it." Taking one last mouthful from the flask she handed it back to him.

He nodded in encouragement, as he took it back and proceeded to finish off the contents, while she told him her story.

Chapter Eight

Her mother had married well and into money. She moved from her home, at Redway Acres stable, to Norfolk. Miss Joy Stockton did not like her childhood at the stable. She hated horses and thought they were smelly, dirty creatures. She married the first wealthy man who crossed her path. Mr. Gregory Billings had not inherited his money, but made it the new way by investments first in mills and then mines. He never got his hands dirty, of course, but he worked hard in making sure he squeezed every penny he could out of them. Helena found out later, that this was often at the expense of the people who worked for him.

She was the older of two children. Her mother having a son two years after Helena was born. As children, they would travel north with their father so he could visit his mills and mines, and when he did so, the children stayed at Redway with their grandparents. Away from the demands of her mother that she *'behave like a lady'*, Helena, as a young girl spent most of those days in the stable with her grandfather. She watched foals being born, helped with the feeding and grooming of the horses, learned to ride and ride well. She stayed up at night with sick horses and read as much as she could in the library. She would have cleaned out stalls, if they had let her. She loved horses, Redway and most especially her grandfather.

As she approached the age of sixteen, her mother refused to let her *'run wild'*, and when her brother went north with her father, she was forced to stay at home and be a lady. Her only respite during these years, was visiting their meagre stable in Norfolk and spending time with the few horses not driving the carriage north. She enjoyed talking to John Robertson, who was one of their stablemen. Sometimes she had even completed chores for John, when he was needed for another task.

These escapades had to be timed well, when her mother was out visiting with local families. Even now, how her mother knew when to go out and when to stay in, was a mystery to Helena, but her mother was never out to a visitor and, whoever she visited, was always ready to accept her. On the occasions she was caught helping John, she was punished severely. She was locked in her room for a day, with no horse books to pass the time and no meals. Her mother was always looking for ways to get her ample figure more to her ideal for society. However, John's wife, Ruth, was the cook and would get food to Helena if she could.

Her father was able to put aside a large sum for her dowry and a number of suitors visited their house in Norfolk. Helena had no interest in being married and could not be cajoled to entertain them beyond the minimum necessary. Most, soon lost interest. On the two occasions she received a proposal, she declined and her father did not force her, much to her mother's disappointment.

After her eighteenth Birthday, the general arrived. He was an older man, close to the age of forty, and an investor of her father's. He had always met with her father in London and this was his first visit to their home in Norfolk. He was quite taken with Helena and made his intentions known. Helena refused. Her mother persuaded her father, that General Alcott was a man not to be spurned. Unhappily, her father agreed, but they came to a compromise. He should wait until Helena was twenty years old. The general's visits were few and far between, due to his military commitments, but her twentieth birthday hung over Helena, like an anvil ready to drop.

The general's only redeeming feature, in her opinion, was his horse. A magnificent grey, with powerful shoulders and haunches, that she visited often while the general met with her father. She groomed him when John was busy and took him his favourite treat. His name was Pegasus and as she groomed him, she noted welts on his hide that had healed into ridges.

Her twentieth birthday came and went, with no sign of the general. She wondered if he had been killed in battle, but scoured each newspaper her father discarded for some news, to no avail. Eventually, six months before her twenty-first birthday, he arrived. She felt trapped, that she had no choice, no way out. It became difficult to breathe, she had to get out of the house, to the place she felt the safest and at peace.

As she approached the stable, she heard a man shouting abuse of the kind that had never assaulted her ears before and a horse whinnying. John and the other stablemen were nowhere to be found. Scared at what she might find, but entering bravely, out of concern for the animal, Helena peered into the stall the commotion was coming from. The general was beating his horse and swearing a torrent.

"Worthless excuse of a beast! You bastard! Startled by a mere fox and trying to shake me off," he railed, his face turning puce with anger and the effort of wielding his crop, "you think I am such a useless rider that you could get away from me, you bugger?" the horse's eyes were rolling and it was pulling at the tether, holding it against the stable wall. Her empathy for the poor horse, trapped in the terrible situation of being owned by this disgusting man, dissipated her fear and she ran toward it. She stepped between Pegasus and the crop, shouting as she did so. Reaching up to the horse and trying to mollify it.

"Stop it! Stop it! The poor thing is terrified," she pleaded.

"Get out of my way, woman," he yelled, "or I will beat you, too. It would not be the first time I have taken a crop to a female." She refused to move and the crop came down hard across her back, ripping her gown and drawing blood. Turning, she saw the look in his eyes had changed, from one of anger, to one she did not recognise. He roughly put his fingers into the torn bodice and pulled her to him.

"Take your hands off me, sir!" she tried to sound authoritative and pull away, but he had an arm around her waist and pulled her back against him. His hot breath in her ear.

"We will be married, I do not see any reason to wait, and you need to learn a lesson," he threw her onto the floor of dirt and straw. Her head banged against the stall wall and dazed her. Kneeling down in front of her he said, "you need to learn to O-BEY."

As he said those two syllables, he pushed one of her legs aside and then the other. He raised her skirts and busied his hands with his trousers. She recovered somewhat, from the bang to her head and sat up crying out the words, "no, please, no!" but they were to no avail. Grabbing her wrists, he overpowered her, pushing her back to the floor and forcing himself upon her. Despite her strength, having worked with horses, she could not hope to get away. Holding both her wrists in one hand, he used the other to rip away her undergarments and thrust himself into her. She screamed and writhed to free herself, but he just laughed.

"Oh, you were worth this long wait. I think you thought you would get away from me, but you are mine now, spoiled for any other, and you will marry me. Tell me you will obey me." Thrust followed thrust and she thought it might never end. She felt she was ripping in two, it hurt so much. Tears streamed down her face and all she felt was despair, at this being her life from now on. Neither of them noticed that Pegasus had been pulling, with all his strength, against the rope that tied him to a stable truss. Finally, the ordeal was over and satisfied, the general rolled away from her.

"You will ob..." but the sentence was never finished. A hoof came down across his head. The sound was awful, blood spattered over the stall wall behind him and he sat there for a moment before his lifeless body fell backwards. Blood spilled from his head that had cracked open from the impact.

Numb, she managed to get to her feet and ran to Pegasus throwing her arms around his neck.

"Thank you," she whispered.

She was crying. She had not even been aware of it, but tears streaked down her cheeks, dripping onto the man's shirt she was wearing. She rubbed the heel of a hand across each cheek. By the light of the lamp hanging on a hook, close to his face she could see Colonel Ackley's face lined with concern for her, and the young girl she had been.

"I am sorry," he stated simply, "it is an awful thing to have happened to you."

"You are the first person I have told that story to, since my grandfather took me in. At the time, it seemed like the end of the world to me, but look at where I am and what I have. I am happier than I ever was before, with the only thing I wish differently, is that my grandfather still be alive. What the general did, spared me from him and Perseus saved my life. Not my physical life, at least not right then, but he saved me from a life of misery with that brute. I cannot regret it, and I have seen and heard of much worse befalling a woman."

"What happened between that incident and now?" he probed further, "how did you become Mrs. Andrews, after being Miss Billings?"

"Well, as Perseus had saved my life, I felt it my duty to return the favour..."

John appeared in the stall doorway, a shocked look upon his face. He took in Helena's shredded clothing, blood on her back from the welt and blood spatter across her face.

"Oh no, Miss, what happened?"

"He saved my life," she held on to the massive grey, he was the only thing keeping her upright.

"He did this?" John asked, pointing at the dead man. She nodded.

"I tried to stop the general beating Pegasus. He threw me to the floor and then took me, right there," she pointed, "no better than an animal, no respect for the marital bed, no waiting. Pegasus was the only one here to stop him, but he was tethered and could not reach me. He tried and tried, look how the bridle has dug into his face, here. He got himself free and as the general withdrew, he kicked him. He had been beating him. I could not let him beat Pegasus. He beat me," she could not fathom how she was telling her story, without collapsing onto the floor, but she was going to be stronger than that. She was beginning to realise, she would have to be.

"They will want to destroy him," John tried to pull her away from the horse, "they will say he is mad and has killed his master. That he will not be controllable."

"NO!" she screamed and tightened her grip around the subdued horse's neck, "I can control him; you know I can John. I cannot let him be slaughtered, I just cannot," she released her hold on the horse and turned to John, pleading, "I owe him."

"Let me take him. I will hide him until it is all settled. No rash decisions will be made that way. Go to your father and tell him what has happened. He will have to explain it to the general's family and possibly the military," he led the horse out of the stable, through the door that faced away from the house. She turned in the opposite direction, to go and find her father. Neither took any further look at the body of the general.

She stood in her father's study, bedraggled and her head bowed. She recited the story of what had happened in the stable. He listened in disbelief.

"I want to keep the horse, Father," she insisted.

"Out of the question, his family will insist on its disposal."

"You could tell them that it was, produce a receipt for it even. I am sure you could get one easily," she was determined, "I think considering my ordeal, this request could be granted."

"I will not have it in my stable," he stated, "you will not have permission to ride it," she nodded in acquiescence. He strode to the door, "I will go and see to the general. The magistrates will have to be informed."

Her father took care of everything. The body was removed, and the receipt for the disposal of the horse produced. Everything was settled. Her mother refused to speak to her. How could she expect a husband now? She had better not think she would live her life there, bringing shame on them and ruining the prospects of her brother. She blamed her daughter entirely for what had happened that day, and would happily never see her again.

In response, Helena insisted that she had never wanted a husband, and stayed in her room as much as possible. She visited Pegasus often, in his hideaway with John and his family. A few months passed and it became apparent to Ruth, that Helena was with child. The kindly woman took the girl aside, when she was visiting the horse one day, and explained what was happening to her. She could not bear to break the news to her family, but she needed money. What could be done, but to tell her father at least? He had promised her a considerable dowry, and as she turned one and twenty within a month, she hoped he could be persuaded to part with it, if she took herself away. She sat at her writing desk and penned a letter to her beloved grandfather.

Within a week, she had her reply and hope soared in her heart. After visiting John and his family, to find out what they thought of her plan, she confronted her father. Revealing that she was with child, convinced him to release the dowry to her grandfather. He agreed John, his family and Pegasus would travel with her, and that he would explain all to her mother. She would probably be pleased, Helena thought.

Once she arrived in Lincolnshire, she was considered a married woman, whose husband was in the military and died in France. Her daughter was born four months later. Her parents told anyone who asked, that she had been so upset at the loss of her betrothed, she had gone to live with her grandfather. They had never visited her, or acknowledged that they had a granddaughter. Her grandfather left her the stable in his will. Although her dowry had been given to him, he had never touched a penny of it.

She became Mrs. Andrews, Pegasus became Perseus, and they were free.

"Your story is safe with me," Colonel Ackley spoke with obvious emotion in his voice.

"I do not wish to deceive anyone," she concluded, "I keep up the pretence for my daughter and to ensure that Redway Acres, on which many depend for their livelihood, continues to do well. You are the only one who has ever questioned how I came to be here."

"Harker would have I am sure, but he is far too in love right now, to see his nose in front of his face. I envy them that."

"You mean Genevieve and Mr. Harker?" she queried and he nodded, "they give me hope."

"Hope that you might find love?" he asked. Why was he holding his breath waiting for her to answer, he wondered?

"Hope for my daughter, that there might be a true love for her. Hope for mankind in general I think. I do not think I could truly give myself that way to another. Not anymore."

"Would it be giving up anything though? You would still have the stable and horses, the money in the bank," he could not understand her reticence, if she believed in love, which she seemed to, by the way she talked of the Harkers.

"It would not be mine, though, would it? If I married, I would lose possession of everything, including myself. I would have to *'O-BEY'*. My husband would make all the decisions. He need not even consult me. I could not ride when or how I wanted, or assist in the barn with any of the chores. If it had been up to you and John today, the foal standing over there could be dead and so would its mother. *He* packed me that gun to take care of it. Men think they know best, but that foal is here today to prove they do not," she had not meant to vent her spleen on her views of how unfair the law is to women, but telling her story had brought the feelings of helplessness back to her. She did not like to feel that way.

Colonel Ackley was surprised by her outburst. At first, he had thought her unreasonable, but when she had pointed out how wrong he had been about the mare and remembered how competently she had dealt with the situation, he knew he could not put this outburst down to a woman being emotional or irrational. To be fair, that was usually his father's point of view. Now she surprised him, by setting the subject aside and asking a question of her own.

"What of you and love, Colonel Ackley?"

"What do you mean?" he hedged.

"Women, Colonel. You do like women, do you not?"

"Of course," he blustered. What possessed the woman to come out with such things? She was laughing at how uncomfortable he was. Why was he? She had revealed her most guarded secret. Surely, he was man enough to return the courtesy?

"You are stalling."

"Women, yes, well, of course there have been…" he stammered, "women."

"And yet no love. No marriage?"

"No."

"But carnal knowledge, yes?"

"What? I mean, yes and all consensual I might add. But no, no love," his voice held more regret than he had intended. She was moved suddenly. She had been teasing him, but felt the mood change. He was looking at her intently.

"You sound sad," she prompted.

"I have seen the happiness of a true love, with Harker and Genevieve. How could I settle for less than that? I would once have been happy to meet a woman of means, whom l could live with compatibly."

"Is that why you decided not to marry your cousin, Grace?" hang the woman, how did she manage to find out so much of him, without him telling her?

"*That* was never going to happen."

"And now?" she prompted.

"Now, I think to find a woman I love, who loves me in return, no matter the circumstance, would be miracle enough," why was he telling her all of this? What was it about her that had induced him to speak of his feelings this way? He looked at her again.

The darkness of the night had crept up and the rain still poured steadily outside. Her face was half-bathed in light from the lantern. Her beauty was not diminished, in fact she looked ever more so. She looked at him in return. Her wariness of him had gone and he hoped never to see it again. He would strive never to give her reason to fear him.

"We should snuff out the lamps before we sleep," he broke the spell, "we do not want a fire to start and become trapped," she concurred and he moved to extinguish them.

"Where are you proposing we sleep? There is only one bed and blanket."

"I will sleep on the floor with my greatcoat for warmth. I have slept in worse conditions."

"I doubt your coat is dry at all!" she exclaimed, "there is nothing for it, but for me to trust you and share the bunk, and the blanket. It will get cold in the night; we will keep each other warm."

He stared at her incredulously, "I could not possibly do that, to risk your honour so."

"What honour?" she asked him, "truly, you are already entrusted with it. Are you not?"

He looked at her openly, seriously, "you will come to no harm from me this night. You have my word, as a colonel in His Majesty's Army."

"Your word as a man is good enough for me, sir." She lay on the bunk facing the wooden wall, taking care to leave room for him to lie behind her. He lay on his back, with one arm behind his head, and did his best to forget a woman lay at his side. A beautiful woman who was challenging, amusing, quick-witted and strong. Her sleepy voice pierced the darkness.

"One more question, Colonel, if I may?"

"Certainly."

"If, upon entering the marriage state, a woman must be pure and a man must be experienced, how is that to be achieved, exactly?" she could feel his laughter, as his body shook gently against her back. She smiled, as her eyes slowly closed and she drifted off to sleep.

The colonel lay awake a little longer, thinking of his interesting ride. He considered her story. Did it change how he had been starting to think of her? No, of course it did not. Why should it? It was not her fault and as a widow, with a child, he had not expected her to be a virgin. Her final comment had made him laugh. She was right about the hypocrisy of society's views. It made him consider the women he had bedded. All of them were willing and compensated in one way or another. None were married, but had there been consequences he was unaware of? He had never considered that before, and felt that maybe he should have.

Her breathing had become even and deeper. He was comforted that she trusted him while she slept. He had known what the general was like, had known his horse better. The sounds of the four horses and the continuing patter of the rain soothed him. He turned toward her sleepily and breathed in deeply the fragrance of her hair, before drifting off to sleep.

She woke in the early hours, with the sun streaming through a crack in the wood and onto her face. How could she have slept so deeply, on this uncomfortable bed, in the arms of this man? She would never have thought it possible. In the night, she remembered waking with him at her back, feeling his muscled body pressed against hers and his arm across her, holding her close to him. Needing to change her position, she had turned toward him and he had lain on his back, so she could rest her head on his shoulder. Half asleep, he had pulled her close to him. She had tensed, wondering what he might do next, but he did nothing more, so she relaxed her head and slept on.

Now, in the early morning sunlight, she studied his sleeping face. In repose, his features were much more boyish. He was certainly a handsome man. Tall, lean and muscular, with sandy, light brown hair framing noble features, but she felt that it was his eyes that drew her to him. They were a piercing blue that could show concern, rage or humour. She had seen all of those, as they talked the night before. But when he had let down his guard and talked of love, she had seen sorrow, and perhaps, loneliness.

She did not wish to wake him, so carefully laid down her head once again on his shoulder. His shirt was open at the neck, and from her vantage, she could see that scar slicing across his chest. *"How brave a man must be to go to war,"* she thought. The sun had shifted, to cast its light directly over the face she had been studying. Its owner awoke with a start and swiped at her hand hovering over his scar, while she wondered if she dared to touch it. Those eyes, she had thought of admiringly, only a moment before bore into hers.

"I am sorry."

"Think nothing of it, madam. Prepare yourself to depart, if you please," he stood up directly and exited out of the nearest barn door.

He had been dreaming of her, of that cascade of red hair and the soft lips. He had embraced her, felt her full figure pressed against his body and brought his own lips down in demand on hers. All the while, he ran his hands through her hair and down her back to those curves. He had awoken in a state that men often do, and felt the need to get away from her as soon as possible, so as not to scare her. In his haste, he may have spoken a little sharply, but that could not be helped. As he stood looking out toward Eastease, he recalled that her hand had been hovering over his chest. What had she been doing? He looked down at his open shirt. So, she was curious, was she? Better than abhorred. He took care of his own ablutions in a small copse and made use of one of the last pails of water remaining from the rain the previous night. Knocking first he entered the barn.

"Are you ready?" he enquired. The horses were restless and ready to be off. She ducked behind him and outside with her own ablutions bucket before he could offer to take it from her. He could see she had also taken care of the horses' needs. All they needed to do was saddle up their respective rides. She said she would send some men out to clean the stalls, later in the day.

The trickiest part, was going to be the conversation about what should be said to their two households. He imagined she would favour saying nothing of it to either. Hers could assume she had managed the foaling on her own. His that he had found shelter for the night, alone. He made a start saddling Thor and upon her return, she saddled Perseus. They worked in a friendly, quiet atmosphere. When they were ready, they moved out of the shelter and he cleared his throat.

"I will ride with you to Redway Acres."

"No, I am quite capable of getting there alone and we do not want anyone to see us together."

"If they do, we need only say I met you out on my ride this morning," he boosted her up onto Perseus' back.

"At this hour?" she questioned. With the sun just up in the sky, she had a point he supposed.

"A compromise then," he conceded, she certainly was not a woman to be told what to do, "I will ride with you to the point just prior to becoming visible to your house and stable. Would that suit you, madam?" she nodded and took the rope he handed to her, after he had attached it to the halter around the dam's head, the foal should follow, but they would have to ride slowly.

Apprehensively, he said what needed to be said of the situation. He looked up at her on the back of that fine stallion, "I know you do not wish to marry, but if anything is discovered about last night, please know that I *would* do the honourable thing," she nodded, not sure if that was something he wanted, but appreciating him saying it nonetheless. He mounted Thor and they headed to Redway.

As they approached the point at which they had agreed to part ways, the colonel asked her one more question, "Harriet tells me, that you had something to say about why men did not want women to ride astride, but she would not tell me what it was. Will you share it with me?" She smiled at him over her shoulder as she continued to ride forward, glad that their parting words should be humorous. He had stopped to turn back to Eastease.

"I said, that the only beast a man wants a woman to have between her legs, is himself," with that she turned to Redway and rode slowly over the last rise, before the stable came into view. He was left wondering, why he was surprised that she had managed to shock him once again, and yet wryly having to admit she was probably right.

Chapter Nine

When he arrived, rather dishevelled, back at Eastease, the colonel dropped Thor at the stable, to be taken care of by the only stableman brave enough to work on him.

"Spoil him, young Adam, he kept me safe in the storm. We found shelter, but I was not able to care for him as I should have."

"Yes, sir," was the happy reply. He knew the colonel would be sure to reward him.

After taking care of his rumpled appearance, he poked his head in the breakfast room. It was early, so he was surprised to see both Harker and Genevieve sitting at the table.

"You see my dear," teased Harker, "our Colonel is a resourceful man and survived the night in the wilderness of Lincolnshire, unscathed." The colonel rubbed the heel of his hand over his chest and wondered if he truly had.

"I know! I know!" acknowledged Genevieve, giving her husband a pained look, "but to survive in battle, only to succumb so close to home, would be a dreadful fate and I am entitled to worry about a dear friend. How did you manage, Nathaniel?" she turned to him.

Flustered, because he had been thinking of a red-haired angel, flying across the fields on a huge stallion, the colonel ran the conversation he had half heard, through his head.

"I saw... I mean, Thor and I found shelter. We spent a companionable evening, with my flask for sustenance," he tapped his coat pocket. Genevieve studied his face. He was being guarded, but she was not sure why.

"We are glad you are safe, are we not, Alexander?" she looked at Harker, but he was lost in his paper and waved at his friend. The colonel was hungry and tucked into a hearty breakfast with relief.

He wandered the halls of Eastease that afternoon, thinking of the previous night and wondering how things were at Redway Acres. He considered borrowing a horse to ride out there and took two strides toward the stable, before realising his foolishness. Then he heard two girlish laughs and some music reached his ears. Knowing that tentative fingering could, in no way, be Harriet's, he pivoted and marched purposefully toward the music room.

The scene that greeted him brought a smile to his face. Harriet sat on her pianoforte stool with a small girl. The young girl was swinging her stockinged legs in time to the music she was attempting. Her shock of red hair was groomed into ringlets, that were swinging, too. The girl turned toward him and a hand gripped around his heart, as he fell instantly in love. Even without red hair, he would have known at once who her mother was. Thank the heavens she had not inherited any physical traits from her father. The cherubic face smiled at him.

"Hello," she giggled, "Harry is teaching me to play!" It was obviously something that positively delighted her.

"*Harry* is, is she?" he replied with a sunny smile of his own. 'Harry' was a nickname his friend, Mark Wyndham, had given Harriet, but when he died she had insisted it never be used again. It felt good to use it. *'Harry'* stood and indicated the young girl do the same.

"Isabella, what is it that I have told you, about speaking before you are spoken to and of speaking first, to people you do not know?"

"Do not do it?" was the reply, with a perfect pout.

"And, what of using the names Harry and Issie?"

"That they are our secret names, to use when we are alone," more pouting.

"Isabella," Harriet continued, this time with a kind lilt to her voice, that magically made the pout disappear, to be replaced with a smile. "This is my cousin, Colonel Ackley. Colonel, may I introduce our neighbour, Miss Isabella Andrews, to your acquaintance?"

"Indeed, you may," the colonel gave a dramatic bow, "I am honoured to make your acquaintance, Miss Andrews." The little girl did a sweet curtsey and giggled again.

"A real life, colonel soldier?" she asked with big eyes, taking his measure admiringly.

"I am," doubt crossed the girl's face.

"But where then, is your red coat and your sword? Have you lost them? Will you get into trouble? I lost Mama's necklace once and I got into dreadful trouble!" Concern crossed her face, of which he directly aimed to relieve her.

"I am not required to wear them, when I am not on duty. They are safe in my rooms, do not worry yourself, madam. May I be permitted to sit and listen, while you are at your lesson?" Isabella looked toward Harriet and got a quick nod.

"Certainly, sir," with one more giggle, she sat down at the instrument with renewed efforts. She thought the colonel wonderfully brave, and imagined him rescuing a princess, from a fire-breathing dragon. She desperately wanted to please him.

Her fingers were slender and long. She certainly had the rhythm of the piece, even if she did not have all the notes. The colonel listened intently, and clapped enthusiastically at the end of every piece she tried. Harriet surprised him with her patience and humour.

As he watched Mrs. Andrews' daughter, the idea occurred to the colonel, that he could take the girl home and have another impromptu meeting with her mother. However, before he could make that suggestion, the girl jumped down from the stool and ran to him.

"Colonel, could you take me home, please?"

"Isabella!" the shocked response came from Harriet, "a lady would never ask a gentleman such a thing. You know full well, that Johnson will drive you home."

She turned, pleadingly to Harriet, "but, Johnson cannot fight off any dragons that may cross our path, hoping to make a meal out of me! The colonel could see them off, with a flash of his sword," with that, she sliced through the air, with an imaginary sword. Harriet primly tutted at the girl's outrageous behaviour.

"I am well known hereabout for defeating dragons, is that not true, Harriet? I am sure I slayed one or two for you, when you were younger."

"Still, these things should be done properly, Cousin," she said, expectantly, and he turned again to the young girl.

"Miss Andrews, would you do me the honour of allowing me to escort you home?"

"I thank you, sir, you may," giggling, she offered him her hand, that he immediately bowed over and kissed loudly, with a smack of his lips, which made her giggle even more.

Colonel Ackley drove the curricle up to the waiting girls.

"Thank you, Harriet. Please inform Alexander, that unlike last night, I will be back for dinner!"

"Did you miss your dinner last night, Colonel?" asked the girl, "Mama missed dinner last night, too. She was caught in the storm and had to spend the night in a barn. I was in charge. She said I was, before she left." Astonished by the coincidence, Harriet could only stare at her cousin. He seemed unperturbed, but she knew from Alexander, when he complained of how often the colonel won at cards, that he was good at showing impassivity. He had made no mention of being caught out in the storm *with* Mrs. Andrews. Their two estates were certainly large enough, that they may not have seen each other.

The colonel leaned into the curricle and pulled out a small step, which he placed on the ground at the feet of Isabella. Usually, she was lifted into it unceremoniously, by Johnson. The stool allowed the colonel to hand the small girl, step by step into the vehicle, with plenty of flourish and aplomb! How thoughtful he was, Harriet thought, with a rush of affection. Isabella loved it and was captivated by the colonel, whom she had firmly placed into the stories she loved to create. The next one she did with her mother would, most definitely, include Colonel Ackley.

With a bow, he left Harriet standing there, with her affection and suspicions. He rounded the vehicle again, to leap into it in one bound and pick up the reins.

"Farewell, Harry!" called Isabella, with a wave.

"Farewell, Harry!" he echoed, "watch out dragons, the colonel is protecting Miss Isabella on her journey home today. You would do well to stay in your caves." His laughter and Isabella's squeals of delight, faded in her ears as the curricle pulled away from her. She stood there for a moment, watching the vehicle disappear from her view, shaking her head with a smile.

The sun was still bright and warm, as they left the grounds of Eastease, heading on the North Road toward Redway Acres. Isabella captivated him with stories of princesses, and the princes, knights or loyal soldiers who saved them from various beasties. Stories she and her mother, told to each other at bedtime. Her mother would often insist, that the princess should save herself from the dragon or an evil witch, but Isabella said, that was not how it was supposed to be done.

He pointed to a distant peak and a thin greyish cloud, that looked like smoke streaming out from it, "I see the Dragon of Lincolnshire is waking up. Can you see his smoke? That is the peak he lives on," he teased. She looked about his person and the curricle.

"Oh no, Colonel! Where is your sword? How will you slay the dragon, if he chases us?"

"Well, firstly, let me say, that I am known in the dragon world, for being the best dragon slayer there ever was, so I do not think he should dare to chase us. Secondly, if he were to chance his arm, or wing, he would find the going rough, because this pair of horses is the fastest in the land," he smiled widely at her, blue eyes meeting green, and elicited another giggle. So, the pleasant journey passed, and before long, they were pulling up to the main house of Redway Acres.

Isabella ran into the house, calling to her mother and talking in a lively fashion of dragons, leaving the colonel to find his own way. He walked into the wide foyer and noticed how it was spacious and unfussy. The housekeeper entered and greeted him, directing him to a well situated and comfortable parlour, in which sat the mistress of the house, with her daughter on her lap. The young girl was relating to her, the story of the Dragon of Lincolnshire and how she had seen the smoke he breathed with her very own eyes. What a picture they made! How was a man supposed to keep his heart within his chest, at the sight of them?

"Colonel Ackley, ma'am," the housekeeper gave a bob and smiled to herself. Her girl had an admirer, she judged, by the way he was looking at her.

"Colonel, you are very welcome in our home. Especially, after saving my daughter from the Dragon of Lincolnshire! Please, excuse me from rising, as I seem to have my lap full," the colonel bowed and moved forward to take a seat, as she had gestured.

"Mrs. Andrews, please do not trouble yourself. Having escorted this princess home, I understand the seriousness of your office!"

"Mama, the colonel missed his dinner last night, too!"

"Did he?" with a slight blush rushing to her cheeks, Mrs. Andrews looked at the colonel. He was looking intently at her, "well, that is a coincidence, is it not?"

"As we are having a picnic, on Sunday, to make up for it. Could we invite the colonel? As he missed his dinner," it seemed, the colonel had made an impression on both Redway women.

"What say you, Colonel? Are you one who enjoys a picnic?"

"I most certainly am! And if you should allow it, I would be happy to supply the provisions."

"It is going to be such a wonderful day!" exclaimed Isabella.

"Do not get too excited, sweet girl," her mother warned, "we have yet to see if the day will be a fine one. Being caught out in one storm a week, is quite enough for me." The housekeeper returned to take Isabella to her rooms and enquire if they needed refreshments.

"Would you like tea, Colonel, or would you, perhaps, be more interested in a tour of the stable?"

"Horses are always my preference, I thank you. Please, lead the way," his luck was holding. A curricle ride, with an adorable, young lady, followed by a tour of her mother's stable and, if the weather held, a picnic with this red-headed duo on Sunday! He was a very happy man indeed.

Redway Acres was a country manor. Bigger than a farmhouse, and not a prestigious house, like Eastease, but large and well situated. Not too grand a house for what it was primarily, a stable. Overall, the colonel felt it was functional and comfortable. He loved it, and that was before he saw the grounds, where the stable buildings were.

Leading him out of the parlour and toward the back of the house, Mrs. Andrews exited through a wide, rich, dark-wood, double door and out to a paved courtyard. They had stopped to fill two large, secret pockets in her gown, with a number of treats from a barrel by the door. She turned and smiled at the colonel, took an additional handful, which she dropped into the pocket of his topcoat. Outside, the functionality, again meshed well with aesthetically pleasing. Two rows of stable buildings extended either side, away from the house, flanking the courtyard. The paving sloped very gently down from each side and to a narrow drainage gulley in the centre. Access lanes between the house and the buildings, allowed for carriages and suchlike, to be brought around from the front of the house or to provide a route to the fields beyond. Indeed, Harker's curricle stood waiting for the colonel's return. The two buildings were joined at the end by the large barn. With a loft and open hatch above. He could see the hay piled up and spilling out.

They wandered down one side, where some horses were stationed with their heads over the half doors. As they approached each one, she gave him a bit of history about them. Their heritage, where she had purchased them, who from and why. She told him which horses were commissioned by a buyer, which were for sale and which certainly were not.

At each stop she gave the horse a treat from her pocket or, if she knew his pocket held the favoured treat, she would let him know and he would dig it out and offer it to the horse in his palm. At first, he felt self-conscious touching her horses, her domain, but she was relaxed, stroking and soothing all the horses herself. It made it easy for him to follow suit. Unsurprisingly, he found himself relaxing. It was always the same way for him with horses. That was why he made his way to the army stable as often as he could.

She pointed out a few horses stationed across the courtyard and then entered the barn doors. Inside, the larger room was divided into several, small store rooms, for equipment, food and an office. Everything was well organised and labelled.

Doors either side led to corridors, that were on the inside of the buildings they had just passed. Taking the one to the right, they came to an inner stall, housing the dam and foal from the previous day. Seeing them again brought the whole afternoon, and night, back into the colonel's mind. Heat rose in his body at the memory, and his chest felt tight. He looked over at Mrs. Andrews and noted an attractive blush had risen in her cheeks. He smiled at her and received a sheepish smile from her in return.

"They look healthy."

"Very."

"And happy."

"Of course," another smile.

"You did a good thing."

"Thank you."

"Who is the foal for?"

"Me, he is mine," she smiled at him again, "his sire is Perseus. It is an experiment. Is Perseus the way he is because of the way the general treated him, or is it just part of his nature? Will his offspring inherit his unpredictability?" she looked very serious when she talked to him of it. The mention of the general made him think of Miss Andrews. He looked around to be sure no one else was there.

"You are thinking of Isabella," the concerned look she gave him, was enough for him to understand that he was right, "she is nothing like him," he reached out and squeezed her forearm.

"Well, we will see how this horse turns out, regardless."

"*We* will?"

"If you wish to come back and see for yourself," her look was more of a challenge. She was testing him to see if he was interested.

"I should like that very much, but first, what did you name him?"

"I have not decided yet, but maybe another Greek god like, Zeus? What do you think?"

"Perhaps you could go with something more along a gambling line. Like Chance or Lucky?"

"Colonel," John approached and pulled his forelock, "she is so full of herself, delivering that foal in the middle of that storm yesterday. I take it she did not mention me having to manage t'other one, all by meself?" the colonel could hear pride in the man's voice for his Mistress.

"Straight forward, the Dam did all the work, you just watched. So like a man. Then you got to sleep in your own bed," she teased back easily, as they moved on a few more stalls to Lady and her foal, "a filly, and so adorable. Just wait until Harriet sees this one!"

"Ruth says, that Miss Isabella told her, you were caught out in the storm, too, Colonel," John's sharp eyes darted between the two faces before him. The colonel was impassive, but he had known his girl a lot longer. Although she managed to keep a blush from her face, she employed her usual tactic when she did not want to discuss a topic, which was to say nothing and look disinterested.

"I am afraid my story is not half as interesting as Mrs. Andrews' adventure. I was out riding Thor, when the storm started, found shelter and we had to stay the night. Luckily, I had my flask with me, but I was hungry when I got back to Eastease."

"Where did you shelter?" asked John.

"I have no idea," the colonel was being indulgent, allowing John to question him. It was obvious the man was protective of Mrs. Andrews and he approved, "I was over the east side. I have been doing a tour around the boundaries of Eastease, but let us talk of more interesting happenings. What time do you plan to be at Old Joe's tomorrow?"

John accepted the change of subject, for now, and they discussed their plans for finishing updating the old man's place, before the colonel left in the curricle.

Dinner at Eastease that night, was a small gathering of Genevieve, Harker, Harriet and the colonel, but as usual it was lively with conversation. He had been asked about his eventful evening sheltering in Eastease grounds and he gave them the same story he had given John.

If it came out that he had spent the night with Mrs. Andrews, he would have to do the gentlemanly thing and marry her. Personally, he did not see that as a problem. He was getting to know her and he liked her. That he found her attractive, was evident by his body's reaction. She was challenging in her actions and her words, but what she said was right. What he loved, was that in making her points she was passionate but sensible. He was beginning to understand why Harker liked talking business with her. She was the best woman he had ever met and he still did not know her fully. He was going to enjoy getting to know her more. No, marrying her would not displease him.

However, he knew enough of her story, to know that she was not ready to marry him, or any man. He did not think, that she had ever had those kinds of thoughts about a man. Who could blame her, given what Alcott had done to her? He hoped that he might be the one she would have those thoughts about. He was confident she was attracted to him, but did she like him? Could she love him? Suddenly he realised, it was very important to him that she did both.

Preoccupied, he had only half listened to Harriet, talking of her music lesson with the adorable Isabella. He missed her small smile before she said, "Mrs. Andrews was caught out in the storm all night last night, too, according to Isabella." Harker turned his head swiftly to his friend, who felt he was getting a lot of practise at keeping his face impassive. His best option, was to have his say before the questions came and he was forced to be defensive.

"I heard all about that when I drove Miss Andrews home. Apparently one of the foaling mares had bolted. Mrs. Andrews had to find it and deal with a difficult foaling. She managed to find shelter and saved both the dam and the colt. She is a very capable woman."

"Did you not see her then, Nathaniel?" pressed Harriet.

"From what I understand, my dear, I was on the other side of Eastease. The other mare foaled, too. A filly. I think John is frustrated, that Mrs. Andrews stole his thunder with a more dramatic event." Harker was appeased and turned back to Genevieve, who was rubbing the large mound of her belly, presumably feeling some discomfort.

The discussion moved to plans for the following day, when many of the hands from Redway and Eastease, would be working with the colonel at Old Joe's cottage. Harker offered to help, said he felt like doing something physical, as he had been stuck behind his desk all week. That was assuming Genevieve could spare him. She assured him she should be fine. He would not be far away, if needed.

"I think it should be nice, if we could get some refreshments to everyone tomorrow," she suggested, "perhaps you could arrange that, Harriet? I expect Jacky Robertson will be there with his father, so you should take Rebecca with you."

"I believe Mrs. Andrews was planning to provide some refreshments, too," the colonel said.

"I will ride over to Redway in the morning and discuss it with her. Then I can see the foals."

"I have been invited to go on a picnic, on Sunday afternoon," he added, as casually as he could. "Perhaps I could trouble you to ask Mrs. Hopkins, for some provisions for that as well?"

"Mrs. Andrews asked you on a picnic?" Harriet asked.

"Actually, it was Miss Andrews. She thinks I am a brave dragon slayer," he brandished his steak knife in the direction of Harriet, who was looking a little put out that she had not been invited.

"As it is for Issie, I will arrange provisions for you."

"Thank you, *Harry*."

The evening at Redway was quiet. Mrs. Andrews and her daughter dined together, and then the tired mother took her daughter to bed, planning to go directly to her own bed afterward.

Isabella was full of talk of Colonel Ackley. She told a story of him saving her from the Dragon of Lincolnshire, as they drove from Eastease to Redway. She talked of seeing him at Old Joe's tomorrow and wanted to make a cake for him. Helena said she would have to ask Ruth, for goodness knows, her own cooking ability was limited at best. She extinguished the candle and kissed her daughter goodnight.

As she got into her own bed, she felt sad that her daughter was longing for a father. She was obviously pinning her hopes on the colonel. She hated that she had lied to her all her short life, but what was she to do? Tell her that she was the spawn of a man her mother had hated. That she was created in violence, fear and death? The girl was such a gift, and that she could not tarnish.

She picked up her diary and decided to write about her feelings concerning the colonel, to see if it would help her make sense of them.

I think he is attracted to me and that has happened in the past. Men see the outside of a woman, and think that the inside is empty, waiting for them to fill, and mould as they please. I have never met a man who does not think he is better than a woman, or knows better than a woman, no matter how highbrow the woman, or lowbrow the man. The best man I have ever known was my grandfather, but I think even he gave me the stable, in the hopes that I should find a husband to run it for me.

Does Colonel Ackley see the 'me' on the inside? I think he does. At least, he is the only one who has given pause to look and listen. I find myself more willing to explain to him how I feel, although I am sure I stumble over the words under that intense gaze. He knows more of me than anyone, even John. He understood my desire to see how Perseus' foal should turn out. Isabella may be spared the meanness of her sire (I hate to say father) but what of her children?

Why do I lie here wishing his arm was around me and I could rest my head on his shoulder, as I did in sleep last night? I feel an emptiness, that I do not experience when he is present. I did not know it has always been within me, until I had experienced time without it. I enjoy just talking to him. Yes, I have to admit, that I do like him, very much.

Chapter Ten

Saturday was a fresh, dry day. The workers at Old Joe's cottage, were warmed by the sun and worked hard. Colonel Ackley and Mr. Harker came to work. They took off their coats and rolled up their sleeves. The tradesmen with the skill for what needed to be done, took over directing the workers. The colonel found himself working next to John, probably by design, as John had more to ask him about the night of the storm.

"Did you find out which shelter you were in, during the storm the other day?"

"No," he grunted as he pulled up an old floor board. Why make it easy for the man? John harrumphed, tackling his own board.

"She is not as tough as she appears," he was protective of Mrs. Andrews, the colonel realised that the other day. How could he not be, when he had been the first on the scene after Alcott had attacked her?

"She *is* tough. Independent."

"Lonely," John said sadly, "will not let anyone help her. Afraid of losing what was hard won."

"Maybe she has to be hard won?" he gave a pointed look at John.

"If someone was willing to try, and was worthy enough," John agreed.

"Trying should prove the worthiness, should it not?"

"And patience."

"Not using an unavoidable situation, as a reason for rushing?"

"No," John had to admit that the colonel had a point there. His girl would not thank anyone who pushed her into marriage.

"So why are we discussing this again?" he asked brusquely, losing his patience with the man. They glared at each other. The colonel might be able to beat him in a sword fight, thought John, but he did not see any swords hereabout. He could never forgive himself for not being there to save the young Helena all those years ago, but he would be damned if this man was going to come in and do the same thing. The colonel put up his hands in a defensive gesture.

"*If* I had been there the other night, nothing would have happened. I am a gentleman before all else," the colonel saw the tension

111

in the other man's body release, but could not resist adding. "I understand your need to protect her. She thought you had packed the gun for Missy." Harker walked in at that moment to see how they were faring. His timing was good, because the colonel was sure the other man was going to swing for him. He actually felt like a bit of a brawl, which is why he had tried to goad John with the last comment. It would do him good to release some of the tension, that was building up in him, thinking of Mrs. Andrews.

Instead, he turned his attention back to the floorboards. John had his answers. His suspicions that the colonel had spent the night at the shelter with Mrs. Andrews were confirmed, but also, he had told him that nothing untoward happened. He had indicated where his intentions lie with regards to her, which until that moment, he had not even admitted to himself.

True to his word, Mr. Brooks arrived to help at Old Joe's place. The garden was a mess and he was put to work directing the younger boys in clearing it. The colonel noticed that he hauled and muscled as much of the rubbish and old machinery, as those boys who were labourers with their fathers out on the farms around Eastease and Redway. He was glad a certain red-head was not there to see the younger man, whose muscles were firm and supple, whereas his own were more steel and granite. He was confident he could flatten the preacher, if only the need would arise, but he could appreciate that his own hardened and battle-scarred body, was not as easy on the eyes.

When Mrs. Andrews drove the Redway cart down the lane, with Isabella, Ruth, Rachel and plenty of food and drink for the men, the colonel was helping the thatcher finish up on the roof. Old Joe's place was single-storey and the thatch finished low past the eaves. She caught sight of him standing astride the pinnacle of the roof, admiring the finished product of Reg Smith's handiwork. He stood in his shirtsleeves, with his sun-streaked hair waving in the breeze and a smile on his handsome face. She was reminded of her dream of being kissed, and sighed. At that moment, he looked up at the cart approaching the front of the house and noticed her watching him.

Suddenly, he lost his balance and started to fall, she screamed, as he rolled over and over, down the slope of the roof.

"COLONEL!" none of the men moved. Leaping from the cart and running the moment her feet hit the ground, she shouted at them, "move, you blaggards, move and aid the colonel, what is the matter with you all?" She rounded the house and realised immediately why they had not moved. At the side of the house was a large cart full of loose thatch. Safe in the middle of the thatch, that had cushioned his fall as he had planned, was a grinning Colonel Ackley.

"Thank you for your concern, madam!" he said, sitting up. Realising she had been hoodwinked, she picked up a large armful of thatch and shoved it at him, none too gently. Pushing him back again and covering his face.

"You bloody bastard. You have easily taken five years off my life," delighted to hear her using such words, he bantered with her.

"Only five? You have hurt my feelings."

"It might have been more, if your face was prettier," she countered, acting up to the crowd of men who laughed heartily. She had learned much of a man's sense of humour, working around them in her stable, but she was also covering up her heart's reaction to thinking he was hurt.

"If prettiness determines years lost, then I should have lost fifty, had you fallen half as far," that got an *'oooh'* from the men that prompted him to add, "but let us deduct ten from that, for the unladylike language!" More laughing was followed by a stern Ruth, sitting with Isabella in the cart, announcing that there was food to be had, so why were they all horsing around?

While they had eaten, many had talked of Helena's expression when the colonel had fallen off the roof and laughingly repeated their banter. She took it all in good humour, but beneath the smile she was concerned. In her mind, she had envisaged, that as she turned the corner of the house, she would see him sprawled on the ground, with a head wound like the general's, seeping his life's blood into the earth. Back then she had experienced relief, this would have caused her grief beyond measure.

It occurred to her, though she had never thought there would be a man that could capture her interest, Colonel Nathaniel Ackley had captured it in a way, she knew no other man ever could. Surreptitiously, she looked at him as he moved easily around the men, laughing with them. He was dirty and sweaty, and his forearms were strong and muscular, and scarred, too, in places.

He made his way to her and the other women, and thanked them for the sustenance. They were packing up and he helped Helena by taking some boxes she was carrying. As he took them from her their hands touched and their eyes locked.

"Mr. Colonel, sir," he turned and looked down at Isabella.

"Ah, the pretty Princess Isabella," he bent down to her, "I have been warning all the dragons hereabout, that they must not attack you or I will hunt them down and cut out their hearts."

"Thank you, Colonel," she was happy to be distinguished, "did you eat some cake? I helped Mrs. Ruth make it especially for you. Can you fall off the roof again? That was a good joke."

"No!" her mother spoke immediately, "that was far too dangerous and the colonel should not have done it at all." He stood again and looked into her eyes, seeing that she had really been afraid for him. His joke seemed less funny, if it had caused her even a moment of pain. Yet it gladdened his heart that she had been worried for him. A commotion broke the tension of the moment, as Harriet was seen riding toward Old Joe's and calling out for Harker.

"Alexander, come quickly, come quickly. The baby is coming!" Harker need hear no more, but sprang from his position of working on a new wooden door frame, to leap on his horse and hurry down the lane. "All is well. Pray, do not break your neck," the young woman called after him. She turned to Mrs. Andrews, "Gennie is asking for you. Mrs. Hopkins says the midwife is in Nottingham for a few days, visiting her sister. She thought, given your experience, you could aid them?"

"Of course," but Harriet was already retreating back up the lane. She looked around for transportation. Why did Harriet not think to bring a spare horse? She turned to Ruth, who was preparing to take Isabella back with Rachel on the Redway cart. Jacky came over to drive the cart for them and return on another horse, but that would take a while. She was eager to get to her friend at Eastease. As she was considering her options, the colonel had mounted Thor and walked him over to where she was standing.

"May I be allowed to provide you transportation to Eastease, Mrs. Andrews? I understand it may not be ideal, but you know me to be an honourable man."

"It would seem I have no other option, unless I walk. I thank you, Colonel. I will have to sit sideways to accommodate my skirts." John stepped up and with a stern nod at the colonel, provided her with a boost. She had turned to face John and put her hands on his strong shoulders. Holding the reins in his left hand, the colonel wrapped his right arm around her waist and pulled her backwards, helping her land as gently as possible on Thor, and across his own lap.

With her in position, he switched arms. His left arm ran across the small of her back and around her side to hold her, leaving his right arm free to control the reins. He was acutely aware of the feel of her weight on his thighs, the embrace of his arm around her back and the feel of her legs under his right arm.

"It might be more comfortable and safe, for you to put your arm around me and hold on, particularly once we go faster," he suggested hopefully, as Thor started to walk slowly down the lane.

"I am well aware of that, Colonel, but not in front of these men and especially not in front of John. Thank you for holding on to me." He squeezed her more closely to him, causing her to look up at him, and he looked into her eyes as he spoke.

"John knows we spent the storm together."

She looked down, "he suspects, but has not asked me outright."

"He knows."

"You told him!" she looked up at him accusingly, "why would you do such a thing?"

"He would not leave it be. I did tell him that nothing happened and that I was a gentleman. I think he was ready to take a swing at me," she laughed at that and he laughed, too. They turned the corner and out of sight of the men, so she leaned into him and tucked her right arm under his arm that was wrapped around her, grasped his shirted back and felt the rock-hard muscles through it.

"I think it is just as well for John, that he did not," her head rested on his shoulder and she felt very safe on his strong horse, in his embrace.

"If I may say so, I missed sleeping close to you last night," her breath drew in a gasp at his audacity. She tried to pull back from him, but he held her tightly, "I mean nothing by it. I wanted you to know that I felt very comfortable and slept much better, that night with you, than I had for a long time. I suspect that you did, too." She turned her face into his chest, she was embarrassed for him to see her in that moment. She could smell his sweat, and sawdust, as she nodded.

She dared not look up at him again. This moment was so close to her dream of that passionate kiss. Here he was in his shirtsleeves, his strong arms around her, holding her close. He had urged Thor into a trot and the rocking movement was arousing them both.

He was sure, in that moment, had she looked up at him, he could have done nothing but place his lips upon hers. It was just as well that Eastease came into view when it did. Slowing his horse to a walk once again, she was able to sit up safely and appropriately. Harriet met them at the door and called a footman to help Mrs. Andrews. She looked accusingly at her cousin, who was dismounting after releasing her friend.

"How else were you expecting her to arrive, after you rode away?" he asked, as Adam came running around the house to take Thor from him. The women hurried into the house and up to Genevieve, while he took a deep breath to regain his equilibrium, after being so close to her again. Then he strode into Eastease to find his friend.

Helena and Harriet walked past Alexander, who was pacing the corridor outside Genevieve's rooms. Upon entering, Helena saw her friend lying on the bed, looking worried, but when Harriet came in Gennie pasted a smile on her face.

"How are you, Gennie? Sorry, silly question, I know that, but you do forget all of this discomfort and pain once it is all done and your child is in your arms." Gennie looked surprised at her and hoped her friend was telling her the truth. She had been in pain for many hours. Knowing the process would take some time, she had delayed Harriet getting Alexander.

Mrs. Hopkins and Gennie's maid hovered in the room. Helena turned to them and asked for two jugs of hot water, to wash in and for cleaning the baby when it was born, and of course plenty of linens and basins, as there would be a considerable amount of blood. Armed with their duties they left the room, trying to take Harriet with them, saying it was not the place for a young lady.

Helena turned to Genevieve, "it is your decision Gennie, but do you not think that Harriet could be in this position herself one day and it should be better for her to know what to expect?" Gennie nodded at that, agreeing Harriet could stay if she wished. "Would you mind Gennie, if I take a look at you?" Gennie nodded again and Helena pulled back the bedclothes, feeling Gennie's contracted belly and then looking below, noted that not a lot was happening there, "it may be some time yet. Your body is still preparing itself for pushing the child out. You do not need to lie in bed, if you would rather not. How do you feel about walking around the room? It can actually help the process if you keep moving."

"I felt like I wanted to do that, but Mrs. Hopkins insisted that I should lie down. That the proper place to have a baby is in bed," Helena waved her hand at that.

"We women should trust our instincts more. We have been having babies for centuries without being in a bed. I leaned back in a chair giving birth to Isabella, after I had been walking about the whole time. Her great-grandfather caught her, how wonderful is that?" while she was saying this she was helping Gennie out of bed. Gennie was surprised at how strong the woman was as she made light work of it, then she looked at her shocked.

"A man in the birthing room?" was that acceptable she wondered? She looked longingly at the door behind which she knew her husband paced in the corridor.

"Who else would I want in there, except the man that had delivered well over one hundred foals in his lifetime? Added to that, a man who loved and cared for me and took me in when I was alone," at this both Harriet and Gennie stared at her.

"Why were you alone, Helena?" asked Harriet. Helena realised that in this intimate setting with her two closest friends, as she was now happy to call them, she had let down her guard. It seemed, revealing the truth to Colonel Ackley the other night, when it had not been talked of in so long, had caused a crack in the wall that she had built up around the secrets of her life. She would have to be more careful.

"This is not the time for such talk," she tried to wave it off, but Harriet was having none of it, too many people kept too many secrets from her.

"I think this is the perfect time to talk of families and babies. You said it could take some time yet," at this Genevieve gave a shriek of pain and grasped the railing at the end of her bed, she leaned forward. Helena rubbed her lower back remembering how hers would ache.

"Breathe, Gennie, remember to breathe. In through your nose and then blow it out, like you are blowing out the pain. How was that?"

"It helped a bit," she said, straightening again and looking gratefully at her friend, "I should like to hear your story. It would take my mind off things." Mindful that she could not tell these women everything, Helena decided to share what she could. Rather than make up lies about a non-existent husband, she told them her story from arriving at her grandfather's.

"Well, when I heard that I was a widow and I was quite sure that I was with child, my parents were not very happy. I wrote to my grandfather and asked him to take me in. He was a wonderful man, tall, strong and handsome and yet so gentle with the foals and Isabella." Genevieve was wracked with pain again, but did not shriek this time. Again, she leaned forward gripping the bedrails, as this seemed most comfortable and this time Harriet rubbed her back.

"So, your grandfather wrote back to say you could stay with him," prompted Harriet.

"Yes, he did, and it was so wonderful to be back at the stable. John, Ruth and their family came with us, as did Perseus. I grew larger and larger with Isabella. until I thought I was going to burst!"

"I know that feeling!" Gennie was gripped with pain again, this one was much worse and she screamed. The time between the pains was getting less. Helena was sure there would be a new life in the world within the hour. The door banged open and Harker burst into the room, with Colonel Ackley not far behind, smiling at his friend's obvious distress.

"I cannot bear it, Genevieve. I beg you to forgive me. What can I give you to make up for all this pain you are going through?" he knelt before his wife and grabbed her hand, while she held fast to the bedrail with the other.

"There is nothing to forgive, my dearest. This is all quite the natural part of the process," she looked lovingly at her husband and then a pain ran through her body and she leaned once more against the bedrail. Helena took Harker's hand that Gennie had released and pressed it to Genevieve's lower back, moving it in a firm circular motion and then released it, so he could continue to aid his wife by himself.

"Gennie, forgiving him is one thing, but there must be something you can ask of him? You are providing him with the heir of this fine estate. Now is the time for you to press your advantage, as would any woman worth her salt. How about a diamond necklace?" Helena looked up and winked at the colonel, who had sat discreetly, in the corner of the room.

"A new wardrobe," suggested Harriet with a laugh.

"A pair of Yorkshire Coach horses, for a dear friend!" said the colonel.

"I do not think that any of *my* friends want coach horses," teased Genevieve, amused and enjoying this process since her friend had arrived. She did not care that the colonel was there, though grateful he was in the corner. Mostly she was so happy that her rock, her partner, her husband was there beside her. He was looking at her expectantly, awaiting her command of him, "I had hoped, that I might be allowed a small garden of my own to tend. To have it walled for our children to play in and I could teach them all about the different plants and flowers we would grow there." Everyone stopped and paused at the pleasant image that gift conjured, so typically Genevieve.

"Then it is yours, my love, and probably some diamonds, too," at which everyone laughed. Harker was happy to be relieved of some of the worry he had been feeling, hearing Genevieve's cries of pain. That would still happen, but being in the room with her helped. He hoped they would not send him out again. Another pain engulfed her and he moved to rub her back.

"Helena was telling us of the birth of Isabella, please continue, it is taking my mind off this interminable process," Gennie managed to say, when the pain had subsided.

"Not so interminable, my friend," informed Helena, "the pains are getting more frequent and more intense. A sure sign your body is almost ready. It will not be much longer now. Still, I do not want to bore Mr. Harker and the colonel with my tale."

"Please," said the colonel from the corner of the room, "whatever is aiding Genevieve is fine with me. We all find Isabella adorable, we would love to know of the day she came into the world."

"Well, my pains with Isabella started in the night, it was so bad, but she is worth every one of them. Took her time, too, as she did not arrive until the next evening. Her birthday is next month, so nearly five years ago. I tried to keep quiet and not wake my grandfather, but he was used to dealing with foaling in the middle of the night. He heard me moving around and moaning. Ruth arrived in the morning and encouraged me to eat some breakfast. I did not want to, but she was right and I was glad I had forced myself, when I was flagging later in the day," as she was talking she went to the nightstand and poured Genevieve some water from the jug there. She handed it to Harker to help his wife drink.

"Ruth tried to send Grandfather away, but he would not leave my side. I loved him so much for that. He knew there was no other family in my life to love me and the baby I was giving life to. He made that day special, just by being there. It was around seven in the evening, close to this time, that she finally decided the time was right. I had been walking around almost all day, on and off, and it just made sense to me to crouch by the fire, with a chair for support and bring her into the world. Grandfather caught her and wrapped her in a blanket he had ready for her. I asked him what it was and he had looked so surprised and said, *'it is a baby'*. To which I said *'of course it is a baby, what did you expect? A foal?'*" her enraptured audience laughed at that. "*'A filly,'* he said then. My sweet girl. I was a mother. It was the best day of my life."

She looked up into those blue eyes that were staring at her intently from the corner of the room. She hoped he understood, the worst day of her life was bearable, because it had provided the best.

"Tell us," he asked, nodding in understanding and with a smile on his face, "what gift did you persuade your grandfather to part with?"

"Missy," she looked at him and saw that he understood her determination in saving the mare.

"I think I should like to have a chair in front of the fire," Genevieve looked at Harker who moved two from around the edge of the room for them to sit on. Harriet perched on the bed and the colonel remained in his armchair in the far corner. Helena's story had held him captive and affected him more than he cared to admit. He fervently wished that he had been there for her and was so grateful that her grandfather had been present.

"Could I catch the baby do you think, my dear? Would it be appropriate?" thinking if it was his child propriety could be damned, the colonel replied for everyone,

"Damn it, Harker, you are the master of this house. If you cannot do as you wish, who can?"

"Well *I* think this is all highly inappropriate," Mrs. Hopkins had arrived with the linens and water Helena had requested, "you men should not be in here."

"I am not leaving, Mrs. Hopkins," said Harker. So she looked at the colonel expectantly.

"I refuse to be the only person shut out. I am fine over here in the corner, am I not, Genevieve?" Gennie, in the throes of yet another pain, did not care right at that moment, but Helena, who had been kneeling at the foot of Genevieve's chair examining her again, came to her aid.

"It is of no matter. The baby is almost here. Mr. Harker, you and I should wash our hands in this bowl. Leave the other to cool to clean the baby." After washing her hands, she placed a basin between Genevieve's feet on the floor. She instructed her to brace herself with her hands behind her and sitting right on the edge of the chair, told her to push when the next pain came and that in between pains she should take small quick breaths. After three pushes the baby's head was exposed. She gently turned the baby, so the shoulders should make it through the mother's pelvis. Moving so Harker could cup the baby's head in one of his large, strong hands she warned him that on the next push the rest of the baby should come out quickly. He caught his son perfectly and held him up for Genevieve to see. Sensing the sudden cold air, the baby started to cry. Helena tied and cut the cord with the knife she had cleaned and Mrs. Hopkins came over with a blanket to wrap the child in. Seeing how adoringly Mr. Harker looked at his son, she did not take him away. She wrapped him up and handed him back to his father and showed him how to clean the baby with the cooled water.

Helena finished taking care of Genevieve, covered the basin of blood and afterbirth, and helped her over to the bed. She turned at the surprised voice of Mrs. Hopkins, "oh, sir, wonderful luck. He is a caul baby!" She got a piece of paper from a nearby desk and removing the caul from the baby's head, draped it onto the paper for drying and keeping. "He will not drown," she claimed.

"Alexander Jacob Nathaniel Harker." Colonel Ackley rode with Mrs. Andrews, across the fields of Eastease and toward Redway. They had named the baby after his father, his mother's father and, of course, the colonel. The sun was low in the sky and soon should be setting. They had offered for her to spend the night, but she had much to do tomorrow, and she and the colonel still had Isabella's picnic to attend. She had said that the girl should understand if he had other obligations, but he thought it should be best to allow the Harkers their family time.

"You were wonderful! When we arrived, Genevieve was lying in bed as if ill. Harriet was as pale as ever I have seen her and poor Harker was at his wits end. In you came like light being shone in a dark place. You helped Genevieve enjoy it despite the pain, Harker was involved instead of shut out and Harriet was no longer petrified. Should her time come in the future, she will know how special it can be."

"And you sat and watched in the corner."

"It was good to hear you talk of your grandfather."

"It was good to talk of him. All those foals he delivered and Issie was his only baby."

"How many babies have you delivered?"

"Including Genevieve's? One," she smiled at him and legged Freda into a gallop as they crossed into Redway land. The colonel and Thor easily caught up with them.

"One. That baby was the first baby you had ever delivered?"

"Yes," she laughed, "it was wonderful was it not?"

"I had no idea. Did Genevieve or Harriet know?"

"I do not know what they knew. You make it sound like I misrepresented myself. I have never said that I have delivered babies before. I have had my own baby and my grandfather talked me through that, even though it was his first. The foal the other day was my first difficult foal. I had seen many others delivered," they had arrived at the buildings now.

"But what if something had gone wrong?" he had asked.

"We would have dealt with it as best we could, but what other choice was there?"

"You seemed so confident."

"Gennie needed me to be, they all did. Calming everyone was the most important part. The calmer everyone was, the calmer I felt. I trusted my instincts. Babies have been born for hundreds of years!"

She dismounted and handed him the reins so he could lead Freda back to Eastease with him.

"You are an astonishing woman, Mrs. Andrews."

"Is that something you are only just noticing, Colonel Ackley?" she smiled up at him.

"Not at all," he returned her smile, "I will see you on the morrow."

"Until tomorrow then, Colonel. Please, do not be late or Isabella will be intolerable!"

"That will depend on how many dragons I have to slay on my way here," he gave a laugh and a wave and rode back to Eastease, as she watched him from the outskirts of the Redway buildings. He had a fine riding form, soft hands, strong legs and a straight back. He kept his seat light. Yes, she pondered as he disappeared from her view in the fading light. She did admire his fine seat.

Chapter Eleven

The following day dawned fine and bright. Isabella jumped out of bed and looked out of the window, giggled and ran to her mother's room, where she jumped up onto the bed. She sang a little song about the sun shining, the blue sky and going on a picnic.

"Wake up, Mama. We have to get our chores done, before the colonel gets here," Helena grabbed the light of her life and snuggled her neck. Then she tickled her and enjoyed the little girl's squeals of delight.

"Let us get moving then, my sweet girl."

Several miles away, the colonel was waking up with similar feelings to that of Isabella. Whilst he did not burst into song, he did hum to himself.

His high spirits were not lost on Mrs. Hopkins, who was the only one in the breakfast room when he entered. The new parents were breakfasting in their rooms.

"I have never known a grown man, be so enthusiastic about a picnic with a four-year old girl," she teased. He pointed at her with the butter knife he was using on his bread,

"You will have no effect on my mood today, Mrs. Hopkins. The child is disarmingly charming. In fact, I should suggest to Wellington himself, that we use her to disarm the enemy before going into battle."

"Maybe he should take her mother, too, given that they seem to possess the same attributes," she sparred.

"Mrs. Hopkins, you always seem to manage to be in the right," he allowed her the point. The day was really too good to worry about losing a battle of words. "How is our new family member today?" They talked a little of the baby and the events of yesterday, with Mrs. Hopkins still tutting over impropriety.

Not having chores to complete, the colonel spent his time moving from person to person within the Eastease household. Each of them dismissed him from their presence because he would not keep still. After Mrs. Harker had thrown him out of her rooms, where he looked in on his godson, Harriet begged him to sit still in her music room while she practised, as his pacing up and down was distracting her. Harker was proudly trying to write many letters to family about the arrival of his son. and would not be drawn into a conversation. Mrs. Hopkins was summoned to the kitchen to drag him away from those who were preparing his picnic. He was told she would personally ensure the large saddlebags be brought out to him, as soon as they were ready. Giving him an apple for his horse, she sent him on his way.

Adam had been working hard with Thor, who was so well groomed, he gleamed. The colonel rewarded him with a coin and Thor with the apple. He talked with Adam for a few minutes and then walked Thor around the courtyard to warm up, before mounting him. The kitchen hands arrived with two saddlebags packed with provisions for the picnic, and a large blanket for the ground. Nodding his thanks, Colonel Ackley headed out toward the road. He was paying a visit to his friend's neighbour and should do it via the proper route, rather than over the fields as he had travelled last night with Mrs. Andrews.

Upon his arrival, a red-haired animal seemed to descend upon him and Thor. He held Thor on a short rein and spoke to him in soothing tones, so he did not trample Miss Isabella. Then leaning down, he scooped her up with one strong arm and sat her in front of him, on top of the blanket.

"I was so happy when I woke this morning to a sunny, sunny day! Were you not, Colonel?" the young face looked up at him, with a smile to rival the sun.

"Indeed, I was," he agreed.

"I am so happy to see you again! Did you see any dragons on your way here?"

"I did not. I believe dragons prefer to sleep at noon, far too hot for them." He walked Thor around the back of the house to the rear courtyard and, like her mother had the day before, the girl put her arms around him and held on tight. Although a completely different sensation, he was immensely pleased that she, too, felt comfortable enough to hold on to him.

Helena was loading a saddlebag onto a pretty, copper-red, chestnut mare with a white blaze on her face. The colour of the horse almost matched the hair colour of the rider. A stableman stood holding a small white pony, that Isabella pointed to.

"That is my very own pony, Colonel. We call her Elpis for spirit and hope. Well that is what Mama says. Do you like her?" she looked up at him expectantly. He had been distracted by Helena's strong and efficient hands, ensuring the soundness of the girth and length of stirrups on each horse. He looked down at Isabella,

"I do indeed! How long have you been riding?"

"Mama says, in her arms since I was born, but I first remember riding with my G-G-Papa, a long time ago. Mama says, I was two and a half, but I could not hold on by myself until I was three," she giggled and that was music to his ears.

"Let us get you in the saddle then, my sweet girl," Mrs. Andrews moved to help her get down from Thor. The colonel held her firmly, as he lowered her to her mother. He watched them walk hand in hand until they reached the pony, she then linked her hands to give the girl a boost. Isabella easily stepped into her hands and put her other leg over the horse. Colonel Ackley smiled, as he saw she wore riding breeches underneath her skirts. Her mother moved quickly to arrange the skirts more modestly. She turned and saw him smiling,

"It makes sense for her to learn to ride astride first. It is more difficult and takes longer to master. It is also safer," he nodded. Isabella took up the reins from the stableman, thanking him politely, before turning the pony toward the opposite gap, between the stable and the house.

"Wait for me," her mother warned, and the tone of her voice, while calm, was firm enough that it stopped the colonel from urging Thor on. Seeing him halt his slight movement, she bit firmly on the inside of her cheek to stop herself laughing out loud. She stepped into the waiting hands of the stableman with a, "thank you, Dom," and swung her other leg over the mare. She, too, was wearing breeches.

They steered their mounts out into the waiting green fields, keeping their riding to a walk, so they could enjoy the scenery and talk. Mrs. Andrews pointed out Redway houses in the distance and told him to whom each was rented. A larger two-storey home that was John and Ruth's, the next one that had been empty, was a small single storey that Mrs. Dawley, James' mother, was moving into today.

"James, who works at Eastease?" he asked, remembering that he had been allowed a day off.

"Yes, his mother lived in a property in the village, that the landlord did not tend to. She had been sick and there was damp and mould. I happened to be visiting her last Sunday, luckily for me, as it turns out that she is a wonderful seamstress. We are always in need of help with mending, horse blankets and suchlike. I am terrible at that type of thing myself. Now we have someone on staff, to do those jobs for the house and the help that need it. She gets a stipend and will live in the cottage. It had just become available. James is hoping to be the one to ferry Isabella to her music lessons with Harriet. He can visit with his mother at the same time." He looked at her incredulously. How did she do it he wondered? He had told her how James had come to him, when his father was heading to her rooms at Eastease and now she had returned that good deed to him tenfold at least.

The other houses that she pointed out, housed other staff members at Redway and some of their family members also worked at Eastease. Redway's land to the northeast was farmland, that was on a long-term lease. Most of the fields visible in the distance were now stripped of their grain and haystacks rested on the stubble left behind by the threshers.

"No Perseus today?" asked the colonel, as the horses walked.

"He would not be tolerant of this pace, or be very good walking in close proximity to your stallion. I was surprised, and impressed, last week, when you were able to walk them both to the shelter. I suppose their horse sense was telling them to get to safety and never mind rivalries."

He nodded at the mare, "she is beautiful, like her owner, your hair colours almost match," the mare nodded her head up and down.

"We both say thank you, Colonel. Persephone is good at keeping pace with Isabella's pony. I apologise if it is difficult for your horse. Please, feel free to ride circles around us if it pleases him. Issie and I are always happy to do what pleases horses."

"Could I trouble you to call me Nathaniel, do you think? I know it is not strictly proper, but we are alone here."

"Nathaniel," she almost whispered it, "I am afraid I am unable to do so, even though I may wish it, as we are not *completely* alone," with that she looked pointedly at Isabella, who was happily singing a song to her pony, "what do you think she would tell Rachel and Ruth, the moment she arrived back at the house?"

"Well then, I will respect your decision and, with your permission, will only think *Helena* when I say Mrs. Andrews," he whispered her name, as she had done with his and he could see that it had the same effect on her, as she had on him. He rode ahead a way, before swinging back around and bringing Thor back to the other side of the two women, so he and the stallion towered over the young girl and pony.

"Is this not fun, Colonel?" the small girl smiled up at him.

"It most certainly is, Miss Andrews, and may I be so bold to say that you are a very accomplished rider?" she giggled, as usual and he asked, "where are we heading?" Isabella pointed ahead of them, where he could see a small copse of trees, surrounded by luscious, green grass and cut through by a small stream.

"It is our favourite place." It certainly looked idyllic.

Upon arriving at the copse, the colonel helped both ladies off their horses and spread out the blanket. He laid down the packs and excused himself, and his horse, for a quick run before eating. Isabella and her mother, ducked into the cover of the trees and removed their breeches, to avoid becoming too hot. Then they sat on the blanket and investigated the colonel's provisions, arranging everything in the middle. It was a veritable feast and Mrs. Hopkins had added some sweet treats especially for Isabella.

They sat and watched Colonel Ackley riding along the bank of the stream and up a hill. Careening back down it again, rider and horse jumped a couple of old, felled trees to come to a halt at the blanket. Their audience applauded loudly, while the colonel jumped down and bowed. His horse bowed, too. He then led him to the stream for a drink.

"That was wonderful, Colonel!" exclaimed Isabella, "can we teach Elpis to bow?"

"I am sure we could, if Elpis is willing, but not today. I am much too hungry and luckily we have a feast waiting for us." He tied Thor's reins to a tree in the same way that Mrs. Andrews had done with Persephone and the pony, so they were loose enough to allow the horse to eat some grass if he wished. Removing his coat, he sat down on the blanket.

An hour flew by as they ate, talked and laughed. Isabella entertained them with tales of when she was young, and of her G-G-Papa, as she called her great-grandfather, because he worked with horses. It was obvious to the colonel that she had adored the old man and missed him. Some of the stories she could not have possibly remembered, so he concluded they were stories that her mother had told her often. No stories of her father, he noted. The mother did not talk of him, so neither did the daughter. Of course, he knew now, that Captain Andrews did not exist, but the child did not. He wondered if her mother realised what a void that was for Isabella, but of course, even if she did, it would not be a good idea to make up stories about a man that did not exist.

Once they had eaten, Mrs. Andrews encouraged the youngster to close her eyes for a short while. The girl had not slept much the night before, with her excitement of the coming day. She rolled up the girl's breeches and put them in front of herself, so Isabella could lie beside her and use them as a pillow. Deciding to do the same with her own, they both lay looking at the colonel. He lay on his side on the other side of the blanket, with his head resting on his arm.

As was usual before she slept, Isabella started a story…

"Long ago, there was a young princess, called Isabella. Her mother was the Queen of the land, because her father, the King, had died in battle, bravely protecting the kingdom and his family."

"Was the Queen very beautiful?" Helena asked, as was their want when they were making up stories. Nathaniel smiled broadly and nodded. Isabella gave a tired giggle and continued.

"The Queen was beautiful, with red hair and green eyes. But she was sad, because the King had died."

"The greatest happiness in her life, was her precious daughter, the Princess." Helena gave the little girl a squeeze and kissed the top of her head. Isabella took up the story again.

"Then one day, the terrible Dragon of Lincolnshire, woke from his one-hundred-year sleep, and he was very hungry. A passing soldier saw the smoke from the dragon's nose, rising from the hilltop where it had slumbered. He feared for the life of his Queen and her daughter, and rode his horse…" she paused while she tried to think of a suitable name.

"Thor," her mother provided, without thinking. Nathaniel smiled broadly again, he was enjoying this glimpse into the relationship between mother and daughter.

"Oh yes, what a wonderful name, Mama!" she turned and planted a sweet kiss on Helena's cheek, *"he rode his horse, Thor, in a gallop across the countryside. Faster and faster they went until they were a blur of redcoat and horse,"* she yawned and her mother took this as her cue.

"*The mighty dragon spread its wings and took to the air. Its favourite things to eat, were Princesses and Queens. The soldier stopped his horse at the palace gates, and the two stood firm, as the dragon landed in front of them,*" she looked into those beautiful, blue eyes and playfully lifted her eyebrows for him to provide the soldier's words. The colonel played his part,

"*'You will not pass here today,' the soldier said bravely, although he was afraid of the dragon, 'I will protect my Queen and Princess to the death. Your death,' and with that he plunged his sword into the dragon's heart. As the dragon died, it reached out a claw and sliced the brave soldier across the chest. He fell off his horse.*"

"Oh no, the poor soldier! He does not die, does he, Mama?" Isabella sat up in sudden horror at the turn her story was taking. Nathaniel looked so panic-stricken, that Helena felt sure, in that moment he would have preferred to face down an actual dragon. So like a male to make a story gruesome.

"Of course not!" she gave the colonel a reassuring smile, as she encouraged her daughter to lie down again, "*the Queen and Princess had seen his bravery and used their secret, magical powers to heal him with a kiss. The princess kissed him on his cheek, but his injury was so bad that it was not enough! The Queen bent down and kissed his lips. Magic stars spun around them both, as they kissed until he was completely healed and stood up again.*"

She had thought her daughter asleep, but her voice spoke out again, sleepily, "*now that they had kissed, they had to get married. The soldier became King and kissed the Queen every day, and she was happy again. The Princess called him Papa and they all lived happily, forever.*" Yawning, her eyes fluttered and suddenly she was asleep. A talent that Colonel Ackley envied.

He looked up from the child to the mother, who was looking at him embarrassed, presumably by her own description of the kisses and then the story ending Isabella had provided. Thankful she had saved Isabella a nightmare, over his part of the story, he aimed to lighten the moment.

"I wish kisses would have worked on me. It took much longer for me to heal and kisses would be much more pleasant," Helena smiled, but her own eyelids were becoming heavy. With her daughter awake late into the night and the excitement of the birth yesterday, she was tired. She looked at him. He smiled and said, "sleep, Helena."

"Thank you, Nathaniel," she thought how pleasant it was to be sleeping with him again, before exhaustion took over.

When she woke, she saw he had cleaned up the food and repacked the saddlebags. What had woken her, was her daughter squealing with giggles, as Nathaniel raised her up above his head while he lay on his back in his shirtsleeves.

"Kisses, kisses," she said and his strong arms brought her down to his face, which he burrowed into her neck making loud smacking noises with his lips. Delighted, she giggled and laughed. Helena lay still, watching and thinking this was how a father would be to Issie. She was sad that she could not give that to her daughter. They both turned to look at her with wide smiles.

"You have woken your Mama," his voice was throaty, as the sight of her lying beside him again was overwhelming. He had watched them both sleeping and had given rein to ideas of marriage and fatherhood, but shaking himself out of that reverie, he had cleared up the picnic. He was a soldier, a bachelor and she had made it clear she did not want to marry.

"Kiss Mama! Kiss Mama!" squealed the girl. He wondered if he could, she lay there with sleepy eyes and looked at him. He leaned over, with the four-year-old still in his arms and with his blue eyes looking into those bright green ones, he brushed his lips, ever so lightly, over hers, "and they all lived happily, forever and ever!" Isabella shouted, pulling away from the adults and getting to her feet, dancing and spinning in her happiness.

Nathaniel looked at Helena, keeping eye contact, he remained still, waiting for her reaction. His lips had been warm and light on hers. Her first kiss. She wanted a second, but did not know how to go about getting it. Allowing him such liberties was not fair. She still did not want to be married. She lifted a hand to touch his cheek and then nature intervened, as the sun slipped behind a cloud. It was getting late in the afternoon and the temperature dropped more in the evenings, now that they were in September. The spell was broken, then they heard a splash and a shriek.

Nathaniel jumped to his feet and raced to the stream. Helena knew the stream was not too deep for her daughter at this time of year, so she was not worried, but she gathered the blanket and rushed after him. As she reached the bank a smile crossed her face. Her sopping wet child was being carried from the water by the gallant colonel. This would provide her daughter with many storylines in the coming days.

"Are you hurt?" she asked the girl who was smiling in happiness at being carried by her hero.

"No, Mama," she was already shivering, "I fell."

"I heard."

"The colonel saved me."

"So I see. You can put her down now," gently he put the girl down on her feet. Helena quickly unfastened the girl's gown and removed it before wrapping her in the blanket. She looked up at Nathaniel, who was looking perplexed, "if I left her in the wet gown, she would be very cold by the time we got home. This way I can carry her on Persephone with me, lead Elpis behind us and keep her warm in the blanket."

"I will carry her with me, if you can manage the saddlebags and the pony," unused to relying on others she hesitated, "let me help you," he said it slowly and deliberately, remembering how John had said she was not one for allowing people to help her. She nodded. It made the most sense. Her arms would be aching on the ride home and he was much stronger. Isabella, of course, agreed that the colonel should carry her.

"You are wet, too, Colonel," Helena gestured to his shirt observing how, in sticking to his chest, it contoured his muscles.

"I will survive," he smiled at her staring at his chest and strode off to mount Thor.

Helena bundled her daughter up well and handed her up to Nathaniel. He made sure he had Isabella, as securely as possible on his horse, and after confirming that Helena could manage to mount the mare by herself, headed back to Redway leaving her to catch up.

Isabella snuggled into his chest. His wet shirt was still plastered to him. Through the wet material, she could see the scar and following the ridge with her fingers, she could tell it went right across his chest. He felt her small fingers exploring and then heard her gasp and she looked around at Thor.

"I forgot to ask you, Colonel. What is your horse's name?"

"Thor," she gasped again. He wondered why and looked down at her face. She was looking back up at him in awe. Then he remembered the story, that was peppered with facts about him. From the child's perspective, it must seem like a character from a story had come to life.

"You kissed her and now you must marry," she almost whispered it.

"No, sweet girl," he said as gently as he could, "you have to think of your mother's feelings on this. You had a father once, who was a soldier."

"He died, before I was born," she was matter-of-fact.

"Yes, he did," he was not going to lie to her, "when that happened, your mother was very upset. It is hard to be alone. She runs the stable on her own and she looks after you."

"No, John helps in the stable, Ruth in the house and Rachel takes care of me."

"But you are *all* her responsibility, and you have been since your G-G-Papa died. When you are the one who makes all the decisions, all of the time, it is hard to let someone take that from you. She would feel that would happen if she married me," was he beginning to understand her a little better?

"When G-G-Papa died, I remember her crying a lot, but she is happier when you are here. I am happier," her pout appeared and she buried her head into his chest, just like her mother had done the day before.

"I am happier with you, too, sweet girl," he had taken to using Helena's term of affection for her child and held her closer to him. He did not want her to be upset and, in the same way of a father, would have done anything to relieve her of it, "sometimes, you have to be patient for good things to happen. Do you think you can be patient for me, and for your mother?"

"Yes, Colonel. I will try."

"Thank you. Here is your mother with the other horses. Hush now."

They completed the journey with very little said. When they got to the stable he carried the 'drowned rat' as he termed her, up to her rooms. As he left her with Rachel, Helena was coming out of another bedroom, that he presumed was hers and he caught a glimpse of her large bed, with a wooden headboard, ornately carved with horses. He swallowed hard and followed her down the stairs.

He was still in his shirtsleeves and she tried not to think of kissing him. Helena had picked up his coat once he was out of sight of her at the stream, she had hugged it to her and buried her face in it to smell his distinctly male smell. She handed it to him now.

"Please thank Mrs. Hopkins for her preparations for the picnic, and let her know we will get a clean, dry blanket back to her at the earliest opportunity," he nodded, "thank you, Colonel, for retrieving Isabella from the stream and bringing her home on Thor."

"You are both very welcome. Thank you for the wonderful day. If I am featured in any new stories, rescuing drowning Princesses, please let me know," he bowed and made to leave.

"I certainly will," she curtseyed.

Isabella had another lesson with Harriet, but Colonel Ackley did not show his face in the music room to hear the girl play, although she had asked after him. He made himself scarce knowing he had fallen in love with the little girl and possibly with her mother. Some distance was what was called for and he anticipated his orders would be arriving soon.

True to his word, Harker had produced a diamond tiara for Genevieve, to commemorate the birth of the heir of Eastease. Harriet had declared that it must be worn at a Christmas ball. It had been so long since there had been at ball at Eastease. Nathaniel decided that he would return then and see if his feelings were still the same for the red-headed Helena.

He received his orders the following day. After informing Harker and Genevieve, that he would be leaving for London, he rode over to Redway to say goodbye to Helena. In the same familiar way that Harriet had done, he crossed the fields of Eastease and Redway to arrive at the stable. He saw her astride either Perceval or Grenville, he could not tell them apart easily. She was putting the horse through its paces in the paddock behind the stable. John was watching and nodding, calling out instructions. Nathaniel tied Thor to a post, away from the paddock to avoid distracting the horse she was riding, and approached John. Looking at the notes, he ascertained that they were just finishing with this horse.

"Colonel," John pulled his forelock.

"John," the colonel nodded. Were they ever to be on friendly terms he wondered? Maybe not until they had tried to knock each other's teeth out, "he is a wonderful specimen."

"Indeed, got to get t'other one out in a minute. Buyer is taking possession at the end of the week," he looked over at Nathaniel, who was staring glumly out at Helena, "you are leaving."

"Yes, tomorrow," he turned to the man who was throwing up his hands in disgust, "I have orders. I am a soldier you know. I will be back."

Helena had halted the horse and dismounted. Bringing it over to John, "Perceval next then?" he took the reins and retreated, muttering.

"Are you two ever going to be friends?" she smiled at Nathaniel.

"I was wondering the same thing myself," he smiled back at her, "could I talk to you, please?"

"Yes, of course," John came back around with Perceval, "could you ride him today, please, John? I need to talk to the colonel."

"Yes, ma'am," the man entered the paddock with the horse and mounted him easily.

She looked at Nathaniel and suddenly wondered if he was going to ask her to marry him. She had been surprised the other day, that Isabella had not talked of it after they had kissed at the picnic, but the little girl had been surprisingly quiet, about that at least.

"I received my orders," he noticed that the panic he had seen in her face, when she had probably thought he might ask her to marry him, dissipated. Then, quickly it returned.

"You are not going back to Spain, are you?" she looked horrified and it gave him hope to know that she cared about him.

"Not yet. I am to report to London. I expect to be involved in strategy, training of officers and horses. At least until Christmas, when I hope to return to Eastease. I am to tell you that there will be a ball, to which you will be invited. Should I make it back for it, I would be honoured if you would save the first two dances for me."

"Yes, of course, and are you a good dancer?"

"I am the son of an Earl, of course I am a good dancer. What about you?"

"I am suddenly glad that my mother insisted on lessons. Actually, those lessons were the only thing my mother made me do, that I enjoyed." He looked in her eyes then, very seriously and held them for a long time, as if drinking her into his memory.

"Mrs. Andrews, Helena, do I ask too much? I mean, could you possibly see your way to write to me?" she made to speak, "no, no need to answer right now. This is the direction should you choose to write. It will find me wherever I am stationed. I would love to hear how things are going here, with the foals and with Miss Isabella. As well as any other musings you might like to share," he handed her a note.

"I do not need to think about it. I would love to write to you, as a dear friend. Is that acceptable?"

"Friends, then."

"Take care of yourself, Nathaniel," she curtseyed and offered her hand.

"Until Christmas, Helena," he bowed over her hand, turned it over so the palm faced upward and brushed it with his lips. Then he turned to leave. She curled her fingers around where he had kissed, as if to hold it in and brought her hand up to her heart.

Chapter Twelve

When James Dawley brought Isabella home after her music lesson later that day, Helena asked him if he would take something back with him that she had for Colonel Ackley. She need say no more. James was willing to help Mrs. Andrews in any way he could. Now that his mother was in a well-maintained house, her health had improved and he could visit her often. He agreed he would hide her gift within the colonel's luggage, so that he should find it after he left Eastease.

Nathaniel did not actually see it until he arrived at the Aysthill London House. One of the servants had unpacked his bag and left the shop wrapped gift on a side table by his bed, with a piece of folded paper and a sealed letter on top.

Curious, he sat on the side of the bed and opened the gift. A silk cravat in dark blue was nestled within and fixed to it sat a gold pin with the shape of a running horse embossed on it. The pin looked old and a little worn, but shone nonetheless. Unfolding the paper, he was surprised by the quality of the drawing of a scaly dragon. One of its sharp talons dripped with blood and a sword was embedded deep within the dragon's chest. The unfortunate dragon of Lincolnshire he presumed with a smile. Leaving those items on the bed, he picked up the letter and fingered the seal of Redway Acres. Knowing it must be from Helena, he savoured the moment before breaking the seal to read it.

Dearest Colonel Ackley,

Nathaniel, if I still have your permission.

I hope you will accept this cravat as a suitable replacement for yours, that was stained too much to clean. The darker blue will show your eyes even brighter. The pin was my grandfather's, a gift from my grandmother, and I rarely saw him without it. I searched for it recently, with the intention of giving it to you on our picnic, but it was so tarnished you had to wait for me to clean it. It shines well enough now, although a little dented, which adds some character in the same way of scars.

My grandfather would have liked you. He had your sense of humour and would enjoy playing tricks on his wife; much like you did to me, falling off Old Joe's roof last week. So, I think he would be happy for you to have his pin, as thanks for your assistance with Missy in the storm. The foal is doing nicely and I did decide to call him Chance.

Isabella has asked if she may write to you with her stories. Many of them include the brave soldier, Colonel Ackley! I hope you like the picture she put in with the cravat. That part of the storyline was yours, still I hope it is not too close to bad memories for you.

Isabella and I hope you travel safely to London, and think of Redway fondly, as Redway will be thinking of you. Your friend,

Helena Andrews

He ran a finger over her name and reread the letter. He was touched that she should give him something of her grandfather's, and it pleased him that she related scars as character. He hoped that when she said *'Redway will be thinking of you'*, she actually meant she would, as he had thought of her often on the ride south.

Striding out of the bedroom, he made his way to the study to pen a reply that was already forming in his head.

Dearest Helena,

I hope I am not being too presumptuous using your given name. Of course, you still have permission to use mine.

You are far too generous buying me an elegant cravat, and very secretive hiding it within my belongings. There was no need for a replacement; my other one was certainly lost to a good cause. It is gratefully received, however, and when I am unable to wear it, due to uniform regulations, be assured that I will have it safe in a pocket about my person, with the pin and an artistic rendering of the Dragon of Lincolnshire.

I am honoured to wear something that was your grandfather's and I would love to hear more of him in our letters. I believe that I would have liked him, too. I should apologise for the trick of falling off the roof. I saw the pain in your eyes, when you talked to Isabella of how dangerous it was. I had not considered that you had witnessed violent death before, albeit in different circumstances. Not realising in those few moments, that I was safe, you would have had a fair picture in your mind, of what you might turn the corner to find. Please accept my sincere apology, dear lady.

Chance is an excellent name. Of course, I would say so, as I was the one to suggest it, but given the circumstances of his birth, chance played a large part.

I would love to read Isabella's stories. She has a wonderful imagination, something that, too soon, the realities of life can tear from us. Her gift is to share what she loves and I would be honoured if she were to share them with me.

I do not have much to report, except that I am arrived safely in London. I report for my duties tomorrow and promised my mother that, when I had time, I should visit Bainbridge in Norfolk. My Father's cousin, Lady Agnes, is a widow and the whole family concerns themselves with her business interests. However, it seems I am the only one who can be pressed upon to report on them.

Please continue to write with more news of Redway and Eastease. I am only gone a few days and I feel it could easily be two months. Your's

Nathaniel Ackley (Col.)

In Lincolnshire, September moved into October uneventfully. Time at Redway Acres was spent caring for and training of horses. The foals continued to grow and flourish, as did the new heir at Eastease. His parents doted on him. He had the dark curly hair of his father, but in striking contrast, the pale blue eyes of his mother.

Having chosen the piece of land where she wanted her teaching garden, Genevieve started to plan. The Eastease gardeners got underway with walling and gating the large area, so it should be safe for young children to run around in and not escape to the lake beyond.

Harriet continued to teach Isabella the pianoforte, and the girl was getting competent very quickly. She often lamented to Harriet, how she missed Colonel Ackley. She reminded her how he had sat and listened to her play, and then, when he had driven her home, they had seen the smoke of the Dragon of Lincolnshire. Sometimes she would embellish on that story, saying they actually confronted the Dragon and the colonel saw him off with a flash of his sword.

At least once a week Helena, Harriet and Genevieve would meet at Eastease for some luncheon. They would coo over Master Harker and talk of their plans for the Christmas ball. Harriet had been horrified to learn, that Helena had intended to wear the same gown, that she had worn to the dinner at the end of August. She insisted that they find one of her own ballgowns, which would certainly be long enough, and arrange to let the bodice out to accommodate Helena's curves.

Trying it on in Harriet's dressing room had been embarrassing. Most of the time she completely forgot about the scar on her back, a reminder from the general, when he had brought the crop down on her as she had protected Pegasus. The cream gown that, Harriet declared perfect for her, had a low back and the top of the scar was visible.

Naturally Genevieve and Harriet had been horrified to see it, but Helena told them the truth, so far as they needed to know it. She had been protecting a horse from a beating, when the man had brought the crop down on her back. When they asked what had become of the man, she said simply that the horse had kicked him in the head and killed him.

After that they turned to the problem of concealing it. Powder would disappear over the course of the evening, and Harriet insisted wearing a shawl would spoil the neckline completely. So, they agreed that she could have one swath of hair fall from the top of her head and wave down her back. It should swish sufficiently that no one should be sure of what they had seen, if it was noticed. Harriet secretly felt it was a talisman of her friend's bravery.

As they perused and tweaked the guest list, Gennie and Helena teased Harriet about whom she might dance with. Certainly, there were some eligible men who should be attending, but no one had caught her eye. In retaliation to their teasing, Harriet did a little teasing of her own.

"Helena will probably want to dance with Cousin Nathaniel all evening," she had exclaimed.

"Well, he has asked me for the first two," she confessed. Harriet was thrilled, "but we are only friends my dear," Helena had told her, "so no meddling!" However, an idea had occurred to Harriet and she planned to write to Nathaniel as soon as she may. She may even be prepared to visit Bainbridge while he was there, to see her plan through.

A fortnight later, Helena was disturbed from her work, by the arrival of an unexpected delivery. Two men came into the house carrying a small pianoforte. Ruth asked her where to put it, so they found room in the formal sitting room, moving some furniture around to fit it. The older man in the crew handed her two letters and departed with a handsome fee, for helping them with the furniture rearrangements. One letter was addressed to Helena and the other to her daughter.

Isabella came running down from her rooms with Rachel, to see what had arrived. She was thrilled with the instrument and wondered whom it was for, and where it had come from.

"I should imagine it is for you, sweet girl. I do not know of anyone else here, who plays the pianoforte. What does your letter say?" she handed it to her, surreptitiously placing her own letter in her hidden skirt pocket. Her daughter would want her to read it aloud with Ruth and Rachel present, and she did not want to deal with their suspicion of there being more to her friendship with the colonel. The girl sat on the instrument's stool, kicking her legs in happiness, and read out the letter, with the aid of Rachel.

Dear Five-year old Miss Andrews,

I have been given to understand that you recently had a Birthday and that you have no instrument of your own, upon which to practice your lessons.

I hope you will accept this gift, as my effort to rectify this situation, and that you have many happy hours playing your sweet music. My only payment, would be to hear your improved playing upon my return to Eastease and Redway. I am, as always, your dutiful dragon slayer.

Colonel Ackley

The rest of the day, she did not get a moment alone to read her letter and had to wait until she was in her own bed. Retrieving it from her pocket and climbing into bed she read it by the light of her candle. In her last letter, and they had exchanged several since he had left, she had not had a lot to say but had talked of her latest meeting with Mr. Brooks. As he had requested after the dinner at Eastease, they discussed the bible and she asked him pointed questions about it. She was curious about the way the bible could be interpreted and put some of her own interpretations to him. It was interesting to have these conversations, but she, in no way, was interested in Mr. Brooks as a man and it seemed his fleeting interest in her, as a woman, had passed. She was unsurprised therefore, when her visits to the clergyman were one of the things Nathaniel addressed. From his words, particularly at the end, she could be in no doubt that he was not happy about it.

Dearest Helena,

I hope that you are not angry with me, for presuming to purchase such a large piece of furniture for your home. I know from personal experience, that practise every day is the best way to learn an instrument. My only wish, is that I could have been there to see Isabella's reaction to its arrival. If you can indulge me with a description, that will have to be sufficient.

How are things at Redway? It is very cold, although it is only October. I hope you have things in order for the winter. I would be happy to advise you in any of this, though I am sure John has it all in hand.

Have you been back to visit Mr. Brooks? I wonder how often you visit each other? Please be careful of people talking, village news can soon turn into expectations of more from a friendship. Unless of course, that is the way you are thinking, which I admit would be a surprise to me. If so, you had better stop writing to me, though I confess, that I would miss our interactions.

By the time you read this, I will be at Bainbridge Hall, visiting Lady Agnes Bainbridge, and you may send your reply directly there. You know of my family's desires for me to marry her daughter, Lady Grace. I loath to visit and encourage their views, however, I promised Mother that I would report back to the family on how the businesses of Bainbridge are faring.

I am back writing this letter after my evening meal. I admit, that I did drink more glasses of wine than I usually might, as the thought of you thinking of that idiot Brooks, in anyway other than your local clergyman, is disturbing my peace of mind. Please, assure me that you will not consider a proposal from him until I return to Lincolnshire at Christmas. Do not forget, that you have promised me the first two dances at the Eastease ball. I will hold you to your word, even if you are married. Always, Your's

Nathaniel

Lying back against the pillows, she hugged the letter to her nightgown-clad chest and smiled. The man could charm, annoy and please her all in one letter. Charmed by the gift he had given Isabella, when she knew he did not have a lot of money to spare and asking her to describe her daughter's reaction when it arrived. Annoyance at his assumption, so typical of a man, that she would not have the stable in hand for the winter, when they had started their preparations even before he left for London. Pleasure in the last part of his letter, when, obviously inebriated, he had allowed his feelings to flow through to the quill and did not discard this version in the light of day before posting it.

She set the letter aside, deciding she should write a reply first thing in the morning. As she willed sleep to come to her, her mind spun out the words and phrases she should write to him. She would have to write to him at Bainbridge Hall. The thought came to her then, that if he thought she was interested in Mr. Brooks, he may change his mind about marrying his cousin. What difference would that make to her though, when she insisted she would not marry? Not sure of that answer, but sighing in frustration, as she knew she would not sleep until she had the words down on paper to ease his mind about Mr. Brooks. She relit her candle and padded down to the drawing room, to sit at the desk and write to him.

The fire had been banked down, but soon lit up again as she burned draft after draft, dissatisfied with her efforts. Finally, she felt she had it right. The easy part had been describing her daughter's happiness over his generous gift; easier still, given her annoyance, she took him to task over doubting her abilities to prepare Redway for winter. The harder part was her response to him exposing his feelings. She felt his bravery at doing so, deserved that she should respond with honesty of her own feelings, but she could not raise his expectations of a future with her either. At some point, he would want to marry and, as it would not be to her, it would break her heart. But there was nothing she could do about that, she was already in love with him. Finally, she allowed the words to flow as he had. Then, without rereading it and before her courage deserted her, she folded and sealed it, giving it the direction to Bainbridge as he had advised.

Leaving the letter on the desk and burning the remaining discarded drafts on the fire, she lay down on the couch and finally, exhausted of the words and phrases that had consumed her, she fell asleep. In the morning, Ruth found her there and seeing the letter to the colonel on the desk she scooped it up to get it to the post coach with the child's own letter of thanks; leaving her mistress to sleep a little longer.

The last time Nathaniel had visited Bainbridge, was after the Harkers' wedding the previous year. He had brought Harriet with him, so the newlyweds could be left in peace for a while. He shared guardianship of Harriet with Harker, but often the responsibility fell more to the other man, because of the colonel's military commitments. Harriet was not keen on visiting her Great Aunt, who was Aunt to her stepfather, but she always referred to her as 'Aunt Agnes'.

Lady Agnes was a rather timid person, who had become more so after her husband's death. Her daughter, Grace, an only child who had enjoyed all the love and no censure of both her father and mother, found fault in everyone except herself. Her own mother was not immune to her criticism, although she did try to temper it when Nathaniel was present. Her way of making herself seem more attractive or accomplished was to find fault in those around her. So, although he knew Harriet would not be happy, he wished she was there, as Bainbridge without her was a dismal affair!

He had arrived the day the pianoforte was delivered to Redway, and began with his ritual of touring the grounds. Two days later, Helena's response to that gift and his own revealing letter, arrived. As was her want, his cousin perused the post that was brought to her on a tray, before waving the butler over to Nathaniel. He picked up the three letters for him and though his heart was beating fast, it thankfully was belied in his expression.

"I see Harriet is writing to you. What does she have to say?" he had not even broken the seal.

"When I have read it, Cousin, I will read out anything pertinent to you," ignoring his surliness, she got to her real interest.

"Are the others very interesting? I do not recognise the seal."

"Not at all, I assure you."

She noticed him pocket them and narrowed her eyes. "'Not at all'?" she thought, "he lies confidently I can give him that." She would know the content of those letters before the day was out, or at the very latest the following morning. Unaware of his cousin's plans, the colonel read Harriet's letter. She teased him about asking Helena for the first two dances. It pleased him to know that Helena had been speaking of him to Harriet, and no doubt Genevieve had been with them, too. His smile was not lost on Grace.

"What does Harriet say that is so amusing then, Nathaniel?" she demanded. He had read on and thankfully came to a part of the letter he could share.

"She is to visit here. Actually, she arrives today. Has Cousin Agnes received a letter to that effect?" he was surprised she had not shared it if she had.

"No, indeed she has not," she was cross now, although the arrival of her cousin could hardly cause her distress. Bainbridge servants would have to make some swift changes to air out rooms, but certainly Grace should have little to do, "this is the ill-breeding of that Hopwood girl rubbing off on her. Harker would never have let her travel without informing Mother first."

Grace was not happy that Harker had married a woman with little to her name and one that did not defer to her regarding her own cousin's upbringing. She felt that Mark should have appointed her mother and then herself, when she was of age, as guardian to the two young girls, rather than two men. Nathaniel thought she had aimed to marry Harker, joining Bainbridge and Eastease together and sharing his guardianship of her cousins.

"You mean Mrs. Harker I believe," he said mischievously, knowing she would start a rant about Genevieve, that he need not listen to and could, therefore, focus on the rest of Harriet's letter. She had decided that she had had enough of Alexander and Gennie cooing over their son and making 'moon eyes', as she called them, at each other. She planned to stay with him at Bainbridge and when he left, she would, too. From there she would travel to Thornbane Lodge, in Cambridgeshire, to collect Genevieve's sister, Martha, who should be staying at Eastease until it was warm enough to travel back in the New Year.

Whilst at Bainbridge, she wanted to practise some music for the ball and she wanted him to help. He was not sure what his cousin was up to, but he had a feeling she was meddling.

Nathaniel really wanted to read Helena's letter in private, as soon as possible. So, making noises to the effect that he was going to go and talk to the groundskeeper, he left his cousin still muttering about the 'insufferable girl'.

He decided to take a brisk walk where he remembered a large felled tree trunk, he could sit upon it and read his letters. He hurried to keep himself warm and get there as soon as possible. He hardly remembered what he had written in his own letter about her relationship with Mr. Brooks, but he knew that he had overstepped the bounds of friendship and hoped she did not push him away because of it. Finally, here was the log.

Dearest Nathaniel,

I wonder how you manage to please, vex and perplex me in a single missive?

Firstly, let me thank you for your kindness to my sweet girl. Isabella has already written you her note of thanks. I think the gift might make an appearance in a new story, as we talked of how the princess who played it might make magical music and the effect of the music will depend on the mood she is in when she plays. But I fear I have already given away too much of the storyline.

When it arrived, she was astounded and wondered whom it was for and who it was from. Both questions were answered swiftly by your letter and she was thrilled beyond measure. Immediately she had to play a tune for us. I was astonished to find that she could play a piece by heart, that she learned from Harriet! My daughter is far more talented than I.

Suffice to say that you have made a young, five-year-old feel very grown up and special, to receive such a present. Anything that can make her smile gladdens my heart, so your gift has made two people very happy.

Having garnered my favour thus, you then proceed to vex me into throwing up my hands and declaring 'How can men be so insufferable?' I think that it must be something you are taught in your education, while women are taught posture, sewing and an instrument.

Here at Redway, plans for the winter were started BEFORE you left for London. John and a team of half our staff, had been working on setting the property straight and making sure of our supplies. He certainly does have it all in hand, as you say, but it was under MY direction, whilst I worked with the remaining staff on the daily duties of the stable. I do thank you for your concern, but I certainly do NOT thank you for your assumptions.

You perplex me with your comment of Mr. Brooks. I agree that he possibly had some interest in me at first, but thankfully, it was short-lived. I certainly have no interest in him as a man, but we have lively discussions about God, the bible and the church. I think he hopes to save my soul, whereas I find these visits more interesting than attending church. A negligence for which he no longer reproaches me. If there is a God and He is good, and if I am as good a person as I can be, because I firmly believe that we all have a responsibility to help the people we meet, then I see no reason He should spurn me. However, if He were to, then I do not want to know HIM.

I am able to assure you, that I will not consider a proposal from Mr. Brooks. As I have told you several times, I have no intention of marrying anyone, so the first two dances of the ball remain safely, yours.

Confusion is disturbing MY peace of mind, regarding your situation with your cousin, Lady Grace. Surely it would be of greatest benefit for you to marry her and live comfortably at Bainbridge Hall? My parents live on the outskirts of a village southeast of there, so I know it well, although we were never in the sphere of receiving an invitation.

You say you hate the thought of me thinking in terms of marriage to Mr. Brooks, and I find it equally detestable that you might think of marrying your cousin, and yet how can I ask you not to, when I have set our boundaries to friendship and will not marry. I wish I had the power to change the law, so that a married woman did not lose her very existence to her husband. It was not something I gave much thought to with regards to myself, but then I had never met a man that I could feel that way about, because I had not met you.

I am saying too much and do not have the excuse of too much wine. It is the middle of the night, and I am sitting at my desk in my nightgown, by the light of one candle and the fire, that is burning brightly with all my discarded drafts. I will do you the same honour, of sealing this letter before I change my mind on what I have said, and feed it to the hungry flames.

Although I belong to no one, I am only... Your's

Helena

Chapter Thirteen

Harriet and Mrs. Cornock, her travelling companion, arrived at Bainbridge later that day. Harriet was hoping that her resolve to be a little bolder, would hold firm in the presence of her cousin, Lady Grace Bainbridge. Helena and Gennie had made her practise holding herself straight and using a stronger voice, while speaking to Lady Grace. Gennie had held court, with an admirable imitation of her, and Harriet, with encouragement from Helena, had tried out some things to say.

Opportunity came more quickly than she had expected, when she was directly summoned to that Lady. Nathaniel came out of the Bainbridge study, where he had been perusing the mountains of papers Lady Agnes neglected, to greet his cousin, only to see her retreating form heading into the afternoon sitting room. He scampered after her, eager to protect her from the scathing comments Grace had obviously been working on since her discovery of the impending visit, only to be brought up short by Harriet's usually gentle voice reaching his ears from right across the room.

"I apologise, madam, that you did not receive a personal letter from me informing you of my arrival. I am sure you must have assumed that I did write one, as would be proper, and that it must have been mislaid in the post coach. I am grateful that I thought to mention it in my letter to Nathaniel and that he was able to inform you, so that my arrival was not a complete surprise. I hope that gave Smythe and the chambermaids sufficient time, to make their usual, excellent arrangements for myself and Mrs. Cornock," she turned to the Bainbridge butler at this and received a nod in affirmation. Satisfied she added, "if you would excuse me, Cousin. It has been a long journey, Mrs. Cornock and I would like to refresh ourselves in our rooms. I hope if we return in an hour, that would be acceptable to you?" without waiting for an answer, she turned and exited the room, passing Nathaniel at the door.

"Colonel," she said, with a small smile that only he could see. He gave her a quick wink and followed her out, before a stunned Grace could call either of them back.

He headed back to the study and stood looking at the papers he had been trying to concentrate on. He ran a hand over his face breaking into a huge smile, as he realised the work of Genevieve and Helena, in Harriet's dealing with her cousin. He was thrilled for the young woman. He knew she had a spine of steel, now she was learning how to wield it.

As Harriet's guardian, he was proud of her and profoundly grateful to the two wonderful women he and Harker had found.

He was, getting ahead of himself again. Helena was not his, not yet, but perhaps at Christmas. He wished her letter was clear, but it was not. Probably her ideas were not clear, because she still talked of not marrying and yet implied that if she were to marry, she would be willing to marry him. Not only that, but only him, as she had never considered a man before, had never thought she would. He wished that he could show the letter to Harriet to discover what another woman thought of it. In truth he should burn it, given its content and the location in which he found himself. He resolved to keep it on his person at all times, even in sleep.

After dinner that evening, he elected to forgo his usual cigar and withdraw with the women. Harriet, who had continued to speak in what he now termed her *'Bainbridge voice'* throughout dinner, disappeared to her rooms momentarily and returned with her music papers. Rifling through them, she found the piece she wanted and asked his assistance in turning the pages.

He recognised at once that it was a piece from the same Beethoven opera that Helena had sung from. This piece was the aria of Florestan, the husband of Leonore, whom she was trying to rescue from political prison. He looked at her pointedly.

"I have been practising this piece for the Eastease ball," she gave him an innocent look, "what do you think, Cousin?" she started to play and he followed along, turning the pages as needed, but realising, quite quickly, that she could play the whole piece by heart. The words, in German, as they had been before, were written below the notes and as he followed, he translated. The imprisoned man was desolate, pleading to God and accepting his fate as his duty, but then toward the end saw an angel who looked like his wife. As he knew from Helena's aria that the wife was dressing as a guard to rescue him, he supposed that it was actually his wife that he mistook for an angel.

"I think, as always, that your playing is magnificent," she came to the end of the piece and Grace called from the other end of the room that she needed to practise more.

"Quite so, ma'am," she said easily, allowing her voice to carry across the room, "that is why I brought the piece with me. It is a tenor piece and I was just telling Nathaniel, I was sure he could sing it. What do you think?" she smiled sweetly at him as he rolled his eyes, out of the view of Lady Grace.

"I think you should," the other lady was saying, "you could cover up Harriet's mistakes with a voice like yours, Nathaniel." Grace had been watching the two of them interact, *'thick as thieves'* was the term that came to mind. He was far too indulgent of the young girl. She would put paid to that once they were married, as she would be the one he would indulge. She did like the way his eyes shone brighter when he wore that dark, blue cravat. She imagined it was a new purchase for her benefit, and smiled.

"I think that might be the other way around, Cousin, but I see I am outnumbered, so I will try my best," they practised the piece two times and even managed a smattering amount of applause from the ladies. During the second performance, Nathaniel noticed Smythe come into the room and speak in a quiet voice to Lady Grace. As he did so, she looked over at Nathaniel and narrowed her eyes. She whispered something quietly back to Smythe and he had exited.

"I should invite the local Doctor, who is the son of Mr. Grosvenor, over for dinner and you can garner his opinion," she offered, when the piece ended again, "he is in need of a wife Harriet. You would be lucky to make a connection there and you would live closer to me, so I could take care of your interests."

It was Harriet's turn to roll her eyes and he read her mind easily, *"why would I want to live closer to Cousin Grace?"*

That night, the colonel lay in bed, contemplating Helena's letter once again. He had reread it many times and now it lay under his pillow. He was sure his belongings had been searched, but as both Helena's and Isabella's letters had been in his coat pocket, with all the others from Redway, they had not been found. He had worn the blue silk cravat, but had hidden the pin behind the knots to avoid answering questions about it.

He was getting used to sleepless nights, he supposed it came with being in love, because as surely as it was dark outside, he was in love with Helena Andrews. As much as he thought of her declaration of marrying him, had she the inclination to marry, he thought of her sitting at her writing desk, clad in nothing but her nightgown, as she wrote to him. He could summon up the image to his mind easily, from his memory of her at the window of an Eastease bedroom. His body reacted to the picture in his mind and he moved his hand around his hardness, but stopped as the door of his bedroom opened with a slight creak.

Had he not been awake already he should not have heard it. He closed his eyes, as a young boy with a single candle crept into the room and set the candle on the dresser. He began to search through the colonel's clothes from that evening.

Finding nothing, the boy turned and looked toward the bed. Nathaniel had closed his eyes enough to look asleep, but still be able to peer through his eyelids. He kept his breathing even. Leaving the candle where it was, the boy stepped lightly toward the bed and looked at the sleeping man. He had seen him striding around the house in the past few days. The man seemed a bit soft, he thought, smiled a lot. It should not be too hard to slip his small hand under the pillow and feel there for the letter Smythe wanted. If he was caught, the colonel *might* beat him, but if he did not find this letter, Smythe definitely would.

The man's hand moved quickly and grasped his wrist in a vice like grip. He did not utter a sound, but tried to pull free. Nathaniel had him fast. Davy was impressed at the colonel's speed. He was light and quick with his own hands out of necessity. It was the only way to get enough food.

"Stop struggling, Davy. Is Smythe outside my door?" he whispered. Davy nodded, surprised that the colonel knew his name. Nathaniel had seen him often. He was such a small boy, that they used him to clean the many chimneys of Bainbridge. He had already developed a cough, that Nathaniel had heard over the few days he had been there and he doubted the boy's chances of making the age of ten. He had talked to Lady Agnes before, of new devices that could replace the need for a child. She had refused. "He wanted you to find a letter?" he got another nod.

Nathaniel looked the boy over. He needed an ally, but an ally needed incentive for allegiance. He took in the sharp, blue eyes, sandy blonde hair curling slightly and full of coal dust. A thought came to him, "who is your mother?" he was half afraid of the answer.

"Mary Beckett, she was a servant here, but died having me. They said she was only young. No other family." He released a breath he had been holding. He did not know a Mary Beckett, so this child was not his. Since his night in the storm with Helena, he had found a few of his assignations, to be sure there had been no consequences. It had never crossed his mind to do so, until he found out about her experience. Such was the effect she had on him.

He put his finger to his lips, slipped the bundle of letters out from under his pillow and tucked them into his nightshirt pocket. He let go of Davy's arm as he got out of bed, confident that the boy would not leave without the letters, and moved to the desk in his room. Picking up a few pieces of paper, he moved to the fireplace and put a corner of a page to the dying embers. It caught alight immediately. Competently, he blew out the flame to leave the corners he held intact. He moved back to the boy, who had been watching him intently.

"Take these to Smythe. Tell him you searched my things and under my pillow, but could not find the letters. You did however find this in the hearth and wondered if I had burned them," he smiled at the boy, who returned the smile thinking it fun to trick Smythe, who was a bully, "do this and keep stumm, and I will take you with me when I leave."

The boy looked at him warily, "do you like horses?" another nod and a grin, "I am going to Lincolnshire at Christmas, to a place where they raise horses. I can get you some work there and somewhere to live. What do you think?"

"Do they not have chimney boys, sir? Is that why they need me?" he felt suddenly protective of the boy and angry at his cousin for her treatment of him.

"No more chimneys, Davy. Horses. You would learn to take care of horses. Be outside a lot," a huge smile cracked the boy's face, and then he unexpectedly hugged the colonel, "I will take that as a yes. Be ready, I will give you the nod when I leave."

On the second day of Harriet's visit, she took a walk out with Colonel Ackley. It was cold, but sunny, and they walked the path from the house that skirted the boundary of Bainbridge, along the Fairfield Market Road. Nathaniel assumed that was the one that led to Helena's parents' house. There were trees on either side of the pathway and leaves crunched under their feet, making a pleasing sound. Nathaniel commended Harriet on her newfound bravery when speaking with her cousin and she told him of the help she received from Helena and Gennie.

He told Harriet of his encounter with Davy the night before and his suspicions, that Grace was trying to find his letters from Helena and Issie, "she may try to get intelligence from you, of Mrs. Andrews."

They discussed how much she should reveal about her. She agreed only to talk of her as her friend and nothing of his interest in her, providing he told her something of their interactions. As she already suspected them of being caught in the storm together, he told her of that day. He talked of the birth of Missy's foal, but left out Helena's story from before she came to Redway.

"Nathaniel, you should have offered to marry her!" she exclaimed, horrified.

"Dearest Harriet, you are young yet and see things so simply. If you know your friend at all, then you know her to be an independent woman. I did of course offer, if it were to become known, to do what was honourable. I was a gentleman that night Harriet, you must know that of me. Why would I want to force her into a marriage she does not want?"

"Why would she not want to marry you?" her loyalty made him smile.

"It is not that she does not want to marry me, but that she does not want to be married. In law, when a woman marries, she is considered under the protection of her husband. Everything she is, everything she has, becomes his. You should understand this, for when the time comes that you wish to marry. I have to give her time to get to know me and know that I would be good to her. She needs to know that she can trust in me."

Harriet was thrilled that Nathaniel was in love with her friend and absolutely believed her friend returned that love.

She asked him about the horse pin she had noticed in the folds of his cravat, as they sat close together at the pianoforte the night before. He confirmed Helena had given it to him. "The cravat too I imagine, as it makes your eyes look even bluer."

They had dinner that evening with Doctor Grosvenor as promised. Even Lady Grace would not discuss family matters with company present. He was a pleasant man whose particular interest was amputees. After dinner when partaking of a cigar with the colonel, they discussed the matter. Nathaniel was able to talk to him of Tommy. He had received letters from his friend thanking him for the money, telling him of his father's passing and of his own experiments in making himself a wooden leg. He gave the Doctor Tommy's address so that he could contact him.

It was not until the following afternoon, when they were having tea, that Lady Grace got her opportunity to broach the subject of Harriet's friend, Mrs. Andrews. Nathaniel and Harriet had not expected such a direct line of attack and looked at each other shocked. Satisfied to have finally cracked Nathaniel's implacable façade when asked personal questions, she went in for the kill.

"I understand there is to be a ball at Eastease, this Christmas."

"Cousin Grace, have you read my letter?" she shuddered at his voice and avoided looking at him.

"If you will leave it lying around," she pulled Harriet's letter out of a concealed pocket and waved it in the air. Knowing full well he had left it in his rooms and Smythe had probably found it on his first search, he stood up and retrieved it from her, saying it did not mean that she had to read it, "I did not know it was not mine, until I had read the first few lines."

"Madam, the *first* line reads *'Dear Nathaniel',*" she waved dismissively at him. He was as furious with himself as he was with his cousin. He had thought to conceal Helena's letters and those of her daughter, as well as the pin, but did not even consider Harriet's letter. Therein, it mentioned about him asking Helena for the first two dances.

"What does it matter when we are all family, Nathaniel?" she turned to the young woman, "Harriet, tell me of Mrs. Andrews."

"There is not much to tell, Cousin," Harriet had never seen Nathaniel so angry and she aimed to help him by talking of Helena as they had discussed the previous day, "she is a widow and runs the stable situated next to Eastease. Her grandfather died a year ago and left it to her. You know how much I love to ride and she has the most delightful foals right now."

"What is her age?"

"I am not exactly sure. At least five and twenty, I should think. Her daughter is five years old."

"She is invited to this Christmas ball?"

"Yes, many of the neighbours are invited," here Harriet listed several and talked of them hoping Nathaniel, who had marched to the window and was looking out, was getting his temper back under control. She was losing her nerve, as she had just recalled that her letter had mentioned her teasing Helena about Nathaniel asking her to dance.

"And Nathaniel here, sees fit to ask her for the first two dances?"

"Well, Mrs. Andrews does not go to dances and was rather nervous about attending a ball, what with Eastease being so grand. Nathaniel was being gallant and putting her at ease. I am sure that is all."

Lady Grace let the matter drop. She could see that Harriet had found her spine and she did not want to push Nathaniel into declaring something for this woman. Hopefully, he was only sowing some wild oats. He would see sense, once he was done playing soldier, and settle down with her at Bainbridge. She should keep her eye on him though. She was not pleased, not pleased at all!

At Redway, Helena had been waiting for a reply, to her letter to Nathaniel. When she had awoken the morning after writing it, she had lain on the couch wondering why she was there and recalled the letter. She would have to rewrite it. She could not possibly send it, given its content. He would be horrified. What if the letter was to get into the wrong hands? She had walked over to the desk, but the letter had not been there. Looking out of the window she had realised how late it was. Ruth must have come in and picked it up.

For the umpteenth time, she groaned and rested her head in her hands, when would she get a reply? Harriet would be with him at Bainbridge Hall by now. She wondered if he would get time to reply to her from there. He was to be there for a fortnight. She could not wait that long. It might be easier to get into a carriage and drive down to Norfolk.

What was she thinking? Ever since she met this man, her life had seemed in turmoil. She was preoccupied with thinking of him, when she had more important Redway Acres business requiring her attention. She still felt she was leading him toward a proposal that she could not accept and that was unfair. Her feelings were such, however, that never seeing him again seemed unacceptable. It was as she was pondering this last thought, that the post finally arrived.

Ruth smiled as she pounced on it. She had railed at her housekeeper for most of this past week for picking up that letter. Ruth, however, did not regret it. Her girl needed a push toward this handsome soldier, in her opinion. He was good for her, would be good for Redway and certainly good for Miss Isabella, who already adored him, as much as he obviously did her.

Running up to her bedroom for privacy, Helena sat in the upright chair in the corner and brought her knees up to her chin in a childlike pose. She rested the unopened letter on top of her knees and placed her cheek on it, grasping her hands together, as she wrapped her arms around her legs. This was a moment that was exquisite, between happiness and pain, with the outcome decided as soon as she opened the letter. If she did not open it, then the pain would not come, if he had not been happy with her reply. If she did open it, she might not experience the pain, as he may be happy and her own happiness could burst forth. Huffing out a breath, she broke the seal and unfolded the letter.

Helena,

Firstly, let me say that your last letter was most gratefully received. I am sure that you have waited with trepidation for this reply, as I did your last one. I am endeavouring to keep our correspondence in friendship, but you know what I feel for you is more than that. I am afraid to push you if you are not ready, because I do not want you to push me away. I am satisfied to know, that if there were to be anyone significant in your life, you would want it to be me.

I want you to know that I feel the same way. While in London, I looked for the women that I have taken before. Not for the same purpose, but to be sure that I had not left them with consequences. I am not sure what I would have done, had I discovered any, but I hope that I would have done something to aid them. One or two of the women were happy to see me and to offer more of the same, but I declined. If I were to lie with another woman, I would only wish I was with you and how would that be fair? If there is not to be you, then how can there be anyone else? See how you have affected my behaviour. I would have considered myself an honourable man before.

I assure you, that I will never propose to my cousin. Let that thought trouble you no more. She has been trying to get hold of your letters to me. She hates to think that something is going on in my life, that she knows nothing of. I thought I had been outwitting her, however I forgot to keep Harriet's letter about my person and she found it in my rooms and read it. It contains how Harriet discussed our dancing at the upcoming ball with you and now my cousin is pursuing information about you. She is displeased and that is when she is at her most formidable. She barely hid the fact that she had my things searched for your letters. The woman has no shame.

I know you will hardly be able to believe this, but she sent a small boy to my rooms one night, to retrieve your letters from under my pillow while I slept. I stopped him, of course. My sleeping of late has not been that deep, something you have a considerable amount to do with. I burned some paper in the fire and gave the boy burned pieces to show the butler. I should have burned your letters so she has no hope of reading them. Although I have committed them to memory, I cannot bring myself to do it.

Davy, is about six years old and I am ashamed to tell you, that they use him as the chimney sweep, for the many flues here at Bainbridge. He already has a cough and they keep him underfed so he fits in the chimneys. I plan to abduct him! He is in favour. I have promised him stable work and horses by Christmas and I hope that is favourable to you. I think he needs you.

Please know that I am not his sire. He looks so like me, that I had to ask who is mother was, but I did not know her. She died in childbirth. He says she was very young. What do you say to a new apprentice?

Please would you accept my thanks and pass them on to Genevieve, too, for helping Harriet face her cousin. She has been respectfully outspoken, held her ground, when questioned about you, and played the pianoforte marvellously. Lady Grace, of course, still finds fault, as she always will, but Harriet bears it well and does not let it affect her, which of course takes the wind out of Grace's sails.

I have not partaken of too much wine this time. I want you to know, that my feelings for you are not conditional on whether you return them, nor are they dependent on marriage. They just are and forever more will be. I do not believe that our story has played out to the fullest yet, so let us move forward, step by step until we see it through to the end. Whatever that may be.

I am as always, Your's,

Nathaniel.

Happiness was the outcome. Her fears of his displeasure washed away with his wonderful words, and tears of relief coursed down her cheeks. *'My feelings for you'* he had mentioned, although he had not stated clearly what they were. That they were not conditional in anyway, alleviated some of her concern over his expectations. But if not marriage, how would their story end, if not in heartbreak? A man like Nathaniel would not want only friendship forever, and her body's reaction to the dreams of kissing him, that were happening almost every night, seemed to demand something that she suspected was only permissible between husband and wife.

Christmas seemed too far away.

Chapter Fourteen

Colonel Ackley rode out from Bainbridge, to find the house of the Billingses. Helena had said they lived on the outskirts of the village over to the southeast, so she must have meant Fairfield Market. He was not sure this was his wisest course of action and felt some unease while he travelled the few miles. However, while he had the opportunity, he was determined to find out what he could of the family that had produced the woman who had captured his heart, and why they had deserted her in her time of need.

He was wrapped up well as it was a cold, late October day. Arriving at the village he found the local tavern, and decided to warm himself and partake of a rousing beer. He asked the barkeep if he knew of the Billingses and where he might find their house. The scrawny man looked down at the coin the colonel was flicking between his fingers and pointed to a young man of about twenty, who he called Master Billings.

Master Billings was not a tall man, but he was certainly large in other areas of his person, as his belly stuck out far enough to touch the table rim and his fat fingers did not all fit in his tankard handle. So, this was Helena's brother. He could see no resemblance at all between the siblings. The colonel estimated he could take the man down in five seconds, but would have to be sure to avoid him toppling on him. He nodded to the barkeep and spun the coin into the air, to the man's outstretched hand.

As Master Billings rode his horse slowly home, Colonel Ackley followed him. His task was made much easier because the man was oblivious of his surroundings and slightly inebriated. He located the Billings household two miles out of the village and took in his assessment of it. Certainly, it was small in comparison to Bainbridge or Eastease, but it was a good-sized country home. Riding around a few hedgerow-bordered lanes, he ascertained it had a reasonable amount of land with it, but no small holdings. All the family money, therefore, must come from the mills and mines she had said her father owned. It was not as substantial as Redway, but if you added in the mills and mines, the estate probably earned more money.

He rode up to the front of the house, dismounted and rapped loudly on the door. It was probably a good twenty minutes since the younger man of the house had returned from his drinking. He gave the maid his card and asked to speak to Mr. Billings. He waited in the hallway, which although large, was crammed with small tables and

163

cabinets, that were covered with knick-knacks. He felt if he knocked one thing over, that small action would send one thing after another crashing to the ground, until nothing was left but shards of glass and china. He could not imagine Helena here at all.

The maid returned and showed him to a stuffy room that served both as Mr. Billings' study and library. It was also full, but unlike the hallway, it was full of books and papers on every surface, stuffed animal heads on the walls and dark, bulky furniture. Behind the enormous desk a tall, lean man stood and bowed stiffly toward the colonel. His dark hair was greying at the temples and his face was very lined.

"Colonel Ackley, I am honoured to make your acquaintance."

"Mr. Billings," the colonel tried to shake off a feeling of guilt, over kissing this man's daughter. However, in Nathaniel's opinion, the man had lost all right to be indignant over that, when he sent her away as if the attack on her had been her fault. Even now, he left her to fend for herself. He was not here to judge Mr. Billings, however, he wanted to pose as a potential investor and so he put on his amiable persona.

"Please take a seat," Billings indicated the seat on the opposite side of the desk to himself, "would you like some refreshments? Tea perhaps? Or is it too early for something stronger."

"It is a bracing day, something stronger will be warming for me, providing, of course, you are joining me," the older man smiled, and reached for the decanter and two glasses behind him. He poured, then handed one glass to the colonel. They both drank, Mr. Billings rather more heavily than prudent. It would seem that the saying, *'like father, like son'* was as true in this household, as it was opposite, when it came to himself and his father.

"How may I be of service?"

"I was acquainted with General Alcott. I understand he was here when he died," the man blanched visibly at the mention of the general's name, but nodded, "he mentioned that he had good investments with you, in your interests in the North, and I wondered if you were still taking on investors? My father is generous and I would like to make some money work for me, in the long term."

"I am sorry to have wasted your time, Colonel. Right now, I have all the investments I need. I can certainly contact you if the situation changes," Nathaniel had no interest in investing. He had wanted an excuse to see the house that Helena grew up in and meet her family. In reality, she was as far removed from them, as anything he had expected. Still, he should not mind a bit more information, as he was there already.

"Not at all, I was nearby anyway visiting my family."

"Ah, yes, my wife often speaks of Bainbridge. Perhaps if you have a little more time you could indulge me and allow an introduction? She would be honoured to meet you."

"Of course, but first, can you tell me what happened to the investments the general made? Did you pay them back or did the family keep them? I might see if they are interested in selling."

"No, the family has kept them, but I hear nothing from them. Silent partners really," he rose to show the colonel out of the room. The colonel followed the older man back through the hallway and into a parlour where his wife sat. She stood when she saw them. Mr. Billings made the introductions loudly, in an attempt to wake his son who was asleep on the couch, but to no avail. The colonel showed his good breeding by ignoring the son and turned to the mother with a bow.

"Mrs. Billings, a pleasure," though it was nothing of the sort. He saw a mean looking woman, who was rake thin. Her brown hair was pulled back tightly on her head. He could tell her gown was refined but there was no lustre to it, because there was no lustre to her. Helena dressed in a rag would have more shine.

Tea was ordered and pleasantries were talked of. The parlour was as fussy and as crammed with furniture and ornaments as the hallway. Although now, he was at least warm, the colonel felt itchy to be out of the house. Understanding of Helena's need to escape to the stable, came to him easily.

"I thought I understood from my cousin, that you have a daughter as well as a son?" the exchange of looks between husband and wife was not missed by him. Mrs. Billings spoke,

"Our daughter lives in Lincolnshire, with her grandfather. Her husband was also in the army, Colonel, but died in battle."

"I am sorry to hear that. You must get to visit often, with your business being in the north, Mr. Billings?" Billings was shifting in his chair, obviously uncomfortable. It seemed they liked to forget they had a daughter, a fact that sickened him, given what a wonderful woman she had become. They should be proud of her not ashamed. Look at the oaf that they did acknowledge and would leave everything to. He could not even be awake to acknowledge a distinguished guest. It did irk him when people with such high hopes of their own importance, as Mrs. Billings obviously had, could not acknowledge him properly. Again the wife replied,

"I do not travel well I am afraid Colonel, so when my husband goes north I stay here. In an effort to get back to me, he does not indulge in a diversion, to see our daughter." Indulge! What was the woman talking of? She was their daughter for goodness sake and they had not seen her in over five years. Had not seen their granddaughter. Did not acknowledge Isabella existed.

He had met the adorable child two months ago, spent a fortnight in the vicinity of her and her mother and already missed them terribly. He put his hand to his coat pocket, wherein he kept Helena's letters. Six so far, one a week, and he had replied to each and every one. He did not think he could contain his temper, if he had to sit there a minute more. There was a knock. The maid entered and addressed the colonel.

"I am sorry, sir, your horse is very upset in the stable and no one dare go in. We think he might sense..."

"Mary, that is enough!" Billings shot to his feet and headed out to the back of the house. Happy to escape and eager to make sure Thor was unharmed, the colonel followed him, grabbing his greatcoat from the maid, who had it ready as he passed. He assumed that Mary was referring to the ghost of General Alcott.

They approached the small stable, that had been the haven of a young, red-headed girl, that did not fit into this family. Within twenty yards of the doorway the colonel heard Thor. He was whinnying so loudly it was almost a scream and his hooves were battering on the stall they had contained him in. The colonel lengthened his stride and overtook Billings to reach his mount quickly.

"Please leave," he shouted over the men in the stable, who were all giving advice to the stable manager. They quieted, but did not move, "LEAVE!" he bellowed. Hearing the colonel's voice, Thor stopped thrashing his hooves, but he still whinnied, pacing in the stall. The men scattered at his command, but the colonel could tell that eyes were peeping around every corner they could, to see what he would do.

"Colonel, can I just say..."

"No, you cannot," he shot it at the man, "I take it this is where the general... died," Billings nodded.

Ignoring the eyes on him, and Billings to his right, he approached the stall door that had been completely closed. Cautiously he opened the top half of it, talking to Thor with a soothing voice.

"Hey there boy, it is me. Whoa there, whoa there. Come on now, we are leaving, but you have to calm down. Come here boy, there now," still in full tack, Thor continued to pace, but the whinnies had stopped and with each word from the colonel his pacing calmed. Although Thor was a battle horse he would not be cooped up like this in battle. Blood spatter still stained the wooden slats from the general. Blood was like that, it hung around for years. Thor could probably smell it.

As he continued to sooth his horse, Nathaniel looked over the stall door and around the stall where Helena's virginity had been forcibly taken from her. The metal rings attached to the walls that Pegasus had been tethered to while he was beaten. The floor the man had thrown Helena to after he had whipped her for trying to protect the stallion. The wall she had banged her head against. The general over her, taking her, he could see it all happening in his mind's eye, but was powerless to stop something that had happened over five years ago. Pegasus had strained and pulled against his ties, finally he got free and then... a loud crack seemed to go off in Nathaniel's ears as, in his mind, saw a hoof connect with the general's head. Without realising it he had opened the lower door and stepped in to reach Thor, grabbing hold of his bridle to steady his head.

"I know boy, I know, she was here, it happened here. You know. Our boy saved her though. He saved her and she is safe now, safe. There you are, there you are," he hardly knew what he was saying, but tears stained his face at the thought of all that Helena had gone through. He held on to Thor, who rubbed his face against the colonel as they comforted each other. Silent now, he marched Thor out of the stall and out of that dreadful stable. If he had been Helena's father he would have burned the whole building down, preferably with the general's body inside. Billings followed him, but he did not care. He mounted Thor.

"Wait! You know my daughter?"

"I have nothing to say to you, sir," he swung his leg up and over his horse, "you have no right to call her that, as it is plain to me that you do not know her, or care about her at all."

Colonel Ackley received a letter from Dowager Alcott within a week of visiting the Billingses. Mr. Billings had written to her directly, after the colonel had left Fairfield Market, as he decided he should be better off, at least in terms of his peace of mind, if he purchased back her interest in his properties, cutting off all ties to the Alcotts. His offer had been pitiful, he knew that, but thought that with her husband now dead, she should not realise that and simply be glad to sell.

The letter gave the colonel the perfect opportunity to make his excuses to leave Bainbridge. Grace was becoming more and more obvious in her questioning of Harriet about Helena. He tried pointing out a few eligible and well-connected bachelors that might be more suited to his cousin. It was to no avail. He had to make his escape and this was his opportunity.

He saw to Harriet's arrangements with the Harker carriage, in which she and Mrs. Cornock had travelled to Bainbridge, and saw them safely on their way to Cambridgeshire to collect Martha Hopwood. He had hunted up Davy and asked him to meet him out front in ten minutes with his belongings. He suspected the child would have very little, but when the word "belongings" brought a confused look to Davy's face he said, "do you have anything other than what you are standing up in?" The boy shook his head.

Gathering his own bag and helping himself to a blanket, as he realised the boy would be cold riding on Thor, he bid his cousins farewell and left. As he strode out of the door to the welcome sight of Thor waiting for him, a slight figure came running around from the side of the house with Smythe in hot pursuit. Smiling Nathaniel affixed his bag to the back of the saddle, mounted Thor and reached down to swing the running Davy up in front of him. Though over a year older, he weighed no more than Miss Isabella had last summer. He wrapped the blanket around the boy and addressed the butler.

"Goodbye, Smythe. I am afraid this little fish is jumping out of the net and coming with me. Tell Lady Bainbridge not to use any more children in her chimneys." Davy, who was thrilled to be so high up on the enormous horse and felt very safe with the colonel, gave Smythe a cheeky wave from within the blanket.

They arrived at Harker's London house, the colonel was grateful his friend allowed him free reign there, as he had not wanted to take Davy to the house of his family. He asked Harker's butler to see to the needs of Davy. The boy needed feeding up, more clothes and to start working in Harker's London stable, as he would be moving to Lincolnshire and working with horses there come Christmas. Jenkins had received word from his Master in Eastease, to provide the colonel with whatever he needed for the boy.

"May I also recommend a bath, sir?"

Colonel Ackley arrived at Dowager Alcott's large, London property, promptly and was shown into her parlour. He was extremely surprised at the woman who greeted him. The general had been a bull-like, barrel-chested man, but the sight that greeted him was completely opposite. She was a slender, delicate, but certainly not frail, woman of about sixty years old. Her blonde hair showed only slight vestiges of silver-like grey and her smile was warm and genuine.

The house had large windows, letting in plenty of light, and brightly-coloured cushions, on sturdy, but decorative furniture, that was not overly ornate. The colonel bowed toward the lady who had stood graciously to meet him and curtsey herself.

"Colonel Ackley, I am so happy that you were able to find time in your busy schedule, to fit in a visit to Alcott House," when she spoke he could hear an accent, slight though it was, as she had obviously lived in London for many years.

"I thank you for the invitation, madame, though I was surprised to receive it," as soon as she was seated again, she indicated that he should sit on the opposite couch, "I hear an accent, am I right in thinking you are French? Parlez-vous français ?"

"J'ai commandé quelques rafraîchissements si cela convient, Colonel ?" he nodded and waited for her to continue.

"I have received a letter from Mr. Billings in Fairfield Market, with whom my late son, General Alcott, had investments. In fact, before he died, he had informed me that he was engaged to Mr. Billings' daughter. Not the best match for a man of his stature, but he was taken with her apparently, although I understand she was very young," she had noted the colonel's mouth form a thin line of distaste for her son, "did you know my son, Colonel?"

"I did not have reason to talk with him at length, but I knew him by reputation. I knew his horse better, as I was often in the stable," he observed her reaction to him mentioning Pegasus, but she merely nodded.

The ordered refreshments arrived and they both partook of tea. The dowager continued with the conversation, "he was a fine animal, but like many things my son laid a hand on, he was ruined," the colonel was surprised by this. She was his mother and usually mothers forgave all, especially to an only son. He had only to look to the Billingses for that example.

"As I was saying, I received a letter from Mr. Billings, who mentions that you visited him and asked him about my son's investments. He was concerned that you might attempt to swindle me by offering very low. After which he proceeded to offer me an extremely insulting, low amount himself," she paused to gauge the colonel's reaction to her disclosure. He was impassive, and calmly, at least it seemed on the outside, waiting for her to continue. She would have to be more direct with him, "Colonel, would you please enlighten me as to your purpose at the Billingses?"

"Curiosity," he had been pondering, while she spoke, how much he should tell her. He obviously could not tell her of Isabella. To the world, the girl was the daughter of Captain Andrews, but he saw no reason not to mention that he knew Billings' daughter, "I met their daughter while staying with friends at Eastease in Lincolnshire. Her grandfather left her his stable when he died. She had been staying with him after the death of her husband in France. She does not have any contact with her parents. She had mentioned the general had visited due to investments he had with her father, and I knew that he had died visiting friends in Norfolk. As I was close by, at Bainbridge, I thought I should pay them a visit."

"I see," she said and he felt she saw a lot more than he really cared her to, "so she married another military man instead of my son and he died, too. That is very unlucky. What is the name of the stable?"

"Redway Acres."

"Interesting. Well, now that my husband has died, everything falls to me. I am still working out what investments he had that I am truly interested in and I do not believe that I am interested in mills and mines. I am tempted to sell. Am I to understand that you are not actually interested in buying, Colonel?"

"No, I am a second son and do not have that kind of income at my disposal. However, I understand from Mrs. Andrews, that her father's businesses squeeze out every penny of profit at the expense of the workers. So, even if I did have the money, I would have to politely decline. My recommendation, if it is of interest to you, would be for you to sell back to Billings and squeeze *him* for every penny."

She laughed out loud. She had not met Mr. Billings, but given what the colonel had just told her and what she could glean from his letter, she did not think he would be the kind of man she would wish to be in business with. Yes, she liked the colonel and she liked his advice. Her husband had been dead almost a year. With her mourning almost at an end, she was experimenting with spreading her wings. Lincolnshire might be just the place to do that.

They spent the rest of his visit talking of some of her husband's other investments and he gave her his opinion of them, glad that he had listened to Harker. He agreed that she could use his name to glean more money from Mr. Billings and promised to visit again when he was in town. She wished him good luck, if he found his way back onto the battlefield.

Once the colonel left, Dowager Alcott asked her butler to request Mr. Davis visit her. She had some instructions for her solicitor regarding her investments, including selling back to Mr. Billings for as much as possible. She also wanted to find out more of Mrs. Andrews and Redway Acres. Mr. Davis had an investigator on staff who could be discreet.

Mr. Davis reported back to the Dowager Alcott a month after her orders. He had dispatched his man to find out more of Mrs. Andrews and Redway Acres stable, without drawing attention to himself. His man had posed as a horse buyer and received an invitation to visit the stable. He was impressed with what he saw and heard, and his discussions with Mrs. Andrews herself had been fruitful, if he was interested in horses. He had also had the fortune to meet the cherubic Miss Isabella Andrews who had turned five years old in October.

All he found out from those who lived in the area, was that Mrs. Andrews was a private person, good at raising her child and horses, kind to her neighbours, especially women who were down on their luck and held the interest of one Colonel Ackley, who met her when visiting his friend, Alexander Harker of Eastease, during his convalescence after an injury in battle.

He had tried to find out more about the unfortunate Captain Andrews, but he had apparently died before Mrs. Andrews made it to Lincolnshire. His contacts in the army, could find no record of him.

The dowager thanked and paid Mr. Davis, and then sat down to work out when exactly Mrs. Andrews, as she was apparently known, had fallen with her child. Given her own best calculations, she realised that it was very likely, that she had a grandchild. Knowing that her son died violently and that he was a violent man, she wondered if her grandchild was begot in violence.

She spent several weeks pondering her next move. Finally, she called Mr. Davis back to her. She asked him to look into the possibility of buying land in the same area his man had been to, in Lincolnshire. Then, just before Christmas, she put pen to paper to write a letter to Mrs. Andrews.

Chapter Fifteen

Colonel Ackley turned Thor into the Eastease estate. Davy sat in front of him and had not complained the whole journey. At least this time he was wearing suitably warm travel clothes, although they still had the blanket with them. He had talked to Davy of Eastease and Redway. The boy would stay at the Eastease stable until after Christmas, which was tomorrow. The ball was the following day. The day after that, Helena planned to take the boy back with her, if he agreed. Harker had arranged that Adam would take care of the boy.

More important to Nathaniel at that moment, was seeing Helena again, but that would not happen until the ball. Christmas would be family time and he would see his godson, who was now three months old. The day after Christmas, Helena should be busy with her horses in the morning and then should come to Eastease. Harriet had planned to whisk her away to get ready for the evening, so the first he would see her, after more than three months, would be when she made an appearance before the ball started. He felt tightness in his chest just thinking of seeing her again.

What were two more days he wondered? But those two days seemed to take as long as the three months before them. Everyone was busy with preparations and Thor did not need to be ridden after the long journey from London. His only respite from his own impatience, was a trip in the afternoon of Christmas Day to Old Joe's. He gave the man the new pipe and tobacco he had bought for him and shared a considerable amount of the bottle of whisky he had taken from Harker's supply.

Things changed, however, in the early afternoon of the following day, when a resplendent carriage and four arrived at Eastease. Lady Bainbridge and her daughter, Lady Grace, descended from the vehicle with the assistance of one of the footmen they brought with them. They had obviously spent Christmas at Aysthill.

"Lady Bainbridge and Lady Grace Bainbridge, welcome. I am afraid you find us in a state of upheaval this afternoon, as we are preparing for our Christmas Ball tonight," Genevieve and Harriet greeted the women, when they were shown into the parlour where tea would be served. Martha deliberately remained in her rooms, out of sight.

"Oh, a Christmas Ball, how wonderful and festive," declared Grace, "you must be excited Harriet." There was nothing to be done, but invite both ladies to the ball and to stay overnight. Colonel Ackley was not going to be pleased.

"My Ladies, we would be honoured if you would join us. We could send to Aysthill for your clothes," offered Genevieve. Harriet had informed her, that Lady Grace was well aware the ball was taking place that evening. Unsurprisingly, suitable attire was produced from their carriage and taken up to their rooms. Harriet's maid was pressed into service of these two women, while Harriet agreed that she and Mrs. Andrews would share the service of the less experienced Rebecca.

"Ah, then I will finally have the pleasure of meeting this, *Mrs. Andrews*," though Grace sounded like it would not be a pleasure at all.

Upon the arrival of the women, Harker had stopped Nathaniel from marching into the parlour and demanding to know what his cousin thought she was up to getting herself invited to the ball. He had taken him into his study and shoved a calming brandy into the man's hands, demanding he drink it and sooth his temper.

Carefully, Harker pointed out, that if he was as serious about Mrs. Andrews as Gennie and Harriet seemed to think he was, then his cousin was going to be disappointed tonight. Despite her attempts to manipulate him by turning up uninvited, he should try and be nicer to her and let her down gently.

"I am still dancing the first two dances with Helena, Grace will be disappointed if she thinks otherwise and then I will need to dance with Gennie and Harry."

"No need to worry about that, Ackers. As host, I will insist I dance the first two with Lady Grace and you can dance the second two with her. Gennie and Harriet have already decided upon it," he said before Nathaniel could protest. They went to greet the ladies.

"Lady Agnes, Cousin Grace, what a surprise to see you both here today," after Harker had formally greeted his guests, Nathaniel bowed to them, with a pointed look at Grace, who at least managed a sheepish smile.

"Colonel, Mrs. Harker has kindly extended us invitation to the ball tonight," she could tell he was not pleased, but she had plans. Since hatching them after his visit in October, she had been to London to the best shops and purchased a gown in the latest fashion. The Bainbridge diamonds had been cleaned and shone brightly in their velvet box, nestled within her belongings. She would dazzle in comparison to this stable owner who had distracted him. With them side by side, he could be in no doubt which of them was the right lady for a man of his stature.

"Thank you, Mrs. Harker," Nathaniel addressed Gennie with feeling and a smile, knowing she had given up the first dances of the ball with her husband so that he could dance with Helena, "*you* are all benevolence and grace."

Finally, it was time to dress and join Harker to wait for the ladies. Genevieve and Harriet descended the stairs with Martha and gracefully received the gentlemen's compliments. Lady Agnes followed shortly after and turned to look up the stairs at her daughter. All eyes followed the older lady's lead and watched Lady Grace live up to her name, as she moved fluidly down toward them.

Begrudgingly, Nathaniel had to admit, that she was indeed a very handsome woman. The gown floated around her and made the most of her figure. Diamonds sparkled, almost blindingly, at her throat, in her hair and at her wrists. As she reached the group, he bowed formally and paid her a compliment. She linked her arm into his and tried to pull him into the ballroom, but to no avail. Instead she heard him gasp and turned to see his eyes once again, looking at the top of the stairs. Everyone looked toward Helena.

Helena did not see why Harriet insisted she make an entrance like this. She was embarrassed, especially when she found out that Lady Grace was going to be there and would, indubitably, be making a very grand entrance to impress Colonel Ackley. She was not able to compete with the resplendent and noble woman, who could outdo her own borrowed ballgown and jewels, with her regular day gown.

Harriet had told her, that Grace would want to be the last to make an entrance and that she should wait until that Lady had descended, before making her own entrance. As planned, Lady Grace must have assumed that Martha was Mrs. Andrews, forgetting she had met her before, and thought she was making the last entrance.

It seemed like a lot of fuss to Helena, but then she saw the look on Nathaniel's face when he saw her and her cheeks heated. She smiled and decided Harriet was right, that look was worth the nearly four-month wait. Despite his cousin standing next to him, a glimmering vision in white, his eyes stayed on her, with a look in them that she could only interpret as hunger.

Nathaniel had involuntarily gasped, quite audibly, when he saw her. Her red hair was piled high and one long thick tail of it came from the top to cascade down her back like a horse's tail. The cream gown was off her shoulders and the neckline scooped low, skimming the top of her ample breasts. Nestled between them was her only jewellery, a large teardrop of jade on a long, simple chain. Cream flowers were in her hair and her skirts were full and moved with her body as she walked down the stairs. Nathaniel could have licked his lips. Her skin looked like cream and he wanted to taste.

For her part, Helena felt caught in those beautiful, blue eyes. The stare of them, as he drank in her appearance, seemed to cause her to vibrate from head to toe. She felt like she was a tuning fork and would not have been surprised, had she put her ear to it, to hear her skin hum. He reached the bottom of the stairs at the same time she did and bowed, "Mrs. Andrews, it is an absolute pleasure to see you again. May I say you look beautiful tonight?"

"You may, and I thank you. It is wonderful to see you, too. It has been too long."

"Far too long," he agreed, looking into those bewitching, green eyes and offering her his arm so he could walk her over to greet everyone.

"Cousin, would you allow me to present to you Mr. Harker's neighbour and owner of Redway Acres stable, Mrs. Helena Andrews. Mrs. Andrews, my cousin, Lady Grace Bainbridge."

"Mrs. Andrews, a pleasure to meet you."

"My Lady," Helena curtseyed and received very little in return, "your gown is beautiful."

"Naturally. I purchased it from the best tailor in London recently, so it is the latest fashion, in case you did not recognise that. Where did you get your gown?"

Standing beside the woman, she felt keenly how the Lady sparkled in the candlelight and wondered at her own choice of wearing only the large, jade pendant her grandfather had bought her. At the thought of her grandfather she felt her confidence and courage rise. She had been looking forward to this evening, admittedly a new sensation for her, and this woman would not spoil that. With a smile, she straightened her back, rising to her full height of an inch or two taller than the other woman.

"Actually, you will have to ask Harriet that question. I have borrowed it from her. Of course, we had to let it out somewhat, but I have a wonderful seamstress in my employ, who managed it rather well."

Colonel Ackley, who had been dreading the moment of these women meeting considering what they knew of each other, smiled at Helena's mettle in dealing with Grace's set down. All they had to do now, was negotiate her expectations of the first dances.

The guests began to arrive and as the ballroom filled, Nathaniel walked in with Helena and Grace, leaving Harker with his wife, Martha and Harriet. Mr. Brooks was going to walk in with Martha and Harriet when he arrived, leaving the Harkers to make their formal entrance before the dancing started.

The colonel found seats and left the ladies together, while he obtained some refreshments. He hoped to get back to them quickly, but at every turn there seemed to be someone else greeting him and saying how good it was to see him in Lincolnshire again.

When he could, he looked back to see how things were fairing between Helena and Grace. Sat side by side, he tried to determine what he thought of each, and why Helena was the one that had captured his heart when Grace had failed to do so. They were both very handsome, but whereas one glimmered and shone from the diamonds about her person, the other glimmered and shone seemingly from within. Her only jewel was the jade that hung between her breasts. He could not determine if the green of her eyes was brought out by the jewel or if it was the other way around. Her red hair gleamed like a horse's coat, and the long tail of it down her back reminded him of the copper-red, chestnut horse she had ridden on their picnic.

People were approaching the two of them often and each time Helena would rise, curtesy and make the introduction between her neighbours and Lady Grace. The Lady seemed little pleased and did not even rise out of her chair, despite the fact that all present were very respectable families. Between greetings the two women seemed to have little to say to each other.

"Mrs. Andrews, I hope you understand that my cousin will, ultimately, do what his family desires and ensure Bainbridge is kept within the family. I only warn you, as I would hate to see you disappointed."

"If that is what you think, I do not think you know your cousin at all!" exclaimed Helena, knowing full well that Nathaniel had no intention of marrying Lady Grace.

"It is you who do not know him. Your arts and allurements are distracting him, that is all."

"Arts and allurements!" Helena laughed, "My Lady, you do not know *me* at all. I think if you are talking of allurements, you could do no better than to look in the nearest mirror," more guests approached them, introductions were made and the guests moved on.

"I think I know you better than you would like, madam," there was anger in Grace's grey eyes now. This upstart woman should be cowering before her and realising how far short, of the level of a wife for Colonel Ackley, she was. Instead, the woman was insulting her, "I visited your family in Fairfield Market. Your mother was most anxious to assure me that she had cut off all ties from you, to ensure the respectability of the family name. She hoped that one *'bad apple'* would not ruin the reputation of the name Billings. I was sympathetic, and she told me everything that happened. Perhaps I should tell my cousin? I wonder what he would make of the lie of your 'marriage' *Mrs.* Andrews."

"My mother only knows the lies she chooses to tell herself, because she cannot face what she allowed to happen to me. Your cousin knows the truth, and has known for many months. He does not seem to be perturbed by it." Yet another family approached and Helena dutifully made the introductions. Realising what this awful woman's next move would be, she planned ahead. The Lady did not disappoint.

"What would all of these respectable families, that seem to hold you in such regard, make of this news however? I insist that you step aside, and leave my cousin to do his duty to his family and to me. Otherwise, I can start tonight, while they are all assembled. This ball has made my task very easy."

"What do you think you will achieve by doing so?" Helena said with some satisfaction, as the vicious woman looked shocked at how calm she was, "you will alienate your cousin, who will never forgive you and you will force his hand in offering for me."

"He would not offer for one so disgraced."

"He would, when it was a member of his family who had exposed her to that disgrace and, if he was in love," as she spoke she watched Nathaniel's progress around the room, he turned and their eyes met. "As

I said, you do not know your cousin, My Lady. He *is* an exceptionally, dutiful and loyal man, but to those he considers more than family."

Once all had arrived, Mr. and Mrs. Harker entered the room to great applause. True to his word and with the permission of his wife, Harker walked over to Lady Grace, bowed and asked for the first two dances.

"Surely, Alexander, you should dance with your wife. Nathaniel will dance with me."

"My Lady, I insist. As your host, I do not think you can refuse me," he smiled warmly and gave her no choice but to accept his hand so he could lead her to the top of the dancing lines. He gave the musicians who had been playing quietly, a nod to start the dancing music.

Formally Nathaniel stood in front of Helena and bowed, "Mrs. Andrews, I believe some time ago you promised me the first two dances," she smiled, acknowledging what the Harkers had just done to allow them these first two dances together, stood gracefully and accepted his hand.

They looked across at each other as they lined up for the first dance. Mr. Brooks and Genevieve had joined them, as well as Harriet and Luke Parker, and Martha with that man's father, a sprightly widower, in his fifties. The Parkers were a wealthy family who lived locally.

Helena was not sure how she made it through those two dances without missing a step or falling over. All she saw were his eyes and all she felt were the sensations that ran through her at being in his presence again. Every time their hands touched it was like sparks running up her arms and through her body, from the looks he gave her, she thought it was the same way for him. No words passed between them, but his words from his letters ran through her head as if he was saying them in that moment and maybe his ideas ran along the same lines...

"Do not forget, that you have promised me the first two dances at the Eastease ball. I will hold you to your word, even if you are married."

"As I have told you several times, I have no intention of marrying anyone, so the first two dances of the ball remain safely, yours."

"I want you to know, that my feelings for you are not conditional on whether you return them, nor are they dependent on marriage. They just are and forever more will be."

"I wish I had the power to change the law, so that a married woman did not lose her very existence to her husband. It was not something I gave much thought to with regards to myself, but then I had never met a man that I could feel that way about, because I had not met you."

"I am as always, Your's."

"Although I belong to no one, I am only... Your's."

The dancing continued and, as he must, the colonel danced the two next with Lady Grace. She was an exceptional dancer and they were well matched, but their dancing was formal and technical. Flawless, but devoid of emotion. It held no joy for him, as had the previous two dances with Helena. When he danced with her he was aware of every part of him that touched her and their dancing had flowed.

He danced the third pair with his hostess and the fourth pair with Harriet. Both Gennie and Harriet teased him about Helena, as he watched her for most of the time he was dancing with them. This was particularly the case when he was dancing with Harriet and Helena was dancing with *'that damned fool'* Brooks.

"Is my dancing so bad, Cousin, that you have to scowl through the whole process?" she had teased.

"My apologies Harriet, my thoughts were elsewhere."

"Mr. Brooks holds no interest for Mrs. Andrews. Though I fear you would scowl even if she danced with Old Joe!" he laughed at that and paid her more attention.

After dancing with Martha, he managed two more dances with Helena, before the music stopped and everyone took a welcome break for refreshments. Tables of food lined an adjoining room, and while they moved to that room the servants speedily set the tables around the ballroom for eating at. As people sat down, servants milled around with wine to fill glasses and help with requests. Nathaniel spent much of his time sitting with Helena and talking to her. Harriet and Martha joined them with the Parkers and much merriment was had.

As the conversation took a lull when bellies were full, Harker called for some entertainment. Harriet rose to take her position at the pianoforte, as they had agreed earlier and Nathaniel joined her as promised. He cleared his throat and as he spoke his commanding voice reached right across the room, "some time ago, at a dinner here at

Eastease, Mrs. Andrews treated those in attendance, to a beautiful rendition of the aria of Leonore from Beethoven's opera. Miss Wyndham recently informed me of the aria of Florestan, Leonore's husband. He has been imprisoned unjustly and Leonore is trying to save him. Harriet persuaded me to sing it tonight, so I apologise for inflicting my singing upon you, but the blame must fall on Miss Wyndham. Thankfully her playing is marvellous and should more than make up for it," everyone laughed and as silence fell, Harriet started her playing. He searched out those beautiful, green eyes he loved so much and began singing.

Helena was shocked at his announcement. Harriet had told her about having the music for the Florestan aria, but did not mention getting Nathaniel to sing it. She must have practised it with him when she was in Norfolk. She had explained how Florestan sang of his despair over his imprisonment and his resignation to his fate, as he prepared to die. Then, how he saw what he thought was an angel who looked like his wife, but in truth was Leonore dressed as a guard who had come to rescue him.

Nathaniel's voice was rich and powerful. She had no idea he could sing so wonderfully. She knew he could speak German so he was able to emote the words because he understood them. He sang to her, his eyes locked on hers. Tears sprang to her eyes at the thought of the man in the song, who was suffering so much. When he had stopped singing, there was silence for just a moment and then the room erupted in applause. She felt a pinch on her arm and looked to her right where Genevieve sat and clapped. That brought her fully back to the room and she clapped with everyone else.

"I had to pinch Nathaniel the night you sang, too."

Having thanked Harriet, with true feeling for making him sing, Nathaniel graciously accepted praise from people, as he gradually made his way toward her. Gennie turned to her sister as he approached to allow him to talk to Helena alone.

"Colonel Ackley, I had no idea you could sing so beautifully," he stopped in front of her.

"Neither did I! I think I was inspired by the view I had of an angel of my own," she smiled warmly at the compliment, but his eyes were suddenly looking concerned and beyond her.

"What is it?" seeing his concern, she turned toward the door. Adam from the stable with his cap in hand, was trying to catch his attention from around Johnson's large body, as the bigger man tried to prevent him from entering.

"I think it might be about Davy," he strode toward the door and she scurried after him.

Grace watched them exit with a scowl on her face. Harriet was a minx. They had practised that song in her very own drawing room. She had known it was for this ball, but she had no idea that Mrs. Andrews had sung the wife's aria. Lady Aysthill had mentioned in a letter to her some time ago, about Mrs. Andrews singing at a dinner and that her voice in no way compared to Grace's. Grace had planned to sing and play tonight, but with Nathaniel out of the room what was the point?

"Colonel, it is Davy, he fell asleep in the stable and now he is screaming and will not stop," Adam was breathless.

"Is he hurt?" the question came from Helena, who had followed Nathaniel to see what was happening.

"No, ma'am, he does not seem to be, his eyes are wide open, so not sleeping, but screaming. Mrs. Hopkins is trying to comfort him, but he is not having any of it," they started toward the stable as this conversation was going on. Helena was right there keeping pace with them in her finery. It was not appropriate, but Nathaniel was glad she was there.

It was cold, but not far to the stable. As they rushed in they heard the screaming, *"poor child,"* was all Helena could think. There was a crowd around the stall that Davy was in, and within it he was rigid in the arms of the Eastease housekeeper, who was sitting on a stool. Nathaniel had no idea what to do.

"Make everyone leave, Nathaniel. Please," Helena looked up at him, as she placed a hand on his arm to get his attention.

"Everyone about your business please, we have this in hand," his commanding voice cut over Davy's screams. All the men, and the women from the kitchen, who had been talking and giving advice, scattered; leaving him alone with Helena and Adam, with Mrs. Hopkins still holding tight to Davy, trying in vain to comfort him.

"Nathaniel, you said he was a chimney boy?" confirmed Helena.

"Yes, that is correct."

"Mrs. Hopkins, I do not know for sure, but if he is still captured in a nightmare, despite his open eyes, it could be of being in a confined space like a chimney. Although you are trying to help, it might be adding to the nightmare. What do you think? Should you perhaps let him go?"

"Oh, I hate to, ma'am, I just want to make him feel better, poor, poor child."

"Indeed, Mrs. Hopkins, but please, could we try it? This does not seem to be working."

"Yes, ma'am," the housekeeper released Davy and placed him on the floor, where it was well banked with straw. Helena stepped forward and sat down near him. Mrs. Hopkins moved to protest, but Nathaniel stayed her with a hand on her arm. Davy continued to scream, even though the screams were hoarse and his breathing laboured. His body was still rigid.

"Davy," Helena said, firmly but kindly, "Davy, I am Helena. You are safe. You are safe, Davy. You are not in a chimney, you are in a stable, with wonderful horses. Can you hear me, Davy?" still screams came, "Davy, listen to my voice. You are safe. The colonel is here. Hear my voice and wake up. Wake up Davy, you are safe," the screams were not so loud now. Encouraged, Helena continued talking to the boy but not touching him. Gradually, the screams lessened until only the panting of his breathing remained. And then…

"Mama," a sob hitched in Helena's throat. She had been near to tears for this boy, who she knew to be almost two years older than her own child, but was so small and undernourished.

"Yes, it is me. Come here, Davy. Come to me. You are safe," the boy sat up and threw himself into her outstretched arms. Then the sobs came. She leaned back against the wall as the boy's tears soaked her breasts and her gown. Nathaniel looked at her in her fine gown and large jewel, sitting in the straw and dirt, leaning against the rough wooden wall, with this ragamuffin boy crying in her arms. Would any woman back in the ballroom do what she was doing here? Would any of them have known what to do, as she seemed to so instinctually? Grace certainly would not. Look at what her family had done to the boy already, "the blanket, Nathaniel," she pulled him out of his reverie, and he strode over to pick up the Bainbridge blanket from the floor and place it around her and the boy.

"You cannot possibly be comfortable," he murmured, trying not to be jealous of Davy, who was crying more quietly, but still had his face resting on Helena's breasts. The picture they made was disturbing given how much Davy looked like him. It could almost be his wife and child sitting there.

"It is of no matter," she smiled, but he moved her away from the wall so he could sit behind her and she could rest on his chest, "thank you, Nathaniel."

"Colonel, this is highly inappropriate," Mrs. Hopkins was most put out that this slip of a gal had managed to calm the boy when she had not.

"Propriety be damned, Mrs. Hopkins. Davy is calm and that is all I care about. Please inform Mr. and Mrs. Harker of the reason for our absence. I will explain all to him tomorrow. Adam, get yourself to bed. Davy can sleep on the couch in my dressing room tonight, in case of any more nightmares. Thank you both for your assistance."

"Yes, sir." They left.

From her vantage point, looking out of a window at the back of the house, Lady Grace saw the comings and goings of the stable. Seeing Mrs. Hopkins returning, she headed her off as she exited the kitchens, on her way to inform Mr. Harker of whatever the situation was out there.

"My Lady, the Bainbridge boy was having some difficulty, but Mrs. Andrews seems to have it in hand. She remains out there with Colonel Ackley, while the boy gets settled again." Despite being put out over Mrs. Andrews handling a situation she could not, Mrs. Hopkins was loyal to her Master and the colonel, and all the Eastease staff knew how badly those at Bainbridge had treated this sweet boy. She was not going to tell this woman more than necessary, no matter her status. Lady Grace allowed her to pass and decided to take a look at what was happening in the stable herself.

Nathaniel looked over Helena's shoulder at Davy who seemed to be falling back to sleep. It afforded him a brief glance at those creamy-white breasts the boy rested on.

"This is not how I had hoped to get a chance to talk to you alone, Helena, but I am not particular. You were wonderful with him. He has not had a spell like this before. I wonder why it happened now?"

"Maybe it is because this is a grand house like Bainbridge and it brought up old nightmares for him?"

"Or perhaps he saw the Bainbridge carriage and footmen. How did you know what to do?"

"I did not. I thought of an idea and tried it. If it had not worked, I would have thought of something else and tried that."

"Thank you, and thank you for giving him shelter at Redway. I have grown quite fond of him; I have to admit. He is smart and funny."

"He looks so much like you, Nathaniel. I know you said he is not your son, but have you considered he might be your father's? He has visited Bainbridge," she could feel him tense against her back. He obviously had not thought of it, "he could be your brother. Well, half-brother I suppose."

"My father would never acknowledge him."

"He called me Mama. Perhaps I should take him in as my own. He would still learn of horses and be a big brother. Rachel could teach him, too. What do you think?"

"Well this is new," he laughed, "Mrs. Andrews of Redway is asking for my opinion!" she laughed, too.

"I believe I asked your opinion of the name for Missy's foal," she pointed out.

"That is true. Well it seems my answer is the same. Chance. Take a chance on this boy and take him in. Like you said, he already seems to think you are his mother. Life so far, for him, has not been good. He deserves a better stab at it."

Unseen by either party, Grace had entered the stable and listened to this last exchange. Nathaniel was so different with Mrs. Andrews than he was with her. His voice, though still deep, was gentle and soothing. There was humour between them, as they teased each other. She could see him looking at the woman as if he could hardly believe that she was in his embrace. She had suspected the chimney boy was Lord Aysthill's bastard, so she had instructed Smythe to do as he wished with the child, providing he was not seen or heard. The boy was lucky to get that much. They could have turned the girl out, and she *and* the baby would have died. It could not be borne that the boy should be allowed to grow up close to Aysthill, or worse, if Nathaniel married this woman, he would be Lord Aysthill's grandson. She turned away to go and find her footman, they would have to take him back to Bainbridge.

Warm in Helena's arms, Davy was not asleep, as they thought

him. He had been confused when he woke and had thought he heard his mother calling to him, though he had never known her so that could not have been right. Instead, he saw this beautiful woman holding out her arms to him and felt such a pull in his chest, he could do nothing to prevent himself from sobbing and falling onto her. She had held him while he cried, and not cared that his eyes and nose had run all over this soft gown she was wearing.

She had continued to stroke his head and play with his hair, even after his crying had eased. It was so comforting and warm, with the blanket that the colonel had put around them both, that he feigned sleep so he could stay there as long as possible. The woman had shifted when the colonel had sat behind her and he had dismissed the others, so there was just the three of them sitting on the floor, one leaning on the other, like a family. It was the happiest moment of his life.

They had talked and he found it soothing. They had a friendly way and were bantering. Then the woman had suggested he might be the colonel's brother. Could that be possible? It would be wonderful to have a brother like the colonel and to think that he could grow up to be like him. It did not matter to him when he had said his own father would not acknowledge him. To know it was so was enough. She said he had called her Mama. He thought he had dreamt that part, but he must have spoken aloud. Then she said she could take him in. What did that mean? From what she said, it seemed to mean that he would be her son. She asked the colonel what he thought and Davy held his breath. What would the colonel say? Finally, he said she should. That settled it then, *this* was now the happiest moment in his life.

Davy had been carried from the stable to the colonel's rooms by the colonel himself. He had truly fallen into a deep sleep, shortly after hearing that Helena planned to take him in. She and the colonel had continued to talk for a while, until they became too uncomfortable on the floor. She had bid them both goodnight and had gone to her own rooms. They had been so long in the stable, that no guests remained and everyone had gone to bed. They might get three or four hours of sleep before the sun was up.

Helena got undressed in the same room she had been in the night of the dinner, when she first met Nathaniel. After help with her hair and her dirty gown, for which she had received surprised gasps from Rebecca, she dismissed the girl and changed into her nightgown. As she brushed her hair she was reminded of that night nearly four months ago, when she had seen the colonel from her window while he played cards with his father and brother.

Her hand reached out to the curtains, but she hesitated. Would he be there? Of course not, everyone had gone to bed. If he was, would he see it as a sign to come to her? No, he would not do that, although the nearness of him in the stall had not gone unnoticed by her. It had been so wonderful to lie against his strong body. If it had not been for the hard floor causing discomfort, she would have stayed there all night with a wonderful man at her back and a small boy in her arms. She definitely wanted to take Davy in, but she had to admit that was partly because he provided a connexion to the colonel she would never have, unless she married him. Nathaniel was infuriating, opinionated and loved to tease her. He was also handsome, thoughtful with Isabella and now Davy, and he was courageous. She loved him and was at a loss at what to do about it.

Regardless, she wanted the curtains open so the early morning sun should wake her. Decidedly she pulled them apart and looked down to the games room. He sat there as he had before in his shirtsleeves with his waistcoat undone and cravat hanging loose around his neck. The decanter of brandy and a snifter were in front of him on the table. His face rested in his hands and he rubbed at it, as she had seen him do many times when he was agitated or frustrated. Usually with her she thought with a smile.

He had wondered if she would come to her bedroom window, as she had after the dinner at the end of August. He had left the boy in his dressing room with James, after a brief explanation and a promise to return shortly. He needed a drink anyway he told himself, but had been disappointed when she had not directly appeared at her window. He had sat down with the brandy to calm his nerves. He could still smell her on his clothes where she had leaned back against him for support. From that position, he had seen the top of the scar on her back where Alcott had struck her for protecting his horse. Fury bubbled within him but it had not been the time to talk of it with the boy there and being in a stall, which was where it had happened.

He had been alive for over thirty years and had never met a woman who challenged him the way she did. She was opinionated, loved to shock him and was frustratingly often right. She was also kind, beautiful and thoughtful to those closest to her and to those in need. He loved her. He wanted to share in all aspects of her life. He hoped that she would see that. He had to at least find out. If only she would come to the window. He dropped his face in his hands and rubbed it.

As he lifted his face from his palm, he looked up to the window once more. She was there. He stood and smiled. He never tired of drinking in her beauty. Red hair and a white nightgown, kneeling on the window seat for him. The same feelings stirred in him, as had stirred that night back in August. He wanted to rush to that room and claim her for his own, but this time he loved, too, and it was even harder to look at her and not take any action. She smiled and put her hand to the window. He did the same, then stepped back and bowed. Standing, she bobbed a curtsey and stepped away from the window. He downed the remaining brandy and headed to the emptiness of his own bed.

Chapter Sixteen

In the morning, Helena made her way to the stable to ensure her curricle was waiting for her. Rebecca had seen to her things and a footman had loaded them. The small bag fitted nicely under the seat.

James had woken Davy and the colonel. Dressing quickly, Nathaniel walked the boy out to Helena. Davy was wondering if he had dreamed everything that had happened the night before and he was not to be taken in after all, but he said nothing and kept the small, warm kernel of hope trapped in his heart. He would not let it fly out until he was sure. There she was, no longer in the fancy gown he had cried over but a regular gown and a warm hat, coat and gloves. She was like the Lady at Bainbridge, in that she had an air of being in charge, but other than that she was completely different. She was beautiful, kind and smiling at him.

"Are you to come with me then, Davy?" she asked, "what say you?"

"Yes, ma'am," he gave a look to the colonel, who was giving him an encouraging nod.

"Mrs. Andrews, may I call on you tomorrow?" the colonel asked her with a pointed look, "I would love to see how Davy is settling in."

"Yes of course, Colonel, until tomorrow then."

Helena and Davy rode in the curricle the few miles to Redway. She was preoccupied with ideas of Nathaniel and what he was planning to say to her the next day. Davy was getting impatient with the woman. When was she going to tell him of the *'taking him in'*? He could not wait any longer, "what does it mean to take me in?"

Surprised, she looked at him, "you were not asleep then?" she got a cheeky smile at that, "well, it is when a child who does not have any parents, finds a new parent. The child then becomes a part of that family."

"You want to make me part of your family?" he looked incredulously at her.

"Yes, I do. I do not have a husband, but I have a daughter, Isabella. Her father died. He was a soldier. She is five years old, so you would be a big brother."

"And your son."

"Yes. If you wish it."

"And the colonel's brother?" my goodness the boy was sharp she thought.

"You have big ears young Davy," she swiped gently at an ear, "we were only speculating there." He looked confused, so she rethought her wording, "we thought it might be possible because you look so much like the colonel, but he did not know your mother. His father is Lord Aysthill, he would never acknowledge you. Lord Aysthill, may have been with your mother and made you, but was not married to her."

"At Bainbridge, they called me a lot of names and said things about my mother, too, because she was not married. I hated them for that."

"I think the best thing you can do for your mother is to think fondly of her, even though you did not know her. She gave life to you when she died and she would have wanted you to do your best with that gift, do you not think?" he nodded. He liked the way this woman thought of these things.

"The colonel is a good man."

"Yes, he most certainly is," she agreed with a sigh.

"If he is my brother then can I be like him, even if he is only my half-brother?"

"I think you can choose to be like the colonel, whether he is your brother or not. Do you have any more questions? We are almost there."

"When can I call you Mama?" there was the cheeky smile.

"Whenever you are ready." she smiled back at him. Not long ago, she thought she could never lose her heart to a man and now she had lost it to two.

Isabella and Davy had accepted each other immediately. They had run away so she could show him the rest of the house, after which Helena was going to take them both out to the stable and the learning would begin. She had spoken to John, Ruth and Rachel of the new addition to the family at Redway and they all seemed happy about it. Obviously, they had known he was coming, but now that she had decided to take him in things would be different. She gave them all additional pay given the new workload, particularly for Rachel, and she warned them of his nightmares.

After that, she went to her desk to attend to her letters. One was addressed in a neat hand that she did not recognise and the seal had a large A pressed into it. She had seen that A before; she would never forget it. It stood for Alcott. The walls of the room seemed to press in on her, she grabbed for the side of the desk to steady herself and sat with a thump in the chair. Ruth had walked into the room with the tea tray and quickly put it down on the nearest surface to rush to her mistress.

"Are you well, Helena?" she showed the letter to Ruth who looked at her questioningly.

"Alcott," that one word had the housekeeper collapsing on a chair, too. Whatever could the ghosts of the past be wanting with her mistress, she wondered? Helena reached over and clutched the older woman's hand for a moment. She seemed to gain courage from it and broke the seal on the letter.

Dear Mrs. Andrews (née Billings)

Please allow me to introduce myself. We have never met and I know it was never announced, but I understood from my son, before he died, that you were engaged to him. Then he died and I heard no more from you or your family, once matters were resolved. My son's investments in your father's businesses reverted to my husband's portfolio and remained there untouched. When my husband died last winter all of his property and investments fell to me.

Imagine my surprise when I received a letter from your father, who had a visit from Colonel Ackley, with whom I believe you are acquainted. He felt that the colonel might be interested in buying the investments and wanted to offer to buy them first. To say his offer was insulting, is not saying anything at all. I think he assumed, that as a woman, I would not know much of money matters. He soon found out to the contrary and I have now cut all my ties with Mr. Billings.

Prior to selling, I met with Colonel Ackley to ask him if he was interested in buying. I was unsurprised when he confessed that he did not have the income. Despite being in mourning, I do keep up with social circles. It did prompt me to ask, why then was he visiting your father?

'Curiosity' he said, as you have no contact with your family and he knew that my son had died in Norfolk. He mentioned that you now lived in Lincolnshire, at the stable you inherited from your grandfather.

My curiosity was now peaked. I wondered why you had left your family after my son had died. Colonel Ackley is under the impression that you married another military man and had a child by him before he died in France. Men do not understand these things the way women do, or perhaps he does, because he did not mention your child. I found out about her when I sent a man to inquire about you. I am sorry to inform you that you will not be making a sale to Mr. Dawson.

Let me say, that I understood more about my son than he thought I did. His father was a cruel man to both of us and his son learned to be the same way, if not more so. I am under no illusions that my son imposed himself upon you, but died before he could marry you. As I know he beat that fine horse of his, too, I would not be surprised if it lashed out in self-defence. I was sad when my husband insisted that handsome beast be destroyed. Its life was too short and very hard.

I have worked it out and am sure that I am not without family, as I thought I was. That I have a grandchild and not only that but she is a pretty, talented and sweet child. I am sure all of that is a credit to you and the fact that she knows nothing of her father.

Please, do not be fearful that I wish to expose your secret. Neither do I wish to take the child from you. I know both of these things have crossed your mind reading this, as I would be thinking the same in your situation. However, I find I do not like living alone here in London. I have only bad memories in this house and my preference would be to find land and purpose further North, close to the only family I have left in the world, even if the connexion is not acknowledged for the sake of the child.

I have met with your Colonel Ackley and I find that I like him very much. I think he likes me, too, as he has promised to visit me again. Perhaps you can speak to him of me and make your decision as to whether I could visit Lincolnshire in the spring and wait on you and your daughter.

I wish you the best felicitations for the season and hope to hear from you in due course. Your's

Janine Alcott

Helena scanned the letter and then let out a breath of relief and handed it to Ruth to read. The housekeeper scanned it herself, nodding a few times.

"Well that is something, is it not?"

"It certainly is," Helena agreed, then added, "the audacity of the man! To see my father, to meet with this woman!" she gestured at the letter. "I thought he was beginning to understand me and then this."

"You should give him a chance to explain."

"He is visiting tomorrow afternoon. I think he might ask me to marry him, but I cannot."

"Why child? Is he not the best man you have ever known?"

"Yes, he is, but I cannot give everything to him and leave nothing for myself. He would control me, be in charge of you Ruth, and John. Look what he does before he even has that right?" she shook the letter.

"But you need someone to love you my dear."

Colonel Ackley had received correspondence of his own. He had orders. He was to report to London in the New Year and he was going back into battle. He would have to get into the right frame of mind for it. He had to ask Helena to marry him and get that part of his life settled.

He rode from Eastease to Redway the following day, as agreed. The low sun and chilled wind felt good on his face. Around his neck, he wore the cravat and pin Helena had given him. He had seen her at the window, the night of the ball and it had made his hopes soar that this was the right time to ask her to be his wife. He had always felt it would be simple to ask a woman, even one of means, to marry him, despite having little to offer in fortune or property. He was a distinguished gentleman and soldier, from a well-connected and powerful family. However, Helena cared nothing for any of that, so he hoped she cared enough for him, to accept him. He hoped she would share her life and daughter with him, for he could love that little girl no more if she had been of his own loins. They would have a son, too, in Davy. A son that he had brought to her and a daughter to whom she had given life. With these thoughts, he turned into Redway.

"Colonel Ackley, ma'am," her housekeeper bobbed.

He stood formally in front of her and bowed, "Mrs. Andrews," he smiled stiffly at her aware of his own nerves, as he suddenly wondered if she would refuse him.

"Colonel Ackley," she curtseyed, "would you like some refreshments?"

"No, I thank you," Ruth bobbed again and left, wondering what the outcome would be.

"Mrs. Andrews," he began, "I do not think you can be in any doubt that I am in love with you. You have captured my heart almost from the first, with your singing, your riding, your caring, your headstrong opinions and logical arguments, and most especially your strength in overcoming some harsh realities. If it is within my power, I will never see you feel pain again. I love your daughter and Davy as if they were my own. I would lay down my life for any one of you and think it worthwhile. Please, Helena, would you do me the honour of allowing me to be your husband and the children's father?"

He could not have asked her in any better way than he had, but why did he have to ask her at all? Every beat of her heart said, *"say yes, say yes, say yes,"* but she knew that she could not. She could not give herself up to any man, not even him. She had to say no, but in doing so she knew, that she would be breaking both their hearts.

"Thank you, Colonel Ackley. If there was any man I could marry, it would be you, but I have always maintained that I cannot. I *will not* marry. I cannot give everything I have and everything that I am over to the control of a man, even if that man is you. No matter how much I love you. I do love you, Nathaniel," he stood and stared at her, frustration showing in his face. He rubbed his hand over his face as she had seen him do several times before, but this time it did not amuse her.

"I do not understand, why you do not trust that I will allow you to continue as you have before. That we would work together, side by side. Raise our children together. Live here in our house together. Your life need not change, except that I would be a part of it."

"Yet, you said, *'I will allow you'*. I would have to ask your permission. No decisions would be mine. You could decide that John and Ruth should go. I know you have had your disagreements with him. You could decide whom Isabella should marry. You love how I care about people and yet I would have to ask your permission before every good deed."

"I would prefer to think that we would discuss all of these decisions. I do not want to rule over you, I want to share in your life and I want you to share in mine." Her eyes narrowed, in an expression he recognised from their verbal sparring before, he wondered what was coming next.

"Is that so, Colonel Ackley? You would consult me before taking actions that would affect me, if we were married? Why should I believe that, when you show no sign of consulting me even when we are not?" she turned to a small desk behind her and picked up a letter. Although there was fury in her face, she walked calmly to hand it to him.

It was a letter from Dowager Alcott, inquiring after the possibility of Isabella being her grandchild. He was astounded. He had not told the dowager of the child, but he could see from the letter how she had come to that conclusion. He cursed her timing, although he was not sure that it would have made a difference to the outcome of this conversation.

"Three times you have meddled in my life without consulting me. First you inquire about the existence of Captain Andrews, then you presume to visit my family and now you put my relationship with Isabella at risk, by talking to her grandmother. Not one time did we have a *discussion*." Seeing his shocked expression, she realised, he had not thought through his actions in visiting the dowager, "what if Dowager Alcott had decided that she should be the one to raise Isabella? She could easily take her away from me. I am an unmarried mother, who has lied to all around her about a non-existent husband. She has the money and power to do it, but I can see you did not think of that."

"I did not. Forgive me," he handed the letter back to her.

"I do forgive you. It seems my fears were unfounded, as you see from the letter. However, it remains that you still did not consider my opinion or even inform me of what you were doing. If we were married, you would continue to make decisions and take actions, because you think you are right. It would not cross your mind that I might have a viewpoint you had not considered. Men will always think they know better than women, and you have not shown yourself to be any different. The only difference if we were married, is that I would be wrong in taking you to task over it. I would belong to you. My opinion would have to be yours."

"I have not done these things in the best way, but believe me when I say I have done them with the best of intentions. I will learn and I would want you to keep taking me to task. I value your opinions and I have always enjoyed our discussions. I do not want to be your captor. Although I feel that you are mine. You are the captor of my heart. I have no choices because of my feelings for you."

"You are the captor of my heart, too. Please, do not doubt that. I have never allowed a man as close to me as I have you, and I should not have. Now we are here, and neither of us will be happy at the outcome. But what of my free will? If I am married, I will not have free will, I will belong to you. My heart belongs to you, but my free will must always be mine, as yours remains with you."

"Why do you suppose they are exclusive of one another? To me I have no free will because my heart gives me no choice."

"But I would have no free will because *the law* gives me no choice, regardless of my heart, or yours."

"Then, if you will not change your mind, I must bid you goodbye. I leave for France in the New Year." The thought of him in battle, where he would once again be in harm's way, was a knife to her heart.

"If I accepted your proposal, would it change your plans? Would you stay here and not go to war?" How tempting it was to say he would stay if she accepted him, but he knew his duty, and with the allied forces so close to defeating Bonaparte, he could not leave it for others to risk their lives and stay safe at Redway.

"No."

"Please be safe." Tears stung her eyes and poured down her face as she blinked them away, but she stood still, not allowing the sobs that threatened to wrack her body to be released. He turned on his heels and exited the room. Once the door closed behind him he heard the sobs come, but it was not his place to go to her and wrap his arms around her, which was all he wanted to do.

Mrs. Robertson stood to the side looking at him. He stood with his hand still on the doorknob and his forehead resting on the door. She could see how miserable he was, even though he was stoic enough not to allow the tears show.

"Do not give up on her, please, Colonel."

"I do not think my heart will allow me to do that, but I have to leave and return to my duties. My place now is in battle."

"Well, come back safe, Colonel. Victorious and safe. John and I will take care of her for you, the same as we always have. I think you will work out a way to be together." He pried himself away from the door, thanked her and left. She opened the door quietly and went to her young mistress. She was sitting on the floor with her head and arms draped over the seat of the couch, as she wept into the cushion. Ruth sat down with her and did her best to comfort the girl, whose heart was breaking. She had not been this inconsolable when that brute of a General had attacked her. A small pair of arms appeared around Helena's neck, as her daughter draped herself over her mother's back. Davy's hand brushed through her hair as he sat on the couch, next to her head.

"Do not cry, Mama. Please do not cry," it was the only thing that could stop Helena's convulsive sobs.

"What is the matter, Mama? Are you ill? Why are you so sad?" Helena could not tell her daughter, that the colonel had asked to be her father and she had refused. Not when she knew how desperately her daughter wanted a father, and loved the colonel so much. She was, however, not one to shield either child from the realities of the world.

"My darlings. Colonel Ackley was just here and he told me he has to go back to France to fight Napoleon Bonaparte, with the allied forces. I am sad because I will miss him, as I know you both will, and I worry for his safety. He has promised that he will do all he can to come back home safely, to his family and us, his friends." The small girl took in this news and her face screwed up as she began to cry. Her mother pulled her to her lap and held her to her bosom. She made room there for Davy, too. He was not crying, but he was very close. With tears still streaming down her face, she held her family to her, the wracking sobs abated for now. He may not be a father or husband, but their grief was equal to what it would be if he were.

Chapter Seventeen

"Well then, Colonel, a happy New Year to you!" Colonel Ackley raised his glass, at his reflection in the window of Harker's study, in his London Town House. His reflection obligingly returned the toast, with the same grim look, swaying slightly. After picking at a lonely evening meal, he had cheerlessly made a dent in the contents of Harker's port decanter, but he did not feel any better for it. This year was not beginning at all how he had hoped. After a wonderful Christmas at Eastease, his heart was flying high on love, but now he felt only bitter disappointment and pain. It was pain of the heart and that was a new sensation for him.

He closed his eyes, but the image of them laughing gaily, lying on a blanket, on a sunny day came into his mind. If he had been a painter, he could have painted every detail, *"not enough port,"* he thought and walked to the side table to refill his glass. She had let him kiss her that day. The girl had giggled 'kisses, kisses' as he had grabbed her and swung her high above his head. Bringing her down to him, he had snuggled his face into that soft, still babyish neck and smacked kisses there to tickle her.

'Kiss Mama,' she had said, 'kiss Mama, too.' He had leaned over to Helena, who had lifted her face to him in invitation. His lips had brushed in a gentle caress over hers. Emptying the glass in one long gulp, he refilled it... *"no, not nearly enough port."*

When he had returned to Eastease, after Helena refused him, Harker found him, put his arm around him and led him to his study. He poured them both a stiff brandy and they sat down at opposite ends of the couch.

"Did you ask her in the right way?" Harker had asked him, "women like to be asked in the right way. I really botched it the first time."

"I could not have asked her in any other way and received a different answer. She refuses to marry, not refuses to marry me," he had told Harker that he could not understand her. He saw marriage as sharing, but she saw it as giving up her freedom. He could have avoided saying, 'I will allow you', but she should know him by now, know he would not rule over her, but share in decisions.

As he sipped the next glass of port and with a few days of insight behind him, he considered it all further. He had done what she accused him of, had he not? He had gone to see her father without telling her or asking her opinion. The dowager of course had written to him, but his visit to Billings prompted that contact. He had not considered the possibility of her wanting to take Isabella away from her mother, but thankfully she was not the same kind of person her son had been.

He thought of the rest of that day at Eastease. He had brooded around the house and almost everyone had avoided him. Everyone with the exception of Grace, who sought him out in the library...

"I wondered where you were hiding. I wanted to talk to you of Mrs. Andrews before I leave. She refused you I take it, given your mood. She is a fool."

"She has good reasons."

"I know she thinks she does. I went to see her family in November. I had you followed the day you went there."

"Really?" he tried to keep his temper under control. He recalled having an uneasy feeling when riding out to the Billingses, but had put it down to knowing Helena would not thank him for it. Certainly, did not thank him for it today, "whoever it was, was good. I did not spot him."

"Her mother told me all that had happened with General Alcott. How her daughter put herself between him and his horse and made the general angry. How she had allowed the horse to kill the general. Was glad that it had. How she made her father allow the horse to live and give it to her."

"The general forced himself on her, Grace. Threw her to the stall floor and took her. No gentleness, no caring and no marriage."

"They were engaged! It would have happened eventually."

"She was a virgin."

"So she says. It was his right." My God! If she were a man he would hit her.

"For God's sake, Grace. Do you not have any compassion? He had no right, until he had stood up in church with her. He was a violent man, Grace, violent with his horse and with Helena. She had not consented to the engagement."

"It was not up to her to consent," he rubbed at his face. He could not understand her lack of compassion for her fellow woman. Helena had shown sympathy for and provided assistance to, many women who had landed in misfortune. Grace had fallen short in every comparison to Helena he had made the night of the ball, and was doing so again.

"We are not going to see eye to eye on this Grace, I think we would do better not to discuss it."

"I agree. Instead, let us talk of when *we* should be married," he looked at her incredulously. Was she completely mad? His heart was in tatters and she thinks he would marry her instead. Why would she even want him? She seemed to have no self-worth.

"Grace," the time had come to be blunt, "I offered for another woman just this morning and she turned me down…"

"That does not matter, it is all forgiven and forgot," she waved away his explanation, "she was a distraction, that is all. Now you are free to do your duty to your family and to me. We can marry when you return from France."

"Listen to me, Grace, Helena was not a distraction. I love her. There can be no one else. There will never be anyone else. If I cannot marry Helena, I will *never* marry. I will remain a bachelor and a soldier. My only duty is to my brothers in arms and His Majesty's Army," he moved to leave the library, but she blocked his path and put a hand to his chest.

"I understand. You need more time. Go to France, go to fight and work her out of your system. I will take the chimney boy back with me to Bainbridge and when you come to us we can be the family you want. He is, after all, my relation as my Cousin's son, he should remain at Bainbridge where he was born."

"Good God woman, how low will you stoop? You will leave *Davy* at Redway with Helena, you have no rights after your mistreatment of him. If I return from France and find that you have taken him away, you will experience firsthand, just how violent a man can be," he glared at her with his nose right up against her cheek. His hot breath was on her face. She had hoped for closeness like this from him, but in love, not this white-hot anger. He scared her, which is something she thought Nathaniel could never do. She stepped aside.

As he marched away from her, he wondered if he was going to have to protect the inhabitants of Redway Acres from all of his family. He felt so ashamed of them and he wished, ever more fervently, that he could call Helena, Davy and Isabella, his family instead.

He left the library in a foul temper and did not care who knew it. He shouted at James to get packing his things as soon as possible, he was leaving Lincolnshire and had a mind never to return.

After arriving in London, he had visited the dowager. For a reason he could not explain, he told her everything. He could not understand, if Helena truly loved him, why she would not want to marry him. Dowager Alcott had said that she did not think he *could* understand. A man could never imagine life where he did not have freedom of will. Despite the fact that he would not mistreat her or refuse her doing whatever she chose, ultimately, he would still have control over her.

Sipping at his port again, he thought of Ruth Robertson, who had said that he and Helena would find a way to be together. Being together how he wanted, however, would mean being married and Helena would not marry him. He had no solution.

Downing the last of the port in his glass, he put his hand on the decanter to pour another. Then he realised, there was not enough port in the world to make him forget her, so he went to bed.

The second day of the year dawned bright and crisp. Colonel Ackley's breath huffed out of him in a fog, as it met with the cool air. He had slept off the port during most of the previous day and managed his evening with minimal alcohol, to ensure he had a clear head when reporting for duty. With his orders tucked into his breast pocket with a picture of a dragon, a bundle of letters, a silk cravat and a pin of a horse, he trotted Thor purposefully down the street.

Work was what was called for. The discipline of a soldier's life would put all other matters from his mind, by putting his mind and body to work. The mind tested by strategies and plans, and the body by the arts of fighting and riding.

A month passed quickly and, all too soon, he found himself on his way back to battle. Allied forces were advancing into France. He was going to be fighting again. He had not fought in a battle since he had received the injury to his chest. It would still twinge occasionally, but now he had a different kind of chest pain. As they sailed across the channel to the Northwest coast of Spain close to the French border, his mind turned again to the cause, Helena.

He thought through the disastrous proposal once again. He had been confident that she reciprocated his affections. She had smiled at him and teased him, at the Eastease Christmas ball and when they danced their eyes had met, held, and spoken to how they felt about each other. He had ridden to Redway and declared his love for her and her children. With tears in her eyes she had refused him. Said that she loved him but could not accept him, could not accept anyone. He left heartbroken and then left Lincolnshire. If she truly loved him why would she not accept him? He was better off being a bachelor, a soldier. Here at least he knew what he was doing. A memory came to him of a sword slicing up across his chest, but he quashed it. There was no room for those thoughts on the battlefield.

This was the hardest time for a soldier, the long days of travel. It was wearisome and at the end of it you fought the enemy. Colonel Ackley had what might be thought of as a luxury in riding Thor. He would not ride him all the way though and once they camped for the night, he would spend a long time rubbing down the horse. The best way to have Thor ready for battle was to treat him well on this long journey north. His man could be imposed upon to deal with Thor, but most men could not work with the troublesome horse. He missed Tommy.

Rain had stopped the allies' offensive earlier in the year, but with a break in the weather, word was coming back to the troops that the battles had continued and went well. Halfway through their march to the battles, the weather changed again and rain poured down, which made marching and camping a miserable affair. Back in England the ladies saw the red coats as dashing men honoured in battle, but they never knew of the dreadful conditions often suffered. A few days later they reached the allies' encampment in southwest France with temporary relief.

As an officer the colonel was required to report to headquarters, after leaving Thor at the makeshift stable, he made his way to the central French house where they had positioned their headquarters. While men put up tents in the surrounding fields, plans of attack were drawn and plans for later were discussed, depending on outcomes. Life went on in the encampment until it was time to fight.

The winter was hard in Lincolnshire, but life continued. The horses thrived under the expert hands of Helena, John and their stablemen. Martha Hopwood stayed at Eastease, to save a journey back to Cambridgeshire in the cold. She and Helena became firm friends and she was part of the weekly visit that Helena had with Gennie and Harriet. Isabella was doing well with her pianoforte lessons and tried her hardest to pass on her skill to her new brother, but he did not have the same musical bent. He did show talent at other studies and soon outstripped Rachel's level of learning. His reading and writing progressed so quickly he was writing out Isabella's stories, for which she then drew pictures and they sent to Colonel Ackley. Helena tried to write to him, but what was there to say, other than she missed him.

Occasionally, Helena went with Isabella to her lessons at Eastease and talked to Harker about business. It was a mutual discussion. He learned of her business and she learned of his. They both owned farms and properties, she conceded that the business side of running a stable was not her strong point and learned a lot from him. During one of their most recent meetings Harker surprised her with a request from Lord Aysthill. She had not seen or heard from that man since the dinner party last August. She was surprised that he wanted to talk with her and then, with a shock, thought of Davy. At her look, Harker had assured her that in no way would Lord Aysthill be interested in Davy being acknowledged as his son. Swallowing, she agreed to the meeting, which would be at Aysthill House.

Late in February, on a day when, unbeknownst to Helena and Harker, Colonel Ackley was leading a regiment of Portuguese soldiers into battle in southern France, they rode their horses to Aysthill. They were received coolly by Edgars, the Aysthill butler, and shown to Lord Aysthill's impressive study. Helena had hoped to feel brave in meeting the stout man again, but stood slightly behind Harker in her wariness. Also present was a smaller man with a balding head, who held a large ledger. He bowed smartly, but said nothing. When the greetings were made, she only curtseyed and nodded, saying nothing. Lord Aysthill noticed this, of course, but did his best to temper his anger. She had reason to be cautious of him, he supposed. Harker knew the content of the meeting. Lord Aysthill had to explain all to him, before he would consent to bring the woman here. Harker nodded to the man to start.

Lord Aysthill cleared his throat, "Mrs. Andrews, as I am sure you are aware, I am under a request from my son, Nathaniel, and Alexander here, to make amends for my misdeeds with women in the past and provide restitution. My son's part of this request was that I not see you again, and let me say, he was so persuasive in that request, that it is unlikely we would meet like this if he were not in France. This therefore, being my first opportunity of speaking to you in person, I would like to formally apologise for my behaviour at the end of August last year, and assure you, nothing of the sort will ever take place again."

"Apology accepted, My Lord," now she acknowledged him, well better late than never. That was done. He had agreed with Davidson that an apology was sufficient in this case, as he was fortunate that she had locked her bedroom door that night.

Helena barely managed to get the words out. Her mind was whirling over what had been said. They must have assumed that Nathaniel had told her what he had made his father do. All these months had passed since the rattle of her door handle that night and he had never uttered a word. Because of that small incident, which, admittedly, could have been a lot worse than it turned out to be, he and Mr. Harker had insisted that his father make restitution to all the women he had harmed in the past. She recalled correcting Nathaniel, saying that the first time Lord Aysthill had forced himself on a woman was going too far. He had listened to that and knowing him, as she knew him now, he had most likely felt some responsibility for it.

Additionally, Lord Aysthill had said, that Nathaniel requested he not see her again, and was so persuasive, he was only seeing her now because Nathaniel was in France. She recalled Mrs. Ridgefield saying her husband had seen him leave Mr. Harker's study looking formidable. What had he said to his father, she wondered? Whatever it was had ensured her protection. Now the man was talking of his relationship with a young girl at Bainbridge, when he visited his cousin some seven years ago. He admitted she was only fourteen years old. Helena felt physically sick at the thought of it, then the name he mentioned caught her attention.

"Mary Beckett was her name, and I understand from Davidson here, that she died giving birth to a son. Davidson did some asking around at Bainbridge and interestingly found out that the boy worked in the chimneys there, but that he had gone because Nathaniel had taken him away with him. Davidson tracked him down to you, at Redway Acres and I understand you have taken him in. Were you aware he is my bastard? Is this an attempt at embarrassing me?"

"I suspected. He looks so much like the colonel, but he did not know Mary Beckett. So, the logical assumption, given your proclivities, was that he was yours." Helena, by this point, was barely containing her temper. There was no enduring this man, but she was unable to leave. He talked of the people, whose lives he had affected so badly, as if they were nothing. As honourable as Nathaniel had been in getting his father to make this restitution, his father held no such honour, as he felt no remorse for his actions whatsoever.

"And so," he continued with a smile on his face, as though he was bearing some gift, "I would like to give you a monthly stipend for the care of this bastard and provide a small fund for him for when he is old enough to marry and enter into whatever trade he decides upon."

"No."

"No? What on earth is the matter with you, woman?" Lord Aysthill did not bother to cover up his anger now. Surely she did not have so much money, that it would be easy to take in another child. Any assistance would be welcomed. Harker turned to Helena and looked at her questioningly, he knew her well enough, to know that she would not throw away money offered to a child that easily. She must have good reasons and he had a feeling, looking at the fury on her face, that they were about to find out what they were.

"There is nothing the matter with me, Lord Aysthill, but I am seriously considering, that there is something the matter with you! These are people you are talking of, children in fact, and I include in that, the fourteen-year old you forced yourself upon. She probably had no other experience of a man than that, and then because of what you did to her, she bore your child and died giving birth to him. You murdered her with your so called *'misdeeds'* and you think that offering her son money makes up for that? That is your restitution? Where is your shame? Where is your remorse?"

"Now, wait just a minute."

"No, you wait a minute, while I finish what I have to say. She bore your child and you allowed her son, your son, to be put to work in your cousin's household as a chimney boy. He climbed up into hot, narrow chimney spaces and swept them by hand when there was a device that could have been used, but your cousin was too much of a skinflint to buy it. They starved him, to keep him small enough to do that job. He was only four years old the first time they sent him up there. He would not have seen adulthood had his brother, Nathaniel, not saved him."

"How dare you use my son's given name and relate him to that mongrel?"

"I do dare and I dare to call your "mongrel' as you say, by his given name, too, which is Davy, as I am sure you are well aware from Mr. Davidson. Now he is my son, you lost all rights to him when you mated with his mother and left her to die. I have taken him in and he calls me Mother, and my daughter calls him Brother. He is very clever and will not 'go into a trade' as you suggest, but will go to school and be as qualified as either of your other sons, to do whatever he wishes in the world. So I do not need your money to raise *my* son and when Nathaniel returns from France and marries me as he has promised, *our* son, will be known as an Ackley and will be your grandson. You should know Nathaniel well enough to know that he will give the boy his name. If you want to set aside some money for Davy, then you should do it and he can decide what to do with it for himself, when he comes of age."

"Marry Nathaniel? He has said nothing of this to us. It will not be borne."

"I have nothing further to say to you. Please do not contact me again unless you can offer more than money to the people your *misdeeds* have hurt. Good day," with that she turned and fled the room and the house.

What on earth had she done? What on earth had she said? She was so angry, she wanted to make that dreadful man see what he had done to a poor, young girl. That the price she paid for his moment of pleasure, had been the highest price of all. He had then compounded that, by allowing the mistreatment of the baby she had brought into the world, for six years. In her anger, she had said she was going to marry Nathaniel, because she wanted to shock him into realising his connexion with Davy could not be discarded so easily. Now what was she going to do?

Harker joined her outside and they mounted their horses to make the return journey. While they made their way out of Aysthill House grounds they said nothing. Once they had turned onto the main road Harker looked over at her and finally broke the silence.

"Are you going to marry Nathaniel? Have you changed your mind?"

"No."

"Then what are you planning to do? You know they will write to him and demand he does not marry you, so he will know you said you would. You cannot hurt him a second time."

"I do not know. I let my temper get the better of me," she looked at him ruefully and he smiled.

"I do not think that anyone has ever spoken to Lord Aysthill like that, except when Nathaniel spoke to him the day after you came to dinner. You called Lady Bainbridge a skinflint. Wait until I tell Gennie that!" he gave a chortle thinking of her reaction.

"You are not angry with me?" she realised suddenly, and with some surprise, that Alexander Harker's approval was important to her.

"Not at all. You have said many things, many times, that none of us had even considered. Your reproof to Nathaniel back in August, was what spurred me into appointing Davidson, to oversee the restitution we have made Lord Aysthill pursue. Now I see that money really is not enough. I did not know what had happened with Davy's mother. It truly was murder. However, because she had no family and he is who he is, he will not be called to answer for it until he meets his maker."

"Mr. Harker, could I trouble you to relay the events of the day after that dinner back in August? I had no idea that so much had been done, or that Nathaniel had threatened him in any way. I thought that the matter was dismissed, never to be spoken of again."

"Nathaniel never told you himself?"

"No, never, but so like him is it not?"

"Yes, very like him." He proceeded to tell her how Mrs. Hopkins had told Nathaniel of Rachel and others Helena had helped, how it gave Nathaniel the idea of making restitution, the conversation he himself had had with Lord Aysthill, as well as a description of Nathaniel threatening him. He told her everything. If he could help his friend's cause to get this woman to marry him by relaying this information, he would.

She listened in rapt attention. She had no idea her words and deeds, had been taken in such a way by these two fine men. Her heart was breaking again over having to refuse Nathaniel's proposal. She had been angered by his actions concerning her family, but now she was considering his actions, on her behalf, against his own.

He had protected her from his father, gone against his mother's wish for him to marry Grace and against his cousin's own wishes. He had chosen Redway over Bainbridge; a life of hard work with horses over the life of leisure at a grand estate. He had rescued Davy from what certainly would have been a hard and very short existence, and when the circumstances of the boy's birthright had been discovered, he had encouraged her to take him in. After which he proceeded to ask for the honour of being Davy's father. In return she had let him face the battlefield, without the promise of coming back to a life with her.

He certainly was the best man she had ever known. She would willingly *share* everything in her life with him, if only the law would allow it. She would share Redway, her children, her bed, even her body. She had no solution.

She was moved to tears. When she looked over at Mr. Harker, he realised how much she loved his friend and that she must have a very good reason why she would not marry him. Given her affinity with women who have suffered, he wondered about her marriage to Captain Andrews, of whom she never spoke.

Chapter Eighteen

It was early March, Colonel Ackley sat in his 'cell', a room on an upper floor of a French mansion in Toulouse, that had been turned into a prison in one wing and a barracks in the other. The battle south of Toulouse had not gone to plan for him and the men he commanded. Although the allied forces had won and the French had fled, he and his men had been captured and marched north.

His men were Portuguese soldiers. Fifty had survived and were imprisoned here with him, mostly in basement rooms. They had marched for three days and then stopped here. It had been several days and apart from the men bringing food, such as it was, and water he had seen no one but Capitão Duarte Matias, the captain of the Portuguese regiment. When they were captured they were relieved of all their weapons, and their horses were marched with them or ridden by the French. On arrival at the mansion they were stripped of their possessions and coats and left in trousers and shirts. They had talked quietly in English and Portuguese. Learning more of each other's language passed the time for them both.

Finally, Colonel Ackley was brought before the leader of the prison. A primped, but mean looking man called Capitaine Henri Arbour. He sat at a table upon which sat the items taken from the men. Particular to the colonel were the blue cravat and horse pin Helena had given him, her letters and a drawing of the dragon of Lincolnshire.

"I have read your letters Colonel. It seems you have a pretty, young woman waiting for you at home," he spoke in French, but could tell the man in front of him understood him, by the way his eyes narrowed. The man looked like he was not one to give away much though, so it might be some fun being in command of this prison full of Portuguese scum after all. "Bring in the other man," he commanded.

A young soldier from the regiment under the colonel's command was brought in. He was injured and held his arm against his body. There was a lot of blood on his clothes and his face was pale and sweaty. "You will tell me what I need to know of my enemy, Colonel Ackley, or I will kill a man for each day you refuse," with that the Capitaine raised his sword, and pointed it at the young man's chest.

"Por favor, eu imploro coronel!" before the colonel could respond the Frenchman laughed and plunged the sword into the man's heart. As he pulled it out again the blood poured from the wound as the heart pumped the life-blood out of the man and he fell to the floor, dead.

"You did not even give me a chance to respond."

"You would only have said non and I would have had to kill him anyway. Now you know I am a man of my word and you have a day to think about the man I will kill tomorrow. Hold out his arm." Two guards now grabbed hold of Nathaniel who struggled to free himself as he wondered what the man planned to do. Reaching for the colonel's left arm the capitaine almost gently rolled up the sleeve to expose his forearm. He pulled a sharp dagger from a sheath at his waist and sliced a thin line into his flesh. "One slice, for one man, I will see you tomorrow, English bastard."

Nathaniel was feeling nauseous when he returned to his cell. There was blood on his sleeve and Duarte came directly to him, with a worried look.

"Colonel, are you injured? You are bleeding, what did the bastards do to you?"

"It is nothing, nothing at all," he pulled his arm away from the young capitão, annoyed with his fussing. "They killed a young man from the regiment right in front of me. One man for every day I refuse to tell them of the allied forces' plans and strategies."

"Why did he slice your arm, my friend?"

"For the man. Tomorrow I will receive another. I do not even know that much myself and knowing we were captured they may change the plans anyway, but if I were to tell him all I know he may kill us all at once. We have to hope the allied forces break through soon. I think Capitaine Arbour is a man who enjoys himself by making others suffer."

"You can tell them nothing and we cannot attempt an escape with so many soldiers stationed here."

"And what if they bring you into the room?"

"*Nothing.*"

Day followed day, and each day at no particular time, he was taken from the room he shared with Duarte and asked to give information of the allied forces. He refused. He had to refuse, though he wanted to shout it from the roof tops, to stop having to hear one more plea, before a man died and he received another slice to his forearm for remembrance. He would wake in the night sweating, and screaming "No!" then he would lie there and think of Helena.

Helena, who had been so strong in her own life, made him strong. He imagined her talking to him, in the same soft, soothing tones she had used with Davy when he had been screaming. He thought of what she would say to him as she played with his hair, while his head rested in her lap, "Nathaniel, you are safe in my heart. I love you. You must come back to us. Come back to Redway where we need you. I know this is hard right now but you can do it. If there is anyone who can withstand this, it is you. You are strong, Nathaniel."

Then he would talk to her and tell her that he understood, finally, about loss of will. He would never have hurt or abused her if she had married him, and he would have worked every day to make her happy. To give all of yourself to anyone, no matter that person and to never have that back in the eyes of the law, was too much to ask. Duarte asked him who he talked to and he told him of Helena and of free will. His friend told him of his own wife and son in Torres Vedras.

He could do nothing to control what was happening. He just hoped each day, that the allied forces would break through to Toulouse and save him from witnessing one more death, in the same way that Pegasus saved Helena from a life of abuse and sadness at the hands of the general.

The door opened and he was beckoned out. Head high, with thoughts of Helena giving him the strength he needed, he walked out. Capitaine Arbour was in fine form, sitting with his feet up on the table and loading a pistol. He was wearing the blue cravat Helena had given to Nathaniel and the horse pin shone within its folds.

"Ah, here he is! Colonel Ackley, how are you today? Talkative? Non?" he walked around the table and backhanded him across the face. Nathaniel tasted blood. This was not an unusual tactic. He had bruises up and down his body of varying colours from the past week of abuse. The door opened again, "here is our other guest."

"Duarte," he said with a weak voice, "no, not you." Pleased with the response, Arbour pranced around the room like an excited child. He had heard of the burgeoning friendship between the two officers and had thought up something fun to do with his plaything.

"Not you, Duarte," he repeated leering into the colonel's face. In his excitement, he got a little too close, which allowed Nathaniel to rear his head back and butt him. Blood spurted from the capitaine's nose and he reached for the pistol he had laid on the desk, pointing it at the colonel.

"Do it, you bastard, do it," Nathaniel pushed his chest up against the barrel of the gun. The Frenchman wiped at his nose with his sleeve.

"Non, Colonel, you do it. Pull the trigger on your friend or tell me what I need to know. Do neither of these things and I will cut him into pieces in front of you," he pressed the pistol into Nathaniel's hand and stood behind him. Nathaniel's body sagged. He could not kill his friend. He looked at Duarte who had tried to follow the conversation in French as much as he could.

"Eu perdoô você, Nathaniel," I forgive you, as simply as that, but Nathaniel could not do it.

"Forgive me, Helena," he said instead. Bringing the pistol to his head, he pulled the trigger.

Nothing happened. The pistol was not loaded, but he had seen the man loading it. He crumpled to his knees, he had thought he had found an escape and a way to save his friend's life, at least for a time, but it had come to naught. Behind him the manic laugh of the crazed man raged on.

"That one was not loaded, Colonel," Arbour bent over laughing, "a sleight of hand. But this one is," with that he was suddenly silent and stood up straight, raising the loaded pistol from his coats and pulling the trigger. Blood burst forth from Duarte's chest as the bullet struck his heart. He fell forward and his head struck the floor by Nathaniel's knees.

He put a hand on Duarte's head, "goodbye, my friend." He was pulled away from the body by the guards. He did not feel it when Arbour cut his arm to mark Duarte's death. Looking at the lunatic he said calmly and coldly, "when I am freed from here, I will kill you. There is nowhere in France you will be able to hide."

"Then I must kill you before you are freed, Colonel, but not yet. Non, I am not done with you yet."

Back in his cell, Nathaniel had never felt more alone, he lay on the floor and cried. He tried to summon Helena to his mind to sooth him, but why would he want to bring her to such a place, even if only in his mind. The music came to him then. The aria that Harriet had made him sing. The words of the aria flowed in his mind and he spoke them softly in English, replacing Leonore's name with Helena's.

"God! What darkness here!
O awful silence!
My surrounding deserted; nothing,
No living thing apart from me.
O difficult trial,
Yet righteous is God's will!
I do not complain,
The measure of misery stands beside you.
In the springtime of life,
Happiness has escaped me.
The truth, I dared to speak,
And these chains are my reward.
Readily I endure all the pain,
A humiliating end is my fate.
Sweet comfort in my heart,
My duty I have done!
Sweet, sweet comfort in my heart,
My duty, my duty I have done!
And do not I sense a gentle,
Soft-whispering air,
And is not my grave lit up?
I see, how an angel with a rosy scent,
Stands comforting by my side.
An angel Helena! Helena so like my wife.
Who will lead me to freedom,
To the Heavenly kingdom!
And do not I sense a gentle,
Soft-whispering air,
I see, how an angel with a rosy scent,
Stands comforting by my side.
An angel Helena! Helena so like my wife.
Who will lead me to freedom, to freedom,
To the Heavenly kingdom!
To freedom, to freedom,
To the Heavenly kingdom!
Who will lead me to freedom, to freedom,
To the Heavenly kingdom!
To freedom, to freedom,
To the Heavenly kingdom!

To the Heavenly kingdom!
To the Heavenly kingdom!"

There she was. With his head resting on her lap and her fingers running through his hair, he was able to sleep.

March came to Redway, as it invariably does after winter, and was welcomed. While it was still cold and often wet, it was at least warmer. The past winter had been one of the coldest Helena had ever known. On a Sunday toward the end of the month, she paid her usual visit to Old Joe, leaving the children with Rachel as it was so wet. Rachel was happy for the excuse to miss church.

Old Joe's house was much nicer to visit since the work was done on it the previous summer, when Colonel Ackley had been there. The colonel had made a deep impression on Old Joe and he talked of him fondly, which Helena always enjoyed. It allowed her to talk of him without the speculation of Gennie, Harriet or Ruth.

A week earlier, she had blurted out to Lord Aysthill that she was going to marry Nathaniel, and he had been opposed to it. She was sure that he would be writing to his son, advising him against the marriage, and therefore Nathaniel would know what she had said. Having raised his hopes, she could not dash them again. She still did not want to marry, but she really wanted to share her life with him.

She confided in Old Joe about the proposal, her refusal and then her declaration to his father. She wondered what he might make of it all. He looked at her kindly.

"I never could get Bertha to marry me," she was astounded.

"But you were husband and wife and had children together," she knew that the two children Bertha bore died of illness in childhood.

"Well, as far as we were concerned we were. I loved that woman, like I had never loved another before, and never since. I made a vow to her in my heart and she did the same to me. We never needed no church, or law, to say what we were to each other. That made no never mind. God could see in our hearts that we were man and wife. What more mattered? We bought this place, moved in and that was that, husband and wife. No one knew different. No one minded."

"Thank you, Joe. Thank you for trusting me with that. I never met Bertha, but I think from all you have told me, I should have liked her."

"Well I like your young man and when he comes back from France, you make sure he comes and sees me. I need to talk to that boy, and then I need to drink him under the table. I need a soldier for that. The bag o' lightweights around here are no good for a piss up."

Returning home, Helena finally sat down to write a letter that she had been avoiding for a week. After refusing Nathaniel's proposal, she had assumed that he would not want letters from her, but now that she had an idea of what could be done, and knowing that he would get letters from his family, she had to write to him and explain herself.

Nathaniel,

I hope it is still acceptable to you that I use your given name. I have missed our letters and yet putting anything down on paper is so difficult, when I have hurt you so much. I have tried many times since Christmas, but the words did not flow, because I did not know how your heart would accept them.

Now, however, I feel I finally have something to say that might rectify the situation.

Last week, Mr. Harker asked me to accompany him to Aysthill House, to meet with your father and Mr. Davidson. Lord Aysthill told me of your persuading him to make restitution to the women he has wronged. I had no idea you had done this. The fact that you did it because of me is astounding and I am exceedingly grateful. I was, however, less than grateful toward your father, who offered to make monetary restitution for Davy and his mother, but showed no remorse for his actions. He sickened me and I am afraid I told him so.

In my temper, I told him that we were to be married and you would give Davy your name, making him an Ackley after all. He was displeased to hear it, which of course was my aim, and I am certain he has written to you, asking you not to marry me. Your feelings may have changed after my refusal, and if so, then no further action is needed.

However, if your feelings remain the same, and please know that my heart has not changed in regards to you, then, when you are returned to England, I should like to meet with you. I wish to make a proposal that should, I think and hope, make us all happy. Well, all with the exception of your parents and your cousin.

If you are thinking of me, then know that I am thinking of you. If you are in battle, then I wish you strength and skill to defeat our enemies and Thor, fleet of foot.

I love you, Nathaniel. Come back to your home. To Redway, to me and our children. Forever and only ever, Your's

Helena

March passed in a blur of beatings and the killing of men. Nathaniel, however, had new purpose. Revenge. He was going to kill Arbour. He had found a spoon within the blankets Duarte had used. The handle had been ground to a point by his friend. Nathaniel used his time well and, despite the meagre food given to him, he paced the room and worked his muscles. To strengthen his arms, he lifted the only chair in the room, above him. From the barred window, he could see out onto the courtyard of the mansion. Arbour practised his sword fighting with his men and Nathaniel watched his techniques to learn a defence against him. He practised the sword moves he would need. Never before had he planned to kill a man, but with every death of a man under his command, his resolve was strengthened. Saying no to Arbour became easier, for how could he stop the death of another man if he would not stop his friend's? The pleas of the men were more difficult to take and he doubted he would ever forget them.

Thirty-five men were killed by Arbour, before the allied forces arrived in Toulouse. Thirty-five cuts to his left forearm, with many of them now healed, leaving thin, inch-long scars as a permanent reminder. He heard the distant cannon fire and knew release was at hand. Arbour should know it, too, and Nathaniel was in no doubt, that he would try to kill as many prisoners as he could, before they could be freed. He had made his plan and hoped that they should come for him first. He had to succeed, he had to take his revenge and return to England. As long as he remained alive, Helena and the children were safe from his family.

The door opened and he attacked the first guard from behind, he wrapped his left arm around the man's throat and holding the bowl of the spoon in his right hand he plunged the handle into the man's abdomen, then grasped the handle of the guard's sword as he released him. The sword unsheathed as the man fell to the ground. He pointed the sword at the second guard's chest. He had been so quick in his attack, the man had not even reached his own sword, "take me to the prisoners and I will spare your life."

They saw no French soldiers, probably because they had fled or had been sent to fight. He had relieved the guard of his sword and held one in each hand, as they proceeded downstairs. The men in the cells were in poor condition, but eager to fight. The guard unlocked the cells and then was locked in himself. Other guards arrived and were overpowered. Those not killed were locked up.

"Search the house," commanded the colonel, "bring any Frenchman down here," he threw the keys to one of his men, "if you find Arbour, he is mine. I will avenge your Capitão Matias."

He found Arbour as he was trying to exit the house to the courtyard, carrying bags of money and other collectibles. He still wore the tie and pin that belonged to the colonel. The voice of Colonel Ackley in the room behind him, stayed him in the doorway.

"Hell waits for you, Arbour."

The door stood open and he kicked the man outside, sending his booty flying in all directions. Nathaniel followed him out and the man unsheathed his sword to fight. As he had seen him do from his window, Arbour attacked in vigorous, predictable movements. Nathaniel parried each attack with minimal effort, he knew he had little strength and had to conserve it. He nicked the man on the left forearm with an inch-long slice, "un", a second on the right, "deux" and a third across his back as Arbour performed one of his favoured, fancy turns, "trois".

Nathaniel's sword fighting was among the best in the British army and had served him well through many battles. When he had time to study an opponent he was unsurpassed and he had spent weeks studying this man. Slice after slice was made in Arbour's skin, until his shirt hung from him in tatters. "Trente-quatre," thirty-four, and not a mark from this fight on the colonel. Arbour's breathing was laboured and in a final effort to take the weaker man down, he lunged for the colonel who sliced a deep gash over the Frenchman's heart and disarmed him. Blood seeped from the wound and Arbour kneeled in front of him, spent. "Trente-cinq, that one was for Duarte, you bastard. I feel him around here. I think he waits to escort you to the gates of hell."

Holding a sword to the Frenchman's heart, he slipped the other between the blue cravat and Arbour's neck. He sliced the material and put the blade through a loop pulling it and dropping it on the ground by his feet. Nathaniel joined the swords together at the man's heart, "what say you Arbour? Feeling talkative? Want to plead for your life, as you made thirty-five, good men plead?"

"Colonel, I beg…" he got no further, as Nathaniel coldly plunged both swords into the man's chest. Removing them again, he allowed the body to fall to the ground, as he turned on his heel, picked up the cravat, removed the pin and pocketed it. Discarding the fabric, he noticed the bundle of letters from Helena on the ground with the rest of Arbour's collection. He picked them up and walked to his remaining men, gathered at the door to the courtyard. They had been watching his display and as he reached them, they crowded around him to pat him on the back and offer their thanks.

Colonel Ackley led his men back to the allied forces riding astride Thor once again. He reported in behind the battle that still raged outside Toulouse. Only days later, Napoleon abdicated and was exiled to Elba. British troops began to make their way home. Before he boarded a ship to cross the English Channel, Colonel Ackley received three letters that had been waiting for him and read them on the trip home. One in particular he read several times over.

The first was from his father, informing him of a meeting he had with Mrs. Andrews where she had declared that he, Nathaniel, had promised to marry her on his return to England. He expressed that he was most unhappy about the fact that Davy Beckett should then be considered his own grandson and urged his son to reconsider. The remaining two letters he could tell from the seals were from his Mother and Helena herself. He read his Mother's first which held no surprises for him, as she had heard of his apparent engagement and was most displeased. She insisted he do his duty to the family and propose to Grace, the moment he set foot on English soil.

Finally, he turned Helena's letter over in his hands. What had happened that she had declared herself such and would the letter make him the happiest man in the world, or make him want to jump over the side of the ship? He opened it.

Her heart remained his and she had indeed told his father that he was going to marry her. She had not actually said that she would marry him however, but she had said that he was to come home to Redway, to her and to *our children*. A chink of light shone brightly, onto the hope he held in his heart that they would one day be together, and it warmed him in a way that he had not felt warm since he had sat in a stable stall with her and Davy in his arms.

On the horizon, he saw England's coastline appear and smiled.

Chapter Nineteen

She stood at the door of the barn and looked in the direction he would arrive from. She would not see him until he crested the rise and was just moments away from her. Her stomach was in knots and she gnawed on a fingernail. Disgusted with herself she turned away, took her hand away with a jolt and gnawed instead on her bottom lip. Turning back to the door she saw him, at one with his horse Thor. They were riding hell for leather with dark clouds chasing them. It pleased her that he was in a hurry! He reined in the horse to a trot as he approached the shelter.

As he crested the hill at a fast pace, Colonel Ackley saw her leaning in the doorway. She was as beautiful as ever. His chest clenched more painfully than he had ever experienced, even when he was sliced in battle. He loved her and she loved him, and apparently, she had a plan about how they would be together.

He had been to see Old Joe and they had drunk heartily. Under the influence of the ale and whisky, he had told Joe of being captured and the torture he had endured. Understanding Joe had asked him, "having experienced loss of your free will, would you give it up again, for anyone?" Nathaniel had to admit that he would not. Nodding, the old man had spoken of Helena, "she is like my Bertha that one, a man takes what she can give you and no complaining, because she is worth it."

He brought Thor to a stop just shy of the door and dismounted with a flourish. She stood aside to allow him to lead Thor into the barn. Neither of them spoke as he moved the horse into a stall and untacked him. She watched his movements. He was still a little thin. She had heard of his capture after she had sent her last letter. He still gave off an aura of strength though. Finished with his task his eyes locked onto hers.

He desperately wanted to touch her. She stood watching him, after she had closed and bolted the door. The bolt was new he noted. Although she stood stock still, he knew her well enough now, to see the signs of nervousness. Her eyes darted around watching his every move, her hands clasped together at her waist, were so tight, her fingers made her skin white where they pressed and she chewed on her bottom lip. She noticed him looking and stopped the chewing, which released a red and slightly swollen lip that only enhanced her beauty.

He stepped out of the stall and toward her. He had expected her to step back, but she held her ground. He was so close to her that his head almost touched hers with his slight bow. He broke the silence, annoyed that she had not done so first.

"Well, this is highly inappropriate," his tone brought out her own temper.

"Still you came though."

"As you see."

So, he was not going to make this easy on her. She could not blame him. Many could say she had led him to believe his proposal should be welcomed, and if she were the marrying kind, it would have been. She wondered if he believed she did not want to share her property. Well she would make her proposal and see what fate awaited her.

Walking around the area where she had delivered Missy's foal last summer, she cleared her throat.

"I am taking on partners," he stared at her intently but said nothing, "you and John actually." A furrow appeared on his brow. Was he angry?

The colonel was pained by this revelation. He had offered her his hand, his love, his protection, and the prestigious Ackley name and connexions; and she was offering him a business proposition. He was hurt.

"I do not have funds enough to buy into your business," he stated bitterly.

"No, that is not what I meant. I mean to give you forty-five percent of Redway. John would have ten percent, and so when you and I disagree, which I am sure we will, he will be the deciding vote!"

"You want to *give* it to me?" he asked, incredulously, "you would not marry me because you did not want to part with Redway."

"You know that is not true."

"So, this is your plan? We would work together side by side, but not be together as husband and wife? As much as I love Redway, I do not think I could bear it. I love you far too much. I hoped you should feel the same way."

"I do, and that is the second part of my proposal," she had been speaking to the ground as she said this, but lifted her head, looked straight up into his blue eyes and took a deep breath, "I propose that we live as husband and wife. Appear to the world as such, but without the actual ceremony and legality."

The proposition of it hit him like a physical blow. Had she gone completely mad? He would never do such a thing and compromise her that way. His face must have shown exactly how shocked he was, because she was reeling. He rubbed his hand up and down his face, as she had known he would.

"This is what you think of me?" he finally exclaimed, "that I should compromise you. You think this is what I want?"

"What I think, is that I am already compromised, you know that. That does not bother me. I think this gives us both what we want."

"I need to sit down," he became aware suddenly, that there was now a door closed between the stable stalls and the back room, where they had slept the night they had been caught in the storm. "Why is there a door here now? What have you set up beyond here?"

He marched to the door and opened it, slamming it against the wall of the stall with Perseus in it and the horse whinnied in protest. He came to such an abrupt halt after walking through the doorway, Helena almost walked right into him.

"What the...?" his breeding was the only thing that stopped the expletive erupting from him. He took in the changes in the room. The narrow bed was wider, with new bedding. The chimney had obviously been cleaned out and a fire set ready to light. A pretty table contained food and drink supplies needed and a small closet was enclosed for some privacy.

"It seems you were confident that I would agree to this, but I am sorry to disappoint you. This is not what I want. It goes against everything I was taught about being a gentleman and I take my leave of you, madam," as he spoke, the rain started to lash against the barn, there was a flash of lightning and a roll of thunder sounded.

"You cannot leave in this!" she exclaimed.

"Eastease is not that far, I will dry off easily enough when I get back."

"Then go, but realise you leave me stranded here alone, as Redway is too far in this weather. What does your good breeding think of that?"

There was no escape then. Had she planned it? She must have known he would baulk at her suggestion. He had thought her asking to meet him at this location, with rain due was perhaps a coincidence or a female sense of romance. Had he known it was a trap? Who was he fooling? He had hoped they should be stranded again.

"If we are to talk of such a course of action, I suggest we sit and drink a glass of wine," he stood behind one chair, holding it for her to sit in, ready to push her to the table.

"Thank you, Colonel."

"I think given the topic of our discussion, you had better continue to call me by my given name."

She put a hand lightly on top of his and looked into his eyes, "Nathaniel."

His name being spoken by her was like a caress. She had said it before, but here they were alone, with a bed across the room. He willed himself back in control and sat down opposite her. In silence, he poured some wine for each of them and took a sip. After she sipped some herself, she seemed to gain some confidence.

"If we had met when I was still under the control of my father, I would have felt very differently about marriage. Oh, my mother would have loved you! Son of an Earl, she would have insisted on marriage and I would not have refused," she blushed becomingly, "but I have spent so long and been through so much, making my own decisions. I cannot give that away. Still, the two parts of my proposal are separate. I have decided I need partners and have already signed over John's ten percent. I gave Ruth their house in her name, even though that makes no difference, as they *are* married. Those are your papers," she gestured at the thick document on the table.

"It was never about Redway Acres for me," he took a more sizeable drink of the wine and felt better for it, "I would have wanted you if you were penniless. I would have wanted Isabella and Davy, too, to be a family." Tears welled up in her eyes at these words and she covered her mouth to stifle a sob. Old Joe was right. She was worth it. Whatever she asked of him. He would take whatever she could give him. At this thought he rounded the table and pulled her to her feet so fast she gasped. She had wept once before and he had left because she had refused him. Now she was the one proposing, he would not refuse and leave her crying again.

"I love you, Helena," he crushed his mouth against hers. His speed and the force of his kiss stunned her. She could do nothing as his lips moved hungrily against hers. Terror at a memory fought its way up her throat, but she did her best to dampen it down. She wanted a life with him and she knew it would mean giving him that thing that men wanted. She had hoped that he would be more like she imagined in her dreams, not violent, like the old nightmares she rarely had, since meeting him. He had been so tender in his attentions before, small though they were. Well, she had survived and would survive again she thought, so she braced herself for him.

In the heat of the moment Nathaniel had given reign to his desire for her, but she did not respond in the way a woman usually would. She was still and tense. He immediately stopped and pulled back from her. He did not let go, but he did gentle his grasp on her arms. He looked into her eyes and was horrified to see the fear that he had put there.

"Damn it all," he swore lightly at his rash actions and took in a steadying breath. She misinterpreted his anger as directed at her.

"I am sorry. I-I will do better, give me some time. I fully understand a man's expectations. I will not deny you."

"Helena, no. I was angry with myself for treating you so roughly. I should have known better, but I have waited so long to kiss you and hold you, that I let my emotions get the better of me," she felt oddly powerful at the thought that she caused such a reaction in him, "*I will* do better this time."

He put his hands up to cup her face. Bringing his lips close to hers once more, he gently brushed them over her swollen, bruised ones. This time she lifted her hands up to his arms and moved her lips against his.

"Helena, I assure you that you do not understand what a man's expectations are. Your experience was brutal and cruel and I will never treat you that way. You have my word on that, as the man that loves you more than life."

"Does this mean that you are accepting my proposals, Nathaniel? Both of them?"

"It would seem that I am, though I reserve the right to continue to persuade you to marry me and I want our children to have my name. All of our children, that means Davy *and* Isabella. Additionally, you must remove this immediately," he took her left hand in his and took off the plain gold band she had put on in pretence of being married before.

She nodded in agreement, "then you may kiss me again." She tilted her face up to him and he kissed her gently, this time applying a little more pressure and encouraging her to part her lips.

"I love you Nathaniel," she murmured, when the kiss finished and this time she pulled his head down to hers and initiated another.

Realising his earlier mistake, he made sure to be gentle, although her words thrilled him. Truthfully, she was much like a virgin, she had only one violent experience, which took away the physical, but in all other aspects she was virginal and he would consider that when taking her. He would have to stem his own desires and be patient. He had wanted to hold her for such a long time and so, indulged in feasting on her lips, gradually increasing the passion. She was surprised by her reaction to him and realised she wanted him to put his hands on her body, run them over her curves. She did not know how to tell him that or even if she should. It did not seem very ladylike.

Tentatively, she leaned toward him and pressed her body against his. She was pleased when his hands slid down her arms and around her. He wrapped one strong arm around her back to her shoulder and the other slid over her bottom. He pressed her closer to him, as if trying to meld their bodies together. With a groan of pleasure, he released her lips to kiss her face and run his tongue down her neck to her collar bone. Sparks of pleasure shot through her body where it was pressed hard against him. She gasped and he reclaimed her mouth, taking advantage of her gasp to allow his tongue to slide inside.

Shocked she pulled away and looked at him. She could see the desire in his eyes, but also the humour which was never far away. She should rise to the challenge, she decided and she grabbed his face to pull him back toward her. Kissing him passionately, as he had just done to her and with his mouth open in shock, she slid in her tongue. The intimacy of it was wonderful. Pleased with her daring, Nathaniel kept their lips locked together and swept her up into his arms to walk to the bed. He sat her gently on its edge and took off her boots, and while he was at it, his, too. He took off his top coat and waistcoat, then moving over to the grate, he lit the fire.

She watched him lovingly, finally they were together and the obstacles between them were gone. She was nervous about what was going to happen next, but although this felt very intimate, she was fully clothed, apart from her boots. He was in his shirtsleeves, like in her dreams, but this was so much better. Kissing him was wonderful, she should not mind the other thing so much, if kissing happened first. He had moved back to her and was kissing her shoulders, where he had pushed her gown off them. Standing her up again, he reached around her back and started unbuttoning her gown, she was impressed at how nimble and quick his fingers were. While he was at his task, she decided to try kissing his neck as he had done to her, but his cravat impeded her way, so she reached up and started untying the complicated knot. She smiled at him, "James ties a very good knot," he studied her face.

"Are you sure, Helena? Be very sure," she tugged harder at the knot.

"I am sure that if I do not get this knot untied and be allowed to kiss your neck very soon, I shall become very frustrated," she smiled, but he continued to look at her intently. She lowered her hands from the knot and returned his look, "I am sure, Nathaniel." She gasped as her gown fell from her body into a heap on the floor. His eyes flared in desire. Reaching up again, she finally freed the knot and she clamped her mouth on his neck. She licked has he had done to her and was rewarded with another groan of pleasure from him. He reached around her again and untied her petticoat, it joined her gown on the floor. She was enjoying this process. She continued to follow his lead, but was not sure when they should actually get on the bed. Surely, he did not intend for them to get completely undressed. She stood in front of him in her chemise, drawers and stockings, and he was in only his trousers and shirt.

Nathaniel, however, was fully intending to get Helena naked. She had told him how she had been treated before and if he could make this time any different he would. He realised, she was fully expecting that the end result should still be him forcing himself into her and that it would be painful, but he was about to show her how different it could be. He was thrilled with her intuition in copying his actions and now she was pulling his shirt out of his trousers, running her slim, strong hands inside and over the skin of his back. He stiffened, because he was unsure what she should make of the scar on his chest.

"I love your body, Nathaniel. You are so strong."

"You make me strong," he said it with such feeling that she looked deeply in his eyes, wondering why it seemed to mean so much to him. She moved her hands to his chest and ran her fingers along the raised skin of his scar, "can you love even that? It is not a pleasant sight."

"Especially that, because it shows how brave you are. Can I judge the sight of it for myself?" she pushed his shirt up and he grabbed it, reaching up with his arms to pull it over his head. She gasped at the sight of him, so muscular and strong, sinewy. Magnificent, was the word that came to her mind. "You are beautiful, Nathaniel."

He laughed. Leaning in, she kissed the hollow of his collar bone and ran her tongue down his chest to the scar. There, she pressed kisses along its length, right down his rib cage.

"My turn," he said hoarsely, and keeping eye contact with her, lifted up her chemise so he could run his hands inside it and over her back. Then he moved them to the front to cup her breasts. She was shocked as his thumbs caressed her nipples and he captured her lips again, as he continued those ministrations. Then his hands lifted the chemise up over her head. In her embarrassment at being exposed to him in this way, she covered her breasts with her arms. Ignoring her reaction, he unpinned her long hair, ran his fingers through it and pulled it forward over her arms. Gently, he took her hands in his, so he could pull her arms away and allow her hair to cover her nakedness.

Slowly, he picked her up again. Lifting her out of the swathes of her gown, petticoat and chemise, to gently lay her down on the bed. Then he joined her. He did not lie on top of her as she had expected, but passed over her to her right side, leaving her free to get out of the bed if she wanted to. Leaning over he kissed her again and pushing some of her hair aside continued his attentions to her breasts with his free hand.

Surprisingly, after kissing his way down her neck again, he continued to her chest and over one breast, taking her into his mouth to lick, and suckle as Isabella once had. The sensations this action delivered to her body, were highly different to those she experienced when feeding her child. He released one nipple to go to the other and lick in circles, almost driving her mad until finally taking it in his mouth.

So distracted was she, by the new sensations that were running through her body and the familiar throbbing between her legs, she had not realised that he had untied her drawers, until he moved to kneel on the bed and remove them. He took off her stockings, too, and added everything to the pile of discarded clothes on the floor.

"Nathaniel," she breathed his name, unsure and yet not wanting to be anywhere else.

"You are so beautiful," he scanned her body. Her curves were full and soft, although her muscles were strong from riding. Her skin was creamy white and the hair in other places on her body was also red. He wanted to touch her, but waited.

"I am going to take off my trousers so we are both naked, but nothing will happen until you are ready," she nodded and he thought she might look away, but her curiosity got the better of her. She watched him eyes wide, while he unbuttoned his trousers and released himself from their constriction. Lying down he pushed them off his legs and kicked them away. She wondered if she could touch that part of him and how it might feel. While she was considering this, she was biting her bottom lip. He almost whimpered as he found it so erotic. Instead, he recaptured her lips with his and ran his hands over her body.

It was glorious just lying next to him. She was not embarrassed anymore. He loved her, he loved her body and he was just as naked as she was. He was sucking her again and ran a hand down to her thigh, resting it where her legs were pressed together. He did not push to part them though, but caressed up and down, as if he was waiting for permission. Her body seemed to be thinking for her and her legs moved apart before she even thought about what was happening. His hand was still moving slowly, caressing her thigh.

"I will not hurt you, Helena," then he moved his fingers to that private area and started his gentle caressing there. As she gasped, he closed his mouth over hers. His fingers moved expertly, parting her gently and finding a particular point they liked to focus on. That point seemed to be the centre of the familiar throbbing. She was pushing herself against his hand and pulled away from his kiss to take in breath after breath. His actions were making her pant as if she had run all the way from Redway. "Look at me, Helena," she met his blue, deep gaze as his finger slipped inside her. The feeling was not at all like her recollection from her nightmares. He moved the finger in and out, and then a second joined it. His thumb had taken up the circling of that throbbing point. All she could think, was that she did not want him to stop. Had he thought of asking her to marry him at this point, she would have been able to do nothing but agree.

"Nathaniel, what are you doing to me?"

"I am experiencing the joy of giving you pleasure, as my wife. It will peak in a moment. Enjoy it," with that he moved his head down to her breast. It was enough to send her over the edge and the throbbing moved to waves of wonderful sensation that rippled through her body, until finally she found out what he meant by a peak. This was what was missing from her dreams. She clamped her legs together, trapping his hand as her body pulsed several times and then relaxed completely sated. He moved to kiss her, removed his fingers and lay back on the bed.

"I have never experienced that before," she turned her head and looked at him.

"You never thought to touch yourself?" he asked. Although the thought of it drove him mad with desire for her. He desperately wanted to take her right there, but knew he still had to wait.

"No, I suppose it is thought sinful and not appropriate for a woman to do. Do you?" she looked at him and then down at his arousal. If he touched himself, then maybe she could touch him.

"Yes," he almost groaned the word. He closed his eyes. He had to stop looking at her for a moment to regain some control. He felt her hand on his chest, then moving down his stomach. He held his breath. This woman was instinctual. His stomach quivered under her touch. Her fingers were light as she reached for him and stroked his length. He moaned, which she took to mean that was the right thing to do. So she lifted her fingers off him and put them back to the base, to stroke upwards again. This time he captured her hand and wrapping his fingers around hers, helped her make a fist around him and move up and down. She understood. His fingers inside her had simulated his arousal. Her hand around him, simulated her surrounding him, as if he were inside her. His breathing was becoming laboured, as hers had.

"Now I am experiencing the joy in giving you pleasure, as my husband," his eyes flew open and looked at her.

"There is another way," she nodded and lay back in the bed, "I promise you, I will not hurt you." Slowly, so as not to startle her, he moved over her and inserted a leg between hers. Still, he did not push her, but allowed her to open her legs for him, "be sure Helena. I am not sure I would be able to stop myself, but I would try."

"I am sure, Nathaniel," she reached up and ran her fingers through his hair, "I love you."

Taking as much care as he could, he gradually slipped inside her. As he had planned, she was still wet from him arousing her before. With each stroke, he could penetrate her a little further. As he did so he ran a hand from her buttocks down a leg to the back of her knee so he was able to bring her knee higher and allow him deeper.

He had never felt anything like it before. He had known women, but he had waited so long for Helena and loved her deeply. He found that being in love with the woman you were taking to bed, made all the difference in the experience.

Helena was surprised by the feeling of him inside her. It felt wonderful that she was giving pleasure to him with her body, that he wanted her, and had said that he probably could not control himself and stop. She did not want him to stop. In fact, the sensations that he had built up in her with his fingers, were building up again now that he was within her. He had gently lifted up her knees and it allowed him deeper, but she wanted more. Lifting her feet, she wrapped her legs around his waist.

He looked at her surprised, but obviously pleased and continued moving. His strong muscles bulged in his arms with the effort of holding himself above her. He was strong, like an animal taking its mate and as she thought of these things, the pleasure within her increased. It was as if that spot that throbbed, had moved from where his thumb had massaged, to a spot within her that his arousal now massaged with each thrust. She was moaning again, as her pleasure built and when her body peaked the muscles within her contracted over and over. He could feel them squeeze him and could no longer hold on. He emptied himself within her with a series of guttural moans and collapsed on top of her.

"You are an astonishing man, Colonel Ackley."

"Is that something you are only just noticing, Mrs. Ackley?" he said, lifting his head to look at her.

"Not at all," she returned his smile.

Chapter Twenty

They spent the night in the bunk, keeping warm by enjoying each other's bodies. In-between those times, they talked of their plans to 'elope' and come back married.

"I do not want to spend another night away from you," Nathaniel had said and she concurred. As she fell asleep exhausted on her side, Nathaniel ran his fingers along the line of the scar on her back. It was over six years old now and had faded. He kissed along the line of it claiming it for his own. No part of her would ever belong to the general again. She was all his, as he was all hers. Pressing himself close to her back, he slept.

"Não, Duarte!" he had screamed out in his sleep and woken her.

"Nathaniel, I am here. It is me, Helena."

"An angel, Helena. Helena so much like my wife."

"I *am* your wife," then she realised he was still caught in his nightmare of being imprisoned, "Nathaniel, wake up!" she spoke firmly, using the voice she had used with Davy in the stable at Christmastime. "Come to me, Nathaniel, you are in a nightmare. I am real. I am here. You are at Redway. You are home."

"Helena," he woke groggy to see her sitting up in the bunk. She was naked, with her arms reaching out to him. The gasp caught in his throat, as the sob wrenched from his chest, "tell me that I am not dreaming," he threw his arms around her and pressed his face to her breasts.

As he cried, she was reminded of comforting Davy and held him to her in much the same way. He told her in a wavering voice what had happened, told her of Duarte, of the cuts to his arm and of putting the pistol to his own head. Then he told her how he had killed the man responsible.

"You are so brave and strong, Nathaniel. To bear the weight of this alone is too much and I am glad that you shared it with me," she brought his arm up to her lips. She had wondered what had happened to him and now she knew. Gently, she kissed each scar. Thirty-five kisses, "these now belong to me. He is dead and controls you no longer."

He put his head to her breasts and thinking he wanted her to hold him some more she put her hand on his head. She felt his tongue on her skin and then a nipple and laughed, "you are taking advantage of my compassion, sir!" she exclaimed playfully. Lifting his head, he looked seriously at her.

"I kissed the scar on your back when you were asleep, so that no part of you could be *his* ever again."

"You did!" she was surprised they had thought to take the same action, "can you do it again do you think? I would like to be aware of it."

He turned her gently onto her stomach and moving her hair aside spread tiny kisses up and down the scar on her back. Aroused once more, he moved his body over her and pushed a leg gently between hers. Bending his head to her back, he ran his tongue along the scar. She moaned quietly and opened her legs for him. After all their loving, he slipped into her easily and then scooping a hand under her, he lifted her to her hands and knees. As he moved within her, his hands roamed over her breasts and then between her legs, to that spot that he had such a talent to make throb.

When they were spent, they collapsed on the bed, entwined their bodies together and slept, peacefully at last, until dawn.

The next day, Nathaniel headed back to Eastease and packed a bag quickly. He talked to Harker, saying that he was leaving with Helena and would return married. Harker wanted to stop him, to make him agree to a wedding from Aysthill or Eastease, in the proper fashion. Nathaniel told him that he could not bear another night away from her after the previous night together. They had waited too long, to be apart anymore. He and Thor then rode to Redway Acres, stopping in to see Old Joe and telling him the news, adding a wink. The old man was very happy for them both and asked the colonel to give his best to *Mrs. Ackley*.

Helena had arrived at Redway rather dishevelled and Ruth shooed her maid away to help her herself. "We are going away for a few days, Ruth. We will come back married."

"You are getting married or you will come back married?" Ruth asked her. Helena smiled at her.

"Does it matter, my friend? I never knew it could be like this."

"Of course you did not. What experience did you have? Well, I said to him that you would find a way and you have. Jacky will drive the carriage. I should suggest John, but you know that he and the colonel are always butting heads. Jacky will be discreet. Where are you going?"

"He has a friend in Sheffield he wants to see. We will find a place to stay for a few days, so we will have been away long enough to have gone to Scotland, and then we will visit Sheffield on our return journey. I am so happy, Ruth."

"Then I am happy for you, my girl," the two women embraced.

On the journey north, they sat in the Redway carriage driven by Jacky, and talked and bantered, kissed and embraced. Nathaniel had purchased a ring in London on his way north, in the hope that he should need it. As they sat together in an embrace, they made their own personal vows to each other and he slipped the ring on her finger.

"Mrs. Nathaniel Ackley," he said and kissed her passionately.

They spent a week at the Lakes in a secluded Inn, where they arrived as Colonel and Mrs. Ackley. Most of the time they spent in their rooms, but they did take in some pretty walks and rode the horses around the lakes, too. Jacky had his own room and they gave him plenty of money to keep himself occupied at the bar or in the local village, where he was able to purchase a gift for Rebecca.

Helena told Nathaniel of Dowager Alcott's visit to Redway while he was in France. She was planning to buy land in Lincolnshire and sell her property in London. She was inquiring about the land opposite Redway. She was looking for a purpose and was interested in the ways Helena helped people, particularly, women who found themselves in desperate circumstances.

Nathaniel told Helena of Tommy Smithson, how they had saved each other, and that he had very little to keep house with his mother in Sheffield, as he could not find well-paying work. Tommy's father had died recently. Nathaniel had been sending him money regularly to help him, but suggested, as he was so good with Thor, that they could give him work at Redway.

She agreed and they discussed where the Smithsons could live. Building had already begun on adjoining cottages. One was for Jacky and Rebecca, when they married and the other could be for the Smithsons. It would be small with just two bedrooms, and one of those very small, but it should do until something else worked out.

Their happiness lasted only as long as their return to Redway. They arrived expecting to be greeted with congratulations, they were met, instead, with sad eyes. The children ran to their mother and she gathered them to her in her skirts. "What has happened, Ruth?" she asked her housekeeper with fear in her voice.

"Tis Old Joe, Helena. John went to look in on him a couple of days ago, and found him dead. He went peaceful, in his sleep, holding a letter from Bertha to his chest. Even if you had been here, you would not have been with him when he went. Bertha was with him I am sure."

"Bertha was always with him, in his heart."

"No one much accepted him, until you showed them different."

"He was a kind and loving man, once you got behind the gruff exterior... and the smell," she laughed, but with tears in her eyes for the old man, "what is being done?"

"Mrs. Dawley and I went and laid him out. John asked Dom to make up a coffin for him. He is the best we have with wood and is using the workshop here. I hope that is all acceptable. Mr. Brooks has been to see Old Joe and we have put plenty of flowers around the room. Mr. Brooks says he has a plot in the church graveyard for him, next to Bertha. We are burying him on Saturday."

"That all sounds acceptable. There is no other family that we know of?" Ruth shook her head sadly, "I will go and see him myself tomorrow," she looked up at Nathaniel, who had tears in his eyes. He had been fond of him, "*we* shall go and see him tomorrow," she corrected with a small smile and then ferried the children into the parlour. They had some news to impart to them.

Ruth left to get some refreshments and give them some privacy. Before Helena had even begun to talk to the children of her 'marriage' to Nathaniel, Davy piped up in his straightforward way.

"Where did you go on a trip with the colonel, Mama?" Nathaniel smiled at him using the term.

"Well, Colonel Ackley asked me to marry him and I said I would! We did not want to wait, because we had missed each other while he was away, so we went away to get married," she had planned to ask the children if they would want him to be their father, but before she could they both threw themselves at the man.

"Papa! Papa!"

Nathaniel was overwhelmed with emotion. The news that Old Joe had passed had barely sunk in, before the two children that he loved most dearly in the world, were clambering over him and calling him *'Papa'*. His tears flowed as happiness enveloped him.

"Papa, why are you crying?" Isabella was concerned.

"Because I am happy, sometimes you cry when you are happy."

"Even men?" asked Davy, a little concerned. The last time he had seen the colonel was the day after he had cried.

"Even men. Come to us, Helena," he said gruffly and she came, removed the two children from his lap and sat on him herself. Then she gathered their children on her own lap. He wrapped his strong arms around them all.

"Kiss Mama!" squealed Isabella.

"Kiss Mama!" repeated Davy.

Their lips met gently and then more passionately, before Isabella joined in with a kiss of her own to her father's cheek and Davy to his mother's. Just at that moment, Ruth walked in and stared at the happy group. How wonderful it was, she thought, that her girl had a family at last.

They buried Old Joe on a bright, late-May afternoon that held the promise of summer to come. Helena was surprised by how many people had bothered to turn up in the church and at his graveside. Many were the men who had worked on Old Joe's house with Nathaniel, the summer before. Colonel and Mrs. Ackley, had allowed all their workers the afternoon, to pay their respects and there was food and drink aplenty for everyone back at Redway Acres.

All the Harkers attended with many of the staff from Eastease. Nathaniel and Helena had been to visit Eastease the day before with the children and they had all been congratulated. Harriet had been a little put out, that she had been denied a wedding to plan, but everyone was happy that the pair had finally come together.

Mr. Brooks completed the graveside service and as Old Joe's casket was lowered into the ground, Helena sang an old folk song that she had often heard sung in the stable. It was fitting that it was about and old tramp who had not been accepted at the local tavern.

"I'm sitting quietly in my chair,
They think I only sit and stare,

But I don't miss much just sitting here,
'Cos here comes poor Old Joe.

He puts his money on the bar,
Would like to buy us all a jar,
And he always asks ya, ha'ya are,
But they don't ask poor Old Joe.

They seem to think he's a disgrace,
They say he low'rs the tone of the place,
Wasn't born with a silver spoon in his face,
No, they don't like poor Old Joe.

He's on his feet, he's on his way,
And as he leaves us every day,
The only words you'll hear him say,
God bless ya, God bless ya,
No, they don't like poor Old Joe.

I'm sitting quietly in my chair,
They think I only sit and stare,
No, I don't miss much just sitting here,
But I do miss poor Old Joe.
God bless ya, God bless ya,
God bless ya, poor Old Joe.

Chapter Twenty-One

It took a while for Colonel Ackley to settle into the routines of Redway Acres. Helena was used to her way of doing things, but tried hard to make adjustments by asking John rather than telling him now that he was a partner, and by including Nathaniel in discussions and decisions. Nathaniel, as it turned out was very good with figures and papers, and it was a good way for him to learn the business. He had some useful connexions and his name went a long way in greasing the wheels. He worked well with the men, whose respect he had earned by handling both Thor and Perseus. Perseus was obviously the more dominant of the two horses, but Colonel Ackley was the dominant male in the stable.

One person who did not accept the colonel well, was John. He felt that the man had taken advantage of Helena and now lorded over them all, because he had finally persuaded her to marry him. Redway Acres no longer belonged to her and she was no longer his girl. He resented the man for it. He realised Helena fancied herself in love, but this opportunity-grabbing scoundrel did not deserve her.

Things came to a head after they had all been discussing Persephone. The mare was, by Helena's calculations, two months shy of foaling. Nathaniel had been surprised to hear that Thor was the sire. It must have happened when they were on their picnic last September. Thor had managed that day, what had taken Nathaniel several months more, and had his way with a red-head. Afterward, John had overheard Nathaniel congratulating the stallion and speculating whether he could manage the same outcome with his own mare.

"Bloody full of yourself you are," growled John, as he passed. Nathaniel put out a hand to stop him.

"Are we going to do this now, John? This has been brewing since you met me."

"Since you took advantage of her in the storm last year, you mean."

"I thought we had settled that. I did not take advantage of her."

"Did not offer to marry her though, did you?"

"She did not want to get married."

"Then you forced your bastard on her."

"Call my son a bastard again and I will knock you into next week."

"You can try. If you wanted to marry her then, why not do it instead of going to war? She said she would take you! She cried for days and you were off playing soldier."

"I wanted her to *want* to marry me, not as a duty to save me from battle. She had already refused me, but would say yes if I stayed. I was sorely tempted John, sorely tempted, but I had already received my orders. Would you have me desert King and Country and my brothers in arms? How honourable should you think me then?"

"If you are so *honourable*, why did you compromise her the other week, in the shelter, and then have to whisk her off to Scotland to a rushed marriage. Her stable is good enough for you to take from her, but she is not good enough for a lavish Aysthill wedding. You have never introduced her as your wife, to your family."

"My father is not welcome here and I have not taken her stable away. You had better stop talking," he warned.

"I am not afraid of you. You might best me in a sword fight, but I will take my chances with fists."

"You would only have one chance, John. I have let you have your say, now it is my turn. I have wanted Helena since the day my eyes landed on her. She will not marry me. I did not have to marry her to get the stable she gave me half her share. I do not own her. She gives herself to me every night, willingly. You do not like it, because you are not the man she turns to anymore."

John's fist landed squarely on Nathaniel's jaw and it staggered him. The man had a hand like rock. He blocked the next one and landed a punch of his own to John's stomach. Doubled over John charged and took the colonel down to the floor, where they rolled over, fists flying, each trying to get the upper hand. Nathaniel managed to get on top of John and straddled him so he could punch him again. As he pulled back his fist, Helena's arms wrapped around his and hung on, preventing him from using it. She pulled him to his feet. As John was scrambling up, she released Nathaniel and stood between them arms stretched out, keeping them apart. Each was rubbing his jaw or another part of his own body, that had taken a blow.

"Oh, you are such… *men!*" she exclaimed trying to find a suitable insult, but realising that was the one that fit, "you are worse than the horses, fighting to see who is the dominant male. Even they did not resort to that. Well I have news for you, there is no dominant male at

Redway Acres, there is a dominant *female* and you are looking at her!" she stood with her hands now fisted on her hips and glared at each of them, in turn.

Turning to see many other men, who had been watching the fighting and now her reaction to it, she bellowed at them, "all the rest of you take note of that. I am in charge here. Now get about your business and *leave!*"

Turning to John with Nathaniel at her back, she defended her husband, "I will not have you talk of Davy like that, John. If I hear you say it again, I'll have your guts for garters. He looks like Nathaniel because he is his half-brother. Now he is our son and you will give him the respect he deserves, in the same way we respect Jacky. I never want to hear you say, that Nathaniel played at being a soldier. His services to King and Country are considerable, as was his suffering when injured and captured. I will NOT have you belittle that. There has not been a lavish Aysthill wedding because we are not married. I will not give over my free will, John, you know why, and Nathaniel has accepted that, although he is not entirely happy with the situation. The pretence is for society and the children. Nathaniel and I have made our vows to each other and in our hearts. He is the best man I have ever known and would never hurt me or the children. In fact, he would give over everything for us. His father is not welcome here because he threatened me some time ago and Nathaniel swore to kill him if he came near me or Redway again. If you cannot accept any of this, I am sorry for it. If you feel you have to leave I will understand, but be very saddened and we will buy back your share in the stable."

John's shoulder sagged. He had nodded his head during this speech. He had not been aware that she had been able to hear every word he said. He had aimed to hurt the colonel, not his girl. Nathaniel harrumphed and made to turn away from them. His wife's voice stayed him.

"Where do you think you are going, my husband?" with John at her back she turned on Nathaniel, "how dare you fight with John this way? You need to show him some respect. He is no longer a paid worker here at Redway, he is our partner in business and you decide to resolve your differences with fisticuffs? Where is your good breeding now, son of an Earl? That aside, this is the man who has taught me all he knows of horses, helped me keep Redway going and has been more like a father to me than my actual father. You know that to be true, as you have met my parents. At a time when they were more interested in what their neighbours thought, John and Ruth were there to comfort me, not blame me. They left all they had known in Norfolk to travel with me here and protect me and my secrets. They are the rocks I leaned on when my grandfather died. Had your father come to Redway when you were away, John would have stood up to him for me, no matter the cost."

Looking from one man to the other, she finished. "I do not want to see either of you again, until you can be civil to each other," then she turned on her heels and left them to sort it out.

"She set you down," John had humour in his voice, "you had to take it and she is not even your wife."

"She set you down, too and she is no longer in charge of you," John nodded conceding the point.

"I am sorry for disparaging you, Colonel, and Davy. I love that boy."

"I am sorry, too, John. I thought that I did not have to ask permission of anyone to marry her, given her situation here and with her own father, but I was wrong. She has a father, and you have done a fine job of raising her," he moved toward the man and bowed, "it is too late to ask permission, but I hope that you will accept me as her husband. I love her, John, more than life itself."

"Son of an Earl, eh?" he grasped Nathaniel's arms, "she has done pretty well for herself," then he embraced him.

The Dowager, Janine Alcott, made her second visit to Lincolnshire in August of 1814. She was happy on her arrival, to personally congratulate Colonel and Mrs. Ackley. She had purchased the property opposite, as she had hoped, and was planning the furnishings. She still had work to do in London, so was not ready to move permanently, yet. For the time being, she stayed at Redway Acres as a guest.

The children were thrilled to have her there, they had fallen in love with her the last time she had visited, when she thrilled them by speaking French. Davy particularly loved languages. He had inherited that same trait as Nathaniel. He marvelled at the dowager and his father speaking fluent French. Janine adored to speak her native language, as her husband had never bothered to learn. They then engaged Davy in some simple phrases.

She also brought with her a gift for Isabella. The colonel had entrusted her with Isabella's stories, as the young girl sent them to him, and asked the dowager to get them made into a book. A one copy first edition, Isabella was delighted. The woman would have done anything for her granddaughter.

She talked at length with Helena of her ideas for her new purpose. Helena told her of Tommy Smithson and how he had made himself a wooden leg. She had wondered about a place where people who had lost a limb, could learn to find a meaningful purpose of their own. She had commissioned Tommy to make himself a leg with a foot, that could be used with a stirrup so that he could ride again. She and Nathaniel had talked often of how working with horses always made them feel better and how freeing riding could be. If they could show amputees that they can care for and ride horses, she felt it could help them realise they still had more to contribute in life, and Tommy could make the wooden legs. The dowager thought it a wonderful idea and they started to make plans on how to combine it with helping women in unfortunate situations.

The Ackleys had been working, when they could, to clear the contents of Old Joe's house. There were no valuables to speak of, just the house that he had told Helena he had bought with Bertha. He had no family, so she supposed the house should revert to the Crown. As she was looking through a box of papers, she came across a handwritten note, dated the day she had met with Nathaniel at the cabin to present her proposals.

"This paper is to stand as the last wishes of Joseph Baxter of the cottage down the lane off the North Road, Near Eastcambe, Lincolnshire.

I do not have much in this world, except the love that is in my heart for my dearly, departed wife Bertha and our two children, who were taken from us far too early. Since Bertha died, I have sought to live for the day when I could join her, but was surprised to find I still had some room in my heart for a dear woman with a child of her own, who cares for me, I know not why. Mrs. Andrews spurred a village to come together to repair my home, and brought a young soldier into my life that I hope I was able to help by listening to him talk of his soldiering experiences. Something he felt he could share with no one. I advised him to put his pride aside and accept this woman for who she was.

The cottage and its land is all I have to leave behind in this world.

I had thought to leave it to either one of them, but as they already have a home at Redway Acres, they would probably just give it away to a worthy person anyway.

So, it is my last wish that this home, that gave Bertha and I so much happiness and sadness, such as life is, should be given to the young man that saved Colonel Ackley in Spain, in June 1813. I believe his name is Tommy. Such bravery and heroism deserves reward and he is in need.

Thank you, Tommy, and I wish you a good life, and perhaps a Bertha of your own.

Old Joe"

With tears in her eyes, Helena showed it to Nathaniel, who nodded in approval. Tommy and his mother could move to Redway Acres sooner than hoped.

Colonel Ackley loved his married life. He worked hard in the stable and was part of the decision making with Helena and John, with whom he was finally friends. Isabella and Davy adored their new father and every night he shared his bed with the most beautiful woman in the world. There was, however, one problem bothering him and he had an idea how to solve it.

Now and again, in the stable, Helena would flinch in recollection of her brutal experience at the hands of the general. If she were alone in a stall with a man, she would step out and lean over the stall door instead, even if it was him or John. He did not think she was even aware that she did it, but it hurt him that she should, even unconsciously, turn away from him in fear.

He recalled how he had reacted, when Old Joe had gotten on the back of Thor with him a year ago, to go down to the Tavern. He thought of the old man fondly. That had been the first time someone had ridden on the back of Thor with him since his injury in battle, and the recollection had been painful and raw. That was until John had started laughing at them and had brought him back to the present. On the journey to the tavern with Old Joe he had told the old man all about Tommy. That moment had given him another memory, leaving the old one on the battlefield where it belonged. He wanted to do that for Helena, to give her a new memory in a horse's stall alone with a man. Him. Her husband.

He smiled when he thought of his plan, because it was not a completely selfless plan. She had been almost virginal when he had first taken her and gradually he had expanded her horizons. She was certainly an eager student. This was another step on that journey they could take together and one he was planning on enjoying immensely. He had made sure that John should be sure to keep the stable clear of people, while he took his pleasure in his wife.

It was a warm, summer day and he walked out to the stable to find Helena all alone. She was wandering the corridors. She heard him come in and turned to him.

"Where is everyone?"

"I have no idea. Come over here with me," he beckoned her to the empty stall. It was banked with straw, not a sight of the dirt floor, as there had been on that day when she was only twenty. She hesitated at the doorway. He was lying in the straw on a thick woollen blanket and patted the empty side for her to lie on it with him.

"It is the middle of the day."

"As it was when you first seduced me, as I recall," he retorted. He wanted to reach up and pull her to him as she stepped cautiously closer, but he waited patiently, he did not want to startle her. She sat on the blanket and looked at her husband's lean body.

"I love you. Do you trust me?" she nodded.

"I love you, too, Nathaniel," she sighed in contentment and slowly lay down next to him. He moved above her and kissed her gently. His kisses roamed her face and then down her neck to the hollow where it met her shoulders. There he licked with his tongue and sucked gently, she gasped in pleasure. She loved how he would do these things before taking her.

"Taking her!" at the thought of it she tensed and her eyes flew open. She wondered why she felt this moment of panic. She was safe, she was with Nathaniel. He loved her, why was she tense? Because it was the middle of the day? Because any of the stablemen or even John could walk in at any time? No, neither of those felt right. Because it was a stall and that was where *it* had happened. She realised that was it.

She had tensed and he sensed it, but he continued his gentle exploration of her lips, neck and face. He slowly loosened her bodice and flicked his tongue inside to the soft skin of her breasts.

Now that she thought of it, the only part of him that was touching her was his tongue. He was not holding her down, so she could get away. She could escape, but why should she? His exploring tongue had found her nipple and was rubbing across it. Another gasp escaped her and her tensed body relaxed, enjoying only the sexual tension that he brought out in her.

"I do love you so, Nathaniel." He looked up at her from his vocation and smiled. "I love your tongue." She nodded toward her exposed breast and saw desire flash in his lovely, blue eyes.

"Do you?" he asked and after she nodded eagerly he added, "do you trust me?"

"Yes, my love, of course I do," oh, when was he going to put that tongue to good use again? He moved his hand to reach below her skirts and move it between her knees. Slowly, and while keeping his eyes on her, he pushed gently one knee aside and then the other.

"Trust me, my love. You need never be afraid of me," she looked down at her breast, where her nipple waited for his mouth.

"I think," she said tartly, "you should stop talking and put that tongue to a better use."

He smiled broadly, "for once we agree!" He playfully lifted up her skirts and disappeared underneath them.

"Nathaniel, what are you doing?" she could feel his hands exploring up the insides of her thighs and his fingers parting her drawers to expose her to him and then, was that his tongue? She gasped and then again, as he licked again. "Nathaniel, oh my!" she could say nothing more, as his fingers moved from holding her drawers apart to holding her apart and she pushed herself against his mouth. He continued to lick and suck her. Sometimes his tongue would flick quickly and sometimes wash over her. His fingers were moving again and one long, strong finger slipped easily inside her moving in and out while he continued to lick and then a second finger. She was losing control. He had brought her to a peak, as he had termed it, many times before, but never like this. Her skirts were rising up her legs and his head appeared from beneath them. She plunged her fingers into his hair, moaning and writhing. With a final gasp her body bucked and one last big wave of pleasure engulfed her. She clamped her legs either side of his head. Her body continued to wrack with pulses, as he withdrew his fingers and raised his head with a self-satisfied smile on his face. He had enjoyed it, too, it seemed and she was glad, because that meant he should be more inclined to do it again.

Looking at her husband kneeling between her legs, she smiled and then notice a sizeable bulge in the front of his trousers. Oh, she was going to knock that smile off his face and he should enjoy it. A thought had come to her while he was pleasuring her, that she must be able to reciprocate in the same way. She had learned how to hold him and give him pleasure with her hand, but now she had another idea. Sitting up suddenly, she barrelled him over into the straw and straddled him. He laughed with her and pulled her to him.

"Oh no," she said, as he made to roll her over onto her back, "it is my turn to use my tongue." He was not sure he took her meaning, but her hands were getting busy on his body as she pulled his shirt from his trousers and pushed it up so she could kiss his chest. She undid his trousers while she slowly lowered her tongue onto his nipple and teased him. Then she ran her tongue, inch-by-inch, down the middle of his body and found the hair that she could follow in a line, leading down where he strained against the last vestiges of his clothing. Pulling down she released him and saw how wonderfully erect he was. She loved that pleasuring her had made him this way.

He moaned and she looked up at him from all fours. My god, she looked like a temptress, with her red hair falling around her face, bodice undone and revealing those creamy breasts he loved to touch, with her skirts raised high on her thighs. Was she going to do what he thought she might? Was it a sin to pray to God that she would? Or perhaps he would make a deal with the devil?

"Do you trust me?" she asked, with a smile.

"Stop talking," he growled. Obliging, she licked her lips to moisten them and then stuck out her tongue and licked him from base to tip. All the while, she kept her eyes on his and he held his breath. Then she took him into her mouth. Thank you, God, he let out all the air he had been holding in, on a moan.

He could barely control himself, but he tried, how he tried, because he wanted the sensations she was giving him to continue forever. She licked him, sucked him and scraped her teeth lightly along his length as her mouth moved over him. Her hand joined her mouth wrapping around him and moving in time. His hands came to her shoulders and tried to stop her, "you have to stop or I will empty into you," but she pushed his hands away and continued, readying herself.

The warm liquid filled her mouth, as it was his body's turn to buck and moans to escape his lips. It tasted salty and she swallowed.

Thoroughly spent, he lay on the straw unable to move. She lay on top of him and laughed lightly.

"Nathaniel, you are so full of surprises. That was so much fun."

"*I* am full of surprises?" he wished he had his breath back and that he could take her to bed and do it all again.

Later that day, as Helena sat working in the office of the barn, she heard an angry roar, that was unmistakably her husband's voice, "argh! What the blazes? Shit? Get back here you little bugger! I will beat the shit out of you and throw it on your head. Let us see if you find that funny, boy," she saw the small streak of her son run past the door and scamper up the ladder to the loft above.

She stepped out of the office and looked in the direction he had come from. Nathaniel was striding her way, brushing straw and horse dung out of his hair and off his clothes. She laughed, "did you fall for the bucket on the door trick?" he did not return her amused look, but walked into one of the storage rooms and picked up a crop. She looked horrified at him and backed up to the ladder to prevent him from climbing it. She took one step up it backwards, so she was facing him nose to nose. His anger was still bubbling and my god, he did smell foul!

"Get out of my way, woman."

"Or what?"

"I beg your pardon?"

"What are your intentions, if I do not move out of your way?"

"Just move out of the way. I need to discipline my son."

"*Our* son."

"Regardless, he still needs discipline."

"Because he played a trick on you?"

"Because he covered me in horseshit!"

"Well, that will wash off your skin and your clothes, although I imagine you will still be full of it. How quickly will the sting of this crop wash off Davy's skin? Should I warn Issie to expect the same treatment?"

"No, of course not."

"What of me? Will you beat me if I do not let you pass?"

"No, never. I love you. I would never treat you that way. You should know that by now."

"I thought I did, but here you are threatening Davy, whom you also profess to love. A grown man with a crop, against a small boy. Perhaps these are your true colours?"

"You do not understand. It is different with boys. Boys need to experience tough love, to help them face the realities of the world. They are beaten at school and in the army."

"Are they the reasons your father gave, for beating you?" she looked in his eyes and saw realisation there, "Davy is not at school nor in the army. He is at home, where he should be safe. I think he has faced enough of the *realities of the world* for a seven-year old, do you not?"

"Yes."

"He's probably thinking you are going to send him back."

"No, never!"

"I know that, but he does not. You should have done better to laugh when it happened. Rolled around in it with him, cleared it up and then had a bath together!"

"Maybe I will play this trick on you, so we can have a bath together," he moved to press his smelly body to hers, "do not think I missed that *'full of it'* comment." She jumped swiftly down from the ladder, pulling the crop out of his hand as she did.

"You do not need to play a trick on me for that, sir!" she laughed, tapping him on the bottom with the crop, "go talk to him and then clean up the mess together. I will go and ask Ruth to get a bath ready."

"Helena," she stopped on her way out and turned to him, "thank you," she nodded and he climbed up the ladder.

"Davy, are you up here still?" there was no reply, but he heard a rustling that sounded bigger than a rat, so thought it must be his son, "I am sorry, Davy. I will not beat you. Will you come out?"

"No, I do not believe you and I will not go back to Bainbridge."

Nathaniel sat on the edge of the hole with his heels resting on the top rung of the ladder. As was his habit, he rubbed his hand across his face. What was the matter with him that he had thought it acceptable to beat his son? He, who had cursed his father and cousin for their treatment of the boy, was going to do no better by him. Thank the Lord, he had Helena to talk him down from his temper. Why had he not just laughed at it like she said? It was, after all, a splendid trick. Not with horseshit, but possibly water or straw would be funny.

He started to laugh and the more he laughed the funnier it got, "you got me good, Davy," he continued to laugh. A snort of laughter came from the same area of straw that the rustling had.

"Your face was funny!" the boy continued to laugh, with Nathaniel this time.

"Come on out, Davy, we need to talk."

"You will not send me back? You can beat me if you want to, but do not send me back." Nathaniel closed his eyes on the tears he felt forming there, his heart was breaking for his boy. What had he done? Had he irrevocably lost the boy's trust?

"Davy, men do not talk of love much. When I asked your mother to marry me, I did not just ask for the honour of being her husband, but the honour of being a father to Issie and to you. I said that I would give my life for any one of you and it would be worthwhile. I still believe that," he opened his eyes and saw the boy standing next to him, "I love you, Davy, and nothing you can do will ever change that. Nothing."

"What if I were to..."

"Nothing."

"But what if I...?"

"Nothing," he smiled as Davy sat down next to him with his legs dangling into the hole, too, "I am new to being a father, neither of us started this when you were born. I am sure that I will lose my temper with you again and you will get angry with me, too, but I promise that I will never beat you and I will never send you away. One day though, you will leave me. It is what sons do."

"Will you teach me how to fight?" the question surprised him.

"Yes, I will and I will teach you when it is right to fight. That is just as important. Also, I am warning you now, that I am good at playing tricks on people and I will retaliate for today. You will not know when or where, Davy, but I am going to get you good, too!" the boy giggled and his father reached over and ruffled his hair.

"We have some shit to clean up, my boy and then we will have a bath." Nathaniel leaned out over the hole, clasped his fingers on the opposite side and swung himself easily down into the room below. Looking up he was shocked to see Davy follow suit and he hung there, afraid to let go, "let go, Davy, I will catch you."

Davy let go immediately and Nathaniel caught him easily. As his heartbeat steadied itself once again, with his son safely in his arms, he realised that his son's trust in him was restored.

John had been preoccupied with his own ideas for several weeks. The colonel had talked to him of Helena's habit of avoiding being in a horse's stall alone with a man. He had never noticed it before, but once the colonel had pointed it out to him, he noticed it often. Then the man returned to him with an idea for freeing her, from what was obviously the reason for it. He did not give John much in the way of detail, but he had said he wanted to replace the memory of her attack, with a different memory. He implied that it would mean his own taking of her in a stall. He asked John to make sure that the stable was cleared and remained so while he did this.

John was not sure, but Nathaniel had mentioned how it had helped him when Old Joe had ridden on the back of his horse, because the last time that had happened was when Tommy had ridden behind him and he thought he was going to die. What Nathaniel had not contemplated, was that the last time John had cleared a stable like this, was when the general was beating his horse and he had wanted none of the men getting in the way of that, no matter how wrong it had been. Of course, Helena had gotten in the way, instead, and he regretted that action every day. So, he decided he should keep an eye on what was happening, in case things did not go as the colonel planned and he could intercede.

What John did not plan on, because he had not thought the whole thing through, was exactly what he would be seeing. He was no peeping tom, but once things had started, and he could see that the colonel was treating Helena the right way and she was receptive, he could not move without making noise and alerting them to his presence. So, he ended up watching and wondering, because in all their married years together, he had never put his mouth on Ruth in the place that the colonel had with Helena, and he wondered what it would be like.

He had thought of doing it with Ruth now and again, and his body had responded to those thoughts. He had taken Ruth a few times since, and stuck with their tried and true way of doing things. It was certainly satisfactory, but now that this idea was in his head, he could not think of much else.

One particular day, he stopped over at the house with one excuse or another to see Ruth and look into her eyes, sweep her up in an embrace, or run his hand down her back.

"What has got into you today?" she had said laughingly, after he had visited her for the third time that morning, but her eyes looked softly at him.

"You," he kissed her neck lightly, "how about an early night tonight?"

"But it is not even Saturday, John!" she exclaimed. They had gotten into a routine once they had children to make sure that they found some time alone together, though the children were older, they had not bothered to change it.

"How about sneaking home now?" he suggested with a teasing squeeze of her bottom. She batted at his hand with the cloth she was holding and laughed.

"Have you been drinking, John Robertson? We both have work to do, so you had better go and get on with it," she swiped at him again, laughing and then, as he left, she flicked the towel at his behind, giving it a slap. Pleased, he left and headed back to work.

Later that evening, he had finally got her into their bed. She lay on her back waiting for him, as she had done so often. He hoped that she would be receptive to what he now longed to bring her. Leaving their two candles burning, he got into bed.

Leaning over her, he kissed her fondly and then with more passion. She returned his kisses surprised at his attention to her lips, as over the years the time spent just kissing had waned, as it did with married couples she assumed. He was undoing the buttons at the front of her nightgown, well that was surprising, but not unpleasant. He would normally give her breasts some attention through the cotton, but not for many years had he done more. She had not really minded, after feeding two bairn they were not as high up as they once were and honestly, she was a little embarrassed about him seeing them.

He was kissing her neck and then moved down toward her breasts and started suckling like a bairn, he had not done that in a while either and a familiar sensation was building up in her. However, his attentions had continued so long, that those sensations she was experiencing were tingling right down her body, and before she knew what was happening she was opening her legs and moaning slightly. Thrilled, John paused in his efforts and looked up into her eyes.

"Do you trust me?"

"Of course I do, you silly bugger. I married you!" and with that he moved his head lower and pushed her nightgown up. As he disappeared under the blankets she asked, "where are you going?" Suddenly, she gasped, he had just licked her. Down there! What was he thinking of doing such a thing? It was... wonderful! Thrill after thrill soared through her, in a way it had not in a long time, if ever. When she was spent, she pulled her husband up to her and kissed him. Wrapping her legs around him, she pulled him to her so he could enter her. He was harder and more ready than she had remembered in a long time, so she was sure that he had enjoyed the experience, too.

The next morning, Helena noticed a glow about her housekeeper that she had not seen before. It was the kind of glow that she saw in herself, ever since allowing Nathaniel into her bed. She sidled up to Ruth, who had mentioned the day before how amorous John was being, "did you have an early night last night?" Ruth could not help telling her how John had surprised her. She thought the younger girl should be shocked, but she just laughed.

"The first time Nathaniel did that to me, I thought he was mad for about two seconds and then I no longer cared as it felt so wonderful. Did you reciprocate, Ruth?" Ruth just stared at her.

"You mean you...? Really?" Helena explained to her what she had done. Ruth left the room looking thoughtful. Helena chuckled, thinking how John should be getting a pleasant surprise that night!

Chapter Twenty-Two

Summer turned to Autumn, and things continued smoothly for all in the vicinity of Redway Acres. A new governess was appointed for Davy, while Rachel continued to work with Isabella and learn from the new governess herself. Isabella continued to improve on the pianoforte and write her stories, which included a young prince and a loving father, who worked slaying dragons. The new family spent many afternoons riding and picnicking, as Davy learned his horsemanship skills. Persephone gave birth to Thor's foal, a colt, who they named Mjöllnir.

In September, Tommy and Enid Smithson moved into Old Joe's place, as it should forever be known. Their horse, Bessie, divided her time between Redway, when her master was at work, and the wonderful stable Dom and some of the Redway men had built for her in Old Joe's garden. Enid started plans for her new, bigger garden for the Spring and worked with Mrs. Dawley on the mending and sewing needed for Redway, and the families that worked there. They added to their workload, now that there were two of them, by taking in washing as well.

By the end of October, the preparations to the property of Dowager Alcott were completed. She sold her house in London and travelled north to her new home. Everyone was happy for her arrival, but Davy most of all, as he had been working on his French with his father and wanted to impress the older lady with his burgeoning talent.

The timing of Dowager Alcott's move was perfect, as Mr. and Mrs. Ridgefield, Genevieve Harker's favourite aunt and uncle, were visiting Eastease once again and this time with their two oldest children. As Martha had visited the previous year, Gennie's youngest sister, Amelia, or Milly as she was known, came with them. For the adults, there should be another opportunity for an Eastease dinner.

The happy group of twelve for the dinner party, included eight that had sat together before, with Mr. and Mrs. Harker of course; Colonel Ackley and his new bride; Mr. and Mrs. Ridgefield and Harriet and Mr. Brooks. The additional guests were the dowager and Milly Hopwood, and to make up the number of men, a local, wealthy widower, Mr. Herbert Parker, and his son Luke.

This was the first time that Helena would be staying the night at Eastease with her husband. She found it oddly pleasing that they were in the same rooms she had inhabited there before. As she readied herself for the dinner, she stood at the window and looked down to the games room, where she had seen her husband twice before and wished herself in his arms. He came up behind her and whispered in her ear how much he loved her, and what a view she had made at that very window.

Gathering before dinner was served, they received the congratulations of Mr. and Mrs. Ridgefield, and those who had not met her before, were introduced to Miss Amelia Hopwood, a handsome, young woman, just shy of twenty years old. Her French was something she was proud of, but it was rather stilted and she enjoyed working on it with the dowager. Janine thought her a bright girl and wondered about taking her under her wing.

Dinner was full of good food, and lively conversation about what had happened since their last dinner. Nathaniel enjoyed watching Helena talking to Mr. Brooks and remembering a time when she had taken him to task over money for some needy children's shoes. At that time, he recalled being happy that he had met a beautiful and interesting woman, and feeling he would enjoy getting to know her better. Now she was his wife and he had two children. How much had changed so quickly!

After dinner, when the gentlemen rejoined the ladies, the dowager turned to Helena, "I understand that a year or so ago, you delighted the room with an aria, Mrs. Ackley, I would love to hear it."

"Well actually, Harriet has persuaded Nathaniel and I to sing together this time." Harriet excitedly sprang up and walked quickly to the pianoforte. Confidently, she stood to its side and waited for a lull in the conversations around the room.

"Many of you were here when Mrs. Ackley, Mrs. Andrews as she was then, sang a moving aria from Beethoven's opera, Leonore. It was Leonore's song, hoping for her love and sense of duty, to give her strength to pose as a guard and free her husband, Florestan, from unjust imprisonment. At our Christmas ball, Colonel Ackley sang Florestan's aria. An emotional song, of his loneliness, suffering and acceptance of death, only to see an angel in front of him who looked like his wife, before realising it was actually her." Helena glanced at Nathaniel at this point, but he seemed to be accepting the description amiably, "and so I have persuaded both singers, now married, to sing together Leonore and Florestan's duet, having finally been reunited. Colonel and Mrs. Ackley."

A light applause followed them to the instrument and they stood side by side next to Harriet who had taken her seat and was ready to play. They had practised the piece often, with Harriet, and alone with no accompaniment. Line after line they alternated Helena and then Nathaniel in German,

"O Nameless joy!
O Nameless joy!
O Nameless joy!
O Nameless joy!
My husband at my breast!
At Leonore's breast!"

Then they sang together, their voices entwining and soaring higher with each repetition.

"After unspeakable suffering,
So great desire.
After unspeakable suffering,
So great desire,
So great desire,
So great desire."

Alternating lines again.

"You again now in my arms!
O God, how great is your mercy.
You again now in my arms!
O Thank You God, for this pleasure!
My husband, my husband at my breast!
My wife, my wife at my chest!
At my breast, at my chest!
It's you!
It's me!
O heavenly delight!
It's you!
It's me!
O heavenly delight!
Leonore!
Florestan!
O Helena!
Florestan! Florestan."

Stunned that he had used her name and not Leonore's the second time, she looked at her husband's face and saw his tears. She faltered with her own tears at the second Florestan, bringing her head down to rest on his chest. He wrapped his arm around her. She could not tell if he had meant to say her name or said it accidentally, but she did not care.

They had missed the repetition of 'so great desire' but Harriet had continued to play. They gathered themselves for the last part, alternating again and then singing the last two lines together whilst in that embrace.

"O Nameless joy!
O Nameless joy!
O Nameless joy!
O Nameless joy!
My wife, my wife at my chest!
You again now at my breast!
You again now at my breast!
O Thank You God, for this pleasure!
For this pleasure!"

Reaching up she gently wiped his cheeks. He brushed away her tears with the back of his fingers and then caught her lips in his, in a quick, but passionate kiss.

The applause, which had held off until they kissed, was now loud and long in appreciation, as much to allow them to compose themselves. Helena looked around and noticed several ladies brushing away a tear, as well as Mr. Harker and of course the emotional Mr. Ridgefield. Both of those men were well aware of the colonel's own imprisonment, even if not the extent of his suffering.

Later, when everyone had gone to bed, Colonel Ackley entered the games room in his shirtsleeves with his waistcoat unbuttoned and his cravat hanging untied around his neck. Helena had gone to their rooms, where Rebecca was helping her undress and prepare for bed. He had looked at her pointedly and said, with a smile, that he would get a drink from the games room, as a nightcap and should rejoin her shortly. She gave a smile of understanding and hurried Rebecca into helping her with her gown, before shooing her away to her own bed, so she could be alone. With one candle lit she went to the window she had looked out of earlier and pulled open the curtains. As before, he was there, sitting with his head in his hand and rubbing at his face. This time she knew he was waiting for her and that he would come to her.

He lifted his face out of his hand, *"what was keeping the woman?"* he looked up for the hundredth time. How often had he fantasised of this moment, when he could see her there and then go to her? There she was on the window seat, as beautiful as ever. Kneeling, she dropped the nightgown from her shoulders letting it fall to her knees. He stood completely still for several seconds, shocked and thrilled, in equal measure, at her brazenness. Raw passion shot straight through him, from his eyes to his loins. He moved to raise a hand, as if he could caress her over the distance, but he heard a noise behind him and spun around, as if caught in the act of something illicit. Harker was in the doorway.

"What the blazes are you doing down here man?" he demanded, "do you not have a wife to see to?"

"What of your wife, my friend?" he smiled at Harker, praying Helena had closed the curtains again.

"I am on my way; you can count on that. First, pour me a brandy and pray tell me more of your imprisonment in France," he glanced down at the scars on Nathaniel's forearm, visible now he had rolled up his sleeves, "from the singing tonight, I wondered if there was more to tell." Yes, of course, Harker could speak German, too, so he knew the content of the song. Before the man could sit down, Nathaniel walked over to his friend and put an arm around him.

"I will tell you, Harker, I assure you. But this kind of talk is not conducive to returning to our wives ready to please them. So I suggest we save this conversation for another day," they walked out of the games room and up the stairs together, parting at the top to go their separate ways.

Helena meanwhile, wondered where Nathaniel had got to. She was hoping he would race to her, such would be his passion at seeing her naked at the window. It had felt very daring and she could feel herself aroused at his stare, even from such a distance. She had seen him spin round and was obviously talking to someone not in her sight, so she quickly closed the curtains and put on her dressing gown.

Peeking back out, she saw him leave with whomever it was he had talked to and moved to her door, to look out for him in the corridor. Here he came around the corner, long legs striding purposefully toward her, with that half smile and half bemused look, only she could put on his face.

He saw her standing there as he turned the corner and strode to her. She was dressed in the white, silk dressing gown he had seen her in, the night he had slept outside her rooms. He remembered wishing then, that he could pick her up and walk into that bedroom with her, and deposit her on the bed to ravish. Well now he could.

"My god woman, you almost killed me with that trick," taking the last stride to her, he scooped her up in his arms without stopping, "you are so very beautiful, wife." He brought his lips down hard on hers. Gone were the days when his rough passion scared her. She felt thrilled that the sight of her naked body had driven him to this behaviour and answered his passion with her own.

Walking through the open door of the bedroom, he kicked the door shut with his boot letting it slam. Striding to the bed, he threw her on it, then joining her, boots and all, continued with his passionate kissing. Ravish her, was exactly what he intended to do, and before he took a single boot off he had her naked on the bed.

Winter was thankfully not as cold as the previous year and the horses, as usual, fared better than the people tending them. All were grateful when March came with the promise of Spring not far behind. The peace, however, would not last.

Very early into March, Helena set out for her weekly luncheon with Genevieve and Harriet. A habit they started when they were planning the Christmas ball, well over a year ago. She had missed a few weeks over the winter with bad weather and several bouts of sickness.

Thankfully that all seemed in the past now, however, Nathaniel insisted on driving her there, and he would visit with Harker, while the ladies lunched together. She planned to talk to Genevieve of her suspicions that she was with child, a fact that she had not told her husband, as the baby had not quickened and she did not want to tell him until it had.

The visit did not turn out to be the pleasant diversion either of them had hoped. Within minutes of Nathaniel leaving the ladies to join Harker in his study, Harriet started crying. Genevieve, by way of explanation, had to tell Helena that they had heard the news that Napoleon had escaped his exile and was already gathering his armies in France once again.

Horrified, Helena ran from the room and toward Harker's study, the door opened before she reached it and Nathaniel stood in its frame looking resolute. She stood just feet away from him and neither of them moved. He knew she would not want him to leave, but he would have to do his duty. She knew he would leave out of a sense of duty, but was scared for his safety.

"Colonel?" she asked, the word catching in her throat. He nodded and held out his arms. She ran to his embrace in tears.

Colonel Nathaniel Ackley's orders came through shortly after their visit to Eastease. In the nights leading up to his leaving, he joined his body to Helena's as often as he could. She would wake in the night and move into his arms. Their joining, which had often been playful and loving, became wistful and tender, with promises of writing letters and returning safely, whispered into the night air. After her first bout of tears in his arms at Eastease she had not shed another, at least none that he had seen. He knew that when he left she would shed more, but she was being strong for him.

He did not sleep well and physical exhaustion from the day's labours and the night's loving was the only thing to give him peace, short-lived as it was. Otherwise he would lie awake in bed and think of a Frenchman slicing his chest open or worse, Duarte and the other men killed at the prison in Toulouse. He was not afraid for himself, but the stakes were higher, for him personally, than they had ever been. If he were to die, he would be leaving Helena and the children, and that hurt him more than any sword could.

On that cold, March day, when he prepared to mount Thor, wearing his red coat and his sheathed sword, she stood with her back straight and her head high. The children had run to him and clung to him, with fresh tears on their cheeks and all she wanted to do was the same. Cling to him and never let go, but she could not. So she called the children to her and held a small hand in each of hers as he bid them goodbye.

"Slay a dragon for me, Colonel," he smiled his wide, bright smile, put his hand over his coat pocket that held a new silk cravat, a dented horse pin and a drawing of the Dragon of Lincolnshire.

"Anything for you, my Queen," he bowed low and Thor did the same, then he mounted him and urged him on, and out of Redway.

In the three months that Colonel Ackley was gone, facing Bonaparte's armies with his brothers in arms and trusty steed, two notable visitors came to Redway. Both part of his family, but not seeking him out. In fact, the visits came because he was *not* there.

Firstly, a visit came in April from Lord Aysthill, with the other man, Davidson, walking close behind him. With Davidson present,

Helena felt safe in accepting his request for a meeting with her. Having shown the two men into the study in Redway's house, Ruth ran out to the stable to inform John. Picking up a knife, John headed into the house. Ruth had left the door ajar and he was able to hear enough, to be able to determine if his services were needed. The conversation seemed amiable enough. Helena, who could see out of the door from her vantage point, facing the two gentlemen, was grateful that John was there and subdued the small smile that crept to her lips.

"Mrs. Ackley," Lord Aysthill began. He seemed hesitant and she was surprised, but waited for him to continue, "I realise that the last time we met, I offended you with the offer of a stipend to assist in raising... ah, your son. Please accept my apologies," she nodded, but said nothing, "I have done what you suggested and set up a fund for Davy Beckett."

"Davy Beckett Ackley," she corrected.

"Ah, quite, well we can add Ackley to it," he looked at Mr. Davidson, who had been reaching in his bag for some papers. Nodding, he returned them to the bag, "and send them to you for safe keeping."

"You could have done that anyway, why come here?"

"At our last meeting, you indicated that monetary restitution is not sufficient and I would like to make an apology to the boy, if you will allow it. Providing he will understand that I cannot admit that he is my..." he paused at the warning look she gave him, "that he came from me."

"He understands where he came from and does not seek that acknowledgement. As far as he is concerned, he is proud of his father, whom he now considers to be Colonel Ackley, your son, which makes Davy your grandson. Perhaps you might consider acknowledging him as such?" she rose to leave, "I will go and talk to him and see if he is willing to listen to what you have to say. I will explain to him that he is under no obligation to accept your apology or acknowledge you as his grandfather."

Moments later she returned with Davy, *"my word the boy looks like Nathaniel,"* he thought. He stood straight beside his mother, defiance in his eyes and a slight pout. He had seen that expression in Nathaniel's face often enough, when he had to discipline him.

"Davy, you know who I am?" Davy nodded, "I would like to apologise to you for what I did to your mother, that is, your other mother. I am sorry that she died. I am also sorry for not doing something about your situation at Bainbridge."

"J' accepte vos excuses."

"He said…" started Helena, but Lord Aysthill held up a hand.

"Je vous remercie, mais pourquoi en français ?"

"Je ne suis pas prêt à accepter en anglais."

"J'accepte vos conditions, monsieur," Lord Aysthill bowed, "if there is anything I can do that might help toward further acceptance, please advise me at once."

"Well, I had been wondering if that old hag at the big house had got another chimney boy. Father told Smythe to be sure she did not and told me there is a new device that can be used instead. I should not want to think that I was lucky to get away from her, but another boy took my place." Lord Aysthill bit the inside of his cheek, to refrain from laughing at Davy calling his cousin an 'old hag'. He loved to call her names himself, so he did not reprimand the boy.

"I will see to it right away and I will ensure that we are using the new devices at Aysthill House, too. Is that acceptable?" Davy nodded, "would it be acceptable to you, if you were to call me Grandfather? I am, after all, Colonel Ackley's father."

"And Issie, too?" the boy asked.

"Yes, Issie, too."

"I will go and ask her," with that he ran from the room.

"Thank you," he turned back to Helena, "He is a tough nut to crack, like Nathaniel. Will only accept my apology in French for now, I expect the English acceptance will be worth the earning. I had no idea how smart he is. I suspect the French is Nathaniel's doing?"

"And that of our new neighbour, Dowager Alcott," he nodded and seemed to want to say more.

"I would like to assure you that my behaviour with his mother, was the only time with one so young. My only defence is that I had drunk far too much that evening."

"Well, let us hope for the sake of all fourteen-year-old girls, you refrain from doing so in the future."

"Will anything I do ever be enough to please you?"

"I do not know, but I do not understand why it is so important to you."

"Neither do I."

The two children raced back into the room. Isabella curtseyed, "Grandfather, I am Issie, would you like to hear me play the pianoforte?" with that they each took a hand of the older man and led him to the drawing room, where the instrument stood waiting.

The second visitor, arrived in the warmer month of May, in a formidable carriage with many footmen in attendance. The Bainbridge crest was emblazoned on the side and the sight of it sent Davy into a panic, thinking that she had come to take him back. Despite his mother's assurances he ran to the stable and shadowed John the whole time the woman visited.

In fact, it was Lady Grace Bainbridge who was announced and stood in the parlour refusing a seat or refreshments. She spotted Ruth's small garden out of the window and gestured to it.

"That seems to be a small but well-tended garden, with no horses roaming around in it, I should like to take a walk there, Mrs. Andrews."

"Mrs. Ackley, Lady Bainbridge," Helena corrected.

"Hmmm. We will see."

Upon reaching the garden, she took a turn around it, criticizing everything. True, it was not a prim garden, rather the various flowers and vegetation were allowed to mix and meld together, to form a complementing whole. Ruth would have been hurt to hear the critical words, but Helena allowed the woman to have her say, and waited for her to get to her real point for the long trip from Norfolk.

"Do you remember who I am?"

"Yes. You are my husband's cousin. We met two Christmases ago, at the Eastease ball."

"I am Colonel Ackley's cousin," she said in a tone that made Helena feel she was being corrected, "being family, I am, therefore, interested in what he is making of himself," she looked back at the house and toward the stable and sneered, "I demand to be satisfied as to whether you are actually married to him."

"I believe that I have already confirmed, twice, that I am," Helena was shocked at the question, wondering what the woman knew. She was not sure exactly how long she was going to tolerate this woman's snide looks and insulting comments about her and her property. If she preferred Bainbridge so much, she should have stayed in Norfolk.

"I understand that you would like the whole world to think that, *Mrs. Andrews*, but I had a man follow the route you took almost a year ago, when you were supposedly gone to Scotland. You never made it further than the Lakes."

"I am of age. There was no necessity to go all the way to Scotland. It makes no difference where we were married."

"My man informs me that no record was to be found of *any* ceremony taking place. You do not acknowledge propriety? You do not give my cousin his due? No respect or trust."

"I have shared everything with my husband. What you see here is our home, our business and our children. I do not understand. Do you want me to be married to him or do you not?"

"It seems you are doing neither."

"You are severely deluded if you think that Nathaniel would marry you, if we were not married. He could have done that at any time had he the inclination. Why do you want to marry him?"

"He is the son of an Earl, from a powerful family, a respectable soldier, injured in battle. If he had married me he would not have had to return to battle. He would own a grand estate, larger than Eastease and with his marriage to me, Granddaughter of the previous Earl of Aysthill, his position in the world would be far greater than that of his friend. He would be accepted in all the best society."

"You mention all of these great places and wonderful society, but you do not know Nathaniel at all. He would not be happy with any of that. You want him only for his name and position, to mould him into something that he is not. You sneer at Redway, but he loves it here. This is his home and it suits him. He works with me and the men, to care for and raise the horses. He teaches our children to ride and work. To achieve something with one's endeavours. I married him because I love him, you mentioned nothing of love. He loves me and our children. He would never leave."

"And yet he is not here."

"Duty calls him away. He could have chosen to stay here, but he is an honourable man. I am proud to call him my husband."

"Perhaps he wishes to remove himself from your brood of bastards," the other woman said with some venom, taking in the swollen belly of her hostess.

Helena felt as if she had been slapped. Without response, she turned to walk away from the woman, around to the front of the house where the carriage was waiting. Lady Bainbridge followed, calling out to her retreating back, "you have no secrets from me, *Miss Billings*. All of your children were born outside wedlock, this one will be no different. How about I spread *that* all around the county? The respectable Mrs. Ackley no more. Unmarried and three children, every single one a bastard, each with a different father. Two of the fathers from the same family. What would Nathaniel do then?"

They had reached the carriage and Helena laughed, which confused the other woman no end. How happy his cousin would make Nathaniel, by putting about the very rumours that would ensure that she would have to marry him.

"Madam, you have left no stone unturned in your insults. I ask that you leave our property immediately."

"Do you admit that you are *not* married to him?" Grace asked after climbing back into the carriage.

"I admit that I have made my vows to my husband and he has done so in return. Where and in front of whom they were made is of no concern of yours. Good day."

Colonel Ackley felt the force of the cannon blast behind him and heard the scream of his horse as half of its rear flank was blown away. Thor landed heavily on Nathaniel's right leg and thrashed around in agony. Nathaniel's sword, which had been drawn in battle, had been thrown from his reach. With each thrash, Thor was moving the saddle and stirrups painfully against Nathaniel's trapped leg, but he could not extricate himself. He tried not to scream with the pain, as he was vulnerable and sooner or later the enemy should discover him, but he would rather it was later. He looked back and saw that Thor's left leg and hind quarter was completely gone. His trusted friend was done for and he grieved.

Withdrawing his pistol, he aimed the barrel at Thor's head. He heard running and hoped it would be allied forces, but heard French spoken. If he shot the first man, the second would kill him anyway. He only had one shot and his sword was out of his reach. Not wishing his friend any more pain, he pulled the trigger.

"Thank you, Thor."

A blade was placed in front of his neck. He closed his eyes and pictured Helena lying on a picnic blanket reaching for him. As he waited for the slice, he hoped the Frenchman's blade was sharp.

The blast of a pistol reached his ears, instead, and the body of the man fell across Thor. Nathaniel grasped the fallen man's sword, but it was not needed. He was surrounded by his own men. They lifted Thor enough to get him out from underneath the animal, but his leg was in a bad way. He screamed in agony as he tried to walk. They carried him back to safety, after he passed out.

Chapter Twenty-Three

Why did they send him back to Aysthill instead of Redway? If he considered her his wife then his place was there, even if he was injured. It was getting into the latter part of June and she was about a month away from giving birth to their child. Travel as far as Aysthill would be difficult. Mr. Harker had been to see him and reported back that his leg had been crushed when Thor had died and fallen on him. She knew that he would feel the loss of Thor badly. The doctor was recommending removal of the leg at a point above the knee, before gangrene set into the damage that had been done, but Nathaniel refused.

She knew why. She had talked to Tommy before, of a young woman from the village who always seemed eager to see him, when her work brought her to Redway. He had said he would not be a suitable husband with a missing limb, Nathaniel would be thinking the same. Tommy, however, did not have a wife already. Nathaniel did. She worried that he was considering that he did not, and what did that say of the vows he made with her, in that carriage on the way to the Lakes?

John had visited the colonel upon his request and returned with papers for Helena to sign. He was relinquishing his share of the stable back to her. All she had to do was sign them, but she would not.

She had written to him several times, but the letters remained unanswered. She was not sure that he had even received them, knowing that his mother had wanted him to marry Grace. John had told her that he asked the colonel to meet with her and that the loss of his leg would make no difference to her love for him. Nathaniel, of course, had decided that he should make the decision for the both of them. He would not be a burden to her and that was that.

Helena stared into John's face. That kind, wrinkled face, of the man who had been more like a father than her own. This was the one man that had been a constant in her life, who had comforted her, protected her and advised her. He had taught her all he knew, as a father would, and now had done the best he could to bring her love back to her.

"I reckon his brain got a knock when he fell down with Thor!" he said, with a sigh.

Fewer than ten miles away was her love, her heart, and he refused her upon the misapprehension that he would burden her. That decided it then, she should go to him and either talk or knock some sense into him.

"Saddle up Colossus please, John," she said with a determined look, "I will talk some sense into him."

"Get some sense into yourself first. You cannot ride in your condition, not even that big ol' softie. That bairn is almost ready to pop out," she stared at the man she had just been considering like a father, and now he was behaving like one! He must have seen the determination in her eyes for he relented, "how about I drive you in the carriage?"

After she had readied herself to be received by Lord and Lady Aysthill, she collected one of the new wooden legs Tommy had made and climbed into the carriage. The new style leg included a knee, to enable an amputee above the knee to ride.

As the journey progressed, she felt that riding the horse might have been more comfortable. She braced herself as best she could in the rocking carriage. Halfway there she felt a dull ache in her lower back, another mile and a pain ripped through her body that was unmistakable. Her child had picked an inopportune time to begin its journey into life. She recollected the painful and long process of birth. Remembering she was nearly a day bringing her daughter into the world, she was determined to see her visit through and get home in time. She worried that the bairn was a little early, but perhaps her calculations had been wrong.

Only one more pain gripped her before her journey's end, and by the time John opened the door of the carriage she had composed herself again. Gathering her skirts and the wooden limb, she walked to the door certain that she had been spotted arriving. Sure enough, the butler, Edgars, she recalled, opened the door promptly and led her to a small feminine sitting room, requesting she wait for Lady Aysthill. Laying the leg on the pretty sofa, she remained standing. She could not fathom attempting to rise from the sofa in that woman's presence, given her condition.

"Mrs. Andrews," Lady Aysthill greeted her as she entered.

"Mrs. Ackley, Lady Aysthill," she corrected.

"That will be all Edgars. *Mrs. Andrews* will not be staying for refreshments," in her hands she held two unopened letters that Helena immediately recognised as her own. She threw them on the sofa next to the leg, "take these and that monstrosity with you when you leave. As you see, they are unopened. My son does not wish to see you."

"He never even saw these letters. You kept them from him."

"No, he did not want to open them. He does not want you."

"I know your son, Lady Aysthill. He thinks giving me up is best for me and because he loves me that is what he is doing. However, he does not know of his child that I am carrying. I told him of it in those letters. If he had read them he would reconsider," the pain of the oncoming child ripped through her once more and she grasped the back of the sofa to steady herself.

"A bastard child, because you refuse to marry him," Lady Aysthill used Helena's pause to interject, as she interpreted the woman's vice like grip on the sofa back, as anger. Helena realised that Lady Grace had been busy imparting her knowledge to Nathaniel's relations.

"I refuse to marry any man and relinquish my property. To become property myself, no matter the man. I do, however, love and respect your son and would marry him in an instant, if the law would change to make man and wife equal, as I believe they should be. I have already shared my property with him as an *equal* partner. I have given him more than his own family has given him. He gets nothing from you, because he is your second son."

"What is the use of ownership of a stable when he cannot run it, when he cannot work with the horses and has to watch others' enjoyment of them, because he can only sit and not ride? I know my son, too, and he would not be happy, when horses and riding are such a passion for him."

"Is he happy now? Is he happy without me? Would he be happy never knowing he has another child? This one from his own loins."

"No, he is not happy now," like an engine that had run out of steam, Lady Aysthill sank into the armchair close to her side, "my angelic boy, with the happy smile and infectious laugh. He no longer laughs or smiles. He will not try and plans only to die."

"I can make him happy again, I know I can. He is a strong man and he can ride with this leg. I have brought a horse for him that will suit him," she hoped she was getting through to the woman and thought to perhaps try and remove a thorn, "I know you cannot be happy that Nathaniel and I took in Davy, but he is a wonderful boy and so like Nathaniel. An angelic boy, with a happy smile and an infectious laugh. It was never his fault what happened to his mother," with a sudden understanding she added, "neither was it your fault."

Lady Aysthill looked at Mrs. Andrews or whatever she was supposed to call this woman now. She had cut right to the core of what had bothered her through all these years of marriage. She felt guilt that she was not enough for her husband, whom she loved, and so he sought solace for his needs elsewhere. Guilt that those needs had caused the death of a fourteen-year old girl. She had not known of it until Nathaniel told her that Mrs. Andrews had taken the boy in.

She had blamed this woman for so many things. Her husband's behaviour at Eastease that had put father and son against each other. His apologising to the women he had wronged, and taking time and money to make restitution, but he had not apologised to her, his own wife.

She resented her fortune in escaping the tyrant she was supposed to marry and successfully hiding behind the story of a dead husband. Most of all she resented her for taking the heart of her dearest son and refusing to marry him.

Lady Aysthill had written to Grace suggesting she visit and tell Nathaniel that he could marry her. All ease would be afforded to him, being her husband and the master of Bainbridge. She had heard nothing in response, despite all her efforts in promoting that woman in the past, even at the cost of her relationship with her son.

All she had done was blame and resent Mrs. Helena Ackley. In return the woman had loved Nathaniel beyond all measure. She had put her pride aside to come here and beg to talk to him, because she loved him and wanted him in her life, regardless of the loss of a limb. She had done right by the son of the young girl, her own husband had wronged so badly, and now stood here telling her, sympathetically that she herself was not to blame, even after all the insults she had just hurled at her.

"He has not apologised to me," she said simply.

Helena knew she meant Lord Aysthill, "men are imbeciles."

"Nathaniel will die if he does not have that leg removed. Do you think you can persuade him to do it?"

"I can try."

"Helena, you should not be here."

"It is you who should not be here," she looked at Nathaniel in his bed in a grand room, "you should be at home, at Redway."

"We are not married, Helena. Everyone here knows it. My home is here."

"I will not sign those papers, Nathaniel," there were tears in her eyes, "Redway is your home, I am your wife and you have three children. This one is making its way into the world right now."

He suddenly noticed that she was carrying his child. In his pain, he had not seen it, "I am sorry, Helena. Once again you have borne so much while I have been away. I cannot burden you with more."

"What I cannot *bear*, is a life without you in it," a pain ripped through her again and tore away all her patience with him. Her eyes narrowed as she looked at him, "my vows to you were real, Colonel, I meant every word. It matters not to me that we were not in a church before your God. No matter that there is no legal document to attest to my vows, so I am under no obligation to keep them. Yet I do, every one, because there has never been another man I have felt this way about and there never will be.

We vowed forever, to each other's hearts, we vowed in sickness and in health, but you are not sick, Nathaniel. You are able to recover from this and you are strong enough to work beside me. You would not be a burden. What of your vows? Were they only words? Did they not matter to you, because they were not bound in law or in a church?"

"Of course I mean them, of course they matter, but if I were to let them do this, it is possible that I will be in pain every day."

"Why do you not understand? If you die, *I* will be in pain every day," another pain ripped through her. She groaned loudly, suppressing a scream and grabbed his hand, squeezing tightly.

"Now is the time to press your advantage wife. Any woman worth her salt should make a request of her husband."

"*You* have to choose this Nathaniel. Ask yourself this, if our roles were reversed and I was the one choosing to die rather that live my life without a limb; willing to leave you to raise three children with no mother; willing to leave you with an empty bed. What would you say to me? I have to leave now and have our child at Redway. Please, choose this, get strong and well again, and come back to us. Do not let this be the last time we see each other."

She bent to kiss him, a soft gentle kiss, and then hurriedly left the room, only to run straight into Lord Aysthill.

"There you are, my dear. Did you talk him into it?" she shook her head, tears streaming down her cheeks, "leave it to me; I think I have just the right thing to say."

"Excuse me, Lord Aysthill. I must leave," she walked as quickly as she could to the stairs, but paused to look back at him, "My Lord, there is a woman you forgot to apologise to... your wife."

Helena all but collapsed into John's arms when she managed to get out to the carriage, "what is it? What happened?"

"The baby is coming, John. Get me in the carriage."

"But you should stay here. They could get you the care you need."

"I will not have my baby here. Get me back to Redway. There is time. Isabella took all day." John got her into the carriage, closed the door and climbed up to start the horses. Halfway home, Helena realised things were not right. She called out to John and banged on the roof of the carriage. It stopped and the door burst open. John stood there looking worried.

"You have to help me, John. Something is not right," she had already taken off her petticoats and started pulling up her skirts, but he took a step backwards.

"No, I cannot do that, Helena. 'Tis a woman's business."

"John, how many foals have you delivered. Get in here and help me, for goodness sake. It feels wrong and I need to know what is going on," John took a look and was shocked to see a tiny foot, small even for a newborn.

"Baby's wrong way round," Helena looked shocked, "do not look like that, we can do this. I could try pushing the foot back in and turning it around. She nodded, but before he could try, she was wracked with another pain and a strong urge to push. John could now see two legs and a bottom, and a tiny hand, but only one. At Helena's nod, he reached inside her and could feel that one arm was tucked up beside the head still inside her womb. Talking her through it, he managed to hook a finger up and around the other arm to bring that down. Hopefully, with the next pain or two, she could deliver the head.

It took two big pushes, but she did it. The baby came out and started crying directly. Aside from being rather small, he seemed healthy, despite his ordeal. Helena wrapped him as best she could in her petticoats, after John had cut the cord. Then she walked into the nearby wood and delivered the afterbirth. John took them both home.

While Helena had been giving birth to his son in the carriage, Nathaniel's father had been to see him.

"I just saw that *'wife'* of yours', boy. Still a fine-looking filly, even with a belly full of your bastard."

"Keep your eyes to yourself, old man," said Nathaniel, tersely, as another wave of pain swept over him. He was in no mood for the man's antics. He remembered though, that Helena had written and told him that his father had apologised to Davy, so had that been play acting after all?

"What are you going to do about it, boy? Once she has had that bairn, I might go and console her on the death of her husband. See if I cannot get her to give me some of what you have been having for the past year."

"She would not have anything to do with you."

"What could she do once I had her or let it be known that I had? Your share of Redway should be mine as your next of kin, unless, of course, she can produce evidence of your marriage."

"Harker would stop you."

"Harker? No, he should not bother me overly. You on the other hand, you were ruthless. I imagine even with one leg you could protect that woman, but you will not be there. I could even get Harker to let me stop with this ledger idea of his."

The older man stood up to leave. He hoped that this tactic was going to be the one that would work. He should hate to lose his second son, just when he was coming to realise what an excellent man he had become, despite his father's example. Then he was stayed by that chilling voice he remembered, from the time his son had threatened him.

"Call the surgeon, Father."

The laudanum had helped, but it did not dull the pain completely, eventually he passed out with it and woke when it was all finished. He had a fever for a day and an infection in the stump of his leg around the scar, but it soon cleared up. He was starting to feel good, except for missing a leg, until Harker walked into his room.

"Harker, how are you? Thank you for coming to visit. Have you heard of Helena? Did she have a boy or a girl?" Harker's sad, brown eyes locked on his. Nathaniel felt like he had been run through with a sword, right through the heart, "what is it, Xander? Helena? The baby? Tell me, for God's sake, man."

"The baby is fine. She had him halfway home from here the day she left you, right there in the carriage. He was the wrong way around and small, but healthy. John had to help get him out and she got an infection. She is in a bad way, Nathaniel, a fever and a tender belly."

"Help me, Harker, I have to go to her," he made to pull back the covers on the bed, but Harker put a hand on his shoulder.

"No, there is no point right now to risk yourself. She does not know where she is or who is around her. You have to get better for your children. Two boys and a girl, you have another son."

"Oh, my God!" he rubbed his hands over his face as the tears welled up in him, he could not hold them back, "how can I live without her?"

"How did you expect she would live without you?" he said it without recrimination, but it hit home much the same.

"This is my fault. If I had been at Redway or had this damned leg removed straightaway, she would not have been visiting here, not had the baby in a carriage and got an infection. I have been so wrong. She called me on it. Said her vows to me meant everything to her regardless of where they were made, but that I did not act the same way because they were not made in a church, with a legal document. I saw it as a way out for her, but she did not want one," he looked at his friend, "we are not married, Harker."

"I know that," he looked at the colonel with a smile, "what woman would take you?"

Nathaniel allowed him the poke, "is she going to pull through?"

"The doctor does not know. We have to wait."

"This is how she felt. I never considered it. Will you keep coming back and let me know how she is? Please?"

"Of course. Every day if I can."

A wet nurse was found for the baby. Rachel helped her and the governess with all three children. Enid Smithson came in when she could, to help Ruth keep the household running and to look after Helena.

Harriet stayed with Helena the whole time. Her own mother had died from an infection after giving birth to a stillborn baby. She hoped just her presence would help her friend pull through it. Helena's fever raged for a week and all three women were kept busy with cold cloths for her head and getting water into her sip by sip. The children were allowed in to read to her, but they did not even know if she heard them.

"Poor babies," Enid had said to Ruth time after time, whenever she laid eyes on one or other of them, "father and mother both battling their problems and who knows what the outcome will be. They need them both, but might end up with neither."

Mr. Harker visited often and brought Genevieve with him when he could. He had updates from Aysthill as to the colonel's progress and took details of Helena's illness back with him. He tried to get Harriet back to Eastease to rest, but the young woman refused.

Nathaniel got stronger over the next few days, but his thoughts were all with Helena. Harker came to visit to let him know how she was. It was a lot to ask of him and Nathaniel was grateful for it. Harker had to ride to Redway and see how Helena was, then ten miles to Aysthill before heading back home again.

Nathaniel's father came back to his room again. He felt he had better confess to his son, before the man was strong enough to hurt him, "I am sorry to hear of your wife, son. I hope she pulls through."

"Do not talk of her, old man. I am getting better, so your plans have come to naught."

"Son, I have come to your bedside to confess. I could not bear to see you throw your life away. I could not bear to continue to watch you die, not when it is only recently that I have come to appreciate the kind of man you have become. I told you the things that would make you take this action to save your life. Your sense of duty is so strong, you would bear anything yourself, to protect your wife and children."

Nathaniel stared at the man before him. Who was he? His father had never spoken to him this way. He assumed he did not really give him any thought at all. He was the spare, not the heir.

"Thank you, Father," was all he could think of to say.

"Heal up quickly son and get back to her. She needs you," he put his hand on Nathaniel's shoulder and Nathaniel leaned his head against the man's arm for a moment. Lord Aysthill left before things got embarrassing for them both.

As soon as he could get out of bed, Nathaniel insisted on getting out to the stable. His mother had told him that Helena left him a suitable horse and he wondered which it was. Using a crutch and followed by his manservant, as were the man's instructions from Lady Aysthill, he managed to get to the stable. It took all his effort and he was breathing hard when he got there. The stable manager was there and he pulled on his forelock, "Colonel."

"Frank, I think my wife left a horse under your care."

"She did indeed, sir. Bit of a handful, not sure you will be able to handle him," Nathaniel snapped his head around to look at the man, and then moved more quickly toward the stall the man indicated further down the row. Could she have left her favourite horse for him? It would be just like her to think of such a thing. He looked in at the stall.

"Perseus!" the horse was thrilled to see the colonel again and came to the half-door, putting his head over it. He nuzzled against Nathaniel, who was nearly knocked over, "whoa there, boy, you have got to be gentler with me now. I only have one leg to stand on."

Frank came over and gave the colonel a letter, "John said to give it to you, when you came to see him," he gestured toward the horse.

"Thank you, Frank. Can you get me some carrots for him?" Frank left him to read the note, that Helena must have written before she visited him. Nathaniel sank, gratefully, onto a nearby stool.

My darling Nathaniel,

I am so happy that you have decided that your life is worth living and to live it with me and our children.

Come to us when you are ready. Tommy can visit and show you how to use the leg with the saddle. He has adjusted your spare saddle to accommodate it. He will help you learn.

Perseus is yours. I give him to you with all my heart. I know you mourn Thor and no horse can replace him. He was so wonderful. Perseus will, I am sure, understand your injury and work with you.

Ride him home when you are ready. We will all be waiting. I love you my husband.

Helena Ackley (Mrs.)

He looked up and saw Harker striding toward him, holding two carrots by the stalks. He had a big smile across his face. He looked at his friend, his heart racing in anticipation of his words. Surely only one thing could make him smile like that right now and it was not the carrots.

"Her fever broke," such was his greeting. Nathaniel blew out a long breath, that he had not even realised he had been holding, "look at you, up and out of bed. Today is a good day." Harker grasped Nathaniel's arm that he had held up for help to stand and retrieved the crutch. Perseus had already reached over the stable door and helped himself to one of the two carrots that Harker had forgotten. He gave the other to Nathaniel to feed to the horse himself.

"Is that not Helena's horse?"

"Mine now, she gave him to me," he handed Harker the note.

"Hell of a woman."

"Yes, she is."

"Are you going to marry her properly?"

"In a heartbeat, but I do not need to own her. She is mine. She has been more of a wife than I have been a husband. We made vows to each other and she took them as seriously as if they were said in church. I did not see it that way and I should have. Do you think she will forgive me?"

"First thing she did was to ask after you and then cried in relief."

"She did? Then I have a chance."

"With all the speculation your cousin unleashed, after Helena threw her off Redway property, you really need to marry her."

"I have something else in mind, but I will need the help of my father and Mr. Brooks."

"Really? Well, let me know if you need me at all."

"Maybe a celebration?"

"Genevieve and Harriet will love it."

"Can you ask Tommy to come and stay with me for a while,

please? I am going to need him if I am going to learn to ride this boy, with one leg."

After Harker had left, Nathaniel made his way back to his room. It was slow going and when the manservant tried to help him he pushed him away. Once he reached the stairs, however, he stopped and allowed the man to help him. Exhausted he fell gratefully onto his bed and slept.

When he woke, it was the middle of the night. A tray of cold meats and bread with wine had been left for him if he woke hungry. He was hungrier than he had been since arriving back home and he was not tired at all, so he sat at his desk eating and setting his mind to writing the letter he needed to.

My dearest wife, Helena,

How can you ever forgive me for the pain I have put you through? Still I know you have a generous heart and therefore I feel brave enough to ask you... Helena, I beg of you to please forgive me.

Your words did reach me, I want you to know that. When I had woken after the surgery, Harker arrived to inform me of your illness. Suddenly, I was the one in the position of possibly facing the rest of my life without you. The pain of my leg was nothing, nothing compared with the pain of my heart and to think that I could have inflicted that upon you, all the while thinking I was doing what was best.

I should know by now that you would be right.

Please forgive me for not honouring our vows as I should have. I put the emphasis on the venue rather than the words. Vows said between husband and wife are what is binding, not the location in which they are said. If God is everywhere, then surely He was in the carriage with us, when we spoke of what was in our hearts, so softly to each other. He should be equally angry with me for breaking the vows of my heart that I made to you then, as He would be if I had said them in church.

You have proven yourself my wife in everything and I only ask you to give me another chance to prove myself equally, as your husband.

I love you more than life. I am ashamed that I was too quick to give up that life, when the most important thing is to live my life as long as possible and spend every breath that I have remaining, with you, with our children and in your arms.

I will return home to Redway and our family, soon. Riding to you on the magnificent horse you have given me when I least deserved it.

Thank you for getting yourself well again and sparing me such pain.

I wish you a speedy recovery, and send my love to our three children. Ever your faithful husband,

Nathaniel

Tommy came the following day and worked with Nathaniel, riding Perseus using the wooden leg. Unlike Tommy's, the leg Nathaniel used had to have a knee, so he could only use it on the horse and would have to switch to a crutch when he dismounted. The doctor had shown Tommy a drawing of a leg with a steel ball knee that could bend and straighten. It could be something that should work for the colonel when his injury had healed more.

Tommy refused to sleep in the house. Instead he shared the stable manager's house with his family. He stayed until Nathaniel was ready to ride to Redway.

Chapter Twenty-Four

On an early August day, Helena sat in the drawing room with her three children; her six-week old son in her arms, her six-year-old daughter at the pianoforte, and her eight-year-old son reading a book and laying on the floor at her feet.

Hooves were heard outside the front of the house and the two older children ran to the window to see who had arrived. "Papa! It is Papa on Perseus!" they sang in unison and ran to the door. Her heart was singing, too. She stood, breathed deeply and then walked to follow them.

He sat straight and tall on Perseus. She could see the wooden leg strapped to the saddle supporting the thigh of his right leg. A crutch was strapped to the side of the saddle, so he could use it when he dismounted. She smiled up at him. He looked strong and healthy, just to look at him was wonderful.

Colonel Ackley was not fully prepared for the sight of Helena framed in the doorway with his three children. He stared at her, trying to imprint this vision into his mind. Despite her recent illness, she was still so very beautiful, cream skin and red hair. He smiled at her and then dismounted as fluidly as he could. He had to lead with his left leg swinging over the horse to the ground and then his stump came out of the hollow of the wooden leg, leaving that still strapped to his horse. Finally, he grasped the crutch and pulled it out of its strappings to use.

"Papa!" Isabella and Davy ran at him. Helena wanted to call out to them to be careful, so as to avoid bowling him over, but she stopped herself in time. She had decided that she was not going to fuss over him. She stared, as he held tightly to the boy and girl who loved him and had missed him so much, afraid that if she stopped looking he would disappear.

She did not move, but held his gaze, as he came toward her.

"Helena, my love, my heart, my wife. Please forgive me," he picked up her hand that was not holding the baby and brought it to his lips.

"There is nothing to forgive, my husband," she moved her hand to his cheek. He looked at the baby. His son, his second son.

"What did you call him?"

"I have not. I wanted to wait for you. I seem to recall you are good with names."

"How about, Nathaniel David Harker Ackley?"

"Perfect."

"Kiss Mama!" demanded Isabella. Nathaniel looked at Davy.

"Could you hold your brother a moment, please, my son?" Davy smiled.

"Then will you kiss Mama?" he asked.

"If she will allow it."

"Nathaniel, be very sure," she handed the baby to his brother, "the infection left me unable to give you any more children."

"You have given me a daughter and two sons, and we have each other. What more could a man ask for?"

"Marriage," she whispered unheard by the children who were happily chanting their *'Kiss Mama'* request, "your cousin…"

"No," he cut her off, "I do not need to marry you. My vows remain the same as they did when I made them to you, they will not be better or stronger if they were legally binding. I will be better at adhering to them though."

"Are you sure, Nathaniel? Please be sure."

He leaned heavily on the crutch and put his hands up to her cheeks. A sob caught in her throat and was smothered by his passionate kiss.

That night, as Nathaniel prepared for bed, he felt as nervous as he had when he was a virgin. How was she going to react to the stump of his leg? She had not worried about the scar across his chest and she had healed the scars of his heart, but this was greater than any of those. He was also unsure of his ability to do what he had been able to before, now he only had one knee for support. Helena had straddled him in the past and may be willing to do so again, but he wanted to take his wife, not just to be ridden himself. He was also unsure how she was feeling. Was she even well enough to receive his attentions? He had not asked.

Putting on his nightshirt, he left his dressing room and entered their bedroom. They had always shared the large bed with the horse-carved headboard. She watched him approach with a welcoming smile, "this bed has seemed too big without you to share it." She frowned as he got into bed still in his nightshirt. They had always been naked in bed before and she was naked now. He was hiding himself from her. She sat up in bed and pulled back the covers then kneeled and faced him as he lay there.

"Look at me, Nathaniel," he was looking at her, how could he not?

"You are extraordinarily beautiful, Helena," his voice was thick with emotion.

"And yet I see how much my body has changed since you saw it last, and I worry you will no longer find it appealing. Whilst I am feeding our son, my breasts are heavier and lower, the tips sometimes sore and cracked. My belly is soft and lined from carrying him within me, and I was stretched once again from birthing a second child. Within, I was so ravaged by infection that I can no longer bear you children and I wonder if that makes me seem less womanly in your eyes."

"None of that makes any difference to me. You are as you have always been, Helena. The most beautiful woman I have ever known, and I will always be in love with you."

"Then why do you not think that I should feel the same way about your body, my love?" she looked at him expectantly.

Smiling, but still nervous, he once again wondered how the woman managed to be so right all the time. He sat up and pulled his nightshirt over his head. She gasped, but when he looked at her eyes, she was not looking at the stump of his leg, but another part of his body that was showing her he did indeed find her beautiful.

Reaching out with a slim, strong hand she stroked his hip and ran her hand down his thigh to the stump. He flinched, but she was looking at him with affection and love. Leaning back on one hand he brought the other up to her face, then down her neck and to her breast and felt the heaviness of it, before running his thumb up and over her nipple. Moving closer, she straddled him and caught his lips with hers, she had ridden him this way before and thought it might be a good starting point for them, as they relearned each other's bodies. It seemed he thought so, too, as he pulled her to him with one strong arm and ran his tongue down to a nipple. Before she could warn him, however, he had sucked her and received a mouthful of her milk for his efforts.

As he spluttered and swallowed, she laughed and he looked up at her, "I am sorry, Nathaniel. My body is not entirely mine or yours for the moment, while our son needs me to feed him. You will have to be a little less rigorous I am afraid," he laughed and she gasped as he moved himself against her.

"Some things are different, some things remain the same," he groaned as she rose above him and slowly took him into her, "I missed you, Helena."

"Oh Nathaniel, I missed you, too."

He lay naked next to his wonderful wife. She had turned to sleep on her side and he had moved his body up against hers, in the same position they had adopted two years ago, when they had been caught in that first storm together. He ran a finger down the now familiar scar on her back. He had kissed that scar to claim it for himself on the night that they had first come together. She had opened up for him then and they had enjoyed an animal kind of mating, which he had fantasised of whenever he spent a night away from her.

He had thought her asleep, but she moved her bottom against him and rolled onto her stomach in encouragement. He pushed his stump between her legs and she allowed him to gradually push one of her legs up with it. She did not flinch or move out of his way. He loved her so much for her acceptance of that part of him, but he was worried about keeping his balance on one knee while he took her.

A pillow hit him in his face, "take me, Nathaniel," she moaned. She had worked it out of course. He rested his stump on the pillow, moved completely between her legs and pulled her up to him. She was strong and gave him some support, too, so he was able to reach a hand around and find that spot between her legs that she loved him to please.

This was right. This was being a man and taking the woman you loved. He had won her trust, her love and the right to her body that no other man had ever had. She did not consent for him to use her body this way because she was married to him and owned by him. She did it because she wanted to; because she chose to; because she loved him. She made him feel strong and whole. He heard her breaths quicken and her moans become more demanding. Thrusting faster and using his fingers in the way she loved, he felt her body peak. Her muscles pulsed around him as he emptied into her.

The following day, Helena could not take her eyes off her husband. She was so happy that he was there and he would not leave again. She had been the strong one for so long that she had forgotten how to be anything else. However, while she was ill everything had gone on without her. Now she was back at the helm, but she realised, in a way that she had not when they were together before, that she no longer had to do it alone in any area of her life.

Every time they came close together they touched somehow, somewhere. He would run his hand down her back, she would touch his hand or cheek, he would tuck a tendril of her hair behind her ear, she would put her hand up to his chest and their eyes followed each other all day. Everyone else kept laughing at the pair, but they were all happy to see them back together.

During their early morning walk around the stalls, when Nathaniel was able to catch up with all that was happening, Helena did her daily inspection of Missy who was close to foaling. On this day, the horse was restless in her stall, swishing her tail and looking at her sides. Helena narrowly avoided a hoof as the mare kicked at her own abdomen.

"Let us keep a close eye on her today. Her udder is distended, too. She could be in the beginnings," she soothed the horse, assuring her they would be there for her, "have you checked the paddock fences, John?" she teased, recalling the last time Missy had foaled. It was almost two years ago that she had escaped Redway's paddock and foaled in an outlying barn, where Helena had then spent the night caught in a storm with Nathaniel. They locked eyes, both thinking of that night and how far they had come.

This was to be Thor's second foal. Mjöllnir was almost a year old. She knew this would mean a lot to Nathaniel. He had told her during the night of his choice in killing Thor, as he had lain trapped under him. She understood because she would have made the same decision, "he knew you loved him, right to the last." Then they had both cried a little for the loss of a dear animal.

Missy gave birth to a filly later that day. They named her Freya. Thankfully there were none of the complications that Missy experienced during her last foaling and the skies remained clear, without a drop of rain in sight.

With the return of Colonel Ackley, the rumours were rife once again about Mrs. Ackley's husband. A man had come to the village when the colonel was in battle and had mentioned to many people, that he had heard no marriage had taken place. No one knew this man and speculation over the truth of the rumours, and how much stock should be put into a stranger's words occurred often. Most of Eastcambe's inhabitants said they should rather believe the word of the colonel and his wife, as they were proven as good people in the village.

Still, there were some who would stoke the fires, for their own amusement, without considering the ramifications to the children of the couple.

Helena had detailed Lady Grace's visit to Nathaniel and the subsequent rumours that had started. While she had no evidence to prove it, she suspected the man she had heard was talking of them in the village, was the same one who had tracked their progress last spring, when they were supposedly on their journey to get married.

With the discovery of his father's continued improved opinion of his wife, the colonel had broached a subject with him that might deal with the rumours, and continue to allow him to be with Helena, without compromising her wish to be a person with her own free will. To that end he met with his father at the house of Mr. Brooks, a fortnight after his return to Redway.

"A pleasure to meet you again, Mr. Brooks," said Lord Aysthill, having been shown into the clergyman's small parlour.

"My honour, Your Lordship, I assure you. Colonel Ackley," he bowed to each man in turn. Various pleasantries were exchanged, while refreshments were served, "how may I be of service?"

"We think you may be able to help with a woman's reputation. As you may know there are some who are saying that my son here, Colonel Ackley, and Mrs. Helena Ackley are not truly married," began Lord Aysthill, "complete nonsense of course! Admittedly, they did not take the more traditional route to matrimony, but I can swear to you they are married. We felt an acknowledgement of the marriage in church, as part of the Sunday service, might put the matter to rest. What say you?"

"Well, it is a little unorthodox, but I suppose I could come up with some suitable wording, to bless the union," Mr. Brooks doubted he could refuse Lord Aysthill anything, however, he should not have refused Mrs. Ackley, if she had asked him, such was their friendship, "I am happy to help friends and neighbours. Mrs. Ackley, if I may be so bold to say so, has made a big difference in my life."

"Mine, too, Mr. Brooks," replied Nathaniel.

"And mine," agreed Lord Aysthill, "quite a woman you have saddled yourself with my boy," he added with some humour and a loud smack on his son's shoulder.

"Father," Nathaniel said, with a wide smile, "you are exactly right!"

Epilogue

And so it was, that two years to the very day of their first meeting, Colonel and Mrs. Ackley attended church. With their family, friends and neighbours cramming the church pews, their marriage was blessed by Mr. Eliot Brooks. Mr. Brooks had not had the pleasure of Mrs. Ackley in his church much since he moved to Eastcambe and it was a sight he enjoyed.

For her part, Helena had submitted herself to the ministrations of her friends and her maid, and was dressed in a lovely gown and small veil. Nathaniel stood by her side in front of the pastor looking resplendent in his regimentals. Using the new leg that Tommy had made for him, he stood without the aid of a crutch.

Mr. Brooks' voice rang out clear and true, "Nathaniel and Helena, you have committed yourselves to each other in marriage, in the will of God, the union of a man and a woman, for better, for worse, for richer, for poorer, in sickness and in health, to love and to cherish, till parted by death. Is this your understanding of the promise you have made?"

"It is," they both said and smiled at each other.

"Nathaniel, have you promised to be faithful to your wife, forsaking all others, so long as you both shall live?"

"Willingly," he said fondly and then in a clearer voice, "I have."

"Helena, have you promised to be faithful to your husband, forsaking all others, so long as you both shall live?"

"Always," she said with a smile and then, "I have."

"Heavenly Father, by your blessing let the ring already given, be to Nathaniel and Helena a symbol of unending love and faithfulness and of the promises they have made to each other; through Jesus Christ our Lord."

"Amen," was heard around the church.

Having bowed his head for the prayer Mr. Brooks looked up at the congregation, "Nathaniel and Helena have affirmed their promises in their marriage here today. Will you, families and friends uphold them in their marriage now and in the years to come?"

"We will," echoed behind them, Helena looked around at the crowd, smiling.

Eastease hosted a lavish celebration. Many local families and friends attended, including Mr. Brooks of course. When opportunity arose, he spoke quietly to Mrs. Ackley, "my first time doing that kind of ceremony, but a special request from Lord Aysthill is not to be ignored. Does this mean I will finally be seeing you more often at Sunday service, Mrs. Ackley?"

"It was very good of you, Mr. Brooks. Well it would seem I have a lot to be thankful for."

"Indeed," he agreed, unsurprised that she had not actually answered his question, so he tried another, "am I right in thinking that you and the colonel are *not* actually married, *Mrs.* Ackley?"

"My vows to Nathaniel are steadfast and I hold them in my heart. Do you think God sees that, Mr. Brooks?"

"Indeed, I do."

~The End~

Acknowledgements

I would like to say an enormous thank you to some important people.

Most importantly to my husband, Richard, and daughter, Emily. "Everything I do, I do it for you."

To my draft readers for your input, suggestions, encouragement and kind praise. Dorothy Beattie, Cheryl Duffy, Melissa Kremmel, Amy McCoy and my sister, Janine Westgate. You are wonderful women and I am lucky to know you.

To Emily Wygod of Endeavor Therapeutic Horsemanship, Bedford, NY for encouraging my girl's love of riding and checking my horse terms.

To Tracey Lusher-Chamberlain for butting in with your English Degree when asked and sorting out my O Level, Grade B mistakes. I will never tell you where to get off!

To my linguists, Maud Piquet, Patricia Widmayer and Jéssyca Santana for checking my French, German translation and Portuguese respectively.

To Barbara Baker, good friend and music therapist supreme. Thank you for asking after my book every week, listening patiently to me rambling on about it and for forgiving me for not practicing your music with my daughter.

To Adriana Tonello for the amazing artwork for the front cover. "I think this is the beginning of a beautiful friendship."

To my Mum "Gal Junie" for Eastease and 'Old Joe', and for pointing me in the right direction in life, even if I didn't always follow it.

To my Mother-in-law, Margaret Butler, thank you for listening to me talk endlessly about my book, when you probably would have preferred to hear about your granddaughter!

To Luis Fernando Jiménez for suffering listening to my singing so he could set out the music for 'Old Joe'. My mum wrote the song when I was young, but never had it down on music sheets.

To Kate Dube of Kate Emilies in Danbury for my hair and make-up and for your wonderful patience with my daughter.

To my wonderful colleagues at Connecticut Family Support Network, all the amazing Mums and Moms out there with children and adults with special needs.

To all women everywhere. I assure you that you all have a bit of Helena's spirit within you.

Thank you all!

Trish Butler

"I don't believe in God, but I believe in Good." ~ *Gal Junie*

About the Author

Trish Butler is the author of Redway Acres series of books.

She was born in Norwich, in the county of Norfolk in England and moved to Connecticut in the US, with her husband, in 1999.

Currently, she works as Communications Director for the Connecticut Family Support Network (CTFSN) a non-profit organization that helps families with children with special needs.

Redway Acres is mostly set in Lincolnshire, Cambridgeshire and Norfolk in the UK, which is an area that Trish knows well.

She has always wanted to write a book and at age fifty, finally realized that dream.

Read her blogs about her process, Redway Acres and its inhabitants at her website www.redwayacres.com

#RedwayAcres

Further books in the Redway Acres series

Redway Acres – Book 2 Maria

Set in early 1800s, England...

Maria Wyndham is the younger and more vivacious, twin stepdaughter of the late Lieutenant Mark Wyndham.

After their mother's death, she and her sister, Harriet, move to Eastease in Lincolnshire, and become wards of the lieutenant's friend, Alexander Harker, and his cousin, Nathaniel Ackley.

Just in time for a ball for the twins' sixteenth Birthday, a friend of their stepfather and guardians, Robert Davenport, arrives bearing gifts and prepared to dance.

Family and friendship bonds are pushed to the limit, as Maria's story plays out. She finds her strength of will to survive and pursue her own happiness.

Maria's silliness and love of life, often hide her intelligence and loyalty, in this story of sisters, and a girl, too soon pushed into the world of a woman.

Redway Acres – Book 3 Martha

Set in early 1800s, England...

Martha Hopwood, who lives with her sisters and parents in Cambridgeshire, meets a gentleman named Mr. Samuel Woodhead, a friend of Alexander Harker of Eastease in Lincolnshire.

Mr. Woodhead takes up residence at the nearby estate of Copperbeeches and pursues Martha both in Cambridgeshire and at Eastease, when her family is invited to visit there.

His sudden departure from Eastease, when all were still asleep, prompts Martha to consider an alternative future. Martha pursues her independence, until the return of the gentleman who stole her heart, and upon whom her family's financial future may depend.

In a time when a woman could not be married and independent, Martha Hopwood has to consider where her true future lies.